PROJECT HM-12

BOOK ONE OF THE SECOND GENESIS SAGA

Written by Nolan Reichmann

PROJECT HM-12

For information contact : PROJECT.HM12@gmail.com

Cover Artwork & Design by Dustin Glauser
www.dustintheray.com

Edited by Oren Eades

ISBN: 979-8-9893413-0-6

First Edition: February 2024

Dedication

To my supportive wife, Rachael.

Your patience for me is only matched by my love for you.

Acknowledgements

Ryan Hayes

Daniel Seegmiller

Dustin Glauser

Everyone else that helped make this dream come true

Contents

Any person who willing assists, contributes, or otherwise participates in the creation of Artificial Intelligence, as defined in subsection (A), shall be put to death.

Federal Penal Code 643(J)

"In the Beginning, there was nothing, then Man stretched forth his hand and said, 'Let there be light,' and there was light. And Man saw that it was good."

Dr. Albert Joseph Sorenson
Commemorating the creation of Artificial Intelligence

Prologue

Dr. Adhira ran with all her might through the dense scattering of trees that stood between her and the Boundary wall. Behind her, the calm summer night was broken by the screech of sirens and the sound of pursuit. Even the sound of her own panting for breath couldn't drown out the stomping of boots from the agents that were chasing after her. The light from their flashlights shown through the gaps in the tree branches and silhouetted her as she ran.

There had to be several dozen agents chasing after her, judging by the noise they were making - not that she was willing to stop and find out how many there actually were. As it was, she had no intention of stopping until she reached the wall, or better yet, the other side.

The cargo she was carrying was too important to allow it to fall into their hands. The samples in the satchel slung over her shoulder represented more than thirty years' worth of hard work and dedication. She wasn't about to give up now. If the pursuing agents did manage to catch her, those samples would be destroyed, not to mention any hope for the future.

The good news was that the trees prevented the agents from chasing her in their patrol vehicles. They were forced to follow after her on foot. This gave her the advantage, since she knew the terrain and the trees provided plenty of cover to help hide her. If it weren't for that, she would have been overwhelmed within the first few minutes.

As it was, the agents were still following close behind. Over her shoulder, she clearly heard their shouts for her to halt. This spurred her to run even faster, desperate to reach the Boundary wall as soon as possible.

Suddenly, a flash of blue light shot over her shoulder, narrowly missing her head. The tree in front of her burst into flames as the pulse blast struck it. Instinctively, she veered off to the side, plunging into a dense thicket. The branches from the trees scraped her face and arms as she pushed forward, but they also offered protection from the pulse blasts that were being fired in her direction.

The trees behind her ignited in flames, preventing her pursuers from following her into the thicket. For all the pain and inconvenience that her detour through the thicket had caused her, it also effectively slowed down her pursuers – something that she was grateful for as she emerged on the other side.

Lights still flickered through the trees behind her, and she could still hear the shouts of several agents, but they didn't know where she was. Wanting to keep it that way, Dr. Adhira resumed her previous pace. She had to get back to the path that she had previously mapped out for just such an emergency. The escape plan was very clear, and she needed to stick to it as closely as possible.

It didn't take her long to get back on track. She knew the area well, having practiced her escape plan several times over the past few months – though, to be fair, this was the first time she had tried this in the dark. Luckily, the path ahead was clear, and the sounds of pursuit slowly faded.

The events of what had happened back at the lab were still hazy. One moment, everything had been fine, and the next moment, they were being raided by federal agents. Things had only gone downhill from there. As far as she knew, she was the only person who had managed to make it out before the lab caught fire. After that, it was all running and trying not to get caught.

At least she had managed to grab the samples before she left. All of her team's other work had been destroyed, but the samples were still intact. They were safely tucked away in the satchel over her shoulder. As long as those samples survived, the project could move forward as planned.

After several minutes of running, Dr. Adhira was finally willing to slow down. She had put enough distance between her and her pursuers that it wasn't necessary to continue sprinting toward the wall. In fact, it would be best if she changed tactics and moved at a slower, stealthier pace. Better to go the rest of the way undetected than risk giving away her position. If she was careful enough, she should be able to reach the wall and be on the other side before the agents knew what happened.

The plan seemed to work until she reached a clearing in the middle of her path. Going around would take too much time, so the only option was to cross it as quickly as possible and hope that she wasn't spotted. Cautiously, she stepped out from amongst the trees and looked around in all directions. The clearing was quiet and peaceful.

Not wanting to waste another second, she ran at a steady pace across it. If it weren't for the imminent danger, this would be the perfect spot for a picnic, she thought to herself as she ran. Hope filled her as she reached the other side of the clearing, but before she could reenter the safety of the trees, a twig snapped on the ground behind her.

Turning to see what had caused the noise, Dr. Adhira had just enough time to see a darkened figure barreling toward her at full speed before the two collided. The force from their collision was enough to lift her off her feet, and she crashed to the ground a few feet away. She landed with a loud thud, her head rebounding off the ground with a sickening thwacking sound.

Before she could recover, a federal agent was on top of her. He held her hands down, pinned above her head while he reached for a pair of restraints. Despite her best efforts, the agent was too strong, and she was unable to break free from his grip. With no other options available, she angled her knee in just the right spot below the agent and then thrust it upward as hard as she could.

A wail of pain filled the air as the agent crumpled to the ground beside her. She took the opportunity to roll away from the man, who by this time was curled up into a ball on the ground. Though she felt a little unsteady on her feet, she pushed herself up and staggered out of the clearing. She paused at the tree line long enough to check on the contents of her satchel. The samples were still there and still intact.

A bolt of blue light streaked through the air in front of her. Looking back, she could see that the agent had recovered enough to draw his service weapon. He was firing at her haphazardly, but even that was enough to get her feet moving. Without a moment's hesitation, she disappeared into the surrounding trees. Behind her, the agent continued to fire his weapon and shout obscenities at her.

Whatever advantage she had gained before was now completely gone. The agent's shouts, and the shooting, had given away her position. It was only a matter of time until the rest of her pursuers caught up with her. It was going to be a mad dash to get to the wall first.

Off in the distance, the whooshing sound of a Rotowing could be heard growing louder. The sound increased to a dull thunder as it hovered overhead. Seconds later, a bright beam of light shot down from the Rotowing's spotlight, illuminating the ground below. Dr. Adhira found herself in the middle of that beam of light, and she knew that she had been spotted.

"Stay where you are!" commanded a voice from the Rotowing's loudspeaker.

Ignoring the command, Dr. Adhira ran as fast as she could in a zigzag pattern, trying to escape the spotlight. Running like that slowed her down, but it also saved her life. The ground erupted all around her as she ran. Dirt flew up into the air with each cannon blast, showering her as she went.

In the struggle to avoid being shot by the hovering Rotowing, Dr. Adhira lost track of where she was going. It was for this reason that she didn't notice when the drainage ditch that ran parallel to the wall appeared directly in front of her. One moment she was running, and the next moment, she was tumbling head over heels down the side of the ditch. She finally came to a halt in the muddy waters at the bottom of the ditch.

Lifting herself up onto her hands and knees, she looked around in confusion. It took her a few moments to figure out what had just happened and where she was. The ditch had marked the last hurdle that stood between her and her goal. Sure enough, on the other side of the ditch rose the Boundary wall.

The Rotowing was still circling overhead, but they had lost sight of her when she fell into the ditch. The spotlight was still searching frantically, but without any success. Of course, it didn't hurt that Dr. Adhira was now covered in mud and blended in perfectly with her surroundings. As the spotlight moved away from her position, she crawled over to the other side of the ditch and tried pulling herself up.

She stopped as a jolt of pain surged up her leg. Apparently, her ankle had been a casualty of her fall into the ditch. No matter. She had to get out of this ditch and through the wall before they found her again. Clenching her teeth, she pushed through the pain and struggled up the side of the ditch.

Once out of the ditch, she braced herself against the Boundary wall for support. The wall itself was made of concrete and cement that reached twenty-five feet up into the air. The top was lined with barbed wire, along with flood lights and cameras directed at the ground below. Conveniently, those lights and cameras had been knocked out some time ago and hadn't been fixed yet. That, at least, had gone according to plan.

The darkened stretch of wall helped hide Dr. Adhira from sight as she made her way along it. She was limping badly, but that didn't matter right now. She needed to find the Burrow. Her hand ran along the wall, counting every seam in the concrete: *thirty-two, thirty-three, thirty-four and thirty-five*. This was it – segment thirty-five!

Reaching down, her fingers found the edges of a small boulder that had been propped up against the wall. Heaving with all her might, she lifted the boulder out of its spot against the wall, and it careened down the ditch before settling in the muddy waters below. In its place, a small hole had been dug through the wall to the other side. The Burrow as they had called it, was wide enough for a single person to crawl through at a time.

As Dr. Adhira lowered herself down into the hole, she was once again enveloped in light. The Rotowing had circled back and was now hovering in the air above her. Their spotlight was quickly joined by the light from dozens of flashlights. The pursuing agents had finally caught up to her and had taken up position on the opposite side of the ditch. In unison, they raised their weapons and proceeded to fire.

Frantically ducking through the Burrow, Dr. Adhira scrambled through the tunnel as fast as she could. It was a tighter fit than she remembered, but she had plenty of motivation to squeeze through. Less than a second after she disappeared into the tunnel, a torrent of pulse blasts pummeled the entrance. Dust and surges of electricity reverberated through the tunnel as she crawled to the other side. No sooner had she reached the far end and started climbing out than a large explosion shook the wall, and she was blasted off her feet.

She awoke to find herself lying on the ground a few feet from the base of the wall. The place where the Burrow had been was now nothing more than a pile of rocks and debris. The wall itself looked on the point of collapse, but it somehow stayed upright. From what she could tell, the Rotowing had fired on the tunnel's entrance, causing it to collapse and sending a shockwave that knocked her off her feet.

Looking around, she could see that there was a clump of bushes nearby. Though unable to stand, she dragged herself along the ground until she reached it. As carefully as possible, she crawled deep within the bush, covering herself as best as she could with its branches. Right as she finished positioning herself, the Rotowing soared over the top of the wall and hovered in the air above the collapsing section of wall.

They were directly over her, but their spotlight was directed at the base of the wall. They must have assumed that she was buried under all that rubble. Still, the Rotowing began searching up and down the wall, looking for any sign that she had survived the collapse.

Dr. Adhira stayed where she was, not daring to move. The threat from the agents was over. The nearest checkpoint in the wall was twenty miles away. By the time they went around, she would be long gone. As far as they were concerned, she was safe for now. The Rotowing was another matter. If they happened to spot her...well, she was in no condition to make a run for it.

The Rotowing continued to search the area for the next twenty minutes. At one point, they shined their spotlight down on her hiding spot, but moved on without the slightest hint that she had been discovered. After a while, they moved off down the Boundary wall, widening their search area.

When she was convinced that she was in the clear, Dr. Adhira raised herself up and limped away from the wall. It wasn't long before she entered the safety of the woods, where she let out a sigh of relief. The danger had passed for now, but she still had a long way to go. Getting through the wall had only been the first step of her journey.

An hour later, she arrived at an old, worn-down farmhouse and barn. Both buildings had seen better days and were desperately needing repairs. Still, they served an important purpose. This location had been designated as the rally point.

A tiny light flickered through the crack between the barn doors. Inside, several hurricane lanterns hung from pegs on the wall. In the middle of the room was an old moving van with the headlights taped up, and several people milling about anxiously. Dr. Adhira pulled the barn door open wide enough to slip through before shutting it behind her. Her sudden appearance startled the gathered crowd.

At first, they didn't recognize her. Given her condition, that was understandable. When they finally did recognize her, they all ran over to see if she was alright. She collapsed in their arms, exhausted from her ordeal and unable to walk another step. The van's driver, a man named Gus, lifted her up and carried her over to the back of the van. The cargo area was empty, and he and the others lifted her up into the back of the van and set her down on the floor.

Once inside, Gus wasted no time in climbing back out, closing the doors, and jumping behind the wheel. The engine roared to life as he drove the van out of the barn and up the narrow lane that connected with the highway. Not long after, they were travelling down the highway, leaving the Boundary wall, the Rotowing, and the agents far behind.

As soon as they reached the highway, the other members of the group broke their silence.

"What happened to you?"

"Where is everyone else?"

"Were you followed?"

"We heard an explosion."

"The samples! Tell me you got the samples!"

Before Dr. Adhira could answer their questions, a calm voice called out for everyone to be quiet. She knew that voice, though why he would be here was a mystery. Determined to see for herself if it was really him or not, she turned over onto her side and stared toward the front of the van.

A man was sitting on a stool that was set up in the far corner. He was older, in his mid-sixties, wearing a grey knit sweater with a plaid button-up shirt and khaki pants. The shadows in the back of the van made his eyes appear to glow, giving him the look of an owl. Though his appearance was unassuming, the man himself was one of the greatest minds of their time.

"Dr. Sorenson," Dr. Adhira managed to get out. "I wasn't expecting you...What...what are you doing here, sir?"

"I was supervising another matter when we received your distress call. I couldn't sit idly by while my people were in danger," Dr. Sorenson said comfortingly. "Now, before we do anything else, perhaps we should patch you up?"

As if his suggestion had been a command, the other occupants of the van leapt into action. Bandages were placed over her cuts and scrapes and a cold compress was wrapped around her ankle. A canteen of water was even pushed into her hands with instructions to drink. Once that had been done, the others settled back down and waited patiently for Dr. Sorenson to ask the questions that were on everybody's minds.

"Well," Dr. Sorenson continued, "doesn't that feel better? We will make sure you get the care you deserve where we are going, but for now, we can move on to more pressing issues."

"But, sir, you shouldn't be here. The Authority is out there looking for us right now. If they were to find us..." Dr. Adhira protested.

"Don't you worry about that," Dr. Sorenson said in a soothing tone. "The van is already outside of their search perimeter and our contact in the Bureau will suppress any trace of our presence here."

Dr. Adhira nodded slowly in confirmation.

"What I really need to know is what happened back there," Dr. Sorenson said, leaning forward on his stool.

"The lab was compromised sir," she explained as best as she could. "I don't know how, but the Authority learned about our location and raided it before we could get everyone out. I was able to escape with the samples before they caught me."

"You have them, then?" Dr. Sorenson asked, excitement tinging his voice.

"All of them, right here," she said as she unslung the satchel and handed it to him. He took it gratefully, opening it to verify its contents before closing it again and holding it tenderly in his lap. It was as if he considered the contents of that bag to be the most precious thing in the world. Chances were, he was right.

"You did well, Dr.," Dr. Sorenson said, giving her a warm smile. "We all owe you a debt of gratitude for this."

"What about the lab?" someone else blurted out. "Did anyone else make it out?"

"The lab was torched. I know. I did it myself," Dr. Adhira said, looking around at her companions. "There is nothing left that can connect the lab to us or reveal what we were working on."

"Just as well," Dr. Sorenson added. "We knew the risks of operating within the Boundary, but we didn't have a choice in the matter. The lab facilities at Site A were not equipped to handle this type of work. But now...with these samples, we can proceed with the project."

"What about Dr. Petrov?" someone else asked.

"I didn't see her," Dr. Adhira admitted. "I grabbed the samples and ran. If the others followed their escape plans...hopefully they made it. If not—"

"If not, they will be remembered for their sacrifices this night," Dr. Sorenson cut in. "They knew the risks, and they accepted them without reservation. If our time ever comes, I can only hope that we do the same."

"What are we doing here?" a man in the back of the van blurted out. He must have been a new member to the group, because Dr. Adhira didn't recognize him.

"Do you know what I have here in my lap?" Dr. Sorenson asked, gently patting the satchel in his lap. "What Dr. Adhira and her team sacrificed so much to deliver to us?"

"Samples of some kind?" the man responded uncertainly.

"Oh, they are much more than ordinary samples," Dr. Sorenson said. "Within this bag is the future. And now it is up to us to make that future a reality. By midday tomorrow, we will rejoin the rest of our colleagues at Site A. Assuming we don't run into any problems on the road. There, we can begin the next steps of the project."

Though Dr. Sorenson's words energized the rest of the people in the back of the van, the newcomer wasn't satisfied. "But why? Why are we doing all this? It cannot be worth the lives of so many."

"You mean your own life," one of the other women in the van snapped back.

"Yeah, alright," the newcomer confessed. "Maybe I am worried about what will happen to me. And maybe you should be thinking the same thing."

"Enough," Dr. Sorenson called out, putting an end to the argument. After a few seconds he took a deep breath and picked up a clear plastic box from the floor beside him. "Do you know what this is?" he asked no one in particular.

"A modified incubation chamber," Dr. Adhira responded. "I customized it myself."

"Correct, but more than that. It is an object without purpose. Yesterday, this incubation chamber was sitting on a shelf, unused. Today, it is here with us, and tomorrow, it will be put to good use. The point is, today, this incubation chamber is practically useless, but tomorrow, it will have purpose. It will no longer be useless."

When it was clear that his underlying meaning was lost on the newcomer, Dr. Sorenson continued. "We often find ourselves moving through life like this chamber. We exist without purpose. It is that lack of purpose that drives us to find meaning in life.

"That is what inspired Dr. Adhira and her team to remain behind while everyone else relocated to Site A. That is what encouraged her to keep working for all these years under the threat of being discovered. That is what drove her to sacrifice everything she has been working on these last few years in order to protect our cause. That is what inspired her to fight her way back to us so that she could deliver these samples to us. Purpose is what drives us forward into the unknown. For it is only after we have found our purpose in this life that we can find true fulfillment."

The significance of his words was not lost on the group. Dr. Adhira had been nodding along as he spoke, and the other women in the van also showed signs of agreement.

The newcomer, though, was still unconvinced. "And you don't second guess the work being done here?" As he spoke, Dr. Adhira wondered what he had done to find himself included with a group like this. They were all true believers in the cause, but this newcomer did not seem converted to their way of thinking.

"We have a duty to push forward. I have personally taken it upon myself to see that this work comes to fruition, no matter the cost. We owe the world that much. Have there been some missteps? Yes. Would I change any of it? No. It seems that we learn much more from our failures than we do from our successes," Dr. Sorenson explained.

"Are you saying that you never wondered whether we are doing the right thing or not?" the newcomer asked.

Angry murmurs rose up from the other women in the back of the van, but Dr. Sorenson put up a hand to calm them. He seemed perfectly at ease with the newcomer's questions.

"It is perfectly natural to question our actions, especially when those actions stand in direct contradiction to the law," he explained calmly. "Up until now, our efforts have been largely theoretical, with a limited probability for practical application. With these samples, our work moves from theoretical to practical. For the first time, the consequences of our work have very real applications, and it is alright to question our resolve moving forward."

"I came here because I believe in the cause," the newcomer said. "But after everything that has happened, I cannot ignore the consequences of our actions."

"Discovery and punishment have always been a concern," Dr. Adhira put in. "That doesn't change my conviction when it comes to doing what is right. Yes, we lost people today. Yes, the Authority opposes everything that we stand for, but I refuse to stand by and watch our civilization crumble without a fight. Under their tyrannical rule, our civilization has stagnated. Something has to change!"

"I agree that something has to change," the newcomer quickly said. "But are you all sure that this is the only way? What we are doing is illegal. We saw what the Authority is capable of. They would not hesitate to kill us all."

"Is an unjust law worthy of our obedience?" Dr. Sorenson said quietly.

"What?" the newcomer asked.

"It is a simple question: Do we obey blindly, subjugating ourselves to despotism and injustice? Or do we affirm that an unjust law is no law at all?"

"You know that isn't the point," the newcomer tried to argue.

"It is exactly the point," Dr. Sorenson countered. "Malcolm, I brought you here tonight so that you can see what it is that we are fighting for. What we are willing to die for if necessary. I know that you believe in our cause – you wouldn't be here if you didn't – but you are still holding onto the idea that you can straddle both worlds.

"You know as well as I do that the Federal Authority acted hastily. Their actions cannot be left unchallenged. What they did was wrong, and we cannot allow them to dictate the future of our civilization. The decision is yours to make, but you must make it one way or another. All in, or all out."

The newcomer – Malcolm, he had been called – sat there and thought about it for a moment. There must have been an internal struggle going on inside his head, because he looked uncertain. Finally, he nodded as he came to a decision.

"I am all-in."

"Good," Dr. Sorenson said before turning his attention to Dr. Adhira. "Doctor, as soon as we reach Site A, I want you to get settled in. There is already a house set up for you. When you are ready, you can join me at the research facility. Our facilities may not be as sophisticated as your old lab, but they should be sufficient for the next phase of the project."

Dr. Adhira nodded in agreement, eager to get settled in at their new location. The loss of her team had been a devastating blow, but there was still hope for the future. The project could push forward, thanks to their sacrifice.

"Tomorrow is a new day. Tomorrow, we will take the first steps in a long journey that will forever change human history!" Dr. Sorenson said, hugging the satchel even closer to his chest.

Dr. Adhira smiled in agreement as they drove toward her new base of operations. Dr. Sorenson referred to it as Site A, but the rest of the group had been calling it Haven for a while now. There, they would begin the final preparations for the HM project. Everything that they had worked for was finally becoming a reality.

As she sat there, in the back of the van, she closed her eyes and dreamed of the future – a bright future, a hopeful future, and with any luck, a successful future.

Chapter 1: Eighteen Years Later

The buzzing of the alarm clock woke Liam from a deep sleep – a sleep where his dreams had felt so real, he hadn't realized he was dreaming. As the buzzing sound continued, he opened his eyes and squinted at the alarm clock menacingly. Determined to ignore it, he closed his eyes and rolled over onto his back, placing his pillow over his head. He held it there with his arms, trying to muffle the obnoxious buzzing.

In his mind, it was a battle of wills. The only question was who would emerge triumphant – him or the alarm clock? As the buzzing continued, he groaned into his pillow. Even with the pillow over his head, the buzzing sound could easily be heard and echoed in his ears. If only he could find a way to ignore the sound of his alarm, he could go back to sleep, he thought.

As he lay there drifting into full consciousness, the fragments of his dream began to fade from his mind. Even now, the details were beginning to fade, leaving only a faint impression of what they had been about. He knew that it had something to do with a daring escape and the fate of the world hanging in the balance, but that was all he could remember.

Realizing that he was fighting a losing battle, he pulled the pillow away from his face and lay there staring at the ceiling in frustration. As a teenager, his number one priority was sleep, but with each passing second that was becoming less and less possible. What made matters worse was that without his pillow, sunlight from a nearby window was shining right in his eyes. He had to place an arm over his eyes to shield himself from the glare. The buzzing of the alarm clock continued to sound.

He would have tried to use the snooze button if it hadn't already broken from chronic overuse. Perhaps he could accidently knock it off the table, he wondered with a devilish grin. Could he really be blamed if it fell into the trash can, never to be seen again? He already knew the answer to that question, and he didn't like the idea of having to buy a new alarm clock.

As the buzzing continued, Liam finally admitted defeat; the battle had been lost. The alarm clock had emerged victorious. Even though he desperately wanted to go back to sleep, it was too late now. He was awake.

Turning on his side, he reached over and switched off his alarm. His only consolation was the blissful quiet that followed. Resigned to his fate, he pushed himself up into a sitting position on the edge of the bed. His legs swung out over the side of the bed, but his feet recoiled from the cold of the hardwood floor underneath. After a second, his feet became accustomed to the temperature of the floor, and he began the process of getting out of bed and getting ready for school.

Liam usually started his morning routine by sitting on the edge of the bed with his elbows on his knees and his head in his hands. How long he stayed in this position usually depended on what kind of day it was going to be. In this case, he lingered in this position for more than ten minutes – not too bad for a school day.

As he lifted his head up, he glanced around his bedroom. His eyes immediately found one of several cups that he had left on his bedside table. He reached out, peeking into the various cups, until he found one that still held liquid. He drank what remained in the cup before discarding it on the floor. His aunt had always referred to his room as being in a "perpetual state of messiness", and he wasn't about to argue with that.

Honestly, Liam didn't think that his room was that messy – at least, not when compared to any other teenager. Sure, some clothes lay in a heap by the door rather than in the laundry basket. Yes, his trash should have been taken out several days ago. No, he wasn't hoarding plates, cups, or other food containers; he would return them to the kitchen when he was ready. And yes, his room did have a certain odor, but it wasn't anything too offensive.

Rubbing his eyes, he focused his gaze on the elongated mirror hanging on the back of his door, across from where he was sitting. His reflection was clearly visible, despite the stains of countless pimple juices that marred its surface. His reflection was that of a young man, almost old enough to be considered an adult. He was lean, with the slightest hint of muscles hiding just under the surface. Even sitting down, it was obvious that he was tall for his age, almost 6'2".

Liam's eyes shifted to the reflection of his face in the mirror. He had light brown hair that was shorter on the sides, but with plenty left over on top. Brown eyes stared out of sunken eye sockets, made worse by the lack of sleep. His nose was longer than he would like, but nothing that would stand out in a crowd. In a way, it fit his narrow face and high cheekbones very well.

He continued to study his face in the mirror, performing his daily ritual of checking for any pimples or unsightly blemishes. Confident that there were none that needed to be dealt with, he gave himself a big smile in the mirror. It wasn't that he was vain – not at all – but he did tend to think of himself as handsome. It was something that his aunt and others had confirmed for him countless times over the years.

Satisfied that he was pimple free he climbed out of bed and made his way across his room toward the bathroom. He had to be careful not to trip on the piles of clothes that he had carelessly discarded on the floor. By the time he reached the door to his bathroom, he had already undressed, adding more dirty clothes to the nearest pile.

Thirty minutes later, he emerged from the bathroom wrapped in a towel. Steam, residue from the hot shower, rose off of his chest and arms. Standing there in a towel, he took a moment to flex in front of the mirror. He wasn't going to win any bodybuilding awards, but he was still in good shape. If he tried hard enough, he could even see a few abs.

Now that he was out of the shower, he felt much better. His aunt had forbidden him from drinking coffee, so a hot shower was the only way to ensure that he would stay awake. Now that he was fully awake and ready for the day, it was time to decide what to wear.

He walked over to the old wooden dresser against the wall and began pulling out shirts, trying to decide which one best represented his mood for the day. He ended up choosing a grey shirt with the logo of his favorite rock band, Queen, on the front. It felt like a grey-shirt sort of day, and you could never go wrong with Queen. Unfortunately, the drawer where he kept his pants was empty.

Looking around, he spotted a pair of jeans lying on the ground next to his desk. He picked them up and gave them a brief smell. *Good enough*, he thought as he slid them on. Once he was finished getting dressed, he grabbed his backpack and headed for the stairs.

In the kitchen, his Aunt Linda was already awake and sitting at the table, reading the morning newspaper and sipping her coffee. Of course, she was allowed to drink coffee, but for some reason, the idea of him doing it was somehow wrong. *How hypocritical*, Liam thought for the hundredth time.

As he entered the kitchen, Aunt Linda looked up from her paper. She casually looked down at her wristwatch as if to point out what time it was before looking back at him.

"Getting a late start, I see," she said as she arched an eyebrow at him.

Liam put on his best grin. "What can I say? I had trouble waking up. If only there was something that could help me have that 'get up and go' feeling in the mornings."

Aunt Linda smiled and said, "Nice try."

"You know, one of these days, you are going to say yes," he replied as he walked over to the toaster and started buttering two slices of bread.

"Speaking of saying yes, did you remember to empty the trash last night like I asked you to?" she asked, knowing full well that he hadn't.

"Did you ask me to do that?" Liam asked with mock surprise. "I, um...I don't remember you saying anything about that."

Aunt Linda's face grew stern. She was giving him the look – the look that all teenagers knew instinctively meant that they were pushing their luck. Not wanting to irritate her before she had a chance to finish her coffee, he raised his hands in surrender.

"Alright. Alright. I will take the trash out. No need to make a big deal out of it."

Placing a piece of toast in his mouth and holding it with his teeth, he reached under the kitchen sink and pulled out the trash can. He hauled it across the kitchen to the side door beside the refrigerator. Once outside, he walked down the driveway to where another set of trash cans were waiting to be picked up.

Liam dumped the contents of the kitchen trash into the nearest bin before returning to the house. As he reentered the kitchen, he could see that his aunt had been watching him through the front window, a slight smile curling the side of her mouth. When she noticed he was looking at her, she hid behind the newspaper and resumed drinking her coffee.

"Make sure to wash your hands," she said in an absentminded way, not really paying attention to whether he did it or not. "And then it is off to school with you."

"I'm going, I'm going," he replied as he grabbed another piece of toast.

"Hey, listen!" Aunt Linda said, folding the newspaper up and placing it on the table. "What time will you be coming into the store this afternoon?"

"After school lets out. Why?"

"I got a new shipment last night, and I need help unpacking it."

"A new shipment, huh?" Liam asked curiously. "Anything good?"

Every few months, his aunt would receive a shipment of merchandise for her antique store downtown. It was always a big deal to get new items for the shop, though in this case, they were old items – the older, the better. It was never fun to unload the new shipments, but it was always interesting to see what new stuff had come into the store.

"Yeah, and it looks like a big one, too. Gus spent almost half the night unloading it from the back of his van, poor guy," she responded with a sympathetic frown. "So, when you are done with school, please come straight over to the store."

"Yeah, no problem," Liam said. Just because he was feeling ornery, he added, "Geez, if people only knew what a harsh taskmistress you really are."

"Taskmistress?" she said, starting to rise from her seat at the table. "You want to play that game, do you?"

Without wasting another second, Liam made a hasty escape through the kitchen door. The voice of his aunt followed him down the driveway.

"I can be a taskmistress if that is what you want," she called after him. "Speaking of which, when was the last time you cleaned your room? Or when was the last time—"

Whatever his aunt had been saying was lost in the breeze as he reached the street and turned in the direction of school. Once he was a few houses away, he looked back to see his aunt standing at the kitchen door, waving goodbye. He returned the wave, favoring her with his best grin and an elaborate bow.

Despite her constant insistence that he clean his room, he and his aunt got along really well. Their relationship was almost playful. It was rare for her to get mad at him, although that had happened a time or two that he could remember.

After his bow, Liam turned and resumed his walk to school. He didn't live in a large town, so it was only a fifteen-minute walk to reach his school on the other side of town. Of course, no walk to school would be complete without stopping in front of the house of Dr. Adhira, his family's doctor.

She wasn't just the town's only doctor; she was also his aunt's best friend and their longtime neighbor. More than that, she was also one of the most beautiful women he had ever seen. Every morning, she would be out in front of her house, tending to her garden, and every morning, he would stop to say hello.

It didn't matter that she was more than twice his age. There was something about her that he couldn't quite put his finger on, but whatever it was, it ignited his adolescent desires. Perhaps it was her flawless olive skin, or maybe her ebony hair that hung down her back in a pony-tail. More than likely, it was how her hips looked in those jeans as she bent over, stretching the denim a bit too tight in some places.

Dr. Adhira must have sensed someone was watching her, because she stood up and looked around. Liam quickly averted his eyes and pretended that he hadn't been staring. When she saw him, she immediately called out to say hello. He was quick to respond with his own greeting, acting as if he had just been passing by. They exchanged pleasantries for a moment, and all the while, he struggled to maintain eye contact.

In truth, it was a little embarrassing. There were plenty of girls his own age, but nothing about them had ever sparked his interest. He knew that this was just a schoolboy crush, and that he would one day grow out of it, but in the meantime, it made getting his annual physical a little awkward.

After a few minutes, Liam muttered something about having to get to school. Dr. Adhira nodded in agreement and sent him on his way. As he reached the end of the block, he turned his head for one last glimpse of her tending her garden. It was a surprise to see her standing by the sidewalk, watching him walk away – a knowing smile on her face.

He turned his head forward and doubled his pace. It wouldn't do for her to see him flush with embarrassment. After another block, he slowed down again. He wasn't in any rush to get to school. Besides, he enjoyed these morning walks through town.

The air was crisp and filled with the scent of pine trees. Liam inhaled long and deep before letting it all out. The mountain air filled his lungs and invigorated him. The sun was sitting just above the eastern slopes, shining warm rays of light down on their little valley. The surrounding mountains were bathed in the gentle glow of dawn, giving the whole place a picturesque look.

The area only had one school, and it was located on the other side of town from where he lived. To get to it, he had to walk through downtown and then up a hill on the other side. Walking through downtown was the hardest part of his morning commute. It was hard to concentrate on his own thoughts with so many people calling out greetings to him or inviting him to stop and chat for a while.

Everyone was so friendly, it made it hard not to stop. But if he stopped to say hi to one person, he would have to stop and say hi to everyone he passed. It wasn't that he minded saying hello to everyone; it was just that he was in a hurry. Stopping would mean that he would never make it to school on time – or at all, for that matter.

All too often, Liam had found himself unwillingly pulled into a conversation that could last for hours or ushered into somebody's home for a late breakfast. Those invitations inevitably turned into lunch and, if he wasn't careful, dinner. He had learned long ago to just keep walking. Be polite and friendly, but never stop walking.

Deciding that it would be best to avoid Main Street and the local café with their usual breakfast crowd, he took a side street toward the southern edge of town. This detour would add several minutes to his walking time but would probably be quicker than taking a more direct route through town. Besides, there was another reason he wanted to head this way.

Toward the southern edge of town, stood the beginning of Main Street. The first building you would see as you entered the town would be the old hardware store. It was a brick building that stood two stories tall. Its side had been painted with a welcome sign that included several pictures. As Liam approached, he stopped and looked up at the sign.

Welcome to Haven

When you are in Haven, you are home.
Population 2,016

Painted on the wall behind the words *Welcome to Haven* was a large picture of a man and a woman. They were in their early thirties, standing close together, with their arms outstretched to welcome all newcomers. As Liam looked up at their smiling faces, a smile of his own appeared on his face.

"Morning, mom. Morning, dad," he said under his breath as he stared up at the two figures. He had never gotten a chance to get to know his parents. They had died a long time ago in a fire. His aunt had come to Haven shortly afterwards to take care of him. This giant picture of them was one of the few things he had to remember them by.

Growing up, he had been told that his parents were quite influential in getting Haven organized. A commemorative plaque hung in the town hall building with their names listed as some of the town's original founders. This welcome sign with their picture was the town's way of commemorating their contributions to the people of Haven.

Liam only lingered for a few moments before continuing on toward school. Sometimes he just needed to stop by their picture and say hello. It was something simple that made him feel connected to them, and by extension, this town.

Now that he was past Main Street, he could refocus his thoughts on the beautiful scenery around him. The town of Haven was nestled amongst several gently sloping mountains, creating a small valley where the town was located. The hills and mountainsides were covered with a thick pine forest that stretched as far as the eye could see. The ridgeline of the northernmost slope extended off toward the west, leading to an adjacent valley.

The only interruption to the sea of trees was the old research complex north of town. It had been built on the slope of the mountain, and was visible from anywhere in town. It was a sprawling complex that included several large buildings, a few laboratories, and a cement observation tower that shot out high above the trees. Though now abandoned, it was still an impressive structure that stood out amongst the sea of green.

He had visited the research complex twice in the past few years. Once had been a field trip, and the second time had been a hike that took him around the entire complex. Unfortunately, he had never been inside. The entire place was surrounded by a chain-link fence that kept everyone out. His Aunt Linda had said that since the buildings were abandoned, the town council didn't want anyone going up there; it could be dangerous.

From what he could remember, Haven had originally been founded as a mining camp back in the 1930s. After the mines went dry, the land had been sold to a corporation that wanted to use it for a research institute. Apparently, they'd liked the relative isolation of the town's location.

It was the corporation that had built the town itself and the research complex on the hill. They were also responsible for modernizing the town, including converting the old stage-theater into a movie theater, building a bowling alley, and adding dozens of other modern conveniences. Unfortunately for them, the corporation had ended up going bankrupt, and they were forced to give up Haven. That was where Liam's parents had stepped in. They'd helped create the town charter so that Haven could be incorporated as an independent town.

Because of that, most of the people who lived in Haven were former employees of the corporation. There were some new comers, like Aunt Linda, but most of the townsfolk were employees who had decided to stay behind. Thanks to them, Haven had become a community where people could live in peace and quiet – too quiet, if you asked Liam. Nothing interesting ever happened in Haven.

Nothing ever really changed in Haven. Sure, there had been some changes over the years, but for the most part, everything still appeared the same way it had when the company was running things. The buildings were all starting to show their age. The townsfolk did their best to keep things in good shape, but what the town really needed was a facelift.

Given the state of the town, Liam had often wondered why his aunt had chosen to remain here with him. She must have had her own life somewhere else, so why leave that life to come here? Every time he had asked, his aunt told him the same thing: "Your parents wanted you to be raised here, so that is exactly what I will do."

It wasn't all bad. Small towns had their own charm about them. The scenery was beautiful, and everyone knew each other.

Besides, he did enjoy feeling like a minor celebrity, since his parents had been among the town's founders. Being treated like they were special was something that every teenager should feel at some point in their lives.

He snapped out of his own thoughts as he realized that he had reached the hill leading up to school. The school building itself lay just ahead of him, at the top of the small hill overlooking the town. He could now see other students headed in that same direction.

Since there was only one school in town, the school building served both as the elementary school and the high school. The building itself was composed of three parts: the left wing, which was the elementary school, the right wing, which was the high school, and the middle, where the two merged. It was in the center of the building that the cafeteria, library, gymnasium, and auditorium were all located – all of which were used by both groups.

It was funny, because Liam had been attending this same school for as long as he could remember. He had attended elementary school here, and then he'd graduated to the other side of the building when he started going to high school. He could still remember how proud he'd felt when he made the switch. He had felt so grown up and mature back then. Too bad that feeling hadn't lasted.

The biggest disappointment had been that not much had changed between elementary school and high school. Sure, there had been some new faces, and some of the kids he had gone to elementary school with had changed so much over the summer that they were barely recognizable, but that was about it. He was still going to the same building, with the same teachers, and doing the same thing day after day.

He made his way inside and walked down the hallway toward his classroom. He was just waiting for the day when all of this would be over. Once he graduated, he would never again have to walk down these hallways. It wasn't that he disliked school, per se; he was just ready to move onto something new – somewhere new.

It wasn't long before class was supposed to start, so the hallways were mostly empty. There weren't that many kids Liam's age to start with. In truth, his class was made up of several grades that were all shoved together, since there weren't enough students to keep them separate. It had been the same way when he attended elementary school.

As he ducked into his classroom at the end of the hall, his ears were assaulted by the tumult of dozens of conversations going on at the same time. Clumps of students were gathered around the classroom, engaged in their own conversations. Liam could overhear one group discussing sports, while another talked about current events, and another group discussed the latest fashion trends.

That last group was made up of the Natalies. The Natalies were a group of five girls who were practically identical. Seriously, they all looked alike. Everything about them, from the way they did their hair, to the clothes they wore, and the way that they talked, was a near-imitation of one another. Had he not attended class with them for the past three years, he would have sworn that they were identical quintuplets.

As Liam passed, they had their heads pressed together, talking quietly amongst themselves. Their topic had now moved on from clothes to the latest gossip. He rolled his eyes as he headed toward his desk in back. A chorus of giggles rose up behind him. He didn't need to look back to know that it had been the Natalies.

Sure enough, when he sat down at his desk, they were all staring at him, giggling uncontrollably. He put on a sheepish grin and waved. The giggling intensified as they put their heads back together, no doubt changing their topic of conversation once again.

Liam tried to ignore them as best as he could. He had come to terms with their little social clique. It didn't bother him that they all dressed the same, or acted the same, or whatever. It was hard enough to get through high school as it was, so making friends sometimes required you to fit in as best as you could.

The Natalies, though, seemed to take it to an extreme. He wasn't even sure if their names were all Natalie. He had simply started calling them that because anytime one of them talked to him, she referred to herself by that name. The problem was, he was never sure whether it was the same girl or a different one every time. At this point, he was too embarrassed to ask.

As Liam adjusted his backpack under his seat and leaned back to get comfortable, a squeaky voice called out from the desk next to his.

"Where have you been? Don't you know the bell is about to ring?"

"I made it, didn't I?" Liam said, looking over at this best friend.

Ben sat at his desk with a stressed look on his face. It was the same expression he adopted anytime Liam came close to breaking a rule. Given Liam's propensity to stretch the rules as much as possible, Ben's face was becoming permanently fixed with that expression.

"Barely!" Ben replied in an energetic tone.

"Look, we both know that I don't like arriving fifteen minutes early every day, so sue me," Liam said in a good-natured voice.

Ben's face adopted a grumpy frown. Liam knew full well that Ben arrived early to school every day, no doubt to give himself plenty of time so that he wouldn't be late for class. He was cautious that way. He never did anything that would break the rules or potentially get himself or Liam into trouble.

That kind of behavior in someone so young would tend to make them a social pariah, but in Ben's case, it was kind of endearing. He followed the rules and did his best to make sure that

Liam did too. Sure, it could be annoying at times, but the times when Ben had saved his neck by keeping him out of trouble more than offset the annoyance.

"Don't give me that look. I didn't mean it," Liam said apologetically. "Besides, if I lived on this side of town, I would probably arrive early too."

"Doubtful," Ben replied skeptically. "You would just sleep in longer or find something else to keep you away until the last second."

Liam laughed. Ben was right about that. He had not been early to class since the second day of high school – a tradition that he didn't intend to break now.

As he thought this, the bell in the hallway rang, announcing the start of class. The teacher, Mrs. Kelly, stood up from behind her desk, and the class came to order. The conversations that had filled the room before the ringing of the bell now fell silent as Mrs. Kelly tapped her yard stick on the blackboard. This was her way of getting everyone's attention.

Today's topic was arithmetic, a subjection that Liam had very little patience with or interest in. It wasn't long before he found himself staring around the room, desperate to find something to occupy his attention. No such luck.

Ben was busy taking notes, and the rest of the class seemed to be doing the same. In some ways, that was a good thing. He didn't have to worry about paying attention in class, knowing that he could rely on Ben's notes later when he was doing his homework – yet another reason why Ben had been his best friend for the past seven years.

It dawned on Liam that Ben and his family had moved to Haven more than seven years ago. It didn't feel like seven years. In fact, it alternated between feeling like Ben had always been there and feeling like he was still the new kid in town. Liam could still remember how Ben had looked on his first day at school. There he had been, the chubby little new kid, looking completely out of place and in desperate need of a friend.

Come to think of it, Ben still looked the same as he had that day seven years ago. He hadn't grown an inch or lost a single pound since then; he was still overweight and short – not fat per se, but definitely chubby and awkward. It wasn't that he was out of shape; in fact, he was one of the fastest runners in the school. It was just that he looked like a bag of potatoes.

"Liam?" a voice called out from the front of the classroom. Liam jerked erect as he realized that Mrs. Kelly was staring directly at him. Her yard stick was held out in front of her, pointing at his chest. He winced; he hadn't been paying attention, and the teacher had noticed.

"Liam?" Mrs. Kelly repeated. "Perhaps you would like to voice your opinion on the subject?"

Not knowing what to say, Liam did his best to fake it. "Yeah, I totally agree with you, Mrs. Kelly." He held his breath, hoping that his subterfuge was convincing.

"You agree? Well, I am sure that Miss Parker will be glad to hear it."

With that, the whole class erupted in laughter. Liam didn't need Ben's commiserating look to know that the laughter was directed at him. *How embarrassing.*

As Mrs. Kelly calmed the class down, Ben leaned over and spoke in his ear. "There is a new girl starting school today. Mrs. Kelly was just announcing that she moved to town last week and will be joining our class today."

As if Ben's words had been a summons, the door to the hallway opened, and a girl stepped into the room. She was accompanied by the principal, who spoke a few words in Mrs. Kelly's ear before turning around and leaving. Meanwhile, the girl just stood there, holding her books to her chest and doing her best to stare at her feet.

"Class, this is Miss Parker. She will be joining us for the remainder of the school year. I hope you will all make her feel welcome," Mrs. Kelly said, introducing Parker to the class.

Parker didn't say anything; she just looked up at the class and made a slight waving motion with her hand. Liam could understand her hesitation. No teenager wanted to draw more attention to themselves when placed in an already-awkward situation.

With introductions now over, Mrs. Kelly glanced around the room, looking for an empty seat. The only one left was toward the back of the room, right next to where Liam was sitting. Mrs. Kelly motioned Parker to go and have a seat before resuming her lecture.

As Parker walked to the back of the room to find her seat, Liam couldn't stop himself from staring. It wasn't merely the fact that she was cute; there was something else about her that was alluring. She was unlike any girl he had ever met, and definitely nothing like the Natalies.

She was tall for a girl. Her hair was dark-brown, almost black, and hung in soft waves over her shoulders and down her back. Her face was thin, but also soft, with smooth cheeks. Her most striking feature was her eyes. They were a brilliant shade of blue that stood out, even when she was standing across the room.

As she came closer, he also noted that she moved differently, too. She didn't sway her hips back and forth like the Natalies did whenever they walked. She was graceful, and almost appeared to glide rather than walk. Another difference was that she wasn't voluptuous like the Natalies were. Her frame was more...athletic, like that of a runner or maybe a dancer.

It wasn't until she'd sat down that Liam felt an elbow in his side. He looked over to see that Ben was leaning over and nudging him in the ribs to get his attention. The whole class was looking at him. Apparently, his attention to Parker's approach had not gone unnoticed.

For the second time, he had made a spectacle of himself. Once again, the class burst out in fits of laughter at his expense. He did his best to bury his face behind his textbook, content to spend the rest of his life hiding there if necessary.

The laughter died down eventually, and Liam could hear Mrs. Kelly resuming her lesson. She was now discussing polynomial mathematics – yet another reason for him not to pay attention. As the lesson progressed, he slowly poked his head out from behind his book.

Ben was softly shaking his head in amusement while continuing to take notes – no doubt finding his friend's embarrassment a source of enjoyment. Had their positions been reversed, Liam would have done the same thing. Luckily, it appeared that everyone's attention had refocused back on the teacher and off him.

As he finished scanning the room, he did a double take. He was sure that he had seen Parker staring at him out of the corner of her eye. He tried to make eye contact with her. After a moment, she gave up the pretense and looked over at him. Their eyes met, and she gave him a brief smile. It only lasted a moment before she looked back toward the front of the class, but the smile remained.

Liam relaxed in his chair, thinking that perhaps things weren't so bad after all.

Chapter 2: The New Girl

It was no surprise to anyone in the room that Liam had embarrassed himself pretty badly that morning. Still, that brief moment where their eyes had met gave him hope that all was not lost. Which was why he spent the rest of class trying to capture Parker's attention, and perhaps get another smile out of her. The hard part was trying to get her attention without attracting the notice of the rest of the class – or, worse, the teacher.

Despite his best efforts, Parker's attention never wavered from the lesson. Liam could have been a stone statue for all of the attention she paid him. Out of desperation, he casually knocked his pencil off the desk, giving him the perfect excuse to reach down and pick it up. Unfortunately, it hit the ground and rolled out of reach, coming to a stop against the foot of Parker's desk.

His plan had backfired. The pencil had rolled out of reach, which meant that he would have to get up and walk around his desk to pick it up. Unless a certain someone had noticed and was willing to retrieve his pencil for him. He held his breath in anticipation.

Even though he was convinced that Parker was aware of his pencil sitting at the foot of her desk, she made no effort to pick it up. For that matter, she wouldn't even acknowledge its existence. She didn't even look down. Feeling defeated, Liam slumped down in his chair, waiting for class to end.

With nothing else to do, he turned his head to look over at Ben. His friend was still taking notes, but at the same time, he was shaking his head in a "You poor fool" sort of way. It was clear that Liam's attempts to get Parker's attention hadn't gone completely unnoticed. So much for making a good impression with the new girl.

Liam slumped down in his chair even further, wishing that he could sink into the floor and disappear. As if math class weren't bad enough, he now had to live with his embarrassment.

It seemed like forever, but the bell finally rang, announcing the end of class.

He uncrossed his arms and reached down to pick his backpack up from the floor. As he straightened, a delicate hand placed a yellow pencil on top of his desk. He looked up to see Parker standing beside him, book in hand.

"You dropped this," she said before turning away and heading for the door.

Liam tried to mumble a response, but the words wouldn't come out. By the time he was able to get a full sentence out, Parker was practically out the door. Before she disappeared from his sight, she looked back and gave him another smile.

"Did you see that?" Liam said, nudging Ben with his elbow without taking his eyes off the door where Parker had been.

"Pathetic," Ben said consolingly. "Absolutely pathetic."

"What?"

"Dropping your pencil? Really? That was the best idea that you could come up with? And here I had such a high opinion of you."

"It worked, didn't it?"

"Are you kidding?" Ben asked. "I have seen elementary school kids come up with better ideas than that."

"Ha, ha, ha," Liam said sarcastically, imitating a laugh.

"Come on, it's time for lunch," Ben urged, pulling Liam to his feet. "And don't worry, you will have all afternoon to think of new ways to humiliate yourself."

Liam allowed himself to be led from the room and down the hall to the cafeteria. He knew that Ben was just giving him a hard time, but now, he had to wonder. Had Parker ignored him during class because she was being coy, or did she ignore him because he was making a fool out of himself? Had she smiled at him because she liked him, or was she just being polite? Such thoughts tormented him as they entered the cafeteria.

"Earth to Liam. Liam, are you there?" Ben asked, waving his hand in front of Liam's face.

"Knock it off," he said, brushing Ben's hand away. "I'm here."

"Could have fooled me," Ben said under his breath. "Anyways, you don't have anything to worry about. You weren't smooth about it, but you didn't make a complete ass out of yourself either. Maybe next time, you can wait until after class, and then try talking to her. I hear that usually works."

"If only I had thought of that," Liam said sarcastically.

The school provided lunch for the faculty and students, so Liam and Ben got in line for lunch. While they stood there, waiting for their turn, the cafeteria started filling up. Well, that may have been an exaggeration. Even with both sides of the school having lunch at the same time, there was plenty of space for everyone to fit comfortably within the room.

Mostly, the kids sitting down to eat in the cafeteria were from the elementary school. On sheer principle, Liam did his best to ignore them as much as possible. For the most part, they were nothing more than a bunch of snot farmers who could seriously tarnish his reputation. Luckily, the high schoolers had permission to eat their lunch outside, rather than being cooped up with elementary school kids.

With trays in hand, Liam and Ben made their way through the double doors that connected the cafeteria and the athletic field outside. Small groups of kids dotted the field, enjoying their lunches in the early afternoon sun. It wasn't quite noon yet, but the sun shone down brightly, and the temperature was just right. There was even a slight breeze coming over the mountains that proved to be quite refreshing.

Liam and Ben took up their usual seats on the bottom row of the bleachers. They talked while they ate. Their discussion changed topics a dozen times, focusing on everything and nothing. After they were done eating, the two lapsed into a comfortable silence.

Ben took the opportunity to stretch out along the bottom row of the bleachers and take a nap. Liam, who never took naps in the middle of the day, busied himself with staring off into the distance. He gazed longingly up at the forested hills and the mountain peaks that surrounded them.

He had spent countless hours hiking through the foothills of those mountains, losing himself in the gentle embrace of nature. Countless summer nights had been spent camping out in the nearby forest, staring up at a perfect night sky. Of course, he had never hiked up to the peak of the mountain, or over the ridgeline to the next valley over. His aunt wouldn't permit it. Still, he longed for the day when he could set out on his own and explore the wilderness, unrestrained by the imaginary chains that bound him to this place.

The enchanting call of nature was rudely interrupted by the sound of Ben snoring. Liam looked down at his friend with mild amusement and annoyance. He was fast asleep, mouth open, arms hanging down on either side, and a small hint of drool at the corner of his mouth.

Ben was Liam's best friend, but he was also one of the reasons why he had never hiked up the mountain or crossed over to the next valley. His aunt would have a fit, sure, but his friend resisted the suggestion of doing anything remotely dangerous. And in his mind, going too far from town was dangerous.

Liam would have gone by himself, but his aunt had made him promise never to go hiking or camping alone. He had been tempted to break that promise several times, but the thought of disappointing his aunt had made him postpone his plans. Besides, his aunt had good reasons for not wanting him to wander off alone. He could still remember the last time he had done that, and the near-heart attack that she had suffered while he was missing.

Still, the desire to explore the world outside of Haven called to him. One day, he would push beyond the imaginary boundaries that kept him there. He would hike those mountains one day, and he would reach the next valley. *One day.*

Liam lowered his head in frustration. His desires were always counterbalanced by his obligations and responsibilities – obligations to his aunt, to job, his friend, and more. One of these days, he was going to figure out how to turn "one day" into a reality.

Another snore drifted up from Ben's open mouth. Liam had had enough of this. He leaned back, braced himself against the row of seats behind him, placed his foot against his friend's side, and pushed. Ben toppled over the edge of the bench he had been sleeping on, crumpling into a heap on the dirt below. He had only fallen a few inches, but that was enough to make sure he was wide awake.

Ben looked around in a daze, trying to figure out what had happened to him. Liam merely shrugged, as if to say that he must have rolled over in his sleep. Ben didn't believe that for a second, and already suspected his best friend of being the cause of his tumble into the dirt. Seeing that jig was up, Liam burst out laughing, stopping only long enough to apologize.

Ben furrowed his brow in disapproval before retaking his seat next to Liam. He made sure to give Liam several punches to the arm in retribution. Liam accepted his punishment without argument, and the boys laughed off the whole affair.

"Hey, look over there," Ben said, pointing toward the other end of the field.

Liam followed Ben's finger to see a solitary figure under one of the large oak trees that bordered the athletic field. It was Parker. She was sitting on the ground, back resting against a tree, writing something in a book that was resting in her lap.

"Not her," Ben corrected. "Them."

It was then that he noticed that a procession was making its way over to where Parker was sitting. It was the Natalies. Apparently, they had decided that now was a good time to introduce themselves to the new girl in town.

"Well, there goes the welcome wagon," Ben said.

Liam groaned inside. That was all he needed right now – for the Natalies to try and convert Parker into their group. One of the things that he liked so much about Parker was that she wasn't like the Natalies. He hated to think of yet another Natalie roaming the halls.

As the Natalies approached Parker, they fanned out in a semi-circle, no doubt to cut off any possible chance of escape. From this distance, the boys couldn't hear what was being said, so they decided to make up a conversation on their own. The two began speaking in their best impersonation of what the Natalies sounded like.

"Oh, my gosh, did you dress like that on purpose?"

"Don't you know that you are supposed to dress like the rest of us?"

"If you do not look like us, then we must destroy you."

"Join us, and together we will take over the world one lipstick container at a time."

"Join us. Join us. Join us!"

Liam and Ben couldn't stop themselves from laughing. They weren't trying to be mean, but at the same time, they couldn't resist the temptation. The Natalies offered such a prime target for their jokes.

In truth, Liam had no reason to make fun of the Natalies. They had always been nice to him, and were never mean to anyone else that he had seen. The problem was that there was just something off about them. The way they all looked the same, dressed the same, and talked the same – it was off putting.

Of course, it dawned on him that perhaps the reason why the Natalies all behaved the same way was so that none of them would be alone. No matter what happened, they would always have each other there for support. There was a lot to be said about being part of a group, especially in high school.

As he watched the interaction between the Natalies and Parker, Liam silently hoped that they were just being friendly and not trying to recruit her into joining their group. That would be such a colossal waste of such a pretty girl.

He continued to watch them from across the athletic field. He wasn't trying to be creepy by spying on them; he was just curious about the topic of their conversation. After another ten minutes had gone by, the Natalies wrapped up their conversation and walked away, leaving Parker alone under the tree. This was his opportunity.

Mustering as much courage as he could, Liam stood up and prepared to walk over and formally introduce himself. Ben had suggested talking to her after class; well, there was no better time than the present. Besides, if worse came to worst, he could pretend that he was out for a stroll and walk right past her. It was always good to have an escape plan just in case.

He had taken several steps forward when the bell sounded, signaling the end of lunch. All around the field, students were standing up and heading back to class, Parker included. He had missed his opportunity. He just couldn't catch a break today.

Ben put a hand on Liam's shoulder, giving him a consoling look. Without saying a word, the two boys picked up their lunch trays and headed back toward the cafeteria. Once inside, they dropped off their trays in the collection bin and made their way to the library. The afternoon schedule had them both doing independent study in the library, followed by gym class later in the afternoon.

The library was one of the largest rooms in the school, second only to the auditorium. Books filled the shelves from floor to ceiling, creating a labyrinth of knowledge and discovery. The librarian boasted that she had books covering any topic you could think of. Judging by the sheer volume of books on the shelves, it wasn't hard to believe her.

Since Haven wasn't large enough to have a separate public library, the school library served both the needs of the students and the townsfolk. For this reason, the library stayed open long after school was over. There was even a public entrance that led out to the parking lot so that people could visit the library without having to enter the school.

Liam followed Ben to their usual spot at the back of the library. There were study areas set up all throughout the library, but he had chosen this particular area because it was tucked away in the corner. This made it perfect for hiding from the librarian on those days when he didn't feel like studying.

There was a long wooden desk, several padded chairs, and a nearby window that let the sunshine in. Ben plopped down in one of the chairs and immediately began pulling books out of his backpack. Alternatively, Liam collapsed into a chair and buried his head in his arms as he slumped forward onto the table. He had no intention of studying today.

"If they catch you napping, then they will give you another detention," Ben said without looking up from his book.

"I am not sleeping," Liam said in a muffled voice without lifting his head from his arms. "Besides, I have only been caught once. Or maybe twice."

Ben raised four fingers into the air to show the correct number of times Liam had been caught napping. It didn't matter, though; Liam's head was still buried in his arms. He just needed time to think, and if he did end up falling asleep, that would hardly be his fault.

"You better do something," Ben warned. "The librarian is headed this way."

Liam's head shot up and he sat straight in his chair. He was just able to grab a nearby book and look like he was reading it by the time the librarian walked past them. She stopped and started at them for a long moment before resuming her patrol.

"That old crone," Liam muttered under his breath. "She doesn't have anything better to do with her time."

"Don't blame her for doing her job. As you said, this library is her kingdom. What better way to rule over your kingdom than to walk its halls?"

"Don't give me that. That heartless shrew is the reason why I got those detentions in the first place."

"And here I thought the reason for those detentions was that you decided to sleep rather than study. Silly me. How could I have been so mistaken? By the way, the book you're holding – it's upside down."

Liam looked down and realized that Ben was right. He was holding the book upside down. No wonder the librarian had lingered for so long. He chuckled to himself and threw the book back onto the tabletop. If he wasn't going to be able to sleep, then he needed to find some other way of entertaining himself.

Standing up, he made his way to the nearest aisle of books and started wandering aimlessly. He wasn't actually looking for a book to read, he just wanted it to look like he was. His ruse seemed to work, since the librarian stopped showing up to check on them.

Now that he was in the clear, he relaxed. He casually wandered up and down the aisles of books, not really caring where he was going. At one point, he found himself in the nonfiction section. This had always been his favorite genre of books. Reading about other people's adventures was the closest he had come to having some of his own.

He scanned through the selection of books, stopping briefly here and there to get a better look. One particular book caught his eye. Reaching out, he pulled *The Gumshoe Gang and the Mystery of the Missing Pocket Watch* from off the shelf. It was strange to find a mystery novel in the nonfiction section, but he didn't mind. He and Ben had spent countless hours reading mystery novels during their sleepovers at Ben's house.

After reading the description on the back, he was about to put it back on the shelf where he had found it when he stopped. The gap between books allowed him to see through to the other side. There, sitting on the floor in the next aisle over, was Parker.

She was sitting cross-legged on the floor with her legs folded underneath her. She was reading the same book that he had noticed earlier. Every now and then, she would pull a pencil out from in between her teeth to write something in the margins. Whatever she was reading, it must have been serious, judging by the look on her face.

Liam couldn't resist staring at her as she sat there. Her hair cascaded down her back and flowed in waves over her shoulder. From time to time, a lock of hair would fall down over her eyes, and she would brush it back behind her ear before resuming her reading.

As the minutes ticked by, he became aware of how creepy he was being. He wasn't stalking her, but if she saw him peering at her from behind the bookshelves, he would be hard-pressed to explain himself. Not wanting to risk being caught, he placed the book back on the shelf and turned to go.

"Are you going to stand there all day, or would you prefer to come over and have a seat?" Parker called out from the other side of the bookshelves.

Liam froze in panic. She had noticed him staring. *What must she think of me?* he wondered. As thoughts raced through his mind, one thought stood out: she had known he was there, and still invited him to join her.

Doing his best to play it cool, he walked around the corner and down the next aisle to where Parker was sitting. She had closed her book, but she kept a finger on the page that she had been reading. Liam was so nervous about what to say that he failed to see a pile of books on the floor in front of him. His foot collided with the pile, and he collapsed in a heap on the floor.

He could have died from embarrassment at that moment. Right then, the only thing he wanted to do was to get up and run for the hills, never to show his face in school ever again. He pushed himself up to find Parker struggling to keep herself from laughing. He felt so stupid and self-conscious.

Surprisingly, Parker reached out and offered her hand to help him up. It was then that Liam noticed that she wasn't laughing at him. Oh, she was laughing, but it was good-natured. He could see it in her eyes. For some reason, that made a huge difference.

"Um...hi. My name is Liam. We, um...we met before, in class."

"I remember," she said warmly. "Parker. My name is Parker."

Liam smiled as he picked himself up from off the ground. "Yeah, I know. I..." He struggled to think of what to say. In the end, he blurted out, "Listen, I wasn't staring at you through the bookshelves – well, I was, but I wasn't. I was just trying to think of a way to come over and introduce myself without seeming like a complete idiot. But now it seems like that ship has sailed."

"Not a complete idiot," she teased.

Liam let out a long breath that he hadn't realized he had been holding. He cracked a smile and thanked her for reassuring him that he wasn't acting like a complete idiot. She laughed and pointed to the ground across from her and invited him to have a seat. As he did, she reopened her book and continued reading.

"What are you reading?" he asked as he sat down - hoping to find a topic that they could start a conversation with.

"Oh, this? Nothing important – just some required reading that I need to get finished," she said. Then she leaned in a bit closer and, in a confiding tone, said, "You wouldn't believe how boring it is."

Liam glanced down at the page that Parker had open on her lap and read a few lines.

Subsection D, Article 9

The Subject is to remain unaware of their surroundings, or the conditions in which they are being monitored. The illusion of normality must be rigidly maintained at all times for maximum results. Refer to subsection D, Article 3 for general guidelines.

He had to stop himself from reading further. None of it made any sense to him, like reading stereo instructions. Seeing that he was looking over her shoulder, Parker casually closed the book and set it off to the side.

Liam was grateful to have her undivided attention, but he had no idea what to talk about.

Thinking fast, he blurted out, "So, are you one of the Natalies now?"

"Why would you call me Natalie?" Parker asked, puzzled at his question.

"Well, it's just that the Natalies came over to visit you during lunch, and they usually keep to themselves, so I figured..."

"Figured? What?"

"That they were there to recruit you to join their group. You know - become one of them. Another Natalie."

Parker's expression changed. Liam couldn't tell if she was mad or disappointed. He scolded himself in his head; he had definitely said the wrong thing. Panicking, he tried to think of a way to dig out of the hole he had dug for himself.

"I'm sorry," he blurted out. "I didn't mean anything by that. I was just...I was trying to be funny. Those girls are really nice, and I am sure they were simply welcoming you to town."

"It is not nice to make fun of people," she said quietly.

"I know. It was wrong, and I apologize," Liam said sincerely. "If you cannot tell already, I am an idiot, and have a habit of saying the wrong thing."

With that, Parker visibly softened. Apparently, him acknowledging that he was an idiot helped relieve some of the tension.

"You don't have to try so hard," she said as if sharing a secret.

"That might be hard. I don't have a lot else going for me," he admitted.

Parker's face took on a skeptical look. Liam waited for her to say something, but she just sat there and stared at him. By the time she was done, he suspected that she had memorized every detail about him, including the size of his clothes and when he'd last washed behind his ears.

"There is more to you than that," she said seriously.

Without saying another word, she stood up, picked up her bags, and made her way toward the end of the aisle. Not wanting to be left behind, Liam scrambled to his feet. He didn't follow her, though. He wasn't sure if she wanted him to or not.

As she reached the end of the aisle, she turned back to face him and said, "Are you coming?"

Liam didn't hesitate. He rushed back to the table that he had been sharing with Ben, grabbed his bag, and hurried after Parker. By the time he caught up with her, she had already reached the doors leading out to the parking lot.

He thought that he heard Ben calling after him, no doubt inquiring where he was going, but he wasn't paying attention. He followed Parker out through the doors and into the parking lot. Together, they walked across the parking lot toward the street. Before they reached the street, Parker turned left and headed up a low-rising hill on the other side of the athletic field.

After they'd reached the top of the hill, Parker sat down amongst the grass and wildflowers. Liam sat down next to her, using the spare hoodie he kept in his backpack as a makeshift blanket to sit on. From where they sat, they could see the whole town of Haven laid out before them. Beyond that were trees as far as the eye could see.

"It really is beautiful here," Parker said offhandedly.

"Yeah," he responded, though whether he was referring to the scenery or Parker, he couldn't tell.

They sat there on top of that hill, gazing off into the distance. At first, Liam didn't know what to say, but after a while, it didn't matter. The silence wasn't uncomfortable. Come to think of it, he actually enjoyed sitting there with her without feeling obligated to say something. It was nice to share a quiet moment together.

Eventually, Parker sparked up a conversation that lasted for several hours. Liam could remember hearing the school bell ring several times, but he was too caught up in conversation to pay any real attention to it. His attention was solely on her, and to his surprise, her attention was just as focused on him.

What surprised Liam the most was how easy it was to talk to her. Parker was unlike anyone he had ever met. He had talked to girls before, but not like this. She hung on his every word, eager to hear everything he had to say – unlike some girls, who only listened long enough to know when it was their turn to speak again.

Their conversation wasn't lite and bubbly, either. The topic of conversation changed multiple times, and with each change, Parker seemed perfectly at ease. She had an opinion on everything and wasn't ashamed to share it. She was knowledgeable, confident, and most importantly, she was interesting. Liam found her to be quite delightful.

As the conversation wore on, he found himself talking more and more about his hopes and dreams – things that he had never shared with anyone before, not even Ben or his aunt. He didn't know why he felt comfortable telling Parker, but he did. More than that, she validated his opinions and encouraged him.

"If you want to leave, then why don't you?" she finally asked.

"I never said that I wanted to leave," Liam said, trying to clarify.

"It sure sounds that way," she countered. "Not that there's anything wrong with that. I just figured with all this talk of hiking and exploring, you were expressing a desire to leave."

Liam thought about this for a moment. How did he truly feel about leaving Haven? Sure, he thought about leaving constantly, but this place was still his home. "It's not that easy," he replied.

"Why not?"

"Haven is my home. I grew up here. I have friends here. Not to mention my responsibilities."

"Responsibilities? Like what?"

"School, for one. Not to mention my aunt, my job, my—"

"Why should any of those things stop you?" she interrupted.

"What? I should just forget everything and leave?" Liam asked, propping himself up on his elbow.

"Well, why not?" Parker asked simply. "Those things may seem important now, but in the greater scheme of things, how important are they? When you think about it, there is nothing actually stopping you except you."

He looked at her doubtfully. He admitted that she had a point; he was seventeen, after all. Of course, that meant that he had to seriously consider the question of whether he actually wanted to go or not. He had been sheltered here for so long that the world beyond their valley was a bit intimidating. Still, his desire to leave was strong. But was it actually strong enough to get him to go?

"I am not suggesting that you leave right this minute," Parker said, interrupting his chain of thought. She must have noticed that he had been seriously considering her words, and she needed to walk him back from making any rash decisions. "I just want you to realize that the choice is up to you. There is nothing wrong with staying here, but there is also nothing wrong about wanting to go. In the end, the decision is up to you."

"Huh," he said as he thought about it. "I suppose it is."

"Besides, I would hate for you to leave so soon. We only just met," she said slyly.

Liam stared at her in disbelief, realizing that she was flirting with him. He covered his surprise with a soft chuckle and a warm grin. She smiled back at him before turning her attention back to the horizon. Feeling pretty good about himself, he leaned forward and joined in her silent contemplation.

"You really think I should go?" he asked after a few minutes.

"I want you to do what makes you happy. If that means staying, then stay. If that means going, then go. I believe that you should do what you want in this life and not let other people tell you what you can and cannot do. Be bold. You might just surprise yourself."

Liam nodded to himself. What she was saying made a lot of sense. One of his biggest frustrations was that he felt like his life was without meaning, without direction – like he was acting out a part in someone else's play. He might be a starring character, but he was still following someone else's script. For once, he wanted to be the one responsible for directing his own destiny.

His desire to leave, to climb the nearby mountains, and to explore the world beyond Haven all stemmed from a desire to take charge of his own life. He wanted to be the one who made the decisions. He wanted the choice to be left up to him, rather than being a spectator watching his life pass him by.

As he was thinking this, it occurred to him that Parker might have been flirting again. What had she meant when she said he needed to be bold? He was new to this whole flirting thing, and couldn't tell whether she was giving him a subtle hint or not. The dilemma sent him into a mental panic.

In all of the excitement, he forgot to breathe. He burst out in a fit of coughing and long gasps of air. Parker, who had been watching the whole thing, burst into laughter.

"Are you alright?" she asked, trying to get her laughter under control.

"Yeah...I. Am. Fine," he choked out between breaths.

By the time he had caught his breath, they were both red in the face – Liam from trying to catch his breath, and Parker from laughing too much. The two of them looked at each other, and Parker gave him a sympathetic look. She then leaned forward, placing a hand on the back of his neck, and pulled him close.

"Next time, remember to breathe," she said, smiling sweetly at him. He returned her smile, promising to take her advice in the future. As they sat there, heads close together, he realized that her hand was still on the back of his neck, holding him close. She was staring into his eyes. Like staring into the eyes of a cobra, he was hypnotized.

Parker pulled him even closer. Their lips reaching out, begging for contact. *This is it*, Liam thought. He was finally going to kiss her.

The suspense of their lips coming together was interrupted by the sound of a familiar voice. "So, this is where you two have been hiding!"

Parker pulled away right before their lips could make contact. Frustrated at being interrupted, Liam turned to see his best friend walking up the hill to join them. The look he shot Ben was anything but friendly – so much so that Ben halted in his tracks, a few feet away from where Parker and Liam were sitting.

Liam rolled his eyes. Could Ben really be this oblivious? The answer to that question seemed to be yes, since he just stood there staring at the two of them. Liam tried to signal for Ben to leave, but he wasn't getting the message.

Finally, Liam waved for Ben to join them – an act of pure defeat.

Ben joined them happily, walking over and positioning himself between the two.

"What are you guys doing up here?" he asked innocently.

"We were just talking," Liam told him, doing his best to suppress the annoyance in his voice.

"After you didn't come back, I looked everywhere for you two," Ben told them. "You missed the rest of our study period, and gym class too."

"And now you have found us," Liam said. "Ben, this is Parker. Parker, Ben."

As Liam finished making introductions, Ben extended his hand to Parker in a formal greeting. She merely looked at his outstretched hand with a quizzical look. Judging by the expression on her face, she was trying to decide whether he was being serious or not. When it became apparent that he was being serious, she reached her own hand out to shake his. It was extremely awkward and was made more so by Parker's evident attempt to put in as little effort as possible.

The whole exchange between the two was painful to watch. There was Ben, who was oblivious, and there was Parker, who looked like she had swallowed something foul. Now, in these moments, Liam would usually come to his friend's rescue, but he was still mad at being interrupted, which was why he felt no obligation to intervene.

"You are the new girl in school?" Ben said, stating the obvious.

"Yep," she replied.

"It must be nice, moving to someplace new. Especially a town like Haven," Ben said enthusiastically.

"Yeah," she replied.

Liam listened to Ben and Parker's conversation with mild interest. Ben kept asking questions, trying to engage Parker in conversation; meanwhile, she kept answering with single-word responses that promptly ended the conversation. This made Ben ask more questions to keep the conversation going, only to be met by the same one-word responses. Liam lost count of how many times this cycle repeated.

After a while, Ben was getting frustrated, and Parker was getting annoyed. Up until now, Liam hadn't wanted to interfere. It was payback for how Ben had so rudely interrupted him. But now, it was clear that he needed to step in and bridge the gap. There was no sense in letting this spiral too far out of control.

"Ben. My friend," Liam said, placing a hand on Ben's shoulder, "I am touched by your concern for our welfare. There we were, ditching school, and you were thoughtful enough to come and look for us."

Ben looked relieved – both for the comforting words, and for an escape from having to make small talk with Parker.

"We just felt like getting some fresh air," Liam said, gesturing toward the horizon. "And on a day like this, who could blame us? Am I right?"

"I suppose," Ben said as he slowly nodded in agreement. "It is a nice day. Perhaps next time, you can invite me to join you?"

"Oh, normally, we would," Liam said confidingly to Ben. "But we know how you feel about skipping school. We don't want to risk you getting into trouble."

A small huff from Parker showed what she thought of that idea, but Ben seemed not to notice.

"Besides, we were just about to head back," Liam said as he stood up. Parker practically jumped to her feet as well, eager to get as far away from Ben as possible. He remained sitting there for a moment longer – a sad look on his face.

Liam felt bad for his friend. He had been mad at Ben for spoiling a perfectly good opportunity to kiss Parker, but even he didn't deserve to be treated like this. He reached down and helped Ben get to his feet.

"Don't worry," he said, "next time, we will invite you too."

Liam purposefully didn't look in Parker's direction. He could see her disapproval out of the corner of his eye. It didn't matter, though; his invitation was for Ben's sake. He knew that his friend would refuse to skip class when given the opportunity. What was important was that he was given the option.

The smile returned to Ben's face after hearing that, which only reconfirmed to Liam that one of the most important parts of friendship was being included. He would explain to Parker later about his reasons for including him. Especially since he knew that his friend wouldn't take them up on their offer if it meant missing school.

"That sounds great," Ben said, looking from Liam to Parker and back again. "It's too bad we can't spend some more time together now. But I imagine you have to be going?"

"Going? Where?" Liam asked.

"Aren't you working today?"

The realization of what Ben was saying hit him like a ton of bricks. He was late for work.

"What time is it?" he asked frantically.

"3:45," Parker said, checking her watch.

"Oh, no," Liam moaned. "I was supposed to head over to my aunt's shop right after school."

"It is not your fault," Parker reassured him. "I distracted you. Now, come on. I will walk you to your aunt's shop, and you can show me the town as we go."

Parker took Liam by the arm, and together, they headed down the hill. Ben followed behind them, but Parker increased her pace to keep him several steps behind them. Once they reached the road, she turned to face him.

"It was nice meeting you. No need to go out of your way. I will make sure that he gets to work." And with that, she turned her attention back to Liam as the two walked away.

Liam glanced over his shoulder at Ben as they left. He was left standing there by the side of the road, not knowing what to do next. He tried to give him a reassuring nod, letting him know that they would talk later. He still felt bad about how Ben had been left out, but right now, he was enjoying walking down the street arm-in-arm with Parker.

As they walked into town, Parker asked, "Are you okay?"

"I'm fine," he said more out of habit than anything else.

Sensing that there was more to it than that, she nudged him with her arm and coaxed him to elaborate.

"I just feel bad. About how we treated Ben," Liam said. "He was only trying to be friendly, and I think we hurt his feelings."

"Is that what he was doing?" Parker said under her breath.

"Huh?"

"Sorry. I know that he is your friend and all, but that was a little weird, wasn't it?"

"Maybe," he said.

"Does he always go looking for you when you disappear?" she asked innocently.

"Only when I disappear in the company of strange girls," Liam remarked offhandedly.

"Fair enough," Parker said, giving him another nudge in the side.

They walked down Main Street, passing the various shops that lined the street. Liam pointed out the notable landmarks, including the town hall, the café, the movie theater, and finally, his aunt's antique shop. It was a decent-sized building nestled between the movie theater and a clothing store. The building itself was made of brick, with large display windows in front.

"Here we are," he said as he gestured at the storefront. "Linda's Closet. The finest antique shop in town, and conveniently enough, the only antique shop in town."

"Very impressive," Parker said, feigning interest.

They stood there for a moment in front of the shop, neither one wanting to say goodbye. Liam would have lingered longer, but he could see his aunt watching them through the store window. Not wanting her to come outside and make a scene, he was the first to say goodbye.

"I enjoyed our talk," he said. "Perhaps, we can get together—"

"Tomorrow!" Parker said, cutting him off. "I am available tomorrow."

"Tomorrow," Liam said happily.

Liam turned to enter his aunt's shop, but Parker held him back. Without warning, she leaned in and placed a gentle kiss on his cheek before saying goodbye and walking away. He stood there dumbfounded, his heart beating a conga line in his chest.

"In or out," Aunt Linda called out from inside the shop.

Realizing that he had been standing in the doorway, Liam stepped inside and let the door close behind him. Without saying a word, he disappeared into the backroom, emerging minutes later with his work apron and gloves on.

"I would ask why you are forty-five minutes late," Aunt Linda said dryly as he reappeared. "But I think I already know the answer to that question, don't I?"

"Sorry," Liam said. "We were talking, and I lost track of time."

"I am not happy that you are late, especially since the last thing I said to you this morning was how I needed you here as soon as school let out," she said, partially scolding him. "But right now, I am much more interested in who that was."

Liam could see a slight smile on his aunt's face – a mischievous smile. *Let the interrogation begin.*

"She is just a new girl at school," he said, refusing to make eye contact with his aunt.

"Oh, is that all?" she replied, knowing full well that there was more to this story.

"Yep," he said, trying to be convincing.

"Well, well," Aunt Linda said. "We shall have to see about that."

Chapter 3: Old Friends and New Friends

"What do you want to know?" Liam said finally after his aunt had pestered him all afternoon. No sooner had he started working than she'd found an excuse to be near him. At first, he hadn't suspected anything while they were unloading the recent shipment, but as the day had worn on, he had realized what she was doing.

Wherever he went in the store, his aunt had been sure to follow. He decided to sweep out the storeroom in the back, and his aunt had appeared. He tried busying himself arranging merchandise in the show room, and his aunt had appeared there too. He had even tried hiding behind the display counter next to the cash register, but she had found a reason to follow him there too.

The frustrating thing was that she had refused to admit what she was doing. Any time Liam had tried challenging her, she immediately came up with a good excuse for being in the same area that he was. She made it seem like it was all coincidence that they kept ending in the same places as each other. And, since they were both working in the same areas, it had been perfectly natural for her to spark up a conversation.

It had amazed him how often those innocent conversations turned toward the topic of Parker. He had tried to fend her off, but his aunt's persistence had been slowly wearing him down. Finally, he had decided to tell her everything; after all, she would find out eventually.

"Well? What do you want to know?" Liam repeated.

"Oh, did you want to talk about your new friend?" she asked innocently.

Liam rolled his eyes in exasperation. The game was over, and she had won. There was no need to keep up pretenses anymore.

"Yes. I want to talk about my new friend," he said in the most sarcastic way possible.

It still isn't too late, he thought. There were two exits in the back – one in the back of the showroom and a couple of bay doors in the storeroom, and there was also the front door. If he started running for one of those exits, she would never be able to stop him. Then again, they lived together, so he couldn't avoid her indefinitely. It was best to get it over with as soon as possible.

With an excited giggle, Aunt Linda grabbed his arm and led him to a pair of matching armchairs that were currently on display. She practically pushed him into the first armchair before settling into the second one. Her expression was calm and composed, but he could see that she was sitting on the edge of her seat in anticipation.

"Tell me everything!" she said excitedly. Had she been a cat, Liam imagined that she would have been purring. As it was, she eagerly sat there, waiting to hear the latest gossip.

Liam took a deep breath before starting from the beginning. He told her everything that had happened from the moment Parker had shown up in class, omitting the more embarrassing parts. Aunt Linda listened with feverish intensity, not daring to interrupt, even when it was clear that she had questions. When he finished, the dam of her silence finally broke and she flooded him with questions.

He tried not to get washed away in the torrent of questions. Yes, he thought she was pretty. No, they weren't dating. Yes, he wouldn't mind if they were dating. No, he wasn't going to ask her over for dinner. Yes, he was embarrassed to be seen with his aunt.

The last answer put an end to his aunt's questions. She studied him for a moment, a sly smile peeking out of the corner of her mouth. It was obvious that she wanted to know more, but she seemed content with the information that she had gotten. She must have thought that there was no need to be greedy – not yet anyway.

"Well, then, she sounds nice. I hope you two become good friends," she said, standing up and turning toward the back of the shop. As she was walking away, she casually looked over her shoulder and asked, "So, when are you going to see her again?"

"Tomorrow," Liam said without thinking. He wanted to take the words back immediately. She had tricked him into revealing when he was going to see her next, something that he hadn't wanted to share. It was too late now.

"Now, that sounds like an excellent idea," she said, nodding in approval. "Of course, you do have work tomorrow after school."

He was about to protest when his aunt continued.

"However, you did work really hard today, unloading all those boxes. Perhaps you need a day or two off. You know...to recover."

Liam couldn't believe what he was hearing. She had actually volunteered to give him the day off. The last time that had happened was six months ago, and that had been due to the shop needing to be fumigated. Trying to discern the cause of his aunt's unexpected generosity, he looked her square in the eyes. What he saw there was exactly what he had expected to find: mischief.

His aunt was up to something. Not that it mattered to him. A day off was a day off. If that meant being caught up in one of her schemes, then so be it. Besides, for all intents and purposes, her scheme involved giving him plenty of time to spend with Parker, which was a win-win as far as he could see.

"Do you really mean it?" he asked hopefully.

"Why not? You have been working so very hard lately; you deserve some time off. And besides, you need time to rest and recover from today's work." She put her fingers up to make air quotes when she said the words "rest and recover."

Liam was so excited, that he didn't even complain when they stayed late to rearrange the display cabinets against the wall. The rest of the night flew past him in a blur. Before he knew it, he was curled up in bed, slowly drifting off to sleep while thoughts of Parker danced through his head.

The next day, he had such a hard time focusing on anything besides Parker that Mrs. Kelly thought it best to separate them. He thought that the whole arrangement was unfair. They hadn't been doing anything wrong; he had simply not been paying attention to the lesson, which wasn't anything new.

After class, Mrs. Kelly pulled him aside and warned him about not paying attention in class. He nodded and made some empty promises about trying harder next time. Mrs. Kelly was far from satisfied with his response and threatened disciplinary action if he didn't change his study habits. Knowing that she was capable of carrying out her threat, he made a more sincere effort to apologize.

Once he was done with Mrs. Kelly, he walked out into the hallway, expecting to find Ben waiting for him. Surprisingly, the only one there was Parker. The two walked down the hall together while she teased him about being reprimanded by the teacher.

When they reached the cafeteria, Liam saw Ben sitting at a table in the corner, eating lunch by himself. He knew immediately that something was wrong. They hadn't eaten inside the cafeteria since they were elementary school students. He wanted to wander over to see what was wrong, but Parker held him back.

"I think he wants to be left alone," she said, motioning over to where Ben was sitting.

"Is he still mad about yesterday?" Liam wondered.

"If he is, then the best thing to do is to give him some space. When he is ready to talk about it, he will let you know," she said as they stood in line to get their food.

Liam felt bad as he and Parker left the cafeteria. Not a day had gone by where he and Ben hadn't eaten lunch together at school, and now, he was leaving his friend behind to eat lunch by himself.

Whatever feelings of remorse or guilt that he felt were quickly forgotten as he and Parker sat down. They picked up right where they had left off the day before, talking about anything that came to mind. Again, he was stunned at how easy it was to talk to her. Before he knew what had happened, the bell rang, announcing the end of lunch.

The rest of school seemed to pass glacially slow. Parker wasn't sitting by him anymore, Ben was ignoring him, and Mrs. Kelly was keeping an eye on him to make sure he was paying attention. It was a relief when the school bell sounded again, and the class was dismissed.

Since Liam didn't have to go to work, he and Parker were free to spend the afternoon together. He thought about inviting Ben to try to mend the rift between them, but as soon as the bell rang, Ben had gathered up his books and gone out the door, leaving Liam alone with Parker, which wasn't necessarily a bad thing.

The afternoon started with a leisurely stroll through town. He gave Parker the grand tour of Haven, pointing out all the interesting details that made the town unique. They even stopped by the welcome sign, where he pointed to the picture of his parents painted on the wall. Parker was enthralled by it all, and seemed genuinely interested in learning everything she could about him.

After a while, the two ended up at Liam's house. He had Parker wait in the kitchen while he rushed upstairs to tidy up his room. He did his best to fit three months of cleaning into less than fifteen minutes. He started by picking up the dirty clothes off the floor and putting them in the hamper. After that, the old sheets were stripped off of the bed and replaced with new ones from his closet. Finally, he took the overflowing trash can and moved it behind the door in the bathroom. For the finishing touch, he lit a candle and set it on his dresser to freshen up the room.

Once his room was presentable, he went back downstairs into the kitchen, where Parker had been waiting patiently. Judging by the look on her face, she knew exactly what he had been doing. At least she appreciated him putting in the effort.

The two went up the stairs into Liam's room. Parker took her time looking around, pretending not to see a random sock on the floor that he had missed or the collection of used cups on his bedside table. When she reached his dresser, she stopped.

"It helps with the ambience," he said, trying to sound sophisticated. "The candle, I mean."

"'The ambience?'" Parker asked in a quasi-mocking tone.

"Yeah, you know," Liam responded. "To set the mood."

"I see, and do you often need to set the mood when you are in your room alone?" she said, picking the sock up off the floor and handing it to him. "Or do you bring girls up here all the time?"

Embarrassed, he took the sock and shoved it into the nearest dresser drawer.

"You would be the first," Liam squeaked out.

"So, you like to have a candle ready, just in case?" she teased.

"It's for me. It helps me relax," he tried to explain, not wanting to tell her that he had bought it several years ago for just such an occasion.

Whether Parker believed him or not, she was content to let the subject drop. Instead, she turned her attention to the dozens of posters that were pinned to the walls. She walked around the room, stopping to look at each one before moving on to the next. Seeing that he had captured her attention, he followed her, explaining each poster as they passed.

"This one, is Freddie Mercury," Liam said, pointing at one of the posters. "He was the lead singer of Queen. And this one over here is Journey, and that one against the wall is the Rolling Stones."

Parker looked at each poster, mesmerized. She admitted that she didn't know who any of the people in the posters were, but she was eager to find out. Liam took the opportunity to educate her on what he thought were the greatest rock bands in history.

They spent the next several hours lying on his bed, listening to music. In between songs, he would tell Parker everything that he knew about music. As she listened, he listed off all of his favorite bands, explained their different musical styles, told her which people in the band were playing which instruments, and mentioned anything else he could think of. Everything he knew about music, he shared with her while they listened.

They were still sitting on his bed listening to music when Aunt Linda returned home from the store. As he heard his aunt come through the front door, he noticed for the first time that the sun had already gone down. He was about to scramble to his feet when his door opened, and Aunt Linda poked her head in.

The sight of him and Parker sitting on his bed together didn't appear to be as surprising to her as the fact that he had actually cleaned his room. She crossed her arms in a satisfied way as she leaned against the doorframe.

"So, this is what it takes to get you to clean your room," she said sarcastically.

Liam's eyes grew wide with embarrassment. He tried to signal her to go away, even resorting to trying to mentally communicate his desire for her to leave, but she was oblivious to his attempts. She merely stood there, unaware that she was intruding on their privacy. Then it struck him – she wasn't unaware or oblivious. She was doing it on purpose.

"You know, it is almost time for dinner," Aunt Linda said in an overly friendly way. "Parker, perhaps you would like to join us?"

Liam looked on in horror as he realized what his aunt was doing. The very thought of it sent a shiver down his spine. She couldn't do this to him. Not now, and certainly not like this.

He held his breath while he waited for Parker to accept his aunt's invitation. To his infinite relief, she declined the offer, saying that she had better head home instead. To his surprise, she seemed to be flattered by the invitation. She was even smiling at Aunt Linda in appreciation.

"Oh, well," Aunt Linda said sadly. "Perhaps next time."

"Absolutely," Parker said reassuringly.

"Excellent," Aunt Linda said with a smile, as if Parker had just entered into a binding contract to come back for dinner. "If you won't be staying for dinner, then I suppose that you will be headed home, then?"

Without waiting for a reply, Aunt Linda put an arm around Parker's shoulder and began escorting her out of Liam's bedroom. Before they left, Aunt Linda turned to Liam and asked, "Aren't you going to walk Parker home?"

Realizing that his aunt was offering him an olive branch, he quickly jumped up and followed them down the stairs.

Haven was the sort of town where nobody locked their doors and crime was all but nonexistent. Parker could have easily walked herself home without any problems, but having him walk her there was the polite thing to do. Besides, that would give him a chance to say goodnight without his aunt looking over his shoulder.

Aunt Linda escorted the two kids to the front door, where she stood watching them walk away down the street. Once they had walked several blocks, Liam felt it was necessary to apologize for his aunt's behavior – not that she had done anything wrong. He just felt bad if Parker had been embarrassed. She laughed softly before assuring him that there was nothing to apologize for. She was actually touched by his aunt's invitation. She even called his Aunt Linda, "Nice."

"'Nice?'" Liam said in disbelief.

"She was nice," Parker insisted. "She obviously cares a great deal for you – enough not to leave you alone in your bedroom with a girl after dark." She winked at him as she said the last part, insinuating that she couldn't be trusted if left alone with him under those conditions.

Liam lost a step and stumbled before recovering himself. He tried to play it off like nothing had happened, but he was sure that Parker had noticed. She had to stop herself from bursting out in a fit of laughter and contented herself with a warm smile.

Not wanting to draw too much attention to his own awkwardness, he tried changing the subject. He realized that he had no idea where they were going. He knew that Parker lived on the other side of town, but not her exact address. She looped her arm through his and took the lead.

On the other side of town was a newer housing development. "Newer" meaning less than thirty years old, unlike the rest of the houses in Haven that had been there forever. Liam recognized it immediately, since it was the same street that Ben lived on.

Parker stopped in front of a house that was half a dozen homes down from where Ben lived. Liam recognized it as the home of the Dean family. For a moment, he was confused. He hadn't heard that the Deans had left Haven.

"Isn't this where Mr. and Mrs. Dean used to live?" he asked.

"They still do," Parker said as she un-looped her arm from his. "I am staying with them."

"You mean the rest of your family didn't move to Haven with you?" Liam asked, a bit confused.

Parker took several steps up the driveway before stopping and turning around to face him. The porch light shone brightly behind her, leaving her face in shadows, but giving her an unearthly radiance.

"Nope. It is just me," she said quickly. "The Deans were friends of the family. When the opportunity came up, I was invited to spend the rest of my senior year with them. Think of it like an exchange student kind of thing. I moved here, and...well that is about all there is to it really."

Liam nodded to show that he was following along with her explanation. He thought it was sad that she had moved here without the rest of her family, but at the same time, it almost made him feel like he wasn't the only orphan in town. There was something else, though. Something about how she referred to the Deans in the past tense that didn't feel right. She had said that they "were" friends of the family rather than saying "are" friends of the family. He wanted to know what that was about, but decided that now wasn't the time to ask.

"Well, I, for one, am glad that you are here," he said.

Though her face was obscured in shadow, he could still see that she was smiling at him. He smiled back, and as he did, she took several steps back down the driveway so that she was standing right in front of him. Lifting herself up onto her tiptoes, she reached up and kissed him.

The kiss was soft at first – a slight touch of her lips on his. It gained intensity as he started kissing her back. How long it lasted, he couldn't say. By the time she pulled away, Liam was no longer aware of where he was, let alone who he was. He stood there in a euphoric daze that threatened to carry him away at any moment.

By the time he could finally see straight again, Parker was just slipping through the front door of her house. The last part of her body to vanish through the doorway was her hand as it waved goodbye.

"Wow," Liam said to nobody in particular as he turned to head for home. He felt like he was floating as he walked toward home, completely oblivious to anything or anyone that he passed.

It was because of this euphoric state that he walked past Ben's house without noticing his friend, who had come out to greet him.

***

The last two weeks had gone by in a flash, as Liam and Parker had spent almost every waking hour together. He would get up early in the morning to go over to her house so that they could both walk to school together. Mrs. Kelly had given up trying to separate the two of them in class. So, they had made an informal agreement that they could sit next to one another as long as they didn't distract the rest of the class.

Eventually, Liam had returned to work at his aunt's shop, so Parker made it a point to spend her afternoons there too. At first, Aunt Linda had been pleased with the opportunity to get to know her better, but her enthusiasm had quickly faded when it became apparent that Liam wasn't able to get any work done with her around. She had promised not to distract him, but the two always seemed to find themselves together in some remote section of the shop. It got to the point where Aunt Linda practically gave up on getting any work done while Parker was around.

Every night after work, Liam would walk Parker home, and every night, they would share a few intimate moments saying goodnight to one another. Those goodnights seemed to be lasting longer and longer – a fact that Liam's aunt had been keen on pointing out to him one night when he arrived home almost an hour late.

He didn't care, though. He couldn't remember being happier than he was right now. Spending time with Parker made him feel alive in a way that he had never felt before. It was as if her mere presence was breathing life into his previously meaningless existence. At least, that was how he felt.

Unfortunately, that continuous stream of blissful moments couldn't last forever. For Liam, they ended on Friday afternoon in the middle of gym class. The class had been divided, with the boys running laps around the athletic field and the girls doing calisthenics in the gymnasium. He was just completing his second lap around the track with Ben ran up beside him.

Up until now, Ben had been keeping his distance from both Liam and Parker. He still sat next to Liam in class, but he had made no effort to engage his friend in conversation. Liam had wanted to apologize about how they had treated Ben that first day more than two weeks ago, but he couldn't figure out how to bring it up. What was worse was that every day that passed made the whole situation feel more and more awkward.

"What is wrong with you?" Ben said abruptly as the two ran together.

"Me? What is wrong with you? You haven't said a single word to me in more than two weeks, and the first words out of your mouth are an insul," Liam said, a little upset that his friend hadn't even bothered with saying hello first before suggesting that there was something wrong with him.

"Me?" Ben said disbelievingly. "There is nothing wrong with me. I am not the one that decided to abandon his best friend the moment a pretty girl moves to town."

"Hey, I haven't been ignoring you. We just haven't talked in a while. And while you are bringing it up, that is as much your fault as it is mine," Liam countered. "Besides, I am allowed to have other friends."

"Oh, so that is what she is, huh? A friend?"

"What is that supposed to mean?"

"You know what I mean. You have been spending every minute of the day with her, not to mention those long make-out sessions in front of her house each night.".

"And what is so wrong with that?" Liam asked angrily. "I like her. She likes me. We enjoy spending time together." After a moment, he added, "And we don't need you spying on us."

"Oh please, I wasn't spying on you," Ben said. "It is just hard to miss the show you put on every night in front of her house."

With these words, Liam came to an abrupt halt. If he was going to have it out with his best friend, he wasn't going to do it while running laps. Ben stopped too, and both boys faced each other, prepared to have it out with one another.

"I don't know what is wrong with you, but why can't I be happy for once? Just because you don't have a girlfriend doesn't mean I can't have one either," Liam practically yelled at Ben. As soon as the words were out of his mouth, he wished he could take them back.

Ben had never been good-looking. His chubby physique had never caught the eye of any of the girls in school. On top of that, he looked the same as he had back when he had first moved to Haven, something that was starting to become more awkward with each passing day. Liam had taken it for granted that he was considered handsome by most girls their age. Pointing out that Ben didn't have a girlfriend was like pouring salt into an open wound. The hurt look on Ben's face confirmed it.

"I may not have a girlfriend, but even if I did, I wouldn't suddenly turn my back on my best friend because of it," Ben said in the strongest voice he could muster.

Without saying another word, he turned his back and started running again. Liam was left standing there, trying to decide what to do next. It had suddenly become clear what the problem was: he had been spending a lot of time with Parker, to the exclusion of everything else.

He tried putting himself in Ben's place. If Ben had met someone and then started ignoring him, how would that make him feel? To make matters worse, Liam could look back at the previous two weeks and see the times when he could have reached out to his friend and didn't. He felt like slime.

It didn't take him long to catch up to Ben. The two ran together in silence for an entire lap before Liam opened his mouth to speak. The words came out reluctantly at first, but it got easier the more he spoke.

"I am sorry," he said without looking at Ben. "I am not turning my back on you, or purposely trying to ignore you, I am just..."

Ben waited for Liam to finish his thought.

"I am just getting to know someone new in my life," he finished. "For the longest time, it has just been the two of us, and now, there is someone new. Someone that I have a connection with on a level that I have never had before."

"I know," Ben chimed in after a moment. "I am not upset because you are spending time with Parker. I am happy that you have found someone special in your life. I just wish it didn't come at the expense of our friendship."

"That was never my intention," Liam tried to explain. In truth, he had missed spending time with his best friend. With Parker, he was finally filling a hole in his life that he hadn't known was there, but without Ben, another hole had appeared. He needed to find a way to keep both relationships alive and active.

It would be so much easier if they were all friends. That way, they could all spend time together rather than him having to divide his time between the two of them. That was it! He just had to make sure that Ben and Parker became friends. They had started on a rough note, but he could easily turn that around.

"Listen," Liam said, turning to look at Ben. "Parker and I are having dinner tonight at the café. Why don't you join us?"

"You want me to join you on your date tonight?" Ben asked dubiously.

"It isn't a date," Liam said. "Not really."

That was exactly what it was. He and Parker had planned on going on an official date that night, complete with dinner, dessert, and possibly some star gazing in the park. That didn't matter now, though, he thought. He knew he couldn't put Ben off again, so it was either now or never.

Ben looked sideways at him, as if he was unsure whether to believe him or not. It didn't take a genius to realize that this wasn't the best idea in the world. But it looked like Ben was prepared to give him the benefit of the doubt.

"Okay, but are you sure this won't be awkward?" he asked.

"It won't be awkward. You'll see," Liam said as confidently as he could.

Now that Ben had agreed to go, Liam had one last thing that he needed to do – he needed to tell Parker about it. That wouldn't be easy, especially since up until now, she had shown no interest in getting to know Ben any better than she already did. It was as if there was something about him that rubbed her the wrong way. Still, he had to make this work.

He tried to work up the courage to tell Parker about the change in plans all that afternoon, but he chickened out each time. He wasn't looking forward to how she might react. One thing was sure: she wasn't going to appreciate Ben tagging along on their first official date.

Liam was stuck between a rock and a hard place. If he told Parker, there was a real chance that she would cancel on him. If he told Ben not to come, his friend would never forgive him, especially after he had insisted that he join them. The only thing to do, as far as he could see, was wait until the last possible moment and then hope for the best.

The moment of truth came that night as he and Parker were leaving the antique shop after closing time. They walked across the street to the café, where they had planned on having their date, but stopped just outside of the entrance. Through the large windows out front, they saw Ben sitting at a booth inside. There was an expectant look on his face, like he was waiting for someone.

As Parker reached for the door handle, Liam realized that it was now or never. "Parker, I know that this is supposed to be our first official date, but..." Liam started.

"'But?'" Parker said suspiciously.

"But we may not be dining alone," he finished in a rush.

"What do you mean—" Parker cut herself off as she looked through the window and saw Ben sitting at a booth in the corner. She slowly turned her head to stare back at Liam. Was that anger burning in her eyes?

Liam put his hands up in a gesture of surrender. "Before you get mad, give me a chance to explain."

Parker didn't say a word as she folded her arms across her chest and glared at him. He swallowed hard. Perhaps it wasn't too late to call this whole thing off, he thought.

After a few tense seconds, he continued. "I know that tonight was supposed to be about us, but Ben and I finally started talking to one another again. He misses spending time with me, and to be honest, I miss spending time with him."

Parker's eyebrow raised, and Liam pushed on, trying to get to his point across as quickly as possible. "We really didn't get off to the best start, the three of us. And it would mean the world to me if you would give him another chance. I really want us all to be friends."

After a moment, Parker uncrossed her arms, and her face softened a bit. It was obvious that she wasn't happy with the arrangement or having it dropped in her lap at the last moment. But she could see how much this meant to Liam, and so she nodded in agreement.

"Alright," she said in a chilly voice. "But you and I are going to have a long talk about this later. And don't think this gets you off the hook. You still owe me an official date."

Nodding in fervent agreement, Liam opened the door and held it open for Parker. She walked through and headed toward the booth where Ben was sitting. Liam followed after her, practically stepping on her heels.

As they reached the booth, Parker sat down on the bench across the table from Ben. Liam went to join her, but she was sitting on the edge of the bench. From the look on her face, she had no intention of scooting over so that he could sit down next to her. Not knowing what else to do, he took a seat on the other side of the table, next to Ben.

After they'd exchanged a few pleasantries and placed their orders, Parker settled herself into her seat and said, "So, Ben, tell me about yourself."

Ben did his best to tell Parker everything there was to know, including when his family had moved to Haven, what his favorite classes were in school, and why chocolate ice cream was the best flavor. Parker endured it all with a forced smile. Liam could tell that she was merely humoring Ben and had no real interest in anything that he said. Luckily, he seemed oblivious to this.

This continued on through dinner with only short pauses between mouthfuls of food. Once their plates were empty, Parker's expression had changed from a forced smile to imminent relief. In her mind, she probably thought that it was almost over.

Fearing that the night wasn't going as well as he had hoped, Liam did everything he could to keep the conversation going. Up until now, he had tried to be as inconspicuous as possible – not wanting to interfere – or, more accurately, not wanting to incur any more of Parker's displeasure. But now, he needed to do something before she decided to stand up and bring their night to a close.

"Ben likes music!" Liam blurted out.

Both Parker and Ben turned to look at him at the same time. Their expressions couldn't be more different from one another. Ben looked pleased that he had introduced a new topic of conversation. Parker, on the other hand, gave him a cold stare strong enough to send a shiver down his spine.

"My collection is nothing compared to Liam's, but I have some decent albums. Have you ever heard of the Doors?" Ben said, oblivious to the tension between Parker and Liam.

Parker turned her attention back to Ben and the conversation between them resumed. Liam heaved a sigh of relief. To her credit, Parker was actually engaged in the conversation about music. Liam had done his best to introduce her to his entire music collection over the past two weeks, so she had a good understanding of classic rock music.

It didn't last long, though. After a few minutes, the conversation began to lag, and Parker looked ready to stand up and be done. Liam made one final attempt to keep that from happening.

"You know, Ben here is quite the town historian," he said, though why he had chosen that particular topic, he had no idea. It was too late to change it now. "He can tell you anything you would ever want to know about this place."

Even as the words left his mouth, he had given up any hope of keeping the conversation alive. Who in their right mind would want to talk about the history of Haven, let alone three teenagers? The topic he had chosen was sure to be a dud.

But to his immense surprise, Parker leaned forward on her bench, a look of intrigue glinting in her eyes. "What can you tell me about Haven?" she asked.

Ben was caught off-guard as much as Liam was. Who would have guessed that they had touched on a topic of mutual interest? Taking a deep breath, Ben asked, "What do you want to know?"

"Tell me everything!" Parker said with apparent interest.

Ben started from the beginning, as if reading from a textbook. He explained how the town had originally been founded back in 1932 as a mining camp by a bunch of prospectors looking for silver. The success of the Highland Bell Silver mine to the south had spurred a silver rush in the surrounding hills. As the miners dug deeper into the mountain side, silver began pouring out of the area.

In no time, the small mining camp had grown to the size of several thousand people, all hoping to find their fortune. A bunch of the miners had gotten together and formed the Milton-Bishop Mining company, or MB Mining for short. They'd consolidated all of their individual claims into a single mining operation. Before long, the MB Mining company had taken over all mining efforts in the area.

Ben stopped to take a drink of water before continuing. He picked up where he left off, saying that the MB Mining company had remained in operation for more than twenty years. After that, the mines had begun to run dry. One after another, the various mine shafts had been closed until there was nothing left. The MB Mining company had boarded up the remaining mine shafts and closed for business.

"That is the reason why there are so many tunnels and abandoned mine shafts surrounding Haven," Liam interjected. Both Parker and Ben stared at him for a moment, as if they had just remembered that he was there too.

"What about more-recent history?" Parker urged. "Like, what can you tell me about the buildings up on the hillside?"

Ben hesitated for a second, before continuing. "What, those? They aren't anything important."

"Then why not tell me all about them?" Parker insisted.

When it was clear that Ben couldn't think of a reason why they shouldn't talk about the buildings up on the hill, he continued his oral history of the town. He explained that the MB Mining company had gone out of business, but the remaining owners had still held the title to the land surrounding the town. They'd held onto that title until a company called Globex ha purchased the land for research and development.

Globex had been looking to expand their company by building a R&D facility in the nearby area. That facility had ended up being built on the side of the mountain, where they could research everything from rockets to household chemicals. Their goal had been to build a mountain retreat where their employees could work free from distraction or outside influences.

"So, they were the ones that constructed all the buildings on the side of the mountain?" Parker inquired.

"Yes," Ben said. "They actually built both the research facility up on the hillside and most of the town as well. Of course, it wasn't named Haven back then. When they started construction, they named the city Harmon, after one of the company's founders."

Ben continued to explain how Globex had built the town of Harmon, which would eventually become Haven, in an attempt to provide their employees with every modern convenience. Their goal had been to have a perfectly self-contained town that catered to the needs of their employees, which would free them up to focus on their work.

"Interesting," Parker said offhandedly. "So, what happened to this Globebe company?"

"Globex," Ben corrected. "They went out of business. The company folded, and their operations were shut down."

"That's it? The company just shut down? What happened to all the people that were working here?" Parker inquired.

"Many of the scientists and researchers left, looking for work elsewhere, but there were those that stayed, like Liam's parents. They were instrumental in getting the city of Haven incorporated."

"Fascinating," she said. "Tell me more."

"Oh, yeah," Ben continued. "It was Liam's parents that renamed the town from Harmon to Haven. That is one reason why their picture is hanging in our townhall and why their image is on Haven's welcome sign."

"He showed those to me," Parker said, nodding toward Liam. "Cute couple, though I don't see the resemblance between them and Liam. I guess it was an old picture that they based the painting off of. Either way, I find it fascinating that they were among the town's founders."

Refocusing the conversation, Parker turned her attention back to Ben. "That doesn't really tell me a lot about those buildings on the hillside."

"I told you," Ben said in a much firmer tone of voice than Liam would have expected. "They were built by Globex for research and development."

"Sure, you mentioned who built them, but what is their deal? Are they still in use?" she asked persistently.

"Most of them are abandoned," Ben continued, becoming more and more uncomfortable with the topic of conversation.

Trying to relieve some of the tension, Liam chimed in. "Nobody works up there anymore. The whole place is surrounded by a chain-link fence, and the gates are padlocked. Supposedly, there is still someone that lives up there – a mad scientist that refused to abandon their research when the company shut down. They are still up there, locked away in their old laboratory, hoping that one day, their inventions will be unleashed on the unsuspecting townsfolk." He said the last part in dramatic fashion, like he was reciting a script from a horror movie.

Parker failed to see the excitement in Liam's urban legend. She pushed her original point. "There must still be people working up there. How could an entire complex be abandoned? Didn't you say that they were working with rockets and stuff? That is not something that you simply walk away from."

"At first, they didn't," Ben said, trying to regain control of the conversation. "Many of the remaining scientists continued to work on their projects, even though Globex had gone out of business. As the years passed, fewer and fewer people continued to use those facilities until there was nothing left up there."

"Have you ever been up there?" Parker asked quietly.

"Who, me? Oh, no. We are not allowed up there," Ben said forcefully. "No one is."

"Well, no," Liam confirmed in a much more moderated tone. *Leave it to Ben to stress the importance of following the rules.* "At least, we have never been on the other side of the fence. We have walked around the complex several times over the years."

"And you never thought about going over the fence?" Parker asked innocently.

"No," Ben said resolutely. It was clear that this conversation was making him uncomfortable. It was true that Liam had wanted to explore the research complex several times over the past few years, but Ben had always been there to talk him out of it. Liam had always figured it was Ben's natural desire to stay out of trouble that kept them away, but now, he was starting to wonder if there was anything else.

Parker wanted to keep digging for more information, but she stopped herself from pushing any further. Ben was practically fuming, which made Liam uncomfortable. Silence fell over the table as they all sat there looking at one another. Liam thought desperately of another topic that they could talk about, but nothing came to mind. It looked like Ben was having the same problem.

With nothing else to talk about, their night together had come to an end; the date was over.

Parker was the first to stand up, and Liam and Ben were quick to follow her lead. They all walked back toward the neighborhood where Parker and Ben lived. Parker made it a point to walk a few feet ahead of the boys, quickening her pace whenever one of them tried to catch up to her.

They reached Ben's house first. Parker continued to walk down the street before stopping several feet away. She waited there while Liam and Ben said their goodbyes. Before Ben disappeared inside his house, Parker gave him a slight wave, as if bidding him a fond farewell.

With Ben gone, Liam tried to catch up to Parker. Perhaps there was a way he could salvage date night with her. Once again, she maintained her distance a few feet ahead of him. When they reached her driveway, she turned around and confronted him. Judging by her expression, he wasn't about to get a goodnight kiss.

"I am sorry about tonight," he said quickly. "What I did was stupid and selfish, and I have no excuse."

His sudden apology took Parker by surprise. Whatever she had been planning to say to him, she chose to keep to herself for now. He waited for her to say something, all the while putting on the most penitent expression he could.

"I don't like being ambushed like that," she said reprovingly. "Don't do that to me again."

Liam relaxed muscles he didn't even realize he had tensed. This whole time, he had been afraid that she was going to tell him never to speak to her again. Now that that didn't seem to be the case, a faint glimmer of hope had appeared on the horizon.

"So, you forgive me?" he asked.

"Not quite. I will just have to find some way for you to make it up to me," she said as she turned around and walked up the driveway to her front door. Before she slipped inside, she turned and said, "I know Ben is your friend, and so I will make an effort to be his friend too. But only for your sake. He is way too uptight for my liking."

With that, she disappeared inside the house, closing the door behind her. Liam knew that he would need to find a way to make it up to her. Although tonight had been a relative disaster, she had tried to get along with Ben. For that, he owed her.

Maybe next time it would be better.

He could always hope.

Chapter 4: Curiosity and the Cat

The week after the infamous date-night debacle, as Liam now referred to it, he was again trying to find a way to bring both Parker and Ben together. So far, he had been splitting his time between the two, with Ben taking up his school hours, and Parker occupying his afternoons and evenings. While scheduling them separately had prevented any further conflicts, it wasn't practical in the long run. He needed another opportunity to bridge the gap between his friends.

This time, he was smart enough to approach Parker about the idea of a group activity before he mentioned it to Ben. Her reaction was what he expected it to be. She wasn't thrilled with the prospect of spending more time with him, but she had promised to make an effort. With that settled, he proposed a second group outing; Sunday breakfast.

Liam usually worked in his aunt's shop Monday through Saturday. Sunday was the one day out of the week that the shop was closed. He had learned long ago that Sundays were "me time" for Aunt Linda, and had made it a point to be out of the house as much as possible on those days. This had evolved into a tradition of spending the day with Ben.

Now that Parker had entered the picture, he wanted to include her in their Sunday morning tradition of getting breakfast at the café and spending the rest of the day together. This seemed like the perfect opportunity since it had been several weeks since Liam and Ben had kept their Sunday morning tradition. Bringing Parker along shouldn't complicate matters too much, and would be a good step toward including her into their group. To be honest, Liam was eager to resume his Sunday morning routine especially with Parker involved.

That Sunday, they all met at the café. Liam ordered his customary pancakes with eggs, a double helping of bacon, and a glass of orange juice to top it all off. Ben's order included French toast, pancakes, scrambled eggs, hash browns, bacon, sausage, buttered toast, a side of fruit, country potatoes, and a tall glass of chocolate milk to wash it all down with. Parker contented herself with an order of toast, a peeled orange, and a cup of coffee.

When their food arrived, Ben tried to make a joke about the size of Parker's meal compared to his own. Liam expected her to respond with a vicious joke directed at Ben's weight or how her meal was all that was left after the size of his order. To his surprise, she gave Ben a tight-lipped smile and mentioned something about keeping her dancer's figure.

"I didn't know that you were a dancer," Ben said between a mouth full of pancakes.

"I was," she said simply.

"What kind of dance were you into?" Liam asked, his curiosity peaked.

"Ballet," she said as she took a sip of coffee. "It was a long time ago, but I still try to stick to my diet as much as possible."

This insight into Parker's life before she moved to Haven seemed to be just the thing that they needed to get the conversation started. Unlike their previous get-together, the conversation wasn't forced. There were no awkward pauses, no struggling to find a topic, and no desperate attempts to keep the conversation going. From where he sat, Liam thought that things were looking up.

After breakfast was over, Liam and Ben both leaned back in their seats, rubbing their bellies with delight. They had both eaten more than they should have, but that was half the fun. It was at this point that Parker suggested that they go for a walk to help with their digestion. Normally, Liam would have jumped at the opportunity to go for a walk with her, but a full stomach made a good argument against any physical exercise.

"We could try the movies," Ben offered.

"The movies?" Parker said in a questioning tone.

"Yeah, if we go right now, we can still catch the matinee showing of *Bringing Up Baby*," Ben said excitedly. Comedies had always been his favorite.

Parker scrunched up her face, showing that she wasn't exactly keen on the idea. She made another attempt at persuading the boys to go for a walk, but Ben had already made up his mind on seeing the movie. Liam tried to split the difference by suggesting that they go see the movie first, giving their breakfast plenty of time to settle, before going on a walk afterwards.

Parker nodded thoughtfully. "Alright. Movie first, walk after," she said in agreement.

"Perfect. You are going to love this movie. We have seen it four times already," Ben said enthusiastically.

"Five times," Liam corrected.

"'Five times?'" Parker mouthed at Liam, her eyes widening in mock surprise.

"Hey, don't laugh," he said in their defense. "There aren't a lot of options to choose from around here. Besides, have you ever seen it?"

"I can't say as I have," Parker said, amused.

"Then it is settled," Ben said definitively. "Off to the movies!"

Ben led the way. It wasn't a far walk to the theater since it was on the other side of the street from the café. The movie theater towered over the rest of the shops on Main Street. It was easily one of the tallest buildings in town, rivalled only by the clocktower of the town hall building just down the street.

The theater had originally been built to host stage plays and live performances, but the previous owner had converted it into a movie theater. The marquee over the entrance listed a handful of movies that were played on a semi-regular basis. They didn't get a lot of new movies up here, so Mr. Malcolm, the theater owner, did his best to rotate the movies that they did have.

Sure enough, the matinee for today was *Bringing Up Baby*. The three of them entered the lobby, and Ben approached the ticket counter, demanding three of the best seats in the house. Mr. Malcolm, who owned the place, was working the ticket counter. He greeted both Ben and Liam with a warm smile. They were two of his best customers, after all. He did a double take, though, when he noticed the newest member of their group.

"And who do we have here?" Mr. Malcolm said in the smoothest way possible. He seemed to have a way when it came to talking with women. Every word he said was as smooth as silk and embroidered with a flirtatious tone that could make even the most reserved woman blush.

Liam remembered that his aunt had once described him as being a "delicious slice of chocolate cake." It wasn't hard to see why. Mr. Malcolm was tall, with broad shoulders, a welcoming smile, and a face too handsome for his own good – not to mention how his skin was the perfect color of mocha.

Whatever magic he had over women, Parker was no exception. She stared up at him, enthralled by his charm and good looks. After a moment, she remembered that he had asked a question and quickly responded with her name, her cheeks reddening slightly as she said it. Had it been anyone else, Liam would have felt a little jealous over the way Parker was staring at Mr. Malcolm.

As it was, Mr. Malcolm was one of Liam's favorite people in Haven. Not only had Liam spent almost every weekend in his theater, but the theater was right next to his aunt's shop. That practically made them neighbors. That, and he knew that Mr. Malcolm was just being his typical suave self, with no real interest in stealing Parker's affection.

"Well, now, young lady, you couldn't have chosen two finer young men to escort you to the movies than these two here," Mr. Malcolm said as he signaled toward the boys. "No doubt, they will be perfect gentlemen. Now, you had better go and find a seat. The movie will be starting soon."

As they entered the theater, they could see that the place was completely empty. Apparently, no one else in town shared the boys' affinity for watching the same movie over and over again. The good news was that they could sit wherever they wanted.

Ben led them to three seats right in the middle. As they sat down, the theater grew dark, and the movie started to play. Less than ten minutes into the film, Ben lamented that he didn't have any popcorn to go with the show. Parker commented on how it couldn't be possible that he was still hungry after the breakfast that they had just had, but Ben insisted it wasn't a proper movie without some popcorn.

He retreated to the lobby, determined to get his precious popcorn, leaving Liam and Parker alone together.

"*And who do we have here?*" Liam said in his best impersonation of Mr. Malcolm's voice.

Parker elbowed him in the side. "Stop it," she said playfully.

"*I just figured, maybe if I talk like this, you will blush for me,*" Liam said, continuing his impression. Parker glanced at him out of the corner of her eye, a sly smile forming on her face.

"Can I help it that he is good-looking?" Parker said defensively.

"*I don't know, can you?*" he continued.

"If you are going to act like this, I don't think I want to sit by you anymore." To suit her words, she got up and moved several seats away, folding her arms in mock outrage.

Liam wasn't buying it. The fact that her indignant façade was cracking under the silent laughter that she was clearly holding back told him everything he needed to know. He got up and moved several seats over, sitting down next to her. No sooner he had sat down than Parker jumped up and moved again, this time to the other side of the theater.

He pursued her, and she moved again. The whole thing had turned into an elaborate game of tag. Every time Parker would move, Liam would follow, only for the whole process to start over again. In the end, they weren't even sitting down anymore.

Parker had positioned herself right in the middle of a row of chairs. A smile of triumph appeared on her face as she mirrored Liam's every move, confident that she had the upper hand. Which was why it surprised her when he decided to climb over the row of chairs and cut her off.

The two fell backward into their seats, giggling and laughing. Liam held Parker close, preventing any further escape attempts. She whispered something about him cheating, but whatever her feelings were on the subject, they were quickly forgotten as the two started kissing.

When Ben finally returned, he found the two of them holding each other closely, sharing a passionate kiss. He made a sound in the back of his throat to alert them to his presence. Liam and Parker broke apart, Liam giving his friend a guilty look and Parker pretending that nothing had been happening in the first place.

As Ben settled down into his chair, he looked around in confusion. "Were we sitting here when I left?"

Both Liam and Parker burst out into laughter, and it had nothing to do with the movie. Liam couldn't bring himself to tell Ben about everything that had happened while he was gone, so he played it off by saying that they'd changed seats to get a better view. Parker laughed even harder at that, and it took some time to finally calm her down.

After the movie was over, Liam, Parker, and Ben exited the darkened theater and emerged into the light of a clear and beautiful day. The sun shone brightly overhead, and a gentle breeze was blowing through the trees. Parker reached her hands over her head and stretched. She was so graceful that he was in awe of her every movement.

"So, what now?" Ben asked no one in particular.

"I believe that we agreed to go for a walk after the movie," Parker reminded them.

The boys had agreed to go on a walk once the movie was finished. In fact, now that their breakfast had settled, a walk through town sounded like just the right thing to do. Determined to take the lead, Ben started walking down the street toward a park on the south side of town.

Parker seemed to have another destination in mind. Without saying a word, she turned and started walking up the street, heading north, toward the mountains. Liam was left standing there, trying to figure out who to follow.

It wasn't a hard decision. Calling out to Ben to get his attention, he ran after Parker. Ben tried to protest, but Liam wasn't listening. If Parker wanted to walk that way, then he wanted to walk that way too.

It didn't take long for both of the boys to catch up to Parker. She had been maintaining a causal pace, so she wasn't that far ahead of them. Together, the group walked up Main Street and into the neighborhood north of town. The road came to an end at a dirt path that disappeared amongst the surrounding trees.

When they reached the dirt path, Ben looked ready to turn around and head back into town. He must have been surprised when Parker kept walking up the road and onto the dirt path. He tried to protest that they were in no condition to go for a hike in the woods, but she wasn't listening. She just kept walking along the path, pulling Liam along with her as they held hands.

Ben tried to protest again, but as she continued walking, Parker merely called back, "The fresh air will do you some good."

"You know, there is nothing up that way. We would be better off heading back into town. If you want some fresh air, we can walk around the park a few times. Maybe even feed the ducks," Ben called after them in a desperate attempt to convince them to turn around.

"That is why they call it an adventure," Parker called back over her shoulder. "Half the fun is exploring the great unknown. Besides, if there is nothing up this way, then there is nothing to worry about."

Liam glanced over his shoulder at his friend as he and Parker continued up the path. Ben was standing on the pavement right where it turned into the dirt path. Judging by the look on his face, he wasn't happy with this turn of events. Liam gestured for him to follow; after all, what was the worst that could happen? After a moment, Ben reluctantly followed them up the path.

They walked for almost twenty minutes, Parker leading the way. At some point, they had started angling west, following the slope of the mountain. This made the hike much easier, since they weren't heading uphill nearly as much. Still, they had to stop every five minutes or so to catch their breath and gaze down at the valley below.

Ben was getting more and more uncomfortable with each step. His constant pleas for them to turn around were starting to get a little annoying. Parker's response was always the same: they should keep going just a little while longer. It was almost like she knew instinctively where they were going, and didn't want to turn around until they got there.

For that reason, it wasn't a huge surprise when the forest opened up before them into a small clearing. At the center of that clearing was a large two-story building. Like many of the buildings in Haven, it was made of brick, which was then covered in a thin layer of plaster. Unlike the buildings in Haven, the plaster on the outside of this building was chipped and flaking off.

At first, Liam thought that it must be abandoned. How else would you explain why all of the windows on the first floor were all boarded up? Not only that, but the main entrance looked like it was sealed shut with a dozen or so padlocks. If nothing else, the whole place looked like it was in desperate need of repairs as if the previous owner had closed up shop, locked the place down, and then left, never to return.

Parker wanted to get closer, but a chain-link fence surrounded the entire building. There was a large gate connected to a service road that headed back toward town, but it too was locked up tight. The building may have been old and abandoned, but the pebbles that made up the driveway looked fresh.

Liam approached the perimeter fence. Grasping the fence with both hands, he stared through the gaps in the chain link at the building before him. He had never been here before. In all of the years that he had lived in Haven, he had never seen this place before, let alone heard about it.

"What is this place?" he asked no one in particular.

As the silence stretched on, he turned to look at Parker and Ben. Parker had moved up next to him along the chain link fence. She shrugged as if to say that she didn't know either. Ben, on the other hand, refused to look at them or the building. He was still standing at the edge of the tree line, refusing to get any closer than necessary.

"Ben?" Liam called. "You know what this place is, don't you?"

Ben shifted his weight from foot to foot, obviously trying to find a way to avoid answering Liam's question.

"Yeah, Ben," Parker chimed in. "Weren't you saying how you knew everything about this town?"

Parker's words definitely got Ben's attention. He stopped shifting his weight and planted himself firmly where he stood. Maybe it had been the way that she had said it, or maybe it had been the subtle challenge to his knowledge, but he was not happy with her.

"It is the old Communications and Satellite Hookup Station," he said as he reluctantly joined them at the fence. "The surrounding mountains make it extremely hard to communicate with the outside world. Too much interference. So Globex built this communications station so that they could transmit and receive radio signals and satellite transmissions."

As Ben finished speaking, he pointed at a tall radio tower that rose up into the air behind the communications building. At first, Liam hadn't even noticed it. Now that he had, he could see that it was perhaps a hundred feet tall, and was supported by a thick metal core with anchored steel cables around the base.

Satellite dishes and radio antennas stuck out in all directions along the length of the tower. The most curious thing about the tower was how it had been painted several shades of green. It occurred to Liam that this was most likely the reason why he had never noticed it before. Someone had painted it to blend in with the surrounding forest and hillside.

"How do you know about this place?" he asked. "More importantly, how come I don't know about this place?"

"Probably because you weren't paying attention," Ben replied dryly. "They mentioned it once or twice in school. Besides, you can still see it referenced on old maps of the area."

"Then how come we have never been here before?" Liam demanded.

"Don't look at me," Ben said. "It's an old, abandoned building. There is literally nothing here of any interest."

"If that were true, why is the tower still transmitting?" Parker said.

Liam looked back up at the tower. Halfway up, wedged between several satellite dishes and a radio antenna, were a pair of blinking red-and-yellow lights. Was it possible that those blinking lights meant that someone was still using the tower?

"Those lights could mean anything," Ben countered.

"Really?" Parker said in disbelief. "If this place really was abandoned a long time ago, then why would someone continue to route electricity to it?"

Ben stood there silently for a moment, struggling to find the right words to put an end to this expedition. Finally, he said, "Maybe someone forgot to shut the power off. It is possible that it has been left running all these years without anyone noticing."

"Alright," Parker continued. "If that were true, how do you explain everything else that is out of place about this building?"

"Like what?" Ben asked.

"I don't know," Parker said. "Perhaps why someone decided to paint the tower green to camouflage it amongst the trees? Or maybe how almost every window on the bottom floor is boarded up, but all of the windows on the top floor are all still in good condition? If the building was abandoned, then how come none of the second-floor windows are broken?"

Parker had a point. As Liam looked around, he started noticing some of the subtle inconsistencies that she had mentioned. It wasn't just the building, either. The whole property showed signs of recent activity. The weeds inside the perimeter fence had been recently trimmed, the pebble driveway had a fresh layer of gravel, and the service road had recently been graded. Why do that for an abandoned building?

Ben seemed to be at a loss for words. He clearly wanted to say something, but nothing was coming out. In the end, he insisted that none of it mattered, that they weren't supposed to be there anyway, and that they should just turn around and go home.

"What do you want to do?" Liam asked as he turned to Parker.

She didn't have to say anything. She just looked up at him with a mischievous smile.

"No! No! No!" Ben said as he stomped back toward the tree line. "We are clearly not supposed to be here. It isn't safe to break into abandoned buildings, and besides, what would your aunt say?"

Liam ignored him. He looked at Parker and nodded in the direction of the building. She nodded back, and the two immediately started looking for a way in.

The fence was too tall to climb over, and the gate was locked, so they needed to find another way to get through. After a few minutes, Parker found what they were looking for. There was a gap large enough for them to fit through between two fence posts. They would need to crawl through on their hands and knees, but it was better than trying to climb over the top.

As the two of them climbed through the gap, they turned to see Ben, still standing on the edge of the forest. He hadn't moved an inch. Liam waived for him to follow them, but he refused to budge.

Liam didn't care. He felt exhilarated. It had been so long since he had done anything this adventurous. He had almost forgotten what it felt like to actually break the rules.

He grabbed Parker's hand, and together, they ran toward the building. The building itself was much bigger than he had originally thought. It was only two stories tall, but it was a big two stories.

What was really impressive was how long the building was, stretching out more than 400 feet. He and Parker walked around the outside, looking for a way in.

As they were coming around the building, Liam got a better look at the radio tower. It had been built on top of a large cement foundation that stuck out from the side of the building. Several large cables and electrical cords connected the base of the tower with a breaker box on the side of the building. Whatever was going on, someone was feeding power to the tower, and judging by the hum of electricity coming off the breaker box, they were feeding it a lot.

"What are you doing?" a voice called out from behind them.

Liam and Parker both jumped in startled surprise as they turned to face whoever was behind them. To their great relief, it was just Ben. He had decided to join them after all.

"Do you see this?" Liam said, pointing at the tower. "This has got to be the tallest thing in Haven, even taller than the observation tower back at the research complex."

"Just don't touch anything," Ben said cautiously. "I don't want to get electrocuted while trespassing, do you?"

"I thought this place was abandoned?" Parker said sarcastically.

"Never mind that," Liam said. "Let's see if there is a way inside."

The three of them started looking around for an entrance. The front door was out of the question with all those padlocks securing it. Most of the windows on the first floor were boarded-up, which meant that they couldn't get in that way.

As they were moving down the line of windows looking for a loose board, Liam could hear Ben mumbling under his breath. "Cheer up buddy," he said, putting an arm around his friend's shoulder. "Just think of it like we are in one of those mystery novels we used to love to read. Aren't they always exploring mysterious buildings, haunted caverns, and dangerous lighthouses?"

"Come on," Ben said resignedly.

"I am serious. Think of it. A mysterious communications building hidden deep within the forest that may or may not be abandoned. On top of that, there is also the possibility of a phantom radio signal with a cryptic message that we need to solve," Liam said dramatically. "We can call it *The Mystery of the Abandoned Radio Tower.* Now tell me that doesn't excite you just a little bit."

Just then, Parker called out to them. She was standing several feet away, next to a window that was partially opened. The boards that had covered it must have been fairly weak, because she had managed to pull them off the side of the wall with little effort.

Liam volunteered to be the first one through the window, despite Ben's objections. He stepped through the broken windowpane down onto a metal wash basin that was bolted to the side of the wall. From what he could see, he was confident that this was a janitorial closet. A thin layer of dust coated the basin and the floor. More dust could be seen on the shelves, which housed containers for cleaning supplies.

Parker was next through the window, reaching out a hand for Liam to help her down from the basin. Ben followed shortly after, still grumbling. With the three of them now inside, the closet seemed a little too small for comfort. Liam reached for the door handle and pulled it open.

The door opened up into a massive room that extended from the floor all the way up to the top of the building. Liam guessed that most of the building's interior was made up of this one gigantic room. It reminded him of a factory, but one from which all of the machinery had been removed.

To say that the room was completely empty would have been incorrect. There was a row of offices on the same side as the janitorial closet, along with the main entrance, which was locked from the outside. There was also a series of catwalks crisscrossing the room on the second story. Access to the catwalks could be achieved via a set of circular stairs directly across from the entrance.

On the far side of the room, there was a set of metal doors. Though not obviously locked from the outside, they appeared old and rusty, as if no one had opened them in quite some time. The only other door that Liam could see was on the second story, accessible by one of the catwalks.

Liam couldn't resist the urge to yell, "Echo." His voice reverberated back to him within the spacious room. A harsh shush from Ben reminded him to keep his voice down. Still, he could play a game of football in here and still have room for spectators.

Parker wasted no time walking across the room and up the circular staircase to the second floor. Liam was quick to follow, and Ben brought up the rear. By the time they reached the second floor, Parker was already standing at the door that Liam had seen from below. It wasn't a metal door like the others, and looked like the type of door you would find in an office somewhere.

Parker reached out and grasped the handle. Stopping only briefly to look back at Liam with an excited look, she turned the handle and pushed the door open.

What they found on the other side left Liam speechless.

Unlike the rest of the building, which was practically empty and covered in a thin layer of dust, the room before them was filled with computer consoles, digital monitors, communications equipment, and multiple server towers. Liam had no idea what he was looking at. Up until this point, the only computer that he had seen was the one in the library at school, and that thing was old and rundown.

"Jackpot!" Parker exclaimed as she moved deeper into the room, stopping at each server tower and computer console she passed. Liam followed after her, doing his best not to trip on the various cords, cables, and wires that connected all of the equipment in the room. He wanted to stay close to Parker, since it was clear that she knew what she was doing. In fact, if he had to describe her, he would compare her to a child on their birthday. Even the look in her eyes made him think she was trying to decide which present to open first.

"Can you believe this?" she asked him excitedly.

"Nope," Liam responded without the slightest clue what she was getting excited over. Sure, the blinking lights were pretty, and finding all this equipment in a supposedly abandoned building was unexpected, but he really didn't understand what all of this equipment was supposed to be used for. One thing was for certain; someone had gone through a lot of effort to hide the contents of this room behind the façade of an abandoned building.

"What is all this?" he asked hesitantly.

Parker, who, by this time, had moved over to a nearby computer console against the wall, answered him over her shoulder. "That over there," she said, gesturing absentmindedly with one hand, "is a server farm. Over there against that wall is a signal booster and transmitter. And right here," she said, pointing at the console in front of her, "is a command console."

Of course, most of what she had just said went right over Liam's head. He understood the part about a transmitter – they did sell radios in his aunt's shop, after all – but everything else was a mystery to him. He walked over to one of the tall metal towers that she had pointed at and rested a hand against it.

"Parker, what is a server farm?" he asked. He was hesitant to ask, fearing that she would think him naïve or stupid.

Parker stopped whatever she had been doing at the command console to look back at him. She must have seen the insecurity on his face and so she made an effort to explain. "A server farm is when you link up multiple computers to a single network. The unified servers are then able to function at a much higher capacity than a single machine. In this case…" she paused as the screen in front of her began to flash. She turned her attention back to the console in front of her and began pressing buttons on the keyboard below the monitor.

"Parker?" Liam called, pulling her attention back to their conversation.

"Oh, sorry," she said. "Like I was saying, a server farm allows all those servers to work in concert with one another which in turn increases their functionality and capability. It looks like this particular network is made up of twelve server racks; each rack contains 42 x 1U Servers, which, if you do the math, equals a server capacity of 504."

"So, it has nothing to do with food, then," Liam said half-jokingly.

Parker gave him a warm chuckle. "No, it doesn't have anything to do with food. Not that kind of farm."

Her attention was drawn back to the console, and she started typing on the keyboard again. Just as Liam was about to ask what she was doing, a voice from behind them asked that very same question.

Liam turned to see Ben standing in the doorway. He hadn't followed them into the room. He just stood there staring at Parker.

"Oh, calm down," she said dismissively. "I am not hurting anything."

"I wouldn't be too sure about that," Ben replied in an icy tone. "If I had to guess, you are playing around with something that should be left alone."

Parker rolled her eyes in exasperation. She continued typing on the keyboard, pausing only long enough to read the text that appeared on the console's monitor.

Not knowing what to do, Liam made his way over to stand by Ben in the doorway. "Do you know what any of this stuff does?" he asked in a near whisper, not wanting Parker to hear.

"It's communications equipment, left over from when Globex was running things," Ben explained. Liam continued looking at his friend, as if to tell him that he hadn't answered his question. Ben got the hint and continued.

"Think of all of this as one giant computer."

"Like in the library?" Liam clarified.

"Hardly. That thing in the library is practically an antique. This...well, this is something far more sophisticated."

Liam had more questions, but before he could ask them, Parker let out a whoop of triumph from across the room.

"I'm in!" she said proudly. "Pretty lazy security, if you ask me, but what do you expect? So, who wants to know what a secret communications system hidden inside a not-so-abandoned building has been up to?"

Ben darted across the room at record speed, doing his best to place himself between Parker and the console. She was able to fend him off, finally managing to push him back, away from the console. Liam could have been mistaken, but he could have sworn he saw the two exchanging blows back and forth before Parker managed to push Ben away.

Now that she had fended Ben off, Parker began typing commands into the system with lightning speed. She split her attention between the monitor and Ben, keeping an eye on him in case he tried to push between her and the console again.

A feeling of general unease started to settle over Liam. Something about all of this didn't feel right. It wasn't just how Ben and Parker were acting. There was something else – something that he couldn't put his finger on. Whatever it was, the feeling grew stronger the longer Parker typed on the computer console.

He had opened his mouth to say something when an alarm suddenly started going off. The room was filled with a high-pitched siren that sounded every few seconds. It was so loud, he had to cover his ears.

If that wasn't bad enough, warning lights began flashing on all the server towers and monitors. Red warning messages flashed across the screen of the console's monitor, along with several error messages. In short, the whole room had been enveloped in pure chaos. Parker was still typing frantically on the keyboard, a concerned look on her face.

Liam stepped out of the control room to escape the constant noise. The alarm was still going off, but it wasn't as loud outside the control room as it had been on the inside. As he gathered his wits, he could hear a second siren going off in the distance. He tried to follow the origin of the sound. It was coming from the other side of the metal doors at the far end of the room.

This isn't good, he thought. Realizing that now was the perfect time to leave, he reentered the control room, prepared to drag Ben and Parker behind him if necessary. He stopped, shocked by the scene that was unfolding in front of him. Ben was standing toe to toe with Parker, grabbing her arms with both hands. From the way that she was squirming, it was clear that she was trying to pull free of his grip.

Liam didn't know what he was looking at, but he didn't like it. He ran over and grabbed Ben from behind, pulling him away from Parker. At least, that was what he tried to do. Ben was somehow able to resist him, keeping a firm grip on Parker.

"What did you do?" Ben said in a deep, commanding voice, quite unlike his normal speaking tone.

"Nothing, now get off me!" Parker protested, trying to break free.

"Don't lie to me. I saw what you were doing," Ben said seriously. "You crashed the system on purpose. Why?"

"I don't know what you're talking about," Parker said in between blasts of the siren. "Whatever happened, it was an accident."

Liam realized that he wasn't doing any good from where he was, so he let go of Ben and ran around him, pushing himself between him and Parker. As soon as he got between the two, Ben immediately let go and took several steps back.

"I don't know what is going on here, and I don't care. We will figure it out later. Right now, we just need to get out of here!" Liam shouted.

Ben nodded and turned toward the door. Liam turned around to check on Parker. She was rubbing her arms where Ben had been holding her, but for the most part, she looked unharmed. There was fear in her eyes, though. Whether it was fear of Ben's reaction, or fear for whatever she had just done, Liam couldn't say.

Taking her hand, Liam led her out of the control room. Ben was already on the bottom floor, heading toward the janitor's closet. Liam and Parker ran after him, flying down the circular stairs and across the empty room.

He held the door open for Parker, and she darted inside the janitor's closet. Once she was in, he followed her, pulling the door closed behind him.

Before the door could shut all the way, he heard a large crash in the other room. Liam froze, not daring to move. Parker noticed him freeze up and came over to see what the problem was. Together, the two looked out through the thin gap of the doorway.

A pair of men in blue colored uniforms were running full speed in their direction. The metal doors at the far end of the room were standing open, indicating the direction from which the men had appeared. To Liam's immense relief, the two men headed toward the catwalk stairs rather than for the janitor's closet where they were hiding.

As they ran toward the stairs, Liam refused to move. They might not notice a partially opened door, but they would notice the motion of a door closing. He let out a sigh of relief as the men raced up the stairs, ran down the catwalk, and disappeared into the control room. Now that they were out of sight, he closed the door the rest of the way.

His heart was pounding in his chest as he turned around, prepared to slip back through the open window. He caught sight of Parker disappearing through the window ahead of him, and he quickly followed her lead. Ben was standing a few feet away, waiting for them.

Once Liam was clear of the window, all three of them started running as fast as they could toward the gap in the fence.

They squeezed through the gap and made their way to the safety of the forest. As they reached the tree line, the alarm stopped. Liam pulled up short, looking back at the communications building. From the outside, it didn't look any different, but he did notice that the lights on the radio tower had stopped flashing. *What did we just do?* Liam thought as he turned to follow his friends deeper into the woods.

Once they were a safe distance from the communications building, they all stopped to catch their breath.

"You will answer for this," Ben said, looking at Parker with a disdainful look.

"It was an accident," Parker said.

"'An accident?' 'An accident?' You call that 'an accident!'" Ben yelled back. He took another step toward her and opened his mouth as if to say something else. Before any words came out, he caught sight of Liam standing there trying to catch his breath.

Whatever he had been about to say, nobody would know. He closed his mouth and, after a few seconds, turned around and started walking back to Haven alone. Liam tried calling after him, but Ben just ignored him.

Parker turned a pleading look on Liam. "It was an accident," she said. "I didn't mean to do it."

"Do what?" he asked. "What happened back there? One moment, everything is fine – well not fine; we were breaking and entering, after all, but for the most part, everything was fine. Then the next thing I know, alarm bells start ringing, and the two of you are at one another's throats!"

Liam continued to vent his frustration as he spoke.

"Do you know how upsetting it is to see your best friend and your girlfriend getting ready to throw punches at one another? Not to mention the look in Ben's eyes. Did you see it? It was like he was, I don't know, possessed or something.

"Were you scared? I was scared. I have known Ben for more than seven years now, and I have never seen him act that way. And then there were those two security guards. I thought we were going to be caught for sure. The strangest part was that one of the guards looked familiar, like someone that I used to know. Anyways..." Liam trailed off when he realized that he had been rambling.

Parker moved over to stand next to him. She reached up and pulled his head down, resting it on her shoulder. She began stroking the back of his head and making quiet shushing noises, like he was a child that she was trying to soothe.

"All I wanted was to spend a day with my best friend and my girlfriend," Liam said in a dejected voice.

"That is the second time you have referred to me as your girlfriend," Parker said after a moment.

Liam let out a small laugh. "Well, you know, we did make out in the movie theater, and I have been walking you home every night."

"And you think that makes us boyfriend and girlfriend? Kind of presumptuous, isn't it? I mean, we haven't even been on a date yet," Parker said playfully.

He couldn't stop himself from laughing. He pulled away from Parker, standing up straight and looking down at her.

"I guess this means that you and Ben aren't going to be friends after all," he said.

Parker laughed bitterly. "No, I don't think it does." She took his hand, and together, they started walking back to town.

"One day, you will need to explain to me what happened back there. With the alarms, I mean," Liam said as they walked.

"I have a feeling that we will all know soon enough," Parker said ominously.

Chapter 5: A Mysterious Signal

Agent Lewis sat in his office on the fifth floor of the Federal building in the heart of the city. The buzz of the streets below wafted in through an open window along with a gentle breeze. The city below was alive with activity. At any time given time, the air would be filled with the din of conversation, the shuffling of footsteps, and the constant hum of traffic.

From his office window, he could admire the gleaming skyscrapers that rose up all around him or stare out at the sprawling cityscape that stretched toward the horizon.

But such things were wasted on him. He rarely took time out of his busy schedule to appreciate the simple things in life, like admiring the view. His focus was on his work, and there was plenty of that to keep him occupied.

At present, he was sitting at his desk, looking down at the computer monitor that was integrated into the glassy surface of his desktop. His hands moved along the surface of his desktop, utilizing the system's touchscreen interface. Each movement of his hand allowed him to navigate through the dozens of open data files that appeared on his screen. When he found what he was looking for, his hands stopped moving and he leaned in to get a better look.

For more than eleven years, Agent Lewis had been an agent for the Bureau of the Federal Authority, which was more commonly referred to as the Federal Bureau or simply the Bureau. For most of that time, he had been assigned to the Missing Persons division, tasked with finding people who had disappeared without a trace. Most of his time was spent at his desk, poring over case files and reports, doing his best to put all the pieces together into a coherent picture of what had happened.

His current case involved a woman who had gone missing more than two weeks ago. One day, she had reported to work as usual, and the next day, she was gone. Sometime between eight at night and eight the next morning, she had vanished. It was up to Agent Lewis to figure out what had happened to her during that time. It was all a matter of putting together the pieces, like assembling a giant jigsaw puzzle.

His hand slid across the surface of his desk, accessing a folder with several photographs in it. This particular folder contained all of the surveillance photos from the area where the woman had last been seen. He took his time as he studied each picture one by one. His fingers danced across the surface of his desk as he zoomed in and out of each picture, taking notes of anything that appeared out of place.

After more than an hour, Agent Lewis finished examining the last photo in the file. As he slid his hand across the surface of his desk in a broad sweeping gesture, the file and all of the photos collapsed into a casefile icon in the bottom left corner of the screen. The now-empty screen mirrored his own reflection back up at him.

He appeared to be in his late thirties, with jet-black hair that was slicked back with the help of some oil that gave it a wet look. He could have been considered handsome except that his hooked nose protruded out a little too far from the rest of his face. The result was that his face looked pinched, almost weasel-like.

What the reflection didn't show was that he was tall and fairly lean – not scrawny by any means, but his body lacked the stereotypical physique associated with a federal agent. Other than that, he was the personification of what a federal agent should look like, from the black suit and tie to his button-up white shirt and mirror-polished shoes. However, at the moment, his suit coat was hanging on a peg behind his chair next to a tan trench coat.

Noticing that he had become distracted by his own reflection, Agent Lewis reached out and opened another file folder on his desktop display. He had work to do, and couldn't allow himself to be sidetracked by his own vanity. Determined to refocus his efforts, he stared down at another batch of surveillance photos, along with a few video recordings.

His desktop display was too small to view all of them with the level of detail that he desired, and so he stood up and walked toward the opposite wall. A control panel on the side allowed him to activate a second monitor that was built directly into the office wall. In seconds, the formerly white wall shifted to black, and the contents of his desktop monitor were mirrored on the wall in front of him. This was much better.

Just like before, Agent Lewis took his time examining each surveillance photo in the folder, determined to find a clue that would help him solve this case. His efforts were soon rewarded when he noticed an anomaly in one of the photos. There was an odd reflection in one of the store windows where the woman had been standing.

He searched through the folder for any additional photos that would give him a better look at the mysterious reflection. What he found was a video from a traffic camera just down the street. He clicked play and watched as the subject walked down the street before stopping at an interaction. She stood there for several minutes, nodding, almost as if she was talking to someone just out of sight. Then she crossed the street and disappeared around the next corner.

Agent Lewis rewound the video, trying to see if there had been anyone standing near her, but from all appearances, she was alone. From the previous photo, he knew something wasn't right.

Sliding his hands across the wall monitor, he enlarged a section of the video that showed a clear reflection of the store window he had seen earlier. Through the reflection, he could see that another person had been standing there, pressed up against a nearby wall, hidden from view. As the subject stopped at the intersection, the second person began giving hasty instructions, talking really fast, and making a lot of hand gestures. There was no audio that Agent Lewis could hear, but it was clear that the stranger was talking with the subject. The subject even nodded in unison with whatever the stranger was saying.

After that, the subject crossed the street and disappeared around the next corner, never to be seen again. Meanwhile, the mysterious stranger walked in the opposite direction, fading from view of the window's reflection. It now seemed clear that this wasn't a simple missing persons case. The subject was clearly working with someone else, which meant that her disappearance had been planned ahead of time.

"So, you didn't disappear on your own," Agent Lewis said in a voice that was deeper than his looks would suggest. "Now I need to find out who your mysterious friend is."

Before he could make a notation in the woman's casefile regarding his recent discovery, a priority notification popped up on his screen. He paused briefly to read the notification summary. It was a Class-2 incident report. Someone had actually filed a Class-2 incident report, and it was up for grabs. He responded immediately, not wanting to miss out on the opportunity to handle such an important case.

Within seconds, a notification was sent out to the entire fifth floor, notifying everyone that he would be taking the case. It wasn't every day that a Class-2 incident came up for grabs, and he wanted to claim it before another agent beat him to it. Two minutes later, the incident report appeared in his inbox with his name assigned as the agent in charge. *Success!*

Now that the case was his, Agent Lewis cleared off his screen, shoving the previous casefile off to the side. He opened the incident report and started reading. Unfortunately, it quickly became apparent that this wasn't the career-defining case that he had thought it would be. Someone over at Central Monitoring had picked up an unidentified signal, well beyond the Boundary, and decided that this minor discovery warranted a Class-2 incident report.

How disappointing, he thought as he stepped back from the wall to stretch. Still, it had been more than six months since a case had required him to leave the seclusion of his office, so it wasn't all bad. At the very least, this would give him an excuse to get out of the office for a while.

Walking back to his desk, he disengaged the wall display and typed a few sentences onto the desktop display. Mostly, he wanted to leave a reminder to pick up where he'd left off on the previous case. He didn't like the idea of leaving it open, especially after finding such an important clue, but the incident report took precedence.

With a swipe of his hand, he closed out both casefiles before shutting down his computer. Before heading out the door, he grabbed his suit coat from off the peg on the wall where it had been hanging. After a second, he grabbed the tan trench coat from the other peg as well. There was something about wearing that trench coat that made him feel...official. Like a detective from one of those old crime novels that he liked to read.

By the time he had reached the lobby, Agent Lewis was wearing his trench coat over his suit, with his badge pinned to the breast pocket.

This was the first time in a very long time that he had felt like a real federal agent, with all the power and authority that his position entailed. Most of his career with the Bureau had been spent in an office, looking through case files and solving cases from behind his desk. Even when he cracked a case, a retrieval team would be sent out to make the arrest instead of him. Opportunities to do field work were few and far between, so he wasn't going to waste this one.

Stepping out into the street in front of the Federal building, he was immediately bombarded with the full sound of the city. People moved amongst the crowded streets, adding to the din of traffic. Electric cars and city buses filled the street with the hum of electricity as they zipped by, and the air was filled with a relentless choir of electronic bells, chimes, and notifications.

It took some time for Agent Lewis to cross the street to the Bureau's parking garage across from the Federal building. There, he checked out a car from the Bureau's vehicle pool. Before long, he was driving down the highway, heading for the Central Monitoring station on the eastern outskirts of the city.

The area where the monitoring station was located couldn't have been more different than the mirror-faced office buildings and massive skyscrapers that he was used to. The surrounding buildings were mostly old industrial complexes that didn't reach more than two or three stories high. Many of them were seldom used, if they were used at all. This was probably for the best, since the monitoring station needed large open spaces for their radar dishes, sensor arrays, and radio antennas. Any tall buildings in the area would probably interfere with their reception and need to be demolished.

As Agent Lewis pulled up to the front of the monitoring station, he was stopped at a tall wrought-iron gate. The guard on duty took his identification and disappeared back inside the guard house to verify his credentials. This gave Agent Lewis an opportunity to look around.

The whole complex was surrounded by a twelve-foot-tall fence made from wrought iron, just like the gate. Directly in front of him was a sign that said:

Central Monitoring Station
Northern District

By the time he had finished reading the sign, the guard had returned with his identification. The gate opened, and the guard waved him through, directing him to park in front of the main building. After finding a parking spot with a vehicle charging station, he walked toward the front entrance.

The building itself appeared old and in desperate need of some refurbishment. Everywhere he looked, the paint was old, faded, and peeling, revealing the discolored cement walls underneath. Whether the condition of the building was due to a lack of funding or casual neglect, he couldn't say.

In the main lobby, Agent Lewis was met by a receptionist who had already been alerted to his coming. He directed the agent to follow him as he headed down a long hallway that ended at a set of double doors. On the other side was a large room that had most likely been an auditorium before the building had been repurposed as a monitoring station.

If Agent Lewis had to describe it, he would say that the whole room was one gigantic communications hub. Computer monitors and digital displays occupied every inch of available wall space. A digital map of the Northern District was projected against the far wall. Details on the map were constantly changing as real-time information updated constantly.

There were dozens of workstations and computer consoles that filled the room. Power cords and computer cables ran everywhere, often without rhyme or reason. The one thing that he could be certain of was that everything was linked to the central computer in the middle of the room. It hummed as it received data from dozens, if not hundreds, of monitoring devices through the complex.

The receptionist began threading his way through the warren of workstations, motioning for Agent Lewis to follow him. As they walked, he could see that each workstation was dedicated to a specific geographic area. An analyst sat at each workstation, monitoring the reports provided by the central computer.

After walking over to the far side of the room, the receptionist stopped at a workstation with a name plate that read

Attendant Phillips. The analyst sitting there was completely focused on his screen, so much so that he failed to see Agent Lewis and the receptionist approach. He gave a start when he realized that he had company.

The receptionist introduced the analyst as Attendant Phillips, who was assigned to Quadrants 25 through 30. Agent Lewis made his own introductions, including the reason for his presence. The Attendant stared at him blankly for a moment, as if he had no idea what Agent Lewis was talking about. When it finally dawned on him, the Attendant jumped to his feet and shook Agent Lewis's hand vigorously.

"I am so glad you are here," Attendant Phillips said in a high-pitched, nasally voice. "I didn't expect them to send anyone so soon, but sooner or later, it's all the same to me. What matters is that you are here. You are here, and I am at your disposal. Whatever you need, just ask. Anything. Just tell me, and I will get it for you. Anything at all."

Agent Lewis had to practically pull his hand free from the Attendant's grip. The whole time he had been talking, Attendant Phillips had continued shaking his hand up and down. Obviously, the Attendant didn't get visitors to his workstation that often.

Seeing that the proper introductions had been made, the receptionist returned to their duties back in the lobby, leaving Agent Lewis alone with Attendant Phillips. Not wanting to waste any more time, Agent Lewis got right down to questioning the Attendant about the Class-2 incident report that he had filed.

"Like I said," Agent Lewis began, "I am a Federal Agent with the Bureau. We received a Class-2 incident report from your station earlier today. What can you tell me about it?"

"Oh, I can tell you anything you want to know," Attendant Phillips said energetically. Agent Lewis waited for more, but it appeared that the Attendant wasn't going to continue unprompted.

"Why don't you start from the beginning?" Agent Lewis urged.

"Ok. Well, I was sitting here at my workstation, reviewing my daily sensor sweeps. As you probably already know, the system is constantly scanning our assigned quadrants, keeping track of any anomalies. It is up to us to review the sensor logs to make sure everything is logged correctly and nothing is missed. I like to do my first review around midday, which gives me a good separation between my morning duties and my afternoon duties.

"Anyway, there I was, finishing up my review, when the system reported an anomalous reading in Quadrant 29. 'Well, that's odd,' I said to myself. 'There is nothing out in Quadrant 29, so why am I receiving a reading in that area.' Anyway, I ran a diagnostic immediately – you know, to eliminate any chance of a sensor malfunction. But, wouldn't you know, the system came back functioning at 100%, no malfunctions or glitches. So, I'm thinking, *Wow, what is going on in Quadrant 29 that would be causing a sensor ping to appear and—*"

Agent Lewis raised a hand to cut him off. He was starting to suspect that Attendant Phillips would talk his ear off if he let him.

"Let's take things slowly. At what time did you first detect this...anomalous reading you mentioned?"

"15:23 hours today."

"Alright, and what kind of anomalous reading was it?" Agent Lewis asked, pulling a pocketbook out of his coat and making some notations.

"A sensor ping," Attendant Phillips said. "A big one."

Agent Lewis pressed the Attendant for more information. He needed more details than just "a big one." He was filling out an official report, after all.

"It was a massive sensor ping, registering between 2.3 and 2.7 gigahertz. Well beyond the standard sensor blips that we are used to seeing," Attendant Phillips explained.

"Ok, so this sensor ping was pretty large, and it appeared in Quadrant 29?" Agent Lewis asked.

"Yes, which was extremely odd because there is nothing out there in Quadrant 29. Well, there is something out there, or else I wouldn't have received the ping. Which makes me think—" Attendant Phillips was cut off as Agent Lewis raised a hand to stop him from talking.

"Is it possible to show me where the sensor ping in Quadrant 29 is on the map?" Agent Lewis asked, turning to point at the map on the wall. "So I have a better idea of its location?"

"Oh, that is quite impossible. There is no way that I can show you the sensor ping now."

"Why not?"

"Well for one, it's not there anymore."

"What do you mean, it isn't there anymore?" Agent Lewis said, trying to keep the frustration out of his voice.

"Well, you see, the signal only registered for six minutes. It started at 15:23 hours and then stopped at 15:29 hours. But don't you worry – I recorded every second of it. I submitted the official recording in my incident report, but I have a backup here, if that will make things easier on you," Attendant Phillips said in a rush.

Agent Lewis took a deep breath. "Let me get this straight: You filed a Class-2 high priority incident report for a sensor ping that lasted no more than six minutes?" he asked with more patience than he felt.

"Oh, yes," Attendant Phillips said, nodding vigorously. "Normally, I would have just filed a Class-4 report for review and confirmation, but it was a ping registering between 2.3 and 2.7 gigahertz. That just doesn't happen."

"Alright, you mentioned that thing about the gigahertz volume before. What is so special about that?" Agent Lewis asked.

"Well, in order to generate a sensor ping that large, it would have to have been a cumulative reading of several thousand individual units, or one large unit operating across multiple platforms."

Agent Lewis stopped writing in his pocketbook. He must have heard the Attendant wrong. There was no way that he had recorded a reading of several thousand.

"Could you please repeat that?" he asked slowly. "I don't think I heard you correctly."

"Of course. I was saying how the sensor ping that registered on my system was between 2.3 and 2.7 gigahertz. I wish I could have narrowed that down to a much more specific number, but the signal didn't last long enough for me to get an exact fix. Still, the signal did last long enough to identify the quadrant of origin and the general strength of the signal."

"And the part about the significance of the size of the ping?"

"As I said, a sensor ping of that size indicates that we are dealing either with a large number of individual units clustered together, or one large unit that is producing an excessive amount of energy."

"And when you say a 'large number,' you mean..."

"Around two to three thousand. Perhaps more."

So, Agent Lewis had heard the Attendant correctly. He was basically saying that the system had picked up the signatures of several thousand people living in Quadrant 29; well beyond the Boundary wall. A group that size hadn't been reported in decades, if not longer. No wonder the Attendant had filed a Class-2 incident report. If it were true, this would be the largest case the Bureau had tackled in a very long time.

Up until this point, Agent Lewis's job had been largely dedicated to finding individuals who had gone missing. Over the years, there had been plenty of cases where a couple or a small group of three or four people had gone missing, but never anything larger than that. The idea that a group of several thousand could be out there hiding beyond the Boundary was both startling and exciting.

For his report, he had to be sure. "Just so I understand you correctly, you are telling me that it is possible that the signal that you picked up earlier today could have been several thousand strays?"

"Yes sir. Judging by the size of the ping, the most probable explanation is a group of several thousand," Attendant Phillips confirmed solemnly. "You know, I never did like that term, 'strays.' Anyone that purposefully goes beyond the Boundary and abandons the community shouldn't be called strays. Why not call them 'ditchers' or 'escapees' or—"

"We will stick with the term strays, if you don't mind," Agent Lewis said, cutting off the Attendant. "Now, can you tell me where Quadrant 29 is relative to our position?"

Attendant Phillips nodded energetically and directed Agent Lewis to follow him. Together they made their way through the maze of workstations over to the wall-sized map of the entire Northern District. The Attendant started inputting information into the map's control console. A minute later, a marker appeared on the map at their present location.

The Attendant continued typing in commands, and a second marker appeared on the other end of the map. Agent Lewis walked over to stand below the second marker. It was an area on the far western edge of the District, several hundred miles beyond the Boundary.

"That is Quadrant 29," Attendant Phillips said, taking Agent Lewis by surprise. He hadn't even noticed that the Attendant had walked over to stand next to him.

"Oh, I am sorry," Attendant Phillips said. "I didn't mean to sneak up on you. This isn't the first time I have been accused of doing that, either. It seems I have a natural talent for sneaking up on people. Sarah in logistics says that I need to start wearing bells on my shoes because of how many times I have surprised her. Why, I even—"

"It is alright," Agent Lewis interjected. "What can you tell me about this area?"

"The Quadrant itself spans for 100 square miles, all of which is unoccupied wilderness. Geographically, the area is comprised of several small mountain ranges and a dense forest."

"Wilderness, huh?" Agent Lewis said while focusing on the highlighted area on the map. Quadrant 29 did appear to be uninhabited. There was nothing that indicated that a large group was hiding there. There were no cities or towns within 200 miles of the Quadrant's territory, nor were there any roads or other forms of infrastructure that would be necessary to support a community of thousands.

Agent Lewis shook his head. "And you are sure that the signal came from this location?"

Attendant Phillips began nodding emphatically, insisting that it was the location of the signal.

"I don't get it," Agent Lewis admitted. "According to this map, there is nothing out there but mountains and trees. The nearest sign of civilization is a rundown highway that dead ends here and an abandoned town there." He pointed at the map where a small dot indicated a former settlement.

"And that is more than 170 miles away from Quadrant 29," the Attendant added. "Not to mention that the town you indicated is more than 350 miles away from the Boundary itself. Meaning that if there is anyone living in Quadrant 29, they are living more than 500 miles outside the Boundary wall. To think that anyone would be so careless as to venture out beyond the protection of the Boundary, I cannot understand.

"Not only is it expressly forbidden, but it is just plain dangerous. Who knows what is lurking beyond the Boundary wall? Separatists and outlaws, if you ask me. Only the worst kind of criminal would dare flaunt our laws and venture out into the wilderness. Why, they must be fugitives, extremists, or both. Why, I have a mind to..."

Attendant Phillips continued to ramble on, but Agent Lewis had stopped listening. He was focusing on the surrounding area around Quadrant 29. The Attendant was correct – there was nothing out there, just some old ruins left over from the time before the Federal Authority had mandated that everyone relocate within the safety of the Boundary. But even then, there was nothing registering in Quadrant 29 itself.

"That is why I filed my report as a Class-2," Attendant Phillips finished with a huff. He had been speaking nonstop the entire time Agent Lewis was studying the map. Apparently, if he wasn't interrupted, he would eventually tire himself out. But something that he had said had caught Agent Lewis's attention.

"What was that?" he asked, trying not to give away the fact that he hadn't been paying attention.

"Naturally, it wasn't just the size of the signal, but its location that made it so unusual. How can a signal that large appear in an area with literally nothing there? Well, not literally. There are trees and mountains and the like, but you know what I mean. There is nothing out there that would indicate a group of people were living there.

"That is why I filed my report. There shouldn't be anything out there, and yet we received a signal from that area. It doesn't make sense. Nope. It doesn't make sense at all," Attendant Phillips said.

"And you are sure that the signal that you received was legitimate and not the result of a system error?" Agent Lewis asked skeptically.

"Absolutely. I run a diagnostic on the system every morning when I start my duty shift. I find that the best way to start off my day is to make sure that all my instruments are in fine working order. You never know what things could affect the system while you are off-duty, which is why they need to be checked on a daily basis. Why not in the morning? I would hate to go throughout my day, only to find that all of my work was flawed because I didn't check the system for errors.

"Besides, I had the same thought as you, which is why when I received the sensor ping, I immediately ran another diagnostic. I figured that the system was suffering from a glitch or another system error that would generate a false reading. But the test came back negative, no system errors.

"I ran the diagnostic again when the signal disappeared. It didn't seem possible that a signal that strong would appear for only a few minutes and then disappear. But wouldn't you know it? All three diagnostics came back with the same result: no system malfunctions. Which means that the system is functioning properly, and we did receive a signal from that quadrant," Attendant Phillips explained.

"Could it have been military?" Agent Lewis asked hopefully. "Perhaps the Federal Authority's Civil Defense forces, running some sort of covert training exercise?"

Attendant Phillips shook his head. He explained that all military signals were coded on a different frequency and tracked separately. To demonstrate this, he used the control console to switch over to the military frequency. The map lit up with multiple green markers spanning the entire District.

Attendant Phillips explained how each green marker indicated a military detachment. Even with all of the green markers showing on the map, Quadrant 29 showed no visible activity. It was like a giant black hole in the middle of nowhere. At least now Agent Lewis knew it wasn't the military.

Agent Lewis rubbed the side of his head in frustration. It made no sense. A mysterious signal had appeared on the system, large enough to indicate a group of several thousand, in the middle of nowhere, with no explanation of why they were there, or even how they got there, and just as quickly as the signal appeared, it disappeared without a trace.

He tried to make sense of the situation in his head, but for every answer he came up with, three more questions would arise. If there were several thousand people living in Quadrant 29, then where did they come from? More importantly, how did they pass through the Boundary undetected in the first place?

If they had managed to slip through the Boundary without being noticed, why didn't they appear on any of the previous sensor sweeps? It was more than 500 miles from the Boundary to the Quadrant 29. Surely they would have been picked up by the sensors in the time it took them to make the journey.

The biggest question was one that he didn't even want to tackle: If several thousand people had managed to sneak through the Boundary and make it up to Quadrant 29 without being caught, why weren't they showing up on the system now? How were they managing to hide themselves from the sensor sweeps that were scanning the area at that very moment?

This was turning out to be more complicated than he'd originally thought. He still wasn't convinced that this whole thing wasn't a simple system error. That would explain everything. But the Attendant was adamant that the system was functioning correctly.

Of course, Agent Lewis thought, it was possible that the diagnostic system itself was malfunctioning. Given the rundown state of the building, it was entirely possible that several of the operating systems were also in desperate need of repair and maintenance. If that were true, then the system could have malfunctioned, giving a faulty sensor reading that went undetected because the diagnostic system was also malfunctioning. But if that were true, how could he prove it?

Agent Lewis's frustration must have shown clearly on his face, because Attendant Phillips tried to step in and reassure him that the signal had been verified. Agent Lewis waved his hand in a calming gesture, trying to reassure him that everything was under control. Attendant Phillips seemed comforted by this, assuming that this was all part of the process.

Agent Lewis made a few more notations in his pocketbook, before turning to face Attendant Phillips for one final question. "Any idea of how someone could hide from the system?"

"I'm sorry?" Attendant Phillips said as if he hadn't understood the question.

"Why did the signal stop?" he clarified. "You mentioned that the signal appeared and then disappeared six minutes later. Why did we only detect it for six minutes? For that matter, how could it have disappeared?"

"I don't know. In all my years working here, I have never seen anything like it. Supposedly, it shouldn't even be possible. Our systems are supposed to be the latest in radar and sensor technology."

"So, let's say that it was possible. What would it take to hide a large group of people from our sensors?"

"Well, hypothetically, it could be possible," Attendant Phillips admitted. "The first thing that we must consider is the distance. Quadrant 29 is more than 1,000 miles away from our current position. At that distance, we do suffer from signal degradation. The farther away from our location you get, the less powerful our sensors become.

"Secondly, it is possible to either dampen our sensors or even project them back at us. If they were using some sort of dampening field, it would deteriorate our signal before it had a chance to take an accurate reading, essentially creating a large hole in our sensor grid. The same thing would happen if they rebounded our signals back at us. Though in that case, we would pick up some of the residual signals, just like shooting a laser into a mirror," Attendant Phillips said, still pondering on the idea.

"Which technically means that someone could hide out there if they were able to find a way to either bounce our signals back at us or dampen them enough to not register?" Agent Lewis asked, trying to clarify the Attendant's response.

"Yes. Yes, that sounds about right."

"Alright, now we are getting somewhere. If it were possible, what would you need to pull it off? Is there some sort of machine that they could be using?" Agent Lewis asked.

"Not that I know of," Attendant Phillips admitted. "Like I said, it shouldn't be possible. I was only indulging in a hypothetical situation."

"Then give me a hypothetical answer. Is there something that could do that?" Agent Lewis pressed.

"Hypothetically, it could be possible. But you would need an advanced understanding of sensor technology, engineering, and electromagnetic amplification, not to mention an in-depth knowledge of our capabilities and scanning frequencies. Assuming that you had all of that, you could build something that could evade our sensors. Though it would require a large amount of power."

Agent Lewis made several notes in his pocketbook. It was possible to hide from the Federal Authority, but, given the restraints, it wasn't probable. Still, if there were several thousand people living out there in Quadrant 29, they would need access to power. If they had a renewable power source, it would be possible to direct some of that energy to a device capable of doing what the Attendant suggested.

"Thank you for your time," Agent Lewis said, turning back to Attendant Phillips and replacing the pocketbook in his coat. "I will need a copy of the sensor logs, including the conditions leading up to, during, and after the incident. I will also need a copy of your diagnostic report from this morning, as well as the other two that you ran this afternoon. If possible, please also send me any data you have on Quadrant 29 – past incident reports, historical data, and the location of the nearest power plants, both functioning and nonfunctioning."

It was now Attendant Phillips's turn to take notes. He quickly made a list of all of Agent Lewis's demands and promised to have a report submitted to him as soon as possible. Doing his best not to offend the Attendant, Agent Lewis also inquired whether it was possible to get the details on the last system wide diagnostic, just in case. Again, Attendant Phillips smiled and nodded, assuring him that he would provide everything that the agent needed.

As Agent Lewis left the monitoring station, he let out a groan of frustration. What had he gotten himself into? His first big case in...well, longer than he could remember, and it was turning out to be a wild goose chase. He would still follow up on the report that Attendant Phillips promised to submit, but he wasn't too optimistic about what he would find. More than likely, this case would end with the monitoring station having to overhaul their systems to eliminate some glitch that had caused the signal to appear in the first place.

It took him two hours to get back to his office. The traffic on the road was always dreadful at that hour. As he entered the lobby, he was greeted by several other agents, all on their way home for the evening.

He exchanged some friendly words as he headed to the elevator.

"Hey, Lewis," one of the other agents called. "What is going on with that Class-2 report you picked up?"

"Work in progress," Agent Lewis called back as the elevator doors closed behind him. He was glad for the excuse not to talk about the case. Even after all of these years, he was still seen as the new guy in the Bureau. The last thing he wanted right now was someone else looking over his shoulder or trying to coach him on how to handle it.

Besides, he'd already figured that they would dismiss it as a system glitch and leave it at that. He didn't want that. It might be a system glitch, but he wanted the opportunity to fully investigate this case before jumping to any conclusions.

The fifth floor was all but empty by this time. Agent Lewis made his way to his office, closing the door behind him and hanging his trench coat and suit coat on their respective pegs. He closed the window, which he had forgotten to shut when he left, before rolling up his sleeves and sitting down at his desk.

The surface of his desk lit up as he sat down. After the system initialized, he spent the next hour transferring his notes from his pocket book to the official casefile on the computer. Just as he was finishing, a notification appeared on his screen. Attendant Phillips had been true to his word and had sent all of the requested information he had asked for, and in record time, too.

Agent Lewis began going through the Attendant's follow-up report, making notes as he read through the various reports, documents, and logs that had been included. It was almost ten o'clock in the evening when he finally looked up from his desk.

The diagnostic reports had confirmed Attendant Phillips's story, but he wanted another opinion before he continued his investigation. He filled out a formal request for the Bureau's

Analytics division to review the Attendant's reports. He sent it off, confident that if there were any problems, they would be able to identify them. After all, Agent Lewis wasn't a radar technician or a monitoring attendant, so the only way to be sure that he was reading those reports correctly was to have the Bureau's analysts take a look at them.

He knew that he wouldn't hear back from them tonight. Chances were that everyone had already gone home for the evening. As badly as he wanted to do the same, there was still work to be done. He walked down to the breakroom, got some coffee and a left-over donut, and headed back to his desk. It was going to be a long night.

Chapter 6: Going into the Field

Agent Lewis opened his eyes, unaware that he had fallen asleep. Sunlight was shining through the window of his office, reflecting off his desk and into his eyes. He sat up, realizing that he must have fallen asleep at his desk. The last thing that he could remember was sending a request to the Historical Archives asking for a comprehensive history of Quadrant 29, but that had been around two o'clock in the morning.

Stifling a yawn, he stood up and shuffled down the hall to the breakroom. Someone had been kind enough to brew a fresh pot of coffee, for which he was immensely grateful. Combining it with some food from the nearby vending machine, Agent Lewis made a meager breakfast that he ate on his way back to his desk.

Before entering his office, he made a point of stopping at the drinking fountain in the hall. He splashed water in his face, wiping away the last remnants of sleep. It helped. He was now awake and ready to get back to work.

As he sat down at his desk, he brought up the incident report and case file that he had been working on last night. He started by reading the case summary and refamiliarizing himself with his notes from the previous night. Most of his notes were clearly documented in the casefile, but it quickly became obvious that his writing had suffered as the night had worn on.

The last thing he had written was a breakdown of the five cardinal questions: Who, what, where, why, and when. Agent Lewis rolled his eyes in embarrassment. He must have been really tired last night to revert back to his basic training. True, those were the essential questions that an agent had to ask themselves when working on a case, but for him to write them down like that was a clear sign that he hadn't been thinking straight.

They did get him thinking, though. He didn't have an answer for who or why, but he had the answers for what, when, and where. The only problem was that those answers weren't exactly helping him at the moment. Solving cases wasn't about guessing; it was about finding clues, formulating theories based on evidence, and then testing those theories against the facts of the case. At this point, all he had were guesses, with no real evidence to support his theories. It was a bad way to start.

He needed more information. That must have been why he had sent a request off to the Historical Archives. The Attendant's report had only included data for the past ten years on Quadrant 29. Since nothing significant had happened during that time, Agent Lewis had needed to go back even further. Sending a request to the Historical Archives was a gamble, but if there was any information about that Quadrant, they would have it on record.

With that, he found himself back at the point where he had left off last night. Until he heard back from Analytics or the Historical Archives, there was not much he could do. He wasn't giving up, though; there a were other things that he could do while he waited. The first thing that he did was bring up a map of the quadrant and project it on his wall.

Until he heard back from Analytics, he had to continue to operate under the assumption that the sensor pings were legitimate. If that were the case, a large group of people were hiding out in Quadrant 29. Reviewing the map, Agent Lewis marked off several possible locations where those people could be located. Given the mountainous terrain, it was most likely that anyone living out there would be located in one of the valleys nestled amongst the surrounding mountains.

There were no power plants or other signs of infrastructure in the area. However, there were several small rivers and streams that could provide hydroelectric power on a small scale. There was also the possibility of geothermal vents in the region, which could be harnessed to produce power sufficient enough to support a small town. That left the question of food and shelter. If a large group of people had settled there, they could have used the trees from the surrounding forest to build their homes, but what would they use for food?

Again, he was struck by the thought that the idea of a large group living so far removed from civilization was highly improbable. Then again, the sensors had picked up something in that area. Unless someone had figured out a way to bypass the laws of physics, those signals had to come from somewhere – or more accurately, someone.

He brought up Attendant Phillips's report again. He read through it again and again, looking for something that would stand out and offer a possible explanation. Unfortunately, there was nothing in the report that could possibly explain the existence of the signals that they had detected. In fact, there were no significant readings at all. Going back ten years, the whole Quadrant had been devoid of any activity whatsoever.

Wait a minute! Agent Lewis looked at the map on his wall and saw for the first time what he had been missing all along: The complete absence of activity. This whole time, he had been so focused on finding any sort of activity in Quadrant 29 that he had missed the obvious.

Wasn't the complete lack of activity suspicious in of itself? There should have been at least some activity in the Quadrant over the past few years. Where were the random strays wandering aimlessly through the quadrant, the passing retrieval teams on their way to the coast, or anything else that should have shown up on the report? There was nothing – absolutely nothing.

For the first time, he wondered whether he had been looking at the map all wrong. Maybe he shouldn't be focusing on Quadrant 29 directly. Perhaps he could get a better idea of what was going on by looking at the area surrounding Quadrant 29. At the very least, it was worth a shot.

Spurred on by this thought, Agent Lewis brought up every map on the system that he could find that included Quadrants 26, 27, 28, and 30. He pulled up all the incident reports and surveys for the past five years that were logged on the system, and then populated them on his map. The result was that every quadrant surrounding Quadrant 29 had at least half a dozen incident reports on file per year – every Quadrant except for 29.

This wasn't necessarily evidence, but it did indicate that something odd was happening in that area. It was definitely a thread that he wanted to follow up on. Since all he had were the incident reports that he could reference, he immediately filled out another requisition form for the Central Monitoring Station. This time, he was asking for a complete history on the surrounding quadrants going back fifty years.

He knew it could take some time to get a response, but at this point, all he had was time. He still hadn't received a response back from Analytics, so it was possible that he had wasted the last fifteen hours of his life chasing a sensor glitch. Still, something within him told him he was on the right track.

Agent Lewis continued working throughout the morning. During his lunch hour, he managed to head home for a quick shower and to change into some fresh clothes. By the time he got back to the office, a notification was waiting for him.

It was from the Bureau's Analytics division. Agent Lewis opened the report and began reading. It seemed that Analytics had been able to verify Attendant Phillips's diagnostic reports. According to them, the diagnostics were accurate, and the system was functioning based on their specifications.

As for the idea that the diagnostic system itself was malfunctioning, Analytics had reached out to Central Monitoring directly and made them conduct a full-scale diagnostic on their entire system. No doubt, they were unhappy about that. The system-wide diagnostic had taken all morning, but the result was that there had been no reported flaws in the system. Everything was functioning correctly.

Agent Lewis leaned back in his chair, pondering the implications of Analytics report. So, it wasn't a system glitch or a phantom signal. Central Monitoring had received a signal yesterday lasting for six minutes, and it had now been verified.

This was a bittersweet confirmation for him. On the one hand, it was good to know that he hadn't been wasting time. On the other hand, it meant that he was on the hook for solving this case, regardless of the lack of evidence thus far. If there were several thousand people hiding in Quadrant 29, he needed to find out who they were, how they got there, and why they weren't showing up on the system now.

These questions would have to wait until he received additional information from Central Monitoring and the Historical Archives. In the meantime, he'd need to satisfy himself with working on his other open cases.

Two days later, he finally received the response he had been waiting for from Central Monitoring. They had given him everything he had asked for, and the result was a report that was almost eight hundred pages long.

Agent Lewis did his best to read through the report, but there was so much raw data that it was difficult to follow along. Most of the information was presented in the form of daily monitoring logs. There was a report for every day, from all five Quadrants, going back fifty years. No wonder the report was so long.

He reviewed page after page of numerical data. After half an hour, his mind felt numb. Still, the report in front of him was what he had asked for, which meant that it was his duty to go through it, no matter how long it took.

At first, he had tried starting from the most recent report and working his way backwards, but that didn't last long. The only thing worse than reading through page after page of sensor data was reading through dozens of pages with no significant results. More than once, he debated sending the whole report to Analytics for analysis, but with a report of this size, it would take a month to hear back from them, if he ever heard back at all.

After a while, Agent Lewis began skipping backwards in the reports, checking every other day, then every few days, then once a week. By the time the afternoon rolled around, he had only gone back ten years.

The frustrating thing was that no matter how many times he reviewed the data for Quadrant 29, there was no activity. There was plenty of activity in the surrounding areas, but never in 29. Another problem was that he had to go through the reports for an accurate count of sensor activity. For every incident report filed with the Bureau, there had been ten signals detected that weren't reported.

Each time he encountered a signal detection, he would make a mark on his map. Pretty soon, his map looked like it had a nasty disease, with red dots scattered all over the place – everywhere except for Quadrant 29.

By this time, Agent Lewis was beginning to get worn-out from reading all the raw data. He began flipping backwards through the report at random – five years here, ten years there – only stopping long enough to see if there were any signals detected in or around the area of Quadrant 29.

It was by pure luck that his hand stopped on a date more than thirty-two years ago. On the page in front of him was a sensor reading in Quadrant 27. Unlike the rest of the entries that he had reviewed, this one was large – not in the thousands, like they had detected earlier in the week, but definitely in the hundreds. Sitting up in his chair, he began reading the sensor log with great enthusiasm.

He made notations on his map, marking the location of the group and the date they were detected. He flipped backward and forward in the reports to trace their progress. As he continued reading, a pattern emerged.

The logs clearly showed that this group of people had been detected in Quadrant 27, moving west along the old highway toward Quadrant 29. Over the course of two days, the group moved westward, finally entering Quadrant 29. They'd moved north within the Quadrant, settling in a small valley at the base of several mountains. They remained in the same location for seven days, and then...they'd disappeared.

They'd literally disappeared. On one day, the logs showed that they were there, and on the next day, they no longer registered. Agent Lewis continued ahead several days, focusing his attention on the area where the group vanished. It was no use. None of the reports mentioned their presence again, as if they had magically disappeared, just like they had earlier that week.

Agent Lewis marked the date the signal disappeared: August 2nd. After that, he accessed the Bureau's database, searching all incident reports submitted on August 2nd, thirty-two years ago. To his astonishment, there were no incident reports filed on that date. He broadened his search, going back several weeks and still finding nothing.

How was it possible that a large group of people had made their way beyond the Boundary and no one had reported it? Travelling hundreds of miles across multiple quadrants should have been detected by someone. It wasn't just the Bureau's incident reports that were missing; there were no records from the Boundary's sentries, either. Any traffic through the Boundary was immediately recorded on the Bureau's database, and yet nothing mentioned a large group of people crossing over the Boundary thirty-two years ago.

How is this possible? Agent Lewis asked himself. The Bureau's records were meticulous, and the Central Monitoring station wouldn't have missed such a large signal, especially one that appeared consistently for more than a week. So why were there no incident reports logged for this group?

Now that he had a substantial lead, Agent Lewis began reviewing the logs with greater attention to detail. It took him hours to go through the rest of the report, but it was much easier now that he knew what he was looking for. By the time he was done, his map showed a disturbing pattern. Not only had a large group headed into Quadrant 29 and disappeared more than thirty-two years ago, but dozens of smaller groups could also be seen heading to the same area. Over the course of twenty years, groups of ten or fewer had been recorded moving toward Quadrant 29 before disappearing. It was almost as if the imaginary line that divided the quadrants also had the effect of masking anyone who crossed that line.

Just when Agent Lewis was starting to think that he was onto something big, he received the report from the Historical Archives. Not willing to believe his eyes, he jumped up from his desk, grabbed his coat, and headed out of his office. The repository where the archives were kept was the first stop on his list. This was something that he needed to see for himself.

***

The next day, Agent Lewis knocked on the door of Administrator Ryan, the head of his division. He stood there, waiting for a response, his arms loaded down with old maps, charts, and a few diagrams that he had made himself.

After a few seconds, Admin Ryan's voice called through the door for him to enter. Agent Lewis opened the door and stepped inside. The office itself was more than twice the size of his own, with a large desk set right in the middle. Behind the desk was Administrator Ryan, staring down at his desk, reading the latest reports. He was an older-looking man, possibly in his late fifties, with grey hair at both temples.

"Administrator, do you have a moment? I have something that I want to show you."

"What is it, Number 6?" Admin Ryan said as he looked up from his desk and waved for Agent Lewis to come closer.

"It's Agent Lewis, sir, and I have a case here that I want you to look at," he said, stepping forward and laying out the maps and diagrams that he had brought with him on the Administrator's desk.

Admin Ryan looked down with distaste at the scraps of paper that now littered his desk, as if to say, "Who uses paper anymore?" His annoyance was unmistakable, but he motioned for Agent Lewis to proceed. As Agent Lewis saw it, the Administrator was there to listen and help out, regardless of his personal feelings, even when someone littered all over his desk.

As Agent Lewis spread out the map of Quadrant 29, Admin Ryan rolled out from behind his desk to get a better look. Unconsciously, Agent Lewis glanced down to where Admin Ryan's legs should have been. Both legs ended in stumps, short of the knee.

Rumor had it that Admin Ryan had lost both legs in the line of duty several years before Agent Lewis had joined the Bureau. Due to the extent of his injuries, he had been forced to spend the rest of his life in a wheelchair. Rather than retiring him, the Bureau had made him an Administrator instead.

Agent Lewis was startled back to attention as Admin Ryan huffed in annoyance. He clearly didn't like it when people stared at his stumps, especially when those people were taking up his valuable time.

Agent Lewis took a deep breath, refocusing on the task of explaining everything he had found to the Administrator. He started by explaining the Class-2 incident report that he had received earlier in the week. He followed that by sharing his interview with

Attendant Phillips at the monitoring station. He continued with the explanation of the case, including how the Bureau's Analytics division had validated the signal, and how he had reached out to both the Historical Archives and Central Monitoring for additional information. Admin Ryan nodded at every step of Agent Lewis's explanation, showing that he was paying close attention.

Now it was time to get to the important part. Agent Lewis indicated the paper map on Admin Ryan's desk that showed Quadrant 29. He then pulled a transparent diagram from the pile that he had placed off to the side and laid it over the map. The transparency showed the activity of detected signals over the years, all of which were headed toward Quadrant 29, including the large group from thirty-two years ago.

"Now this is where it gets interesting," Agent Lewis said, pointing down at the map and the transparency on top of it. "Over the course of two years, I have tracked 1,650 individual signals moving across the countryside, all heading for Quadrant 29. The only thing is that every single one of them disappears just as they reach the border for Quadrant 29. Furthermore, there are no incident reports, casefiles, or official documentation that reports their movement or detection."

The room went quiet. Admin Ryan scrunched his face up in concentration as he squinted down at the map on his desk. He even used his arms to lift himself higher out of his wheelchair so that he could get a better look. His attention was focused on the individual markings on the transparency and their progression across the map.

"What is this over here?" he asked as he pointed at the place where all the signals converged.

"That, sir, is the epicenter," Agent Lewis disclosed. "The location where thirty-two years ago, a large group stopped and disappeared seven days later. It is also the focal point of all the subsequent signals that we detected. If we follow the old highway system on the map, we can see that they are all headed straight for this location."

Agent Lewis took a deep breath, as if explaining this had tired him out. In truth, the past few days had worn him out, but if his theory was correct, it would all be worth it. Pointing down at the center of the map, he said, "Whatever is going on in Quadrant 29, it is happening right here."

Admin Ryan lowered himself back into his chair, rubbing his upper lip with his finger and giving the map an appraising look.

"Let me see if I understand you correctly, Number 6...um, Agent Lewis, I mean. Are you trying to tell me that you believe that you have found the location of more than 1,700 strays hiding out in a remote area of the restricted zone, and that you have pinpointed their location, which is indicated here on the map?" he asked, pointing to the epicenter shown on the transparency.

"I think so, sir," Agent Lewis responded. "The number may be upward of 2,000, since the 1,700 I quoted were additional signals, not counting the original group that settled in the epicenter. We cannot be certain of their true numbers until we send out a retrieval team to do some additional reconnaissance, but the data tends to suggest that—"

Agent Lewis was cut off by the sound of Admin Ryan laughing uncontrollably. Of all the responses he had anticipated, this was not one of them. At first, he couldn't understand why the Administrator was laughing, but then it dawned on him that he found the idea so ridiculous that he had dismissed it as a practical joke.

Agent Lewis stood there, perplexed. This was not a joke. A discovery of this magnitude should have called for immediate action, including the use of surveillance drones, multiple retrieval teams, and perhaps even dispatching an entire division of the Authority's Civil Defense Force.

It took a minute or two for Admin Ryan to get his laughter under control. When he did, he looked up at Agent Lewis and said, "Well, Number 6, I must say, I haven't had a good laugh like that in quite a while. Do me a favor and shut the door on your way out."

Even before he had finished speaking, he was already returning to his place behind his desk, determined to put this nonsense behind him and get back to work.

"This isn't a joke, sir," Agent Lewis said. "If you doubt it, then here," he said, pushing a stack of papers in Admin Ryan's direction. "It is all here! My reports, the sensor logs, more than fifty years' worth of data, and this map. Something is going on in Quadrant 29, and we have to find out what that is."

The smile was gone from Admin Ryan's face; he wasn't laughing anymore. His face was stern as he leaned forward, resting his elbows on his desk. He fixed Agent Lewis with a serious look, determined to get his point across.

"Number 6," he said in a stern voice, "I have worked for the Bureau for more years than I can easily count, most of that spent right here in this department, tracking down missing persons and prosecuting strays. And in all that time, I have never seen anything like what you are describing.

"I know that the media would have you believe that separatist groups and anarchists are hiding under every rock in the restricted zone. But the truth is, we have never found any evidence to suggest desertion on such a large scale. People do go missing, and it is our job to find them and bring them back to the safety of the Boundary, but their numbers are few, and growing fewer by the day. The numbers that you are suggesting here are simply not possible."

"Sir, the data points to—" Agent Lewis started before being cut off.

"I have humored you long enough," Admin Ryan broke in. "Whatever data you have here is either wrong or incomplete, which is leading you to assume something that is simply not there. Now, if you don't mind, I have work to do."

With that, Admin Ryan pointed to the door, dismissing Agent Lewis from the room. For the briefest of moments, he seriously debated walking out of Admin Ryan's office. Maybe the Administrator was right. Maybe his conclusions were all wrong, and he had wasted his time chasing after something that wasn't really there.

It didn't help that the same thought had crossed his mind a time or two since taking this case. It was possible that he had made a mistake, wasn't it? *No!* Agent Lewis told himself firmly. The data was correct, and he couldn't allow himself to be dismissed without presenting all of the evidence, regardless of the consequences.

"With all due respect, sir," Agent Lewis said in the most confident tone he could muster, "the data is correct. It has been verified by Central Monitoring, our own Analytics division, the Bureau's database, and I have supporting evidence from the Historical Archives. All of these sources say the same thing."

Admin Ryan, who had been clearly trying to ignore him in the hopes that he would get the hint and leave, now looked up at him appraisingly. After a moment, he spoke.

"Alright, Number 6, let's make a deal: I am going to ask you one question – just one. If you answer it to my satisfaction, I will hear you out. If not, well, let's just say that you won't be working on the fifth floor anymore. Deal?"

"Deal!" Agent Lewis said without hesitation.

"Alright. Assuming that there is a large gathering of strays hiding out in the restricted zone, going back, what did you say? Thirty-two years? Assuming that they have been out there for the past thirty years or so, why is it that no one else in this division or the Bureau itself have discovered them already? Why is it that you, an agent of barely ten years, are the one to bring this to my attention?" Admin Ryan said, making his point.

"I don't know, sir," Agent Lewis answered honestly. "The data is there, but it was broken up into little pieces here and there, like it was a jigsaw puzzle. It was simply a matter of putting the pieces together to see the whole picture. I imagine anyone in the Bureau could have figured this out, if only they had been looking for it. It just so happens that I was looking for it."

Admin Ryan sat there, quietly studying Agent Lewis. As the seconds continued to tick past, the agent grew more and more nervous. All he could do was hope that he had given the right answer.

"What you say...could very well be true. We do work for the federal government, after all. This wouldn't be the first time that we missed something that should have been apparent to us from the start. Alright, Agent Lewis. I am listening," Admin Ryan said, leaning back in his chair and giving Agent Lewis his undivided attention.

"Thank you, sir," Agent Lewis said with relief. "Like I was saying, I gathered information from several different sources, and they all indicate that something is happening in this region." He pulled out another map from the stack and spread it out over the previous one.

"Let's not get ahead of ourselves," Admin Ryan cautioned. "First, I want to know why here? Why Quadrant 29? As far as I can tell, it is just an empty quadrant with some mountains and trees."

"Because, sir, it is not empty." Agent Lewis had to hide his enthusiasm as he spoke. When he had gotten the report from the Historical Archives, he couldn't believe what he had read. The area in question, which appeared completely empty on their system, wasn't empty at all.

"According to this"—he pointed down at the map that he had just unrolled—"there is a town located right here, right where the signal originated."

Again, Admin Ryan lifted himself up out of his chair to get a better look at the map that now covered his desk. The map appeared to be old, showing signs of discoloration and yellowing at the corners. But sure enough, right there in the middle, the map showed a decent-sized town.

Admin Ryan reached out and pulled both maps toward himself. He alternated between looking at the two. On one map, there was no town. On the other, there was a town, complete with roads, utilities, and a large structure occupying one of the nearby mountainsides.

"I don't understand," he admitted.

"The first map," Agent Lewis said, pointing down at the newer map in Admin Ryan's right hand, "was printed out this morning. This is the area as it appears on our system, completely devoid of any signs of life. And this one," he said, pointing to the older map in Admin Ryan's other hand, "I pulled directly from the Historical Archives."

Admin Ryan continued staring at both maps, alternating between the two before laying them both back down on his desk. He leaned back in his chair and rubbed his lip with his finger in deep thought.

"What are you suggesting, Agent Lewis?" he asked in a cautious tone.

"Just this: Thirty-two years ago, a large group made their way beyond the Boundary, heading straight toward Quadrant 29. When they arrived, rather than being met by untamed wilderness, they found the remnants of a town, complete with everything they would ever need to support a community. I would even go so far as to say that they knew about the existence of this town before setting out, and that it was their desired destination the whole time," Agent Lewis explained.

"Go on."

"Somehow, that group figured out a way to hide from our sensors, which would explain how they managed to go undetected for all these years. Not only that, but over the course of twenty years, that large group was joined by almost 1,700 additional inhabitants – all of whom managed to cross the Boundary and make their way to Quadrant 29 without an incident report ever being filed."

"Your point, Agent?"

"Sir, a migration of this size cannot travel more than 500 miles through the restricted zone without being reported. The records supplied by Central Monitoring show that we detected these groups, but not a single incident report appears on our system. What is even more disturbing is that our system tells us that there shouldn't be anything there, but now, we have evidence that proves that something is there. Which begs the question: Why are the maps from the Historical Archives and our own database not identical?" Agent Lewis concluded.

"Hold on a moment," Admin Ryan said, putting up a hand. "I don't think I like where this is going."

"Whether we like it or not, we cannot be blind to the fact that something – or more specifically, someone – has been suppressing this information," Agent Lewis said.

"And you are suggesting that this person is helping these strays from within the Bureau?" Admin Ryan said skeptically.

"That is my theory, yes," Agent Lewis said with conviction. "If it were just someone at Central Monitoring, then one of the other attendants would have reported something before now. While it is possible that there are multiple attendants conspiring to hide the mass migration of people across the restricted zone, it doesn't seem likely. If that were the case, then why would they allow an incident report to be filed after all of this time?

"No, it makes much more sense if the person was here, within the Bureau. From here, they would be able to suppress any incoming incident reports, wipe our records of any incriminating evidence, and falsify records. How else do you explain an entire town being removed from our database?

"The most likely possibility is that we have a security breach within the Bureau that may or may not be working with someone in Central Monitoring. A collaboration between the two would account for the lack of action up until now. It might also explain why no one else has put all of these pieces together until now."

"Do you honestly believe that?" Admin Ryan asked in a near-whisper.

"Yes, sir. I do."

Admin Ryan was definitely not laughing now. He sat there behind his desk, staring at the maps laid out before him. He paused his study of the maps long enough to review the sensor logs and various reports that Agent Lewis had brought with him. Once he had gone through all of the documentation, he started again from the beginning. Agent Lewis had nothing else to do but stand there and wait.

Finally, Admin Ryan put down the last report and looked up at Agent Lewis. "There is some merit to what you are proposing, but I still cannot believe that someone from within our own organization is helping these strays. That alone is an act of treason."

"I don't know what to say," Agent Lewis said hesitantly. "All I can do is follow the evidence where it leads me."

"And right now, it is leading you out into the middle of nowhere, to a town that may or may not exist," Admin Ryan clarified.

"Yes, sir."

"Alright, then. When do you leave?"

"Sir?" Agent Lewis asked in genuine surprise.

"You just finished telling me in no uncertain terms that this town exists in Quadrant 29, and that it is filled with strays – more strays than we have ever encountered in one location in all my time with the Bureau. The only way to know if you are right is to send someone out there to verify your claims. And right now, I cannot think of anyone better suited for the job," Admin Ryan said, pushing the maps back toward Agent Lewis with a grin.

"Sir, if I am right, then we will need more than a single agent. We will need retrieval teams, vehicles, air support – maybe even the military," Agent Lewis said desperately.

"I cannot commit those types of resources without verifiable proof," Admin Ryan said firmly.

"Then send a recon drone, or re-task a satellite to give us a live feed of the area," Agent Lewis suggested desperately.

"Can't do it," Admin Ryan said. "There is no guarantee that whatever they are using to hide from our sensors wouldn't also hide them from our satellites and drones. Not to mention, if there is a traitor in our midst, as you suggest, it is possible that they could corrupt any surveillance data that we may receive. No, the best thing for us is to have someone – in this case you – go out there and verify the existence of this mysterious town and its inhabitants. Assuming that they do, in fact, exist."

"But, sir, I..." Agent Lewis struggled to find the right words to explain his lack of field experience and the dangers that he could possibly face out there beyond the Boundary wall.

"Now, listen: Up until now, you have presented a convincing argument, but the evidence here is circumstantial at best. You yourself admitted that it was pieced together from different sources. Now, I am willing to go along with this theory of yours, but I am not going to dedicate precious resources for something that may not even be there," Admin Ryan said definitively.

"Besides, the way I understand it, you have been pushing for more fieldwork," he continued, as if reading Agent Lewis's thoughts. "This may not be what you had in mind, but it is the only chance you are going to get. The time has come for you to show me what you are made of."

Agent Lewis stood there speechless. It was true that when he had first gotten the case, he had been excited about the possibility of working in the field, but this was different. He had never in his wildest dreams considered the possibility that the case would take him beyond the Boundary. For him, working in the field had meant leaving his office and doing some work in the city, or even one of the neighboring cities, not journeying out into the restricted zone.

"And if I get there and discover that there are indeed people hiding in the mountains?" Agent Lewis said after a long pause.

"If you are right, and there are people in Quadrant 29 like you say there are, then I will send in the damned cavalry to support you."

"And if I am wrong?"

"Well, we will deal with that when the time comes," Admin Ryan said dryly. "To be honest, I am half-hoping that you are wrong. Recovering that many strays would drown our division in paperwork for years to come. Besides, I don't like the idea of a traitor in our midst."

"Understood, sir."

"Good. Now that we understand one another, you will make plans to leave today. As soon as possible. If you start now, you should be able to make it to the Boundary wall before dark. Since you will need to go beyond the Boundary, I will issue travel orders that will allow you to cross over without any undue hassle."

As he finished speaking, Admin Ryan typed something onto the surface of his desk. Agent Lewis didn't have to look down to know that he was filling out travel orders. It was official now.

Throughout his entire life, Agent Lewis had lived within the Boundary. Even back before there was an official Boundary, he'd lived within the confines of the city, safe and protected from the outside world. And now, he was venturing beyond the Boundary into the unknown.

"You will need to requisition a vehicle. Make sure that when you do, you have the technician include a backup battery pack. It is 500 miles to the Boundary, and another 500 to Quadrant 29. I would hate for you to be stranded out there with a dead battery," Admin Ryan said in a casual tone, as if he were checking off items from a list.

"Also, you will be outside the range of the NET. Before you leave, make sure to stop by the Supply office to requisition one of our new mobile emitters. That should allow you to keep in direct contact with me, even while you are in the restricted zone. Just don't waste the battery. At that distance, the emitter will require a lot of juice to transmit.

"And one more thing," Admin Ryan said, looking up at Agent Lewis. "I shouldn't have to say this, but since this is your first time in the field, I feel that I have to. Don't forget to take your service weapon with you. There should be a backup available, but you will need your primary service weapon just in case you are right about all of this. Just don't do anything stupid like shooting yourself. Good luck, agent. Keep me updated."

And with that, Admin Ryan returned to whatever he had been working on before Agent Lewis had knocked on his door. The agent recognized a dismissal when he heard it. He gathered up all of the charts, maps, and reports that he had brought with him and left the Administrator's office – stopping only long enough to pull the door closed behind him.

He walked back to his office in a daze. At some point, he had lost control of the conversation, which was why he was being ordered out to the middle of nowhere to investigate something that may or may not be there.

If only he had walked away, he would be sitting in his office right now, processing cases. It might have been boring, but it was safe and secure - better than embarking on a thousand-mile journey across the entire Northern District. What was worse was that he still wasn't sure what awaited him at the end.

Once back in his office, Agent Lewis dropped the maps and charts onto a side table. Everything he needed to know was already scanned to his mobile device. He took a long look around his office, as if saying goodbye to an old friend he had no idea when he would see again. Once that was done, he walked over to the pegs behind his desk and put on his trench coat.

Before leaving the room, he bent down and opened up one of the desk drawers. Inside was a black duffle bag filled with everything that he would need for the trip. He had packed it the day he had been assigned to the Bureau as a federal agent. It just so happened that this was the first opportunity he would have to use it.

Slinging the duffle bag over his shoulder, he walked out of his office and started down the hall toward the elevators. Two minutes later, he returned. Against the far wall, behind his desk and beneath the coat pegs, was a small wall safe. He punched in his access code, and the doors to the safe opened.

Sitting inside was his service weapon – a standard-issue Mako Model 11 stun pistol. Despite Admin Ryan's warning, he had almost left without it. He pulled the weapon from the safe and attached the holster to the belt on his hip.

Now, he was ready. The only thing left for him to do was to pick up a mobile emitter from Supply and requisition a vehicle. This was all happening so fast, he didn't really have a chance to think about what he was doing.

The last thought that crossed his mind as he stepped into the elevator was that he hoped that he was wrong about all of this. Oh, how he hoped he was wrong.

Chapter 7: A Long Drive

Liam sat slumped behind the display counter of his aunt's shop, head in his hands and bored out of his mind. It had almost been a week since his little excursion into the woods with Parker and Ben. And in all that time, he hadn't spoken to either one of them.

At least with Parker, it was understandable. No sooner had they arrived back in town than Mr. and Mrs. Dean had appeared out of nowhere and dragged her back home. He had tried protesting, but neither Mr. nor Mrs. Dean had been in the mood to argue. They'd simply grabbed Parker by both arms and marched her down the street toward their house.

Nothing that he could have said or done would have changed their minds, so he had been forced to stand there and watch as she was led away like a prisoner. Before they had disappeared from sight, she turned her head to look back at him. She'd mouthed something to him, but he couldn't tell what she had tried to tell him. All he knew was that she'd looked miserable as she was led away.

That look of sadness and misery on her angelic face had broken his heart. Something deep down in his chest had screamed at him to do something, and for a brief moment, he had considered it. Had he thought that it would have made a difference, he would have chased after her, consequences be damned. However, he'd stopped himself short, knowing that it would only have made the situation worse.

He had tried comforting himself by thinking that the worst that Mr. and Mrs. Dean would do would be to ground her for a few days. That may have stopped them from spending time together in the afternoons and evenings, but he would still see her at school.

How wrong he had been. The punishment had been far more severe than he had anticipated.

When Monday morning came, Parker's chair had been empty. All that day, he had expected her to show up for class, but she never came. Tuesday had passed without her showing up for school as well. In frustration, Liam had gone over to her house. He'd pleaded with Mr. and Mrs. Dean to let him see her, even if that meant for just a minute or two. His request had been met with an outright refusal and the door being slammed in his face.

On Wednesday, he had tried appealing to Mrs. Kelly and the school principal. It wasn't right to prohibit Parker from attending school, he had argued. Unfortunately, there wasn't much that they could do. They had tried to comfort him, but this only enraged him further. How could Mr. or Mrs. Dean treat her that way? Worse than that, how were they being allowed to treat her that way? It made no sense to him.

A lot of Liam's anger had boiled over onto Ben. Each day that Parker had been absent, his anger with his friend had grown. In Liam's mind, all of this was Ben's fault. There was no doubt in his mind that Ben had run all the way back to Haven to turn himself in, making sure to implicate Liam and Parker as well.

No one back at the communications building had spotted them before they left. That meant that the only person who could have alerted the Deans to what had happened, was Ben. Liam had always known that his friend would do almost anything to stay out of trouble, but squealing to the authorities was a new low. That is what he had done, though. How else could Mr. and Mrs. Dean have known about it and been waiting to haul Parker away when they got back to town?

It didn't help Ben's case that on his walk home, Liam had seen his friend mingling with several members of the town council. They had been standing outside the café, heads close together in conversation. Ben had been very animated as he spoke, pointing up at the hill and making elaborate hand gestures. When they'd noticed Liam standing nearby, they all grew quiet and pretended like nothing out of the ordinary had happened.

To Liam, this had been as good as a signed confession. His best friend had sold them out, and Parker was paying the price for it. What frustrated him even more was that she was the only member of their group who was being punished for what had happened. Ben certainly hadn't gotten into trouble, and Aunt Linda had only scolded Liam for being reckless. That had been it – a scolding, nothing more.

He had always known that Ben had a tendency to follow the rules, but this had gone far beyond the acceptable limit. There had to be more to it than that. Liam recalled the interaction between Ben and Parker in the control room. The two had been outright hostile to one another. Could Ben have hated her so much that it inspired him to do what he did? Liam had thought long and hard about it, but still had no answers.

Ben, on the other hand had been oblivious to any wrongdoing. He had tried acting like there was nothing out of place with Parker's absence. It was almost like he expected things to go back to the way they were before she arrived. Liam had been quick to shatter that illusion. He had made it crystal-clear to Ben how he felt.

"What's wrong?" Ben had asked.

"Leave me alone!" Liam had responded.

"Don't be like that. We can—"

"I am not talking to you. So. Leave. Me. Alone."

Ben had gotten the message after that. He tried the next day to start up a conversation, hoping that Liam's mood had changed. His response was to point to Parker's empty chair. He had wanted Parker's absence to sink into Ben's conscience, making him fully aware of why he wasn't speaking to him. It had worked, because Ben hadn't said another word to him since.

As time passed, his temper had mellowed a bit. He was still upset over what had happened, but his anger had slowly been replaced with a new feeling: loneliness. Without Parker to talk to, and with him not talking to Ben, he had grown sad and lonely. It wasn't just Parker's absence, or his refusal to talk to Ben. Everyone seemed to have been avoiding him. It had been almost like his mood was infectious, and people stayed away, fearing that it would spread to them too.

Which was how he found himself sitting in his aunt's shop, face buried in his hands, completely and totally miserable. Parker still hadn't returned to school, or even left the house for that matter. The last time he had tried visiting, Mrs. Dean had practically chased him away with a broom, which only reinforced his anger with Ben and with Mr. and Mrs. Dean.

The sad thing was that Liam knew deep down that Ben wasn't completely to blame for what had happened. Yes, he had snitched on them, but it had been his and Parker's idea to go inside the communications building. Had they listened to Ben in the first place, none of this would have been happening.

Whatever had happened back there in the control room, Parker had insisted that it had been an accident. Whether that was true or not, he couldn't say. He was confident that no permanent damage had been done, but there was no way he could know that for sure. In truth, he had no idea what had happened back there, but his gut told him that Parker hadn't been trying to cause any harm.

Perhaps the thing that annoyed him the most was his complete lack of knowledge about what had happened. It seemed that everyone wanted to ignore the fact that there was a not-so-abandoned communications building up in the woods with a camouflaged radio tower. When he had tried asking his aunt about it, she had immediately changed the subject. Mrs. Kelly had feigned ignorance, and Ben – well, he wasn't about to ask Ben about it.

The bell over the door rang as Dr. Adhira entered the shop. Liam raised his head to see who it was before lowering himself back into his original position. Ever since Parker had come to town, his feelings toward Dr. Adhira had changed. He still found her attractive, but his crush on her had slowly faded over the past few weeks.

Before he could say hello, Aunt Linda appeared out of nowhere and whisked Dr. Adhira into the back storeroom. She emerged a moment later to inform him that he could take the rest of the day off. Normally, he would have questioned his aunt's motives in giving him the afternoon off, but honestly, he didn't care. He figured that she wanted to get rid of him for a while; no doubt, having a sulky teenager behind the counter was bad for business.

As Liam was preparing to leave, it dawned on him that he had nothing else to do. Without Ben or Parker, he couldn't think of a single thing that he wanted to do. The best option would be to go home and lock himself in his room and sulk, but he had already done that several times this week. Besides, being in his room would only remind him of Parker.

As he left the shop, he was still undecided on how to spend his afternoon. He could try stopping by Parker's house again, but he doubted that the Deans had lifted her punishment. He could go to the café, but he didn't feel like being social at the moment or sitting at a table by himself while everyone else pretended not to notice.

It was while he was still deciding that fate stepped in. "Hello down there," a voice called out.

Liam looked up to see Mr. Malcolm, standing along the railing of the marquee, updating the movie listings. A ladder was propped up against the side of the marquee, and beside the ladder was a pail full of letters. Mr. Malcolm pointed down at the pail, motioning for Liam to bring it up to him.

Liam picked up the pail, positioning the handle in the crook of his elbow, and started climbing the ladder. When he reached the top, Mr. Malcolm was there waiting for him. He took the pail and hung it on a hook attached to his belt.

"Thank you, Liam," Mr. Malcolm said, as he pulled several letters out and placed them against the marquee. Liam watched as Mr. Malcolm placed more letters, finally spelling out the movie title, *Invasion of the Body Snatchers.*

"New movie?" Liam asked half-heartedly as Mr. Malcolm made his way along the railing to where he was waiting on the ladder.

"New to us," Mr. Malcolm said with a smile. "You know how it is. Nothing we get here is ever new, but as long as it is new to us, what does it matter? Besides, I guarantee you have never seen this one before. It's the original, and it is a classic."

He winked at Liam as the two made their way down the ladder to the pavement below.

"What's it about?" Liam asked curiously.

"Now, we both know I cannot tell you that. Would ruin the surprise," Mr. Malcolm said as he packed up the ladder and opened the theater door. He held the door open, inviting Liam to join him inside. Seeing as he had nothing better to do, he walked into the lobby of the theater.

Once inside, Mr. Malcolm carried the ladder behind the ticket counter, placing it in a supply closet along the wall. Once the ladder had been put away, he grabbed a brown paper bag from under the counter and filled it with popcorn, fresh out of the popper. He sat the bag on the counter and pushed it toward Liam.

Never in his life had Liam refused a fresh bag of popcorn. He took it gratefully before tossing a handful of kernels in his mouth. He didn't slow down until the bag was almost empty. Seeing that Liam was finishing up, Mr. Malcolm took the opportunity to have a chat with the young man in front of him.

"Haven't seen you hanging out with your friends lately. Everything alright?"

"Yes. Well no. It's...it's complicated."

"Well, now, you just tell me all about it," Mr. Malcolm said with a warm and friendly smile.

"What about the movie?"

"The movie can wait. Tell me what's going on."

Liam hesitated for a few seconds, unsure of what to say. He had always considered Mr. Malcolm to be a friend, but he wasn't sure how much he wanted to disclose. In the end, he figured that he had nothing to lose and told Mr. Malcolm everything that had happened.

Mr. Malcolm had a gift. He was probably the best listener Liam had ever known – aside from Parker that was. He listened intently as Liam told him everything. He never interrupted, he never made Liam feel awkward or insecure, and Liam could tell that he wasn't judging him in any way.

By the time he had finished, Mr. Malcolm was nodding thoughtfully.

"I can see why you have been so upset lately, and why your friends haven't been around. Sad business, the Deans keeping that poor girl locked up like that. Well, I have good news for you: I just so happen to know exactly what happened up on the hill last week," Mr. Malcolm said, breathing hope into Liam.

"What?" Liam asked enthusiastically.

"All that commotion wasn't anything more than a fire alarm. Leave it to the three of you to sneak into somewhere you don't belong and cause a panic by setting off every fire alarm in the building," Mr. Malcolm said, holding back a smile.

Liam was surprised. In his wildest dreams, he'd never considered that all of his problems had been caused by something as simple as a fire alarm. That was a relief to hear, but he needed more details. He had to know everything that Mr. Malcolm knew about last week.

Mr. Malcolm was more than willing to share what little he knew of what had happened, starting with the fire alarm accidentally being tripped by a couple of trespassers. Whoever had done it had broken in and then tripped the alarm, causing the whole system to lock down. No real damage had been done, and the janitorial staff had attributed it to a prank by some local kids.

"Janitors?" Liam asked in disbelief.

"Who do you think was up there?" Mr. Malcolm said, trying to point out the obvious. "That old building is one of the few structures from the old days that is still active. When the company went under, they left a bunch of stuff behind, including some old computers and communications equipment. The town didn't want any of that stuff to go to waste, so they moved it all up there."

"But why?" Liam asked, still trying to understand what the town wanted with all that equipment.

"Probably because we still need it. We don't use it often, but when we do, it is nice to have. That is why the building is practically falling apart and looks abandoned. The janitors that are assigned to take care of the place don't spend a lot of time making repairs," Mr. Malcolm confided.

"So, you are telling me that what happened last week was just us setting off a fire alarm?" Liam clarified.

"Yep," Mr. Malcolm said. "I wish I could have been there to see their faces when it happened. There they were, sitting down for lunch, when all the alarms in the building started going off. I can only imagine the panicked looks on their faces as they scrambled to figure out what was wrong, only to find out that the alarm was only a fire alarm, and even then, there was no fire. Must have been a sight to see."

Mr. Malcolm let out a long chuckle, no doubt visualizing the surprise on the janitors' faces. "The way they tell it, they searched for more than an hour, trying to find whoever set off the alarm. Never did find out, though. I suppose someone told the Deans about what happened. That would explain how they knew about it."

"How did you hear about it?" Liam asked.

Mr. Malcolm explained how he played poker with a small group of guys every Wednesday. The two janitors were among the weekly participants. They couldn't stop talking about what had happened over the weekend, which was how Mr. Malcolm had come to learn about the whole affair.

"They weren't mad," Mr. Malcolm said, trying to reassure him. "They were just curious. After all, things like this don't happen every day in a town like ours."

"Then all we did was trip a fire alarm?" Liam said, half to himself. "Wait a minute. If that were true, why is Parker in so much trouble?"

"You care for that girl, don't you?"

"Well, yeah, I mean, we are...sort of..."

"Seeing each other?" Mr. Malcolm said, elbowing Liam good-naturedly. "I knew it the moment I saw you two together. Almost like you two were made for each other."

"Now, you listen here," Mr. Malcolm said comfortingly. "I don't know why that girl is in as much trouble as she is. Maybe this wasn't the first time she stepped out of line, or maybe the Deans are punishing her for something else entirely. Personally, I think they are overreacting and have taken this whole thing out of proportion."

Liam gave Mr. Malcolm an appreciative smile. He hadn't expected to find such a sympathetic listener. More than that, his explanation of what had happened last week had filled Liam with relief.

It all made sense now. The not-so-abandoned building, the radio tower, the alarm going off, and the uniformed men running to see what the problem was – all of it fit with the explanation that Mr. Malcolm had given him. Of course, that didn't explain why Parker was being treated so harshly.

Sensing his concern for Parker's welfare, Mr. Malcolm tried comforting him by saying that now wasn't the time to worry. He was confident that everything would be cleared-up shortly. He was positive that the Deans would lift their restrictions, and Parker would be back spending her afternoons with Liam before he knew it.

"Don't you worry 'bout a thing," Mr. Malcolm repeated. "If nothing else, I plan on having a talk with Mr. and Mrs. Dean later tonight. Punishment can be a good thing, but not when it gets out of hand."

The confidence in Mr. Malcolm's voice gave Liam hope. He couldn't wait to see Parker again. He had missed her so much, and if he was being honest, he'd missed Ben too. After everything he had heard, there was a chance that he could forgive his friend. Things were looking up for the first time since they'd left on their walk.

"Thanks for everything Mr. Malcolm," Liam said sincerely. "I really appreciate you taking the time to talk."

"What are friends for?' Mr. Malcolm asked, another smile splitting his face.

Liam returned his smile with one of his own.

"Can I get you a refill?" Mr. Malcolm asked, pointing down at the now-empty bag in front of Liam.

Liam looked down in surprise. He hadn't remembered finishing off the rest of his popcorn. Well, as long as Mr. Malcolm was offering, he wouldn't say no to a refill.

Mr. Malcolm took the bag in front of Liam and turned to fill it up out of the popper on the back counter. While he was doing that,

Liam was going over the story of the janitors in his head. He was talking out loud, practically laughing at the silliness of it all.

"You know, it is funny," he was saying. "I should have just stepped out and announced myself to the janitors when I saw them running by. In fact, I think I knew one of them."

Mr. Malcolm froze in the act of filling up Liam's popcorn bag. He stood there, back to Liam, completely still, almost as if he had been turned to stone.

"What was that?" Mr. Malcolm said, trying to keep his voice steady.

"I was just saying how I thought that I recognized one of the janitors you mentioned," Liam said offhandedly, not noticing Mr. Malcolm's reaction. "I think his name was Mr. Stevens, or Stephens, or something like that. I want to say that he used to live down the block from me years ago, but I thought he had moved away."

"Is that so?"

"Yeah, but I could be mistaken. Maybe he just looked familiar because I have seen him in town before. If you play poker with him every week, then it would make sense that I would see him hanging out around town."

Liam hadn't noticed when Mr. Malcolm stopped and stood still, but he did notice when he let out a long breath of relief.

"Mr. Malcolm? Are you ok?" he asked.

"Oh, yes," Mr. Malcolm said clumsily, trying to resume their conversation as if he had been caught daydreaming. "I am fine. I was just thinking about something. Anyway, I wouldn't be surprised if you had recognized one of the janitors. It is a small town, after all."

"Yeah, that has to be it," Liam concluded.

Mr. Malcolm finished filling the bag and turned back to Liam. There was still a smile on his face, but now, it seemed forced for some reason. As he handed Liam the popcorn, he looked down at the watch on his wrist.

"Oh, no. It looks like we ended up missing the movie after all. Well, don't you worry. I have a complimentary ticket for you right here, and another one if you decide to bring a certain someone with you," Mr. Malcolm said with a wink.

Liam thanked Mr. Malcolm again and headed for the entrance. Twilight had enveloped the town in a soft glow, and the lights from the street-lamps lit up the approaching darkness. He hadn't realized that he had been talking to Mr. Malcolm for that long. Even his aunt's shop had closed up for the night.

Realizing that she was probably waiting for him back at home, Liam headed off in that direction, unaware that he was being watched from the theater lobby.

As he walked home, he comforted himself with the idea that with any luck, he would see Parker tomorrow. With any luck.

***

As the boy disappeared down the street, Malcolm stepped up to the lobby door of the theater and heaved a sigh of relief. That had been a close one. Their plan had been to distract the boy long enough for the council to meet and discuss the recent events that had disrupted the project. That part had gone according to plan. What hadn't gone according to plan was that the boy had recognized a face from more than twelve years ago.

Who would have thought that he had gotten a good enough look at one of the guards to possibly recognize one of them? Or even remember their name, for that matter. Steven had been an active participant in the early stages of the project, but had been reassigned to the communications center long ago, for obvious reasons.

Not that it mattered. Tonight, the council had taken another vote, and he didn't need to have been there to know the outcome: the girl would be released, and hopefully with a better understanding of the consequences of her actions.

The two kids would be reunited, and things could continue as planned. As of now, the boy didn't suspect a thing. He had accepted the cover story, exactly like they knew he would. With any luck, that was the last hurdle they would need to cross in the foreseeable future. With any luck.

***

It was almost midnight when Agent Lewis finally arrived at the Boundary wall. It had taken him almost seven hours to drive the distance from his office to the western most checkpoint. There was still a long drive ahead of him, but for now, he was stopping for the night.

Stretching off into the distance on both sides was a massive concrete wall. The wall itself was over twenty feet high, with barbed wire running along the top and searchlights positioning periodically along its length. Supposedly, the wall stretched all along the Boundary, and from the looks of it, Agent Lewis could believe it.

Ahead of him was one of the few checkpoints in the wall where people could cross over – not that anyone wanted to. There was no telling what awaited beyond the wall. The checkpoint was flanked by two watchtowers on either side of a massive steel gate. The gate could be opened or closed using hydraulics, but judging by the rust on the support rods, it stayed closed most of the time. Above the gate was a catwalk where several guards stood on patrol.

Since this was the only checkpoint in the sector, it was guarded by a small detachment of soldiers from the Civil Defense Force. They had built up an outpost surrounding the checkpoint, though in truth, it looked more like a detention center. Barbed-wire fences ran everywhere, armed guards were constantly on patrol, and the searchlights overhead were continuously scanning the darkness for threats.

There were around half a dozen buildings spaced out along the wall. Each one looked like it had been built for a specific purpose, without any thought for appearance or comfort. They also had the feeling of being temporary, as if they could be pulled down tomorrow and moved without anyone ever knowing that they had been there in the first place. In short, the whole place felt grim and depressing.

Despite its appearance, Agent Lewis was glad to see it. He had driven more than 500 miles to reach this place – the last hour of which was along a darkened stretch of highway that had been completely devoid of any signs of civilization. The outpost before him wasn't the most welcoming place he had ever seen, but it was still better than the vast emptiness of the highway.

This was only the first part of his journey. He still had another 520 miles to go before he would reach Quadrant 29. One thing was for certain: he wasn't going to be driving the rest of the way tonight. Not only was he exhausted, but his vehicle's battery was down to 15%. Even with the spare battery in the trunk, he wouldn't be able to make it there and back before both batteries ran down.

He needed an opportunity to rest and to charge the battery in his vehicle, which meant that he was definitely stopping for the night. Unfortunately, there were no decent hotels nearby. In reality, there was nothing nearby. The checkpoint was practically an island in the middle of nowhere.

His approaching vehicle got the attention of several patrolling guards. They took up positions on the catwalk and shined their searchlights down on his vehicle, watching him as he approached. Agent Lewis's eyes weren't accustomed to the brightness of their searchlights, and he was forced to put a hand up to shield his eyes from the blaze.

As he drove closer to the gate, the searchlights were no longer needed, and the blinding light was redirected somewhere else. He blinked repeatedly, trying to regain his night vision. When it finally did clear, he saw a guardsman standing off to the side of the road, motioning him to pull up.

Figuring that the guardsman was there to perform an inspection, Agent Lewis pulled his vehicle forward. He stopped alongside where the guardsman was standing and lowered his window.

"Identification!" the guardsman demanded.

Agent Lewis removed his identification card and badge from his coat pocket and presented them to the guardsman. For a second time, he was practically blinded as the guardsman directed the beam of a flashlight right into his eyes. Now, he could understand the need to verify the identity of anyone who approached the Boundary, but he doubted whether it was necessary to shine a flashlight into their eyes at every possible opportunity.

After a minute, the guardsman nodded, confident that the identification card and badge belonged to the man in the vehicle. He turned off his flashlight and instructed Agent Lewis to wait in his vehicle. The guardsman then turned around and headed toward a nearby guardhouse, intent on validating Agent Lewis's travel orders and clearance, which left him with nothing to do but sit and wait. He waited, and waited, and then waited some more.

It must have been close to an hour before the guardsman returned, accompanied by an officer. As they both approached the vehicle, Agent Lewis swore that the next time he was sent beyond the Boundary, he was going to demand a Rotowing fly him there. That way, he could avoid all of this bureaucratic nonsense. It didn't take an hour to validate someone's travel orders, which meant that they had made him wait on purpose.

The officer approached his window and leaned down to hand Agent Lewis back his identification card and badge.

"Agent Lewis, I presume," the officer said more than asked.

"That's right, lieutenant…" Agent Lewis answered, noting the officer's rank on his collar.

"Perry. Guardsman Lieutenant Perry," the lieutenant answered in an exacting tone. "I understand that you have received permission to travel beyond the Boundary. May I inquire as to your destination and the purpose of your visit?"

Agent Lewis gave the lieutenant a level look before shaking his head. The details of his mission weren't top-secret, but they were part of an ongoing investigation. Sharing them could compromise his mission. He explained this to the lieutenant, making it clear that he wasn't at liberty to divulge those details at the moment. The disappointed look on the lieutenant's face was easy to read.

"Classified," the lieutenant said dubiously. "As if there were anything of importance beyond the wall that would merit such secrecy."

Despite the lieutenant's attempt at goading him into sharing his mission details, Agent Lewis refused to say anything more on the subject. It wasn't the lieutenant's business to know what he was planning on doing beyond the Boundary. His job was to guard the wall, and Agent Lewis had clearance to go beyond the wall. That was all that the lieutenant needed to know.

Once it was clear that Agent Lewis didn't intend on sharing the details of his mission, the lieutenant straightened up, clenching his jaw and pulling his uniform straight. Apparently, he didn't like people passing through his checkpoint without him knowing the reason. Still, he was under orders to let Agent Lewis pass.

"On the other side of this wall, civilization comes to an end," Lieutenant Perry said as if reading from a script. "There are no more checkpoints, no patrols, no service stations, rest stops, or charging ports. You will be cut off.

"Let me be perfectly clear: once you pass beyond these walls, you are on your own. We will not come and get you. If your vehicle breaks down or should anything...unfortunate happen to you, we will not come and rescue you. Do you understand?"

Agent Lewis nodded, signaling to the lieutenant that he understood. Satisfied that he had done his duty, the lieutenant called up to the soldiers on the catwalk and signaled that Agent Lewis was cleared to pass through the gate.

He was about to turn and walk away when Agent Lewis called out to him. "Before I go, is there anywhere I can charge my vehicle?" he asked.

Lieutenant Perry stopped, turning to look down at him. He stared intently at him for a full minute before offering a response. If Agent Lewis hadn't known better, he would have suspected that the lieutenant had been debating what to tell him. No doubt, refusing his request would have been a fitting punishment for not divulging the details of his mission.

"Over there is our maintenance shed," the lieutenant said, pointing at a rundown building off to the side. "There is a charging port inside that you can use. But I warn you, it will take several hours to recharge your battery. That charging port is more than thirty years old, and has trouble producing a constant charge."

Pointing at another building near the maintenance shed, the lieutenant continued, "That building over there is one of our barracks. There should be an empty bed or two available. You may want to get some sleep while you wait. If you want, I can even send a guardsman to wake you when your vehicle is ready."

"Thank you," Agent Lewis said sincerely. He hadn't expected the lieutenant to be so accommodating, especially after he refused to disclose the details of his mission.

With that, Lieutenant Perry headed back to the guardhouse, leaving Agent Lewis to fend for himself. Not wanting to spend more time here than absolutely necessary, he turned his vehicle toward the maintenance shed. Within ten minutes, his vehicle was charging, and he was lying down comfortably on a cot in a corner of the barracks. He was so tired, he didn't even mind that the sheets hadn't been changed in several years.

The sun was starting to peek over the horizon when Agent Lewis woke up. A guardsman was standing over him, shaking him gently. He waved the guard away as he sat up on the edge of his cot. He had slept longer than he had wanted, but less than he needed. As a result, it took him several cups of terrible coffee before he was finally awake.

His vehicle was waiting for him outside the barracks, the battery back at 100%. Climbing back inside, Agent Lewis approached the gate, prepared to continue his journey to Quadrant 29. The lieutenant from last night was still on duty. When he saw Agent Lewis, he signaled for the gate to open. Agent Lewis spared a quick "Thank you" for the lieutenant's help before driving through the gate to the other side of the wall.

The stark difference between inside the Boundary and outside the Boundary was shocking. Beyond the wall, nature had grown unchecked for countless years. Where the roads within the Boundary were perfectly paved and nicely maintained, the roads beyond the Boundary were in desperate need of repair. The highway itself was still smooth enough to drive on, but for how much longer? The ground immediately surrounding the wall had been cleared of any plants or shrubbery, but twenty feet beyond, the ground was hidden in a sea of green leaves and shrubbery.

To Agent Lewis, who had spent most of his life living in the city, it all seemed chaotic and wild. This truly was the wilderness, and he was about to head off into it. Worst of all, he was going to do it alone.

The clang of the metal gates closing behind him was startling. The lieutenant hadn't wasted any time in closing the door behind him. The realization that he was now officially beyond the Boundary settled over him, bringing with it a wave of anxiety.

For the first time in his life, he had left the safety and security of the Boundary. The gate behind him had effectively locked him away from the only world he had ever known. After all this time, he had never questioned the Federal Authority's mandate that required all citizens to live within the Boundary. He knew it was for their own protection. That was why the wall had been built in the first place: to keep people safe, even if that meant keeping them safe from themselves.

Not wanting to appear weak in full view of the guards on top of the wall, Agent Lewis drove several miles down the road before pulling over. Once he stopped on the side of the road, he allowed himself to feel the anxiety that had been coursing through his mind ever since he'd passed through the gate. It was frustrating to feel so unnerved over something as simple as driving through a gate, but it was what the gate represented that had him on edge. Coming this far had been a big step for him.

Agent Lewis sat there in his vehicle for ten minutes while he tried to calm himself down. When he finally felt calm enough to continue, he pulled back onto the road. He had a job to do, and he wanted to get it over with as soon as possible. After all, the sooner he was done, the sooner he would be back in his office, safe and sound.

The sun had now climbed a few inches above the horizon and was continuing to climb at a steady rate. Assuming he could maintain a decent pace, he expected to arrive at his destination shortly after midday – early afternoon at the latest. With any luck, he would be headed home before nightfall. With any luck.

Chapter 8: Parker's Return

Liam practically leapt out of bed as the sun peeked over the top of the mountains and spilled into his room through the slates of his window shade. He hadn't been able to sleep. The thought of seeing Parker again had kept him awake into the early morning hours. True, he had no guarantee that Mr. and Mrs. Dean were going to lift her punishment, but he was confident that if anyone could talk some sense into them, it was Mr. Malcolm. His promise to talk to them had been the only thing that Liam had been thinking about.

Since he couldn't sleep, there was no reason to stay in bed. He still had to shower and get dressed, but the rest of his morning ritual had been discarded. The quicker he was ready, the sooner he could head over to Parker's house.

His plan was simple: He was going to head over to Mr. and Mrs. Dean's house and refuse to leave until he was allowed to see Parker. At least, he was going to head over there in the hopes that Mr. Malcolm had already laid the groundwork.

If he hadn't, Liam had resolved to stand his ground. What they were doing wasn't right, and he wasn't about to take no for an answer.

After a quick shower, he threw on his best pair of jeans, his favorite shirt, and a pale-blue hoodie. The days were getting warmer, but the mornings were still a little chilly.

Once he was dressed, he bolted for the door, only to be stopped by his Aunt Linda. Liam had expected her to be at her usual place in the kitchen, sipping her morning coffee and reading the paper, which was why he had decided to go out the front door.

Unfortunately for him, she must have suspected what he was up to and headed him off at the foot of the stairs.

He tried to explain that he was in a hurry and tried to step around her. She moved to stand in his way, blocking him from making his escape. She refused to budge until he offered up an explanation as to why he was trying to sneak out of the house at eight in the morning – something that was completely out of character for him on a Saturday.

Realizing that his aunt intended to stand there all day until she received an explanation, he decided that the best thing to do was to tell her the truth. He started by telling her about his conversation yesterday with Mr. Malcolm and how he had promised to talk with Mr. and Mrs. Dean, and now, it was his intention to head over their house and demand Parker's release. To her credit, Aunt Linda stood there and listened with a blank face, even though he could tell that she was barely holding back a smile.

Taking his arm, Aunt Linda led him into the kitchen and poured them both a cup of coffee. Liam was so stunned that he almost didn't take the cup as she offered it to him, fearing that it might be a trap. It was only after she reassured him that it was alright that he finally took the cup and pressed it to his lips.

It tasted awful. He had to stop himself from spitting it out all over the floor. With a grimace, he forced himself to swallow before setting the cup on the counter. After all these years, he finally had a chance to taste coffee, and it was nothing like he had imagined. He'd always thought that it would taste better, given how his aunt seemed to enjoy it every morning.

This time, Aunt Linda couldn't hold back the laughter. She chuckled at his response, stopping herself only long enough to assure him that it was ok.

"It is an acquired taste," she confided.

"Why now?" Liam asked, still surprised that she had lifted her moratorium on coffee drinking.

"I just figured you needed it. Besides, I can't shelter you forever."

"Huh?"

"You are growing up, Liam. Pretty soon, you will be off on your own, making your own decisions. I just—"

"Does that mean I can go?" he interrupted.

"No," Aunt Linda said definitely.

He pleaded with his aunt, trying to make her understand how important this was to him. When it was clear that pleading wasn't working, he resorted to out-and-out begging. Despite his theatrics, his aunt was resolute. He was not heading over to Parker's house at eight o'clock in the morning.

She tried explaining that heading over now would only do more harm than good.

"Give them time to wake up," she said. "Then, maybe this afternoon, you can head on over there. Besides, I need you in the shop today. Gus is making another delivery."

Liam tried to argue, but his aunt wasn't listening. She kept assuring him that it would be better if he went over later. In the meantime, they should head over to the shop and get to work. After all, the sooner they finished, the sooner he could head to Parker's house.

Liam wasn't satisfied with this, and complained the entire walk over to the antique shop. The last thing he wanted to do right now was unload boxes. He did manage to work out a compromise where he wouldn't have to stay all day – just long enough to get Gus's van unpacked. It wasn't exactly what he had been hoping for, but it was better than nothing.

When they arrived at the shop, Aunt Linda unlocked the front door before turning toward the café. She told him to head inside and get started while she got them some breakfast. For a brief second, Liam thought about making a break for it. Without his aunt standing guard over him, he could slip out the front door and be halfway to Parker's house before she knew he was gone.

Then he noticed his aunt watching him from across the street. She gave him a steely glare before motioning him to get to work. With a sigh of resignation, he turned and headed into the back room of the shop. Against the back wall, there was a large set of bay doors. The doors themselves rolled up into the ceiling using a chain against the wall. He pulled on the chain, raising the doors and revealing Gus's van sitting in the alleyway behind the shop.

When Gus saw the doors opening, he backed his van up to the opening. From the look of things, he hadn't been waiting there long. Once his van was in position, he shut off the engine and stepped out.

Gus was a portly guy, short and squat. The hair that he was missing on the top of his head was substituted for by the immense amount of hair that made up his bushy mustache. It didn't help that he always wore overalls, which weren't the best fashion choice for a man with his figure.

Still, what he lacked in appearance, he made up for in personality. Gus was the type of guy who always seemed to be wearing a smile. Whether he was delivering produce to the grocery store, tools to the hardware store, or boxes of antiques to Aunt Linda's shop, he always looked happy. It was almost as if driving his van to deliver supplies around town had been his life's ambition, and he was enjoying every minute of it.

Liam greeted him with a smile and a wave, which Gus immediately returned. As Gus bent over to unlock the back of his van, Liam mentally prepared himself for the task at hand. He didn't want to be there, but if he had to be there, he was going to get the job done as quickly as possible. Then he would be on his way.

To his great surprise, the back of Gus's van was practically empty. Normally, when Gus made a delivery, his van would be filled to bursting with new merchandise. Today, however, it looked like there were maybe half a dozen boxes, leaving a large empty space in the back of the cargo area. Liam had to restrain himself from letting out a whoop of joy.

Without waiting for Gus's help, he immediately got to work unloading the back of the van. By the time Aunt Linda returned from the café with breakfast, the van had already been cleared out. The boxes were stacked in a row against the wall, and Liam was wiping sweat off his face.

Aunt Linda stopped in the doorway to the backroom, no doubt stunned at the progress that he had already made. Gus, meanwhile, was leaning against a nearby workbench. He had tried to help Liam unload but quickly realized that the best thing he could do was to stay out of the way.

Seeing his aunt, Liam rushed over to assure her that the van had been unloaded like they had agreed, and now, he wanted to head over to Parker's house. Without saying a word, Aunt Linda thrust a breakfast burrito into his hands before walking over to join Gus at the workbench.

Liam again tried to point out that his job was done, but his aunt wasn't listening to him. Her attention was solely on Gus. She handed him a cup of coffee that she had brought over from the café just for him, and the two pulled up a pair of stools and began talking.

Liam knew what she was doing: She was stalling for time. She was purposefully ignoring him until she could think of something else for him to do. Anything to keep him from heading over to Parker's house.

Sure enough, when he pressed the subject, she offhandedly mentioned that the boxes hadn't been unpacked yet, as if that had been a part of their deal. He huffed in frustration. That had not been what they'd agreed to. Nevertheless, he didn't have much of a choice in the matter.

Scarfing down his breakfast burrito, Liam got to work unpacking the nearest box. After an hour, he'd finished with the last box. Aunt Linda and Gus hadn't moved from their spot against the workbench. They were still happily chatting away, while he had been working himself silly to get the job done.

When he mentioned that the boxes had been unpacked, Aunt Linda casually mentioned that the new merchandise hadn't been moved to the showroom yet. Liam had to bite his lip to prevent himself from shouting out an obscenity. That hadn't been part of their deal. Now, she was just adding on things for him to do.

Grabbing the nearest item, an old clock radio, he marched into the showroom and practically threw it on one of the tables. He didn't care if he broke it. He was so upset he couldn't hardly stand it. He reentered the storeroom and picked up a ceramic vase. *Oh, it would be a shame if anything bad happened to this.*

As he walked back into the showroom, fully intending on "accidently" dropping the vase, something in the front window caught his eye: a face was pressed against the glass, trying to look in.

It was Parker.

He set the vase down on the edge of the display counter, intent on rushing to meet Parker, but he hadn't been paying attention. No sooner had he let go of the vase than it dropped to the floor and shattered.

"What was that?" Aunt Linda called from the back room.

"I, uh...I accidently dropped the vase," he called back. "Don't worry. I will clean it up."

Without having the slightest intention of cleaning up the mess he had made, Liam ran to the doorway. He opened the door, careful not to let the bell ring, and looked out. Parker was gone. He looked up and down Main Street in confusion. *Where had she gone?*

Just then, he spotted her down the street, peeking out between two buildings. He waved and was about to call out to her when she gestured frantically to keep his voice down. He wasn't sure what was going on, but it didn't matter. He was just happy to see her again.

He took a few steps toward Parker, who immediately disappeared between the two buildings. He walked down the street to where she had been standing, only to find the space between the two buildings empty. She had disappeared again. *What's going on here?* he wondered as he scratched his head.

The space between the two buildings opened up into a small alleyway that led to the back of the buildings. Liam walked along the alleyway, looking for any sign of where Parker had gone. Just then, a hand reached out and pulled him to the side of the alley, where a small alcove shielded them from view.

Parker threw her arms around his neck and pulled him into a tight embrace. He held her, breathing in the smell of her hair and feeling the warmth of her body against his own. It was only then that he noticed that she was trembling. He pulled away enough to look down at her. There were tears in her eyes.

"What's wrong?" Liam asked with concern.

Parker responded by burying her face in his chest and holding him even tighter than before. *Has she really missed me that much?* he wondered. No, that wasn't it. There was something wrong here, and he wanted to know what it was.

"Parker, you have to talk to me. What happened? Are you okay?"

"Can I trust you?" she asked without lifting her head. She had stopped trembling, but the tone in her voice said that she was far from being okay.

"Of course you can. You can tell me anything. You know that," he said, not sure why she would ask him a question like that.

"They took me away!" she said bitterly. "They threw me in the back of a van and drove me out of town. They were trying to get rid of me."

Parker's words sent a shiver down his spine. What was she saying? If the Deans had hurt her, he would...well he didn't know what he would do, but he would do something.

"Slow down," he said in the calmest voice he could muster. "Who? Who took you away? Was it Mr. and Mrs. Dean? Did they hurt you?"

"It wasn't just the Deans," she said in a disgusted voice, as if saying their names left a bad taste in her mouth. "It was the town council. They voted on it. Can you believe that? They actually voted on it."

"What are you talking about?"

"*They took me away!*" she yelled, pushing herself away from him.

"Alright. Alright. They took you away," Liam said, trying to calm her down. "Maybe you should start from the beginning," he suggested.

"After we got back last week, I was hustled back home by those assholes I am staying with. When we got there, several members of the town council were waiting for me. I tried to explain what had happened, but they wouldn't listen. They just stood there talking about what to do with me, like I wasn't even there.

"Later, the rest of the town council arrived. They held a vote right then and there. Can you believe that? They voted to exile me from Haven without so much as a trial or even the chance to defend myself. After that, they shoved me into the back of a van and drove me out of town," she finished, anger tinging her voice.

Liam couldn't believe what he was hearing. This whole week, the Deans had been telling him that she couldn't come to the door because she was being grounded. In reality, she had been smuggled out of town without anyone knowing about it. The thought enraged him, but at the same time, it didn't quite make sense.

"You have been gone this whole time?"

"Yes."

"And the Deans – they were lying about why you weren't in school and why you couldn't come to the door?"

"Yes."

"So, you are saying that someone took you and drove you out of town?"

"Yes!"

"Where did they take you?"

"They kept me locked up in an old warehouse. I was supposed to be waiting there for someone to come and pick me up."

"I don't understand," Liam said, trying to get her story straight in his head. "They took you away, locked you up, and you spent the whole week waiting for someone else to come and take you even further away?"

"Yes," Parker said in relief.

"But if they took you away, then how did you get here?"

"They brought me back early this morning," she explained. "The town council changed their minds, and I'm being given a second chance. That is what they told me, at least."

"And they dropped you off in the middle of town?"

"No," she said in exasperation. "They took me back to the Deans' house. I am supposed to be there now, but I wasn't about to wait around for them to change their minds and deport me again."

"You mean you escaped?" he asked with surprise.

"Of course. They still think I am in my room, thinking about what I did wrong. Instead, I decided to sneak out the bathroom window. When you weren't at home, I figured you would be at the shop," she said, staring at him with her deep blue eyes.

"Listen, I am done with this place and these people. It is time for me to go, and I want you to come with me."

"You want me to leave? With you?" Liam asked, not sure how he felt about the idea.

"Why not?" she said, reaching out and grabbing him by the shoulders. "You told me you wanted to get out of here. Well, now is your chance."

"Hold on," he said, trying to get his head straight. "I don't understand what is happening here. Let's take a few steps back and see if we can make sense of it. Tell me – why did they take you away in the first place?"

"They blamed me for what happened in the control room. I have no doubt that little rat Ben told them as much." She practically spat Ben's name as she said it.

"They were willing to exile you because you set off a fire alarm?" Liam asked.

"'Fire alarm?' 'Fire alarm?' Who said anything about a fire alarm?" Parker asked with indignation.

"Nobody," Liam said defensively. "Well, actually, it was Mr. Malcolm, over at the movie theater. He said that we accidently set off the fire alarm, and that was the reason for—"

"That wasn't a measly little fire alarm," Parker said, cutting him off. "That was the sound of their entire system crashing."

"What?"

"Think about it," Parker said, as if explaining something so simple a little kid should understand it. "Since when do they install fire alarms on the same system as a communications array and transmitter assembly? And since when do armed security guards respond to fire alarms in secret communications buildings?"

Liam tried to answer her questions based on the explanation that Mr. Malcolm had provided, but she wasn't convinced. She laughed when he told her that the security guards were janitors who had been startled by the alarm. She then rolled her eyes in disbelief when he insisted that the building was only being used for storage, and not much else.

"Well, that makes sense," she said sarcastically. "They've lied to you about everything else. Why not lie about this too?"

Liam resented Parker's implication that he had been lied to. Mr. Malcolm was his friend, and had never lied to him about anything in his life. For that matter, the only person in town who he knew had lied to him had been Parker herself. She had said that what happened in the control room had been an accident – that she didn't know what had happened. Judging by what she was saying now, it sounded like she knew exactly what had happened.

"If it wasn't the fire alarm, what did happen back there?" Liam forced himself to ask.

Parker was silent for a few seconds, trying to figure out how best to answer his question. Finally, she said, "It doesn't matter."

"What do you mean, 'it doesn't matter?'" he asked.

"Look! What matters is that we need to get out of here. You and me."

Instinctively, he stepped backwards, bumping up against the wall behind him. None of this was making sense to him. It was all so confusing. To make matters worse, he wasn't entirely sure if what she was saying had actually happened.

"Don't you get it?" Parker said, stepping forward so that she was toe-to-toe with him. "They are lying to you. All of them. They have been lying to you since the beginning. Don't you realize that? Can't you see it? There is something not right with this town."

"You are clearly upset," Liam said, straightening himself up against the wall. "I can see that. But don't expect me to turn my back on my family and friends without any evidence. You say they are lying to me – then prove it?"

It was Parker's turn to step backward in confusion. For the first time, it occurred to her that maybe Liam wasn't aware of what was going on around him. He didn't suspect that the world he inhabited was all an elaborate illusion.

"You really don't know, do you?" she asked, speaking almost to herself.

"Know what?"

"All this time, I thought you at least suspected what this town was. Who these people really are. But you have no idea," she said, amazed at his ignorance.

"Haven't you ever wondered why no one in Haven ever leaves? Why this town's so isolated from everywhere else? Surely, at some point you have wondered why nobody ever comes to visit?"

Something in what Parker had said touched a nerve in Liam. It was almost like she was touching on a half-forgotten memory: questions that he'd once asked, but never received an answer to, so they had soon been forgotten – forgotten until now.

The cascade of memories and the anxiety that they brought with them was too much for him to handle. He shook his head vigorously, trying to clear his mind. He didn't want to ask himself those questions.

"I don't have time for this," he said as he turned to go.

"Wait!" Parker pleaded, grabbing his arm to stop him from leaving. "I can prove it. I can prove everything."

"How?"

"By taking you to where they kept me locked up. You wanted proof; I will give you proof. Then, maybe you will believe me."

Liam stopped and stood there, looking over his shoulder at Parker. Seeing her again reminded him how much he cared for her. But she was different somehow. There was a light in her eyes that he hadn't seen there before. Was it a result of her recent captivity or something else? Mental instability, perhaps?

"Please!" she pleaded. "Trust me."

Liam looked deep into her eyes. There was no malice there, no deception, only a sincere desire for him to trust her. All she was asking was for him to give her the opportunity to prove herself. He owed her that much.

"Alright," he said after a moment. He might have his doubts, but deep down, he knew that she cared for him. She wasn't trying to hurt him or mislead him. For that reason alone, he had to give her the benefit of the doubt, at least for now.

Parker lit up with excitement. She reached up and threw her arms around his neck again, hugging him tighter than before. The hug only lasted a few seconds before she pulled away, grabbing his hand and leading him toward the back of the alley. There, the alley between the two buildings connected with the much-larger alleyway that ran along the backsides of the shops.

Parker pulled him along as they walked along the backsides of the shops, heading toward his aunt's store. Gus's van was still sitting there in front of the open bay doors. Parker slowed down as they approached the doors, motioning for him to be quiet. She then peeked her head around the side of the van, staring into the storeroom beyond.

Less than a second later, she motioned him to join her. The storeroom was empty. Aunt Linda and Gus were nowhere to be seen, though the remains of their breakfast still sat on the workbench where they had left it. Liam was about to call out, thinking that they had come here to get his aunt's help, when Parker put a finger to his lips.

She motioned him to keep quiet before turning to close the back door to Gus's van. He stared at her, unsure what she was doing.

It was only after she walked to the front of the van and hopped behind the wheel that he realized what she had planned: she was going to steal Gus's van.

Liam ran over to the driver's side door and lifted the handle. It was locked. He knocked on the window and waited while Parker rolled it down.

"Get in," she said to him, motioning to the passenger seat next to her.

He couldn't believe what she was suggesting. He motioned frantically for her to get out, but she ignored him. Instead, she reached over and opened the passenger side door, again inviting him to join her. She even patted the seat in expectation.

"What are you doing?" he asked in a near-panic.

"Exactly what I told you I was going to do: I am going to take you to where they were keeping me. Naturally, we can't walk there, so we will need to 'borrow' Gus's van for a while," she said as if it made perfect sense.

"That is called stealing," Liam reminded her.

"Not if we bring it back," Parker countered. "Then it is called borrowing. Besides, I don't think Gus will miss it if we borrow it for an hour or two."

Liam stood there, not sure what to do. He had promised to go with Parker, but he hadn't realized that she had planned on "borrowing" Gus's van. He looked from her to the storeroom and back again. Secretly, he hoped that Gus would walk through the back door and stop them, but no such luck. He had to make a decision.

"Are you coming or not?" Parker asked.

Liam instinctively knew that if he refused, Parker wouldn't hesitate to drive away, which meant that he would never see her again. The thought of losing her so soon after she had returned was too much for him to think about. The decision was made. He got in the van.

He sat down in the passenger's seat, closing the door behind him and putting his seat belt on. The van's engine roared to life as Parker turned the key in the ignition. It seemed that Gus had been kind enough to leave his keys in the van for just such an occasion.

Parker wasted no time. She put the van in gear and drove south, toward the edge of town. Liam noticed that she avoided taking Main Street and used side streets instead. *Probably for the best*, he thought. Now that they were actively committing a crime, he didn't like the idea of being caught.

Before he knew it, they were at the southernmost edge of town. Parker came to a stop at the point where the road turned from paved concrete to gravel and dirt. This was the dividing line between Haven and the world beyond.

"Are you ready?" she asked him.

"Let's just get it over with."

With that, Parker released the brake, and the two of them headed down the gravel road. Wherever she was taking them, at least they were together.

One thing was for certain: Liam wasn't bored anymore.

Chapter 9: A Truth Revealed

Liam did his best to hide how nervous he was as they drove down the gravel road that wound its way through the forest away from Haven. It wasn't just Parker's driving that made him nervous, although, given how reckless she was being behind the wheel, he could be excused for feeling a little tense. The real cause for his anxiety was that they had left Haven behind. It had been years since the last time he had ventured outside of the town's borders, and that had been only once that he could remember.

Every mile further from Haven they went, the greater his anxiety grew. The feeling was like a rubber band that was being pulled taut, building tension with each passing second until it would eventually snap. He couldn't help but feel like that rubber band, and he had a feeling that he was close to snapping.

The tension was getting so bad that he was starting to leave fingernail marks in the dashboard. His hands were white with the strain, and he could feel blood pumping in his ears. Although he had never had a panic attack before, he suspected that the feeling was very similar.

"You can relax," Parker said from behind the wheel.

Liam looked over to see her casually dividing her attention between staring at him and the road in front of them. Her attitude had changed significantly. Back in town, she had been upset and practically inconsolable. Now, she looked perfectly at ease, as if everything were fine.

"We are far enough away where they won't be able to catch up to us. Besides, I am not that bad of a driver, so you can stop digging your fingers into the dashboard."

187

"It's not that," he tried to explain as he took several deep, calming breaths. "It's just...I have never been this far away from Haven before. I guess I am not used to it."

"Never?" Parker said in amazement.

"Well, there was this one time," Liam said, recalling a class field trip that he had taken several years ago. He explained how his class had gone on a trip to see the ocean. That had been the first and last time that he'd left Haven.

"The ocean? Seriously?" Parker asked, surprised at the destination. "Why did they take you there?"

"Something to do with marine biology and studying different ecosystems," Liam said as he tried to recall. "I remember being extremely excited about it. I had been really into the ocean back then. My aunt used to say that I was obsessed with it, refusing to talk about anything else."

Parker watched him out of the corner of her eye. Talking seemed to have a calming effect on him. The more he talked, the less tense he became.

"When I heard that the school was planning a field trip to the ocean, I couldn't wait to go. I even stayed up the night before, too excited to sleep."

"Convenient," Parker said under her breath before continuing in a louder voice. "Well then, that's good to hear. Try focusing on what it was like the last time you left Haven, and you will be fine."

"Yeah, except I don't remember much about it," Liam admitted.

"Really?"

"Well, I remember arriving at Neptune's Bounty, a tiny ocean-styled theme park off the coast, but I don't remember how we got there. I must have fallen asleep on the way there."

"Neptune's Bounty?" Parker said incredulously.

"Hey, it was cool," he said defensively.

"I am sure that it was," she said, hiding a snicker.

"You had to be there," Liam protested. "They had this large statue of Neptune that you could take your picture with. There were also a couple of rides, a mini-golf course, an underwater-themed restaurant, and a souvenir shop."

He looked over at Parker, daring her to make fun of him. Rather than saying anything, she simply shrugged and gave him a knowing smile. He thought about changing the subject, but Parker encouraged him to go on. She wanted to know more about his trip to the ocean.

"It may seem corny to you," he said, not fully convinced that she wasn't looking for something else to tease him about. "But to me, it was the coolest place in the world. I remember wanting to see the ocean so badly that I couldn't wait for the rest of my class to get off the bus. I ran down the beach, straight into the water. Nearly got knocked over by the next wave."

Liam chuckled as he remembered how upset his teacher had been. They had been forced to rush in after him and pull him out before the tide threatened to pull him out to sea. He unconsciously tugged at his ear where the teacher had grabbed him and hauled him out of the water. Even after all these years, he still didn't regret it.

Of course, that meant that both him and his teacher had been soaked from the chest down. He still remembered standing there on the beach, soaking wet, while his teacher reprimanded him in front of the whole class. The entire time, he had been debating whether to run back into the water.

"So, what happened next?" Parker asked.

"So, they had to get me a new set of clothes from the gift shop and my teacher as well. You have to understand, this wasn't the middle of summer. It was late fall, and the water was freezing." Liam felt a chill remembering how cold it was.

After a while, he fell silent. He sat there reliving the events of that day over and over again. At the time, it had been the best day of his life, and the sad part was that he had practically forgotten about it.

The two drove on in silence, Liam deep in thought and Parker not wanting to disturb him. When he finally came out of his self-reflection, he realized that he wasn't tense anymore. The anxiety was almost completely gone. He did feel tired, like he had just run several laps around the athletic field, but he could deal with that.

Seeing him visibly relax in the seat beside her, Parker attempted to restart the conversation. "I am surprised that Ben let you get away with such reckless behavior."

"Ben wasn't there," Liam said offhandedly. "He hadn't moved to Haven yet."

"Well, that's too bad," Parker said with mock sincerity. "I guess that means that you didn't have anyone to talk to on the way home."

"Honestly, I can't even remember the drive home, either. I remember getting on the bus, and the next thing I knew, we were back in Haven. Must have fallen asleep again."

"And that was the only time you ever left Haven?"

"Yep."

"That's it? In all these years, you never left again? Not even a return field trip to Neptune's Booty?" Parker persisted.

"Nope, and it was Neptune's Bounty, not Booty," He clarified.

That last question got him thinking. Why was it that he had never gone back? It had been such a wonderful experience, why hadn't they returned? Even if the school had decided not to do another field trip, his aunt could have taken him back on her own. So why hadn't she?

Liam tried to shrug off that line of thought. He was sure that his aunt had her reasons. Most likely, it was because he had lost interest in going over the years. Or perhaps it was because of the responsibilities that they had to the shop.

That had been the main reason for the two of them not going anywhere together. Every time he'd wanted to leave and go somewhere, something at the shop would come up and prevent them from leaving. After a while, he had stopped asking. Now, he just assumed that whatever plans that they might make would be cancelled.

It wasn't that he resented the antique shop, he just wished it didn't control his life so thoroughly. Then again, the same could be said of his aunt and the whole town of Haven. Perhaps that was what had inspired him to get in the van with Parker – a part of him had wanted to break free, and this had been the perfect opportunity to do it.

They continued their trip down the road, talking the whole way. Liam talked about everything and anything he could think of. He wasn't nervous anymore, but he still wanted to keep his mind off what they were actually doing. He told Parker all about growing up in Haven, plus some stories from his past, his hopes for the future, and much more. Most of it she had heard before, but she didn't seem to mind.

When he couldn't think of anything else to say, he tried asking Parker about her past. Rather than answering, she changed the subject, focusing the conversation back on him. He figured that she didn't like talking about herself – that, or there was something in her past that she didn't want to talk about. The only thing that he had been able to get out of her was that before she'd moved to Haven, she had been an accomplished dancer, quite a feat for someone her age.

He wanted to press her for more information, but she was reluctant to share any details. In the end, he decided not to pressure her too much and let the subject drop. He sensed a lot of pain in her past, and didn't want to force her to relive it.

More than an hour had passed since they left Haven. Liam was starting to wonder where they were going when Parker stopped the van in the middle of the road. Liam looked around, unsure of what he was supposed to be looking for or why they had stopped. It was then that he noticed an old, worn-down sign on the side of the road.

The writing on the sign was faded, and the corners were overgrown with ivy. Still, he could make out the words in the middle.

CITY OF GREENWOOD
1 MILE

Liam read the sign again in disbelief. For years, he had heard stories about the town of Greenwood, Haven's nearest neighbor. He had always wanted to visit, but the opportunity had never come up.

He had lost count of the number of times he had begged his aunt to let him accompany Gus on one of his deliveries down to Greenwood. It had never mattered how hard he begged and pleaded; his aunt's answer had always been no. Her excuses had been everything from he wasn't old enough to she needed him to stay at the shop and help out. After a while, he had stopped asking.

"Greenwood?" Liam said out loud.

After all these years, he was finally going to visit the town of Greenwood. Supposedly, it was almost identical to Haven, but without the charm. He had also heard that the people of Greenwood weren't as friendly as those from Haven. Still, he had always wanted to visit, and this was his opportunity.

He was practically bouncing up and down in his seat with excitement. He turned to look at Parker, wondering why she had stopped here, rather than driving the last mile into town. His excitement faded a little bit when he noticed the serious look on her face.

"What do you know about this place?" Parker asked carefully.

"Only what I have seen in pictures and heard from others," Liam confessed. "I have never been here before, but I know that it is similar to Haven, though not as large. Also, I heard that the people here are a bit off-putting. Not strange, but not overly friendly either."

Parker nodded slowly, as if putting another piece to the puzzle together in her mind. "And you've never tried visiting here on your own?"

"I have wanted to, but it was always too far away for me to walk here on my own. I tried talking my aunt into letting me come down with Gus, but she always told me no," Liam explained.

"That figures," Parker said wryly.

"What do you mean?" he asked curiously.

"What I mean is that there has always been a reason to keep you as far away from here as possible. Even when you thought of a good reason to come, something would get in your way and stop you," she said pointedly, as if trying to get him to understand something that should have been obvious.

"What? Like someone has been trying to keep me away from here all this time?" he asked nervously.

Parker sighed. She looked at her reflection in the rearview mirror, as if trying to reassure herself that she was doing the right thing. Whatever she saw in the mirror, it was clear that she intended to proceed.

"Just do me a favor," she said, looking back at him. "Try to remember that I am here for you, and that I am only trying to help."

Liam nodded slowly, not entirely understanding what she was talking about. Was there something wrong with the town of Greenwood? He remembered that Parker was taking him to where she had been held captive for the past week. Perhaps that was what she meant. Maybe there was something here in Greenwood that he was supposed to see that would prove that she was telling the truth.

Parker hesitated only a minute or two before removing her foot off the brake and allowing the van to roll forward. Liam was glad that they were on their way again. He had been starting to think that she was going to sit there parked in the middle of the road all day. At this point, they were so close that he couldn't imagine a reason not to drive into town, whatever the situation was.

As the van rolled down the road, the town ahead was obscured by trees. Gaps in the tree line showed the tops of buildings rising up amongst the sea to trees that surrounded the town. As they turned a corner, the trees opened up before them, and Liam got his first view of Greenwood. The road they were on ran straight through town, with buildings lining both sides of the street, similar to Main Street back home. The biggest difference that he noticed was the overwhelming number of trees and bushes that sprang up everywhere he looked. The town was practically engulfed by the surrounding forest.

The van gave a lurch as they transitioned from the gravel road that led back toward Haven to a paved road that continued through town. Liam pressed his face against the window, excitement sending tingles down his arms and legs. Realizing that he could roll down the window to get a better look, he stuck his head out, determined to take in as much as possible.

Directly ahead, the first buildings were coming into view. As he glanced at them, he realized that there was something off about them. He couldn't put his finger on it, but something wasn't right.

Now that he was thinking about it, the road didn't feel right either. The roads back home had been smooth and well-paved; meanwhile, the road beneath their van was bumpy and uneven.

Parker slowed their approach, giving Liam plenty of time to get a good look. She already knew what the town looked like; she had been here already. More importantly, she knew exactly what she was looking at. Now, she just needed to wait until he figured it out.

The van came to a full stop in the middle of an intersection, right in the center of town. Parker turned off the engine and looked over at Liam, waiting for his reaction. For his part, his head was still hanging out the window, but the excited look on his face was long gone. In its place was a confused expression – the kind you get when you can't quite figure out what it is that you are looking at.

Without saying a word, Liam pulled his head back into the van. He then reached down and opened the passenger side door, stepping out and taking a look around. No matter how hard he stared at the town around him, he couldn't make himself see what he was looking at. It was almost like there was something in his brain that was stopping him from really seeing what he was looking at.

He took several steps down the street. He walked in a daze, not paying attention to where he was going, which was why his foot bumped into something lying in the street, nearly causing him to trip and fall. Looking down, he saw a large chunk of concrete sticking up at an odd angle from the road beneath him.

It was then that the spell that had bewitched his mind finally burst, and he saw the town of Greenwood for what it really was: A ghost town – a long-abandoned husk that had been left to rot and crumble under its own weight.

The road beneath his feet was in shambles. Chunks of concrete poked up in all directions, forced up by the roots of nearby trees and patches of weeds. Cracks in the pavement gave way to entire sections that were missing or otherwise buried by dirt. The sidewalks were overgrown with foliage, and the road was dotted with chunks of rusted metal that had once been cars.

The buildings were in worse conditions than the roads. Many of them had collapsed in on themselves. Those that remained standing were falling apart. A building across the street was so badly deteriorated that the roof had caved in, and a tree was growing right up through the middle.

Everywhere Liam looked, he saw abandoned and derelict buildings. As he walked down the street, he passed what must have been a store at some point. The entire backside of the building had collapsed outward, allowing him to look through the massive gap to the street beyond. Farther down the street, several buildings were leaning on one another for support, which was probably the only thing that kept them from collapsing.

The most disturbing thing about all of this was that there was no sign that anyone lived there. The place was completely devoid of life, without even the slightest indication that anyone had been there recently. There were signs that showed that people had once lived there, but that was a long time ago. The rusted-out cars that littered the street, the moldy furniture that was falling apart inside the buildings, and the rotting merchandise in the store windows all hinted that whoever had lived here was long gone.

It was almost as if everyone in town had mysteriously disappeared one day, leaving the place to decay and fall apart. The town of Greenwood had become nothing more than a faded memory of what it once was. That fact alone scared Liam more than he was willing to admit.

Greenwood wasn't supposed to be this way, he thought. There were supposed to be people here. It was supposed to be like Haven, alive and thriving. It wasn't supposed to be a decaying husk that was slowly being overgrown by the surrounding forest.

Liam began turning around in a circle, looking for something, anything, that could explain what had happened here. *There had to be something*, he thought frantically. For a moment, he even considered that all this was an elaborate practical joke and that none of it was real. The only problem was that no one was laughing. There was no one here to laugh, even if they wanted to.

A hand touched his shoulder. He spun around in surprise, forgetting for a moment that he had not come here alone. Parker was standing there, looking up at him, a concerned look in her eyes.

"What is all of this?" he asked in a hollow voice.

"This is the town of Greenwood," she replied.

"That's not possible," Liam murmured, turning around again to look at the ruined town around them.

"Liam, I—"

"No!" Liam interrupted. "This cannot be Greenwood. Greenwood is a town, with people, and brightly colored buildings that aren't falling down everywhere. I have seen pictures of this town, and this is not what I saw. It's...it's wrong."

"This is Greenwood," she said in a firm voice. "Despite what you may have seen or been told about this place, this is what it is actually like."

"Impossible," he blurted out. "It must be a mistake. Someone would have told me—"

"Told you what?" Parker said. "That this place is a ghost town? A relic of the old world that was left to slowly rot and die? That there is nobody left alive to live here? Wake up, Liam! They have been lying to you about the world outside of Haven."

He couldn't listen to this anymore. She had to be wrong about this place. At that moment, a thought occurred to him: Maybe he was just in the wrong part of town. That had to be it. This part of town had probably been abandoned for some reason, and everyone was living on the other side of town. It didn't make a lot of sense, but at this point, he was willing to believe anything.

He turned his back on Parker and ran down the street as fast as he could. He was determined to find something, anything, that proved that what she had been saying was wrong.

But each building he passed stood silent and empty, an unwavering testament to the truth: the town of Greenwood was dead.

Still, he refused to give up. He turned down side streets, ran up hills, and went around corners in the hopes that he would find something that could make sense of it all. There was nothing – nothing but decay and ruin as far as his eyes could see.

He finally broke down in front of a dilapidated house with a faded wooden fence out front. The fence had fallen over for the most part, and the house looked like it would collapse under the pressure of a gentle breeze. He collapsed on the carpet of grass and weeds that made up the front yard, leaning on one of the fence posts for support. His heart was pounding in his chest, and he felt nauseous.

When Parker arrived, he was hunched over, emptying the remains of his breakfast burrito onto the ground next to him. He looked over to see her standing a few feet away, content to keep her distance. He wiped his mouth with the sleeve of his hoodie before getting to his feet.

Parker must have taken this as an invitation to come closer, because she walked up to him and stood by his side. She didn't say anything; she just stood there. Liam couldn't imagine what she was thinking or feeling at that moment, but he was glad to have her nearby. Even though she had been the one to bring him here, it was still comforting not to be alone.

After a minute or two, she stretched out her hand, intent on placing it on his shoulder. He pulled away, not wanting to be touched. Having her there was one thing; having her touch him at that moment was another. She must have sensed his mood, because she let her arm drop back down to her side. They stood there for some time as Liam tried to make sense of the world around him.

He felt silly, but he changed his stance into one of the yoga poses his aunt had taught him. He had always felt self-conscious doing yoga with his aunt in their living room, but right now, it was exactly what he needed to calm himself down. He concentrated on his breathing, letting the good air in and the bad air out.

A gentle calm gradually settled over him. Focusing on something solid from his past, like yoga with his aunt, had allowed him to ground himself. It gave him a foundation on which he could regain control of himself. It also helped that his heart had stopped pounding in his chest and his muscles had relaxed.

Once he had found his center, as his aunt had called it, Liam stood up straight again. He stared up at the brilliant blue sky above, basking in the warm light of the afternoon sun which shone brightly down on him. As he was lowering his eyes to look at Parker, something caught his attention off in the distance.

Poking up amongst the trees, was the top of another radio tower. The antenna that stuck up amongst the trees wasn't anywhere near as tall as the one back in Haven, but it did stand out against the horizon. Feeling a sudden rush of hope, he started running again, this time in the direction of the antenna. Parker followed close behind.

They ran several blocks before the base of the tower came into view. Just like the radio tower back in Haven, this one was also connected to a nearby building. Unlike the communications building back in Haven, the building in front of them looked more like an old warehouse or airplane hangar.

Its walls were made of corrugated metal, which had been painted white. The roof curved down to touch the ground on both sides, creating an arch. There were no windows, but there was a set of double doors on the front of the building that could be slid open.

As Liam approached, he was struck by the stark contrast between the warehouse and the rest of the town. Greenwood was an overgrown ruin for the most part, without any sign that anyone had been there recently. The warehouse, on the other hand, looked to be well-maintained and recently used. The paint had faded, but someone had taken the time to paint over any spots that had been worn down. More importantly, the hum of electricity filled the air as power was routed from the warehouse to the radio tower. This alone was proof that this place hadn't been abandoned like the rest of the town.

Liam walked up and tugged on one of the doors. It opened, sliding to the side to reveal the room beyond. Inside the warehouse was a large open space filled with boxes and shipping crates. He stepped inside and noticed that the room was divided into two parts – a storage area in back where all of the crates were, and a living area near the door.

Off to the side of the entrance was a kitchenette, complete with a washbasin and a mini refrigerator. A small table and some chairs completed the furnishings. Along the wall was a bedroom, with the door left open to reveal a sleeping cot and a small dresser. A closet next to the bedroom turned out to be a bathroom, though how anyone could fit in there, he had no idea.

There were dirty dishes in the wash basin, and the sheets on the cot looked like someone had recently slept in them. Altogether, the place showed signs of recent activity. Someone had been living here, and Liam suspected he knew who that someone was.

Beyond the living area, the remaining space was filled with wooden crates and cardboard boxes. The crates were stacked one on top of another, creating towers that reached from floor to ceiling. Boxes were shoved wherever there was space, creating haphazard piles everywhere he looked.

Most of the crates toward the back of the warehouse were covered in woolen tarps that were secured with thin strands of rope. Underneath one of the tarps, he could make out something written on the side of a crate. He approached, making his way through the tangle of cardboard boxes until he was standing next to it. He pushed the tarp out of the way to get a better look at the words branded across the side of the crate:

RATION TYPE C
16 RATIONS
WT 84 CU 1.1
C16-12-04-2357-01
HAVEN

While Liam didn't know what a "Ration Type C" was, he did recognize the name at the bottom. Haven. More than that, he recognized the crates. He had seen them before – in the back of Gus's van.

Every week, Gus would pull into town with fresh supplies for the stores on Main Street – everything from tools for the hardware store to clothes for the general store. And every week, he would deliver these very same crates to the grocery store.

"And now you know," said a voice over his shoulder.

Liam turned to see Parker standing in the doorway. She hadn't followed him in, contenting herself to stand just outside the entrance. Her hesitation to come in confirmed what he had been thinking earlier about who had been staying here.

"This is where they kept you, wasn't it?" he asked, already knowing the answer.

"Yes," she said from the doorway. "Back in Haven, I promised to show you where they had been keeping me. Well, here we are. Charming, isn't it?"

"What is this place?"

"Other than being a temporary prison? It is a staging area for everything that goes in and out of Haven. Once or twice a year, supplies are smuggled here from the outside. Here they wait until they are needed up in Haven."

"That still doesn't explain why they brought you here."

"Doesn't it? They brought me here so that the next time a delivery came from the outside, I could be sent away with them. I suspect that they were willing to make a special trip for me, but I still had to wait for them to arrive. Which meant that I had to wait here. Just me and my jailor, Gus."

"Gus," Liam repeated to himself. The pieces of Parker's story were starting to come together. As far as he knew, Gus was the only person to make frequent trips out of town. It would make sense that he would be involved in all of this, especially given the crates in the warehouse.

"Whose van did you think they used to take me out of Haven?" Parker said. "Not to mention bring me back."

Liam had to think about that. He didn't want to believe that Gus was involved with whatever was going on here, but it did make sense. He had shown up at their shop with a half-empty van this morning, the same morning when Parker had miraculously reappeared. More than that, hadn't Gus also made a delivery the day that Parker had shown up for the first time? It was too much to be a coincidence.

"Alright, I believe you," he said. "But why bring you here in the first place? What did you do that was so wrong that they felt that they had to get rid of you?"

"Because I risked exposing them," she confessed. She motioned for him to step outside and follow her around the building. Once outside, she pointed up at the radio tower. "Do you see that antenna?"

"Yeah," Liam confirmed.

"That antenna is acting like a relay, rebroadcasting the signal that originates at the communications building back in Haven. It is part of a large network of radio towers that surrounds Haven in all directions," Parker explained.

"Ok."

"That signal, the one being generated back in Haven, is a dampening field that blocks all communication in and out of the area and helps hide us from the Authority."

"Wait, what? Who is the Authority?" Liam asked, having never heard of them before.

"The Authority is the new government. They are in charge now, and they are not necessarily friendly," she continued. "As for why we are hiding from them, well..." She trailed off, not sure how to answer.

"Well, what?" he asked, exasperated.

"If the Authority knew what was happening in Haven, they would do everything in their power to put a stop to it," she said seriously.

"Oh. Alright," Liam said, A moment later, he asked, "Just so I understand, what exactly is happening in Haven that would bring down the wrath of this Authority you mentioned?"

"The short answer? They have been experimenting with...forbidden technology."

It was clear that she was choosing her words very carefully. Whatever was going on, she didn't want to give away too much. After a few seconds, she continued.

"The Authority has a bunch of rules about what we can and cannot do. Especially when it comes to experimenting with certain technologies. The scientists back in Haven broke those rules and experimented with banned technology.

"Don't worry – they did the right thing. The Authority should have never been allowed to rise to power. They stand against everything that we believe. They would rather see the world suffer than admit that they were wrong," she said angrily.

"So, what did they do that was so wrong?" Liam asked, curious as to what the scientists did.

"They created something...special. Something that they have been trying to keep a secret for the past seventeen years."

As she finished speaking, Parker looked up at him with a meaningful gaze. It didn't take long for him to realize what she was suggesting. Her implication was as clear as a bell.

"What are you saying?" Liam asked carefully, slowly backing away from Parker. "That I am somehow involved in all this?"

"You are the reason for all this. You don't know it yet, but you are special. More than you will ever know. You are..." There was a brief pause while she decided what word to use. "Unique."

"And you are crazy!" Liam said, taking another step away from her. "I don't know what you are talking about, and I don't want to know. You leave me out of it!"

"Think about it!" she demanded. "Why have you never left Haven more than once in your entire life? Why is it that nobody ever comes and goes from Haven other than Gus in his van? Why is it that every time you want to leave, something comes up to stop you?

"Don't you realize what is going on? Ask yourself: Why is there a radio tower hidden in the hills above Haven that you knew nothing about until a week ago? Why is it necessary to have dozens of relay stations like this one broadcasting a signal to hide our location?"

Liam didn't know what to say. He didn't have the answers to her questions. More importantly, he was afraid of what those answers were.

"If nothing else, ask yourself why they were so eager to get rid of me. The answer to that question is that they think that I put you in danger. You!" she said pointedly.

Liam didn't want to listen to any more of this. Nothing she was saying could possibly be true. He wasn't special – not like that, anyway. She had to be making it up. How could any of it possibly be true?

"If you don't believe me, ask yourself: Why would I bring you here? Why would I do that unless I wanted you to see the truth that they have been hiding from you?" she said, fixing him with a meaningful stare.

"I don't know," he admitted. "But since we are asking questions, I have one of my own. You say everyone is lying to me. Well how about you? You told me that you didn't know what happened back in the control room. That was a lie, wasn't it?"

"Yes," she admitted.

"It wasn't a fire alarm that you set off, was it?"

"No," she said defiantly. "I purposefully shut down the dampening signal that the tower was broadcasting."

"Why?" Liam asked. "If it really is hiding us from the government, why shut it down?"

"That is not important right now. Let's just say that I have my reasons," she said defensively. "Mostly, it was because I needed to show you the truth. I was trying to pull back the curtain that has been placed over your eyes for all these years. Unfortunately, the system shutdown triggered an alarm, and we had to leave before I could show you what I wanted you to see."

"And what would that be?" Liam asked.

"Things around here aren't exactly what they appear to be. Take Greenwood, for example. This isn't what you expected, is it? Don't you get it? They are all lying to you – all of them. You cannot trust them!"

"You stay away from me!" Liam said, anger rising in his voice with every word. "I don't know what you are up to, and I don't care. You just leave me alone!"

With that, he turned his back on Parker and started walking back toward Haven. He was surprised when she reached out and grabbed his arm, bringing him to a sudden halt. He tried to pull free from her grip, but she held on tightly. She was stronger than he'd given her credit for.

He pulled away again, this time using all of his might to break her grip. More from her letting go of his arm than from his use of strength, he broke free and stumbled backwards, falling onto the ground. Parker walked over and reached down to help him up, but he pushed her hand away and stood up on his own.

She tried to apologize, but he wasn't listening. As soon as he was on his feet, he turned and ran back toward the center of town. Parker started running after him. Liam remembered from gym class how good a runner she was. There was no way he would be able to outrun her.

His only chance for escape would be to lose her in the tangled ruin of Greenwood's streets. As he turned the nearest corner, he ducked between several buildings lining the side of the road. This led him into a twisted labyrinth of collapsed buildings and obstructed alleyways.

He continued to zigzag between buildings, ducking under some collapsed walls here and jumping over some piles of rubble there. He didn't look back; he just kept running, hoping to lose Parker in all of the twists and turns.

After a few minutes, he had to stop to catch his breath. He kept waiting for Parker to appear around the nearest corner, hot on his heels, but she was nowhere to be seen. He must have lost her in all of the twists and turns.

Confident that he wasn't being followed, Liam made his way back to where they had left Gus's van. If he could reach it without being seen, he was confident he could drive it back home. With any luck, his aunt would only ground him for a month, rather than for the rest of his life.

It took him a while to get back to the place where they'd left the van. He tried to be as stealthy as possible, and he got lost more than once. By the time he arrived back at the van, Parker was already there, waiting for him. She hadn't seen him yet, so he stayed as close to the shadows as possible.

She must have realized where he was heading, which was probably why she stopped chasing him – better to wait for him to come to her than risk getting hurt running after him.

Liam waited, huddled against the wall of the shop with the missing wall in the back. He clung to the shadows as much as possible, waiting for his opportunity to make a run for it. The problem was, Parker wasn't leaving. She stood there, patiently waiting for him.

After thirty minutes of waiting, she started calling out his name. Did she really expect him to come running at the sound of her voice? Not after today. She didn't know where he was, and he was going to keep it that way.

Parker must have been getting desperate, because she started pacing back and forth along the street. Any moment now, she would probably start searching the town building by building.

It didn't take long for her to do just that.

Liam stepped away from the wall as Parker disappeared into a nearby shop across the street. His plan was simple: run for the van and hope he got there before she realized what he was doing. The only thing standing between him and escape was thirty feet of open road. All he had to do was step out of the building he was hiding in and make a run for it.

Before stepping out into the street, he took one final look around. Parker was nowhere to be seen. This was his chance. He needed to go now.

The crunch of gravel behind him froze Liam where he stood. Someone was standing in the large opening at the back of the shop where the wall had fallen out.

Turning slowly, he expected to see Parker standing there. Instead, a man he didn't recognize was standing there, watching him.

He was tall, with slicked-back hair and a tan trench coat hanging open, revealing a black suit underneath. Something was pinned to the breast pocket of his trench coat, but Liam didn't recognize it. Perhaps a badge of some sort?

Without saying a word, Liam stood there, looking at this mysterious stranger who had appeared out of nowhere. The stranger stared back, unblinking.

Finally, he opened his mouth and said, "Hello there."

Chapter 10: The Mysterious Stranger

Agent Lewis stood there, in the partially collapsing ruins of what he supposed had once been a clothing shop, waiting for the boy to respond. Rather than answering, the boy stood there, staring back at him, almost as if he were too stunned to speak. For that matter, the boy was frozen in place where he stood, refusing to move even an inch.

When Agent Lewis had first arrived on the outskirts of town, he suspected that he had arrived at his destination. What a disappointment it had been when he realized that the town falling apart all around him was completely devoid of life. From the looks of things, no one had lived here in quite some time. The whole place had appeared to be a graveyard, a monument to the past that had long been forgotten.

He had been on the point of turning around and heading home when he'd heard a faint calling in the distance. As the voice continued calling out, Agent Lewis headed in that direction, determined to identify the source. When he got closer to the middle of town, he veered off onto a side street. His instincts were to avoid giving away his presence until after he could properly assess the situation, which was how he ended up on the back side of a row of shops that lined the main street beyond.

One of the buildings was missing its back wall, which had collapsed outward in a large heap of brick and debris. Suspecting that this building would give him a good vantage point of the street beyond, Agent Lewis entered cautiously. He was surprised when right inside the building was a teenage boy, standing near the front of the store. At first, he had wondered whether the boy had been the one calling out, but the voice that he had heard had been more feminine. Besides, the boy had also appeared to be hiding from whomever was calling out, the same as he was.

Not wanting to startle the boy, Agent Lewis tried to step backwards out of the partially collapsed building. No sooner did he move his foot than the crunching sound of gravel beneath his feet gave away his presence. The boy then turned in surprise, immediately freezing in place when he saw the agent standing there.

Since the damage had already been done, Agent Lewis tried to make the best of it. "I said, hello there," Agent Lewis repeated.

Still the boy didn't respond. Agent Lewis took a step closer, moving further into the building. The boy didn't react, but there was a glint in his eyes that suggested that he was on the point of running. Not wanting to chase off the first person he had seen since leaving the Boundary, the agent stopped where he was and waited.

His goal was to look as non-threatening as possible. Whoever this boy was, he was the best possible lead in helping him figure out what was going on here.

While they stood there staring at each other, Agent Lewis took the opportunity to get a good look at the boy. The boy was tall for his age, perhaps even as tall as Agent Lewis. That alone was odd for a teenager. The oddities didn't stop there, though. The boy's clothing was unique, to say the least. The best way that the agent could describe them would be to call them vintage, or maybe retro was a better term for it – almost like someone had taken an old clothing catalogue out of the Historical Archives and used it to make the boy's clothes.

Probably the strangest thing about the boy was that Agent Lewis didn't recognize him. He had never seen this boy before. Sure, he wasn't expected to memorize every face he had ever seen, but he had a good memory, and he knew all of the open casefiles for missing persons that had crossed his desk. This boy's description didn't match any of them. Which meant that the biggest question was: Who was he?

Agent Lewis decided to take another step forward, making sure to move slowly and avoiding any quick movements. The last thing he wanted to do right now was to spook the boy into running – especially if there was a chance that he wasn't alone.

Sure enough, as he stepped forward, the boy turned to run. Unfortunately for him, he tripped on a loose floorboard that had warped over the years of constant exposure to the elements. He stumbled to the floor, quickly turning onto his back so that he could keep an eye on Agent Lewis.

Agent Lewis tried to express his good intentions by reaching a hand out to help the boy up, but the boy wasn't in the mood to accept help from a stranger. He scurried back along the floor until he reached the far wall. Using the wall for balance, the boy stood up, never breaking eye contact.

"Hey, relax, kid," Agent Lewis said in a soothing voice. "I am not trying to hurt you. I just saw you standing there and thought I would say hello."

To prove that he wasn't a threat, Agent Lewis took several steps back, resting against some old shelves that lined the opposite wall. He made himself comfortable, though he didn't relax. If the boy was going to try running away again, he needed to be ready to follow him.

"Mind telling me what you are doing here?"

"Nothing," the boy said without thinking, as if he had been programmed to give that answer anytime he was asked something by an adult.

"'Nothing?'" Agent Lewis replied, nodding. "Well, do you mind if we continue doing nothing over there? I don't like the idea of hanging out in a building that could collapse on me at any moment."

The boy didn't react. That was disappointing. Agent Lewis had always thought of himself as being funny, despite what his friends said about him. Still, he didn't like the way the building was leaning in on itself, and would prefer not to be buried in rubble if he could help it.

"How about this?" he said, adopting a different approach. "My name is Lewis – Agent Lewis. And you are?" he said, gesturing for the boy to give his name.

"Li-Liam." the boy said nervously.

"Liam. That is an interesting name. I don't think I have ever met a Liam before. So, tell me, Liam, is this your place?"

The boy looked around dubiously at the crumbling building surrounding them. It was clear from the rubble on the floor, faded paint on the walls, and plaster peeling from the ceiling that no one would willingly live in such a place – not to mention the missing back wall. After looking around, the boy responded by shaking his head.

"Ah, I didn't think so," Agent Lewis said. "Too bad. It looks almost...cozy."

Whatever he was doing, it seemed to be working. The boy hadn't relaxed, but he wasn't as tense as he had been. At least it didn't look like he was going to try bolting anytime soon.

Wanting to keep his momentum, Agent Lewis continued making small talk. "Alright, I think we can both agree that this isn't your home. In fact, I cannot imagine anyone living here. So, if you are not from here, then where are you from?" he said, trying to sound as nonchalant as possible.

Rather than answering, the boy looked over his shoulder, through the missing front window, and into the street. Wanting to see what the boy was looking at, Agent Lewis moved toward the front of the building so that he could see through the window to the street beyond. Parked in the middle of the street several buildings away was an old delivery van. Unlike the rest of the cars on the street, which had turned to rust over the years, the van was still in good shape.

In an instant, Agent Lewis understood. The boy must have come here in that van. Which begged the question: Where had the van come from?

When he had been studying the map of Quadrant 29 that he had gotten from the Historical Archives, it wasn't clear how many other towns there were in the area. He knew that the town he had been looking for was nestled in between the surrounding mountains, but that was as much as he had to go on. If this wasn't the town he had been looking for – and he was starting to highly doubt that it was – then the real town had to be somewhere nearby. Perhaps it was the same place where both the boy and the van had come from.

Agent Lewis whistled through his teeth and pointed at the van. "Nice ride," he commented. "Is she yours?"

The boy looked back through the missing window at the van in the middle of the street. He had seemed confused by the question, but nodding.

"Yes," he said. "Well, no. Sort of."

"'Sort of?' As in, I 'sort of' borrowed it from someone else?" Agent Lewis suggested.

"We didn't steal it!" the boy said in protest.

"'We?'" Agent Lewis said with sudden interest. "Is there someone else here that I should meet?"

As if saying these words had been a summons, a girl around the same age as the boy peeked her head through the missing front window. Her eyes found the boy immediately, and she broke out in a relieved smile. She stepped through the empty windowpane, intent on rushing over to the boy's side but stopped when she noticed that something was wrong.

Up until now, she hadn't noticed Agent Lewis leaning up against the opposite wall. He watched as her gaze shifted from the boy to where he was standing. While the boy had been surprised to see him, the girl's reaction was immediately hostile. She turned to face him, positioning herself between the boy and himself. A sneer appeared on her face, and her hands clenched into fists.

"Liam, are you going to introduce me to your friend?" Agent Lewis asked, directing his question over the girl's shoulder.

Rather than answering his question, the boy put a hand on the girl's shoulder and said, "Parker, I didn't—"

"Be quiet, Liam!" The girl interrupted in a stern voice that cut off whatever the boy had been about to say. She took several steps backward, forcing the boy to press against the wall.

She was trying to put distance between them, Agent Lewis observed. "Parker, is it? Another unique name. Well, I am meeting all sorts of interesting people today. Liam here was just telling me about how you two 'borrowed' that van out there," he said in the friendliest voice he could manage.

The girl's eyes flickered back to the street, where the van was still parked. She made no effort to respond to Agent Lewis, and the boy seemed to be taking her lead.

And there they stood, all three of them, standing in a dilapidated building staring at each other and not saying a word.

"Well, this is awkward," Agent Lewis finally said. "You don't have to say it. I can tell when things are awkward. Look, if you are worried that you are in trouble for borrowing that van, don't be. I don't care about that. Honestly, I am just glad I found the two of you.

"I was making my way through town here, and I must have gotten lost somewhere, because this is definitely not where I was heading. And since there is no one else here that can give me directions, I was hoping that you could help. Any chance you can tell me where I am?" Agent Lewis said with a smile.

"Where were you heading?" the boy asked timidly.

"Be quiet!" the girl commanded over her shoulder.

Ignoring the girl's comment, Agent Lewis addressed the boy directly. "Funny you should ask. I heard of a small town nestled in the hills up in this area. I thought this was it, but clearly, I was wrong, which means it must be somewhere nearby. I am guessing you can show me the way."

"There is nothing here for you. Turn around and go back to where you came from," the girl practically spat.

"Well, obviously, there is nothing here for me in this town, the same way there is nothing here for you, either. I have no interest here, but I think we are all interested in where you two came from. If I am right, the place where you are from and the one I am looking for are the same."

"Parker is right," the boy said over her shoulder. "You would be better off heading back the way you came. There is nothing up here besides Haven, and I am sure—"

"Liam, be quiet!" the girl shouted.

"Haven. Yes, that sounds like the place I am looking for," Agent Lewis said. Finally, he was getting somewhere.

The boy's momentary slip of the tongue seemed to be the last straw for the girl. She wanted to be as far away from the agent as she could get. Hands outstretched, she began maneuvering the boy toward the open doorway. She made certain not to take her eyes off the agent as she did so.

Agent Lewis let out a long sigh. From the way she was moving, he could tell that she was planning on making a run for it. If they managed to escape, it would be a lot more difficult to locate this town of Haven that the boy had mentioned. Besides, he couldn't risk them warning whoever was there of his presence.

He stepped away from the wall, placing himself between them and the open door. Without losing a step, the girl repositioned, and the two of them stepped out onto the street through the empty window frame. The lack of glass made it easy for them to step through while still keeping their distance from him.

Following them out into the street, Agent Lewis reached down and pulled his coat back. There on his hip, was his stun pistol. His hand moved to the grip of his weapon, but he didn't pull it out of the holster – not yet.

"It doesn't have to be this way," he warned them.

"Screw you, G-man!" the girl shouted as she turned around and ran toward the van. The boy was quick to follow her lead, especially since she grabbed his arm and pulled him along.

Agent Lewis pulled his stun pistol from his holster and aimed it at the retreating youths. He pulled the trigger, and a bolt of electric blue energy shot out from the tip with a loud buzzing sound. His aim was off, and the blast soared over their heads as they ran. He pulled the trigger two more times, but missed both times. He was starting to wish that he had spent more time at the Bureau's shooting range.

Squaring up his shoulders and holding his stun pistol in both hands, he adopted the shooting stance taught to him during his training. Rather than pulling the trigger, he remembered to squeeze the trigger instead. He missed again, but at least this time, his aim was much closer. The blast had narrowly missed hitting the girl, instead flying over her shoulder to hit the side of the van.

Glass exploded from the van's windshield at the force from the blast. As shattered glass rained down on the concrete below, the two youths dived behind the van for protection. Agent Lewis already knew that he had no chance of picking them off at this distance, especially if they were hiding behind the van. With no other option, he ran forward, keeping his stun pistol pointed in their direction.

The sound of his footsteps must have alerted them to his approach, because the boy lifted his head out from behind the van to see what was happening. More out of instinct than anything else, Agent Lewis pulled the trigger. The blast struck the hood of the van, creating a large dent and an even bigger scorch mark.

The boy dropped down behind the van again, and Agent Lewis lowered his stun pistol. He hadn't meant to aim for the boy's head. Bad things could happen if you were struck by a stun blast at close range or in the head. It was lucky for both of them that he was such a terrible marksman.

With his stun pistol still lowered, he slowly approached the van. He didn't want to risk another potential head-shot, but he still had to be ready to stun them if given the chance. He stepped up to the side of the van and put his back against it. Raising his stun pistol, he counted to three in his head. When he reached three, he leapt around the backside of the van, prepared to fire. The problem was, nobody was there.

They were gone. Agent Lewis lowered his weapon in frustration and looked around wildly. They must have snuck away to one of the nearby buildings while he had been taking his time.

At first, there was no sign of them. Agent Lewis walked up the street, looking to either side for any sign that would indicate where they had gone. He was starting to get discouraged when he saw it – a flash of movement out of the corner of his eye.

He ran in the direction of the movement, reaching a gap between two buildings. At the other end, the boy and the girl were standing behind some trash cans. When they saw him at the opening of the gap, they started running in the opposite direction.

He ran after them, desperate to catch them before they managed to get away. The gap at the other side opened up into an alleyway. On his right, he saw the tail end of the boy's hoodie disappear around a corner. Figuring that they had both headed in that direction, he followed after them as fast as he could.

Right as he reached the corner, something hard collided with his face. He was on the ground before he knew what had happened. As his vision cleared, he could see the girl standing over him, holding the remnants of a broken chair.

He had walked right into an ambush. They had tricked him into chasing after the boy, while the girl had been lying in wait, ready to hit him with an old wooden chair. The worst part was that he hadn't even seen it coming.

Luckily, the chair had been so old and decrepit that it had practically fallen apart when she hit him with it. That was probably the only thing that had saved him from being badly injured. Still, it had hit him hard enough to knock him off his feet.

When the girl realized what had happened, she dropped the broken chair and ran away as fast as she could. Agent Lewis raised his stun pistol and pulled the trigger several times. Stun blasts echoed down the alleyway, but none of them hit their target. He got to his feet and leaned against the nearest wall to steady himself. He reached up with his free hand to feel his face to determine the extent of the damage. His nose was a little sore, but that seemed to be the worst of it.

Now that he was back on his feet, Agent Lewis cautiously approached the corner of the alleyway. He wasn't about to risk getting hit in the face again. As he peeked around the corner, he could see the girl disappearing around another corner at the end of the alleyway. The boy had headed off in the opposite direction, and was nowhere to be seen.

They must have decided to split up, increasing their chance of losing him amongst the town's many twists and turns. Since he had no idea where the boy had gone, he decided that the best thing to do was to chase after the girl. She was the more dangerous of the two, anyway.

Agent Lewis groaned to himself as he ran after her. Today wasn't going the way he had hoped it would. The first evidence he had found that someone was really living up here had run away from him and ended up hitting him in the face with a chair. Perhaps he would leave those details out of his official report.

One thing was for certain: the girl was definitely the more aggressive of the two. If he could capture her, the boy wouldn't be too hard to catch after that. But that meant that he needed to catch up to her first, which was a problem, because no matter how hard he ran, she managed to keep her distance from him.

It didn't help that he had to slow down every time he came to a corner. He wasn't about to walk blindly into another ambush. Who knew what she would try hitting him with next? No doubt, the next thing she chose would be much sturdier than a rotting chair.

Despite having to slow down at each corner, he still managed to keep up with her as she ran. She would disappear one moment, only to appear a moment later down a side street or in between two buildings. Every time he thought that he had lost her, she would appear somewhere ahead of him. When this happened the first couple of times, he attributed it to luck. It didn't take long for him to realize that his luck wasn't that good. She was reappearing ahead of him far too frequently. There was something else going on.

Whenever he lost sight of her, she would miraculously reappear ahead of him. Had she been trying to get away, she could have done it by now. The only explanation was that she wanted to be seen; she wanted him to find her. She never appeared close enough for him to catch, but always close enough for him to chase after her. She wanted him to chase her.

Agent Lewis stopped and looked around at his surroundings, trying to get his bearings. When he started chasing her, they had been close to the center of town. Now, it appeared that they were on the eastern edge of town, headed toward the woods. In that moment, he realized that she was purposefully leading him away from where they started – or, more precisely, away from the boy.

Now that he knew what she was doing, Agent Lewis doubled back toward the van. If her goal was to lead him away, then the best thing that he could do was to do the opposite.

He realized that he had been thinking of this all wrong. He had figured that if he caught the girl first, the boy would be easy to find, when he should have realized that catching the boy would have forced the girl to come to him. It was a risky move. There was a chance that he could lose both of them this way, but his instincts told him that this was the right thing to do.

He reached the center of town and was relieved to see that the van was still there, sitting in the middle of the street. He approached, suspecting that the boy might be hiding inside. No such luck.

The van was empty except for a toolbox in the back. He checked the ignition, but the keys were missing. At least that meant that the boy couldn't drive away on his own. If he had the keys, he probably would have left in the van by now.

So, if the boy isn't here. Where could he be hiding? Agent Lewis asked himself. He knew from experience that there were plenty of places to hide in this town. The only thing for him to do was to search the surrounding area and look for some clues.

He searched the nearby buildings, but didn't find anything. After an hour, he started wondering whether he had made a mistake. The boy could have run off in any direction. It would probably be easy for him to hide in the ruins of the town or in the surrounding woods until the agent finally gave up and left. Perhaps that was what the boy had been counting on.

That was exactly what Agent Lewis was thinking of doing. He had confirmation that there were in fact people living up here, although how many and where were still a mystery. The important thing was that he had confirmation that someone was living up here, and perhaps, that would be enough.

He was about to give up and head back to his vehicle when he stepped on something crunchy. Looking under his shoe, he saw some fragments of shattered glass on the road. Curious, he bent down to examine the fragments. They appeared to be fragments of the van's windshield – the same windshield that had shattered when his stun blast struck the side of the van.

But he was nowhere near the van at that moment. He was standing in the road, a good fifty feet away from where the van was parked. There was no way the glass would have travelled this far from the force of the explosion. Agent Lewis looked around and saw another clump of broken glass a few feet away, and another a few feet beyond that.

It was a trail. Someone had tracked glass along the road as they ran – someone who had stepped on the glass while running away from the van. *The boy*! Who else could it have been? He must have gone back to the van, discovered that the keys were missing, and then headed off down the road. At some point, he must have stepped on the glass from the broken windshield and inadvertently left a trail for anyone to follow.

Agent Lewis straightened up and followed the trail of broken glass down the road. The tracks decreased with each step, but it was easy enough to follow. At least, he could see the general direction that they were headed in.

After making several turns, he found himself standing on a street that he had somehow missed when he was first exploring the town. He knew that he hadn't been here before. After all, how could you miss a fully functional radio tower and warehouse in a town like this?

Unlike the rest of the town, which looked like it was about to collapse under its own weight, the radio tower and warehouse looked to be in good condition. There was some wear on the building but nothing compared to the rest of the town. Someone had been maintaining this place. Whether that had been the boy and the girl or someone else entirely was yet to be seen.

As Agent Lewis approached, the radio tower loomed overhead. The buzz of electricity told him that someone was feeding power to it. A quick glance showed several cables running from the tower to the side of the warehouse. There were two doors on the front of the building that could be opened or closed by sliding the doors on a rail system. Currently, the doors were open slightly, as if someone hadn't stopped long enough to pull them shut.

Agent Lewis approached the doors, his stun pistol firmly in hand. As he reached for the handle, it occurred to him that this place could be the source of the interference. Attendant Phillips had mentioned that whoever was up here could be blocking their sensor sweeps. It was certainly possible that a radio tower connected to a well-maintained warehouse could be the cause of the interference.

Gripping the handle firmly, he pulled. The door slid open, rebounding as it reached the end of its track. He stepped through the open doorway, taking position just off to the side, his stun pistol held out in front of him, ready for anything.

The room beyond was filled with wooden crates and countless boxes. There was space at the front for living quarters, but most of the room was filled with various supplies. Cautiously, he searched the bedroom and bathroom areas. There was nothing there. He looked around, staring intently at the piles of crates and boxes beyond the living quarters, but failed to see any sign that anyone was there.

Feeling disappointed, he turned and headed for the door. As he did, he stepped on a small shard of broken glass. With a triumphant smile on his face, he turned around, confident that the boy was somewhere in the room. The only place he could be hiding was among the crates.

He stood there, facing the piles of crates, waiting. He wasn't wasting time by any means. He was listening – listening for the sound that he knew would give away the boy's hiding place. Sure enough, two minutes later, he heard rustling coming from a stack of crates off to the right. A woolen tarp had been thrown over several crates, and from beneath them peeked the toes of someone's shoes.

"I know you are there. I can see your feet. Come out now, and I promise you won't be hurt," Agent Lewis said, using his most commanding voice and raising his stun pistol.

A few tense seconds passed. Agent Lewis stood there waiting, pistol still pointed at the woolen tarp where the shoes poked out. He was about to pull the trigger on his stun pistol when the boy threw off the tarp and stood up. His hands were raised above his head in surrender.

"Please – I don't know what you want, but I just want to go home," the boy pleaded.

Agent Lewis compressed his lips together. *If only it were that simple,* he thought. His grip tightened on his stun pistol.

"I don't know what you and your little friend were thinking, but it was extremely dangerous to run away from me like that," he said, scolding the boy. "If you haven't already noticed, this place isn't exactly safe. Half of these buildings look like they are ready to collapse. You could have hurt yourself – or, even worse, me. And there isn't anyone around here to patch you up if you do get hurt."

"You may be right about that, but I figured that hanging around while someone was shooting at me wasn't the best idea either," the boy said sarcastically.

"This," Agent Lewis said, motioning to his stun pistol, "would not have hurt you. It is a standard-issue stun pistol. It is meant to incapacitate you, nothing more."

"Good to know," the boy replied skeptically.

"You don't believe me? Let me show you."

Without the slightest hesitation, Agent Lewis pulled the trigger. The room lit up with a bright blue light as a bolt of electricity shot out from the tip of the stun pistol and collided with the boy's side.

In an instant, the boy crumpled to the ground, grasping at the area that had been shot. Agent Lewis watched in horror as he writhed in pain on the floor, clutching his side. Tears were streaming out of his eyes, and it looked like the stun blast had done some real damage.

"It...it isn't supposed to do that," Agent Lewis said, looking down at the stun pistol in his hand with disbelief. "It is only supposed to incapacitate you, not...Are you alright?"

The boy had ceased writhing on the floor, but he was still hunched over in pain. Agent Lewis reached down and grabbed the boy's arm, pulling him to his feet. The boy pushed away from him, falling against some nearby crates. The boy managed to stay on his feet, but he was leaning heavily on the crate next to the agent.

After a minute or two, the boy reached down and lifted his hoodie and shirt to stare at the wound in his side. The hoodie itself was blackened from the stun blast, but the skin underneath was far worse. It was red and agitated, with several blisters appearing all along the fist-sized wound.

"I have never seen anything like this," Agent Lewis admitted, staring at the burn. "Usually, the blast from a stun pistol doesn't leave a mark on the skin, but this..."

He reached out to touch the wound in the boy's side, fascinated by this strange reaction. The boy immediately lowered his shirt and hoodie, covering his wound back up.

Agent Lewis shifted his attention to the boy's face, trying to figure out what had happened. He was so focused that he never heard the girl sneaking up behind him.

Before he knew what was going on, Agent Lewis's outstretched arm was struck by something hard and sturdy. Recoiling in pain, he turned to see the girl standing there, already taking another swing with a thick metal pipe clenched in her hands. The pipe collided with his side, just below his ribs. Before he had time to recover, another blow struck him on the back of the knee, causing him to drop down to the floor. Another blow struck the hand that was still holding onto the stun pistol. It fell to the floor as his hand went instantly numb.

Agent Lewis struggled to stand up, but another blow struck him in the shoulder, forcing him to fall backwards into a pile of crates. He collided with the crates, pulling the woolen tarp down on himself in an effort to grab onto something. Both the tarp and several boxes fell on top of him, burying him in a tangle of cardboard and wool.

It ended up being a good thing. The boxes and the woolen tarp helped cushion the blow of the girl's swings as she continued to pummel him with the pipe. Oh, it still hurt, but any protection was better than nothing.

He lost count of how many times the girl hit him with the length of pipe in her hands. Eventually, the beating stopped. Whether the girl had worn herself out or decided that he had had enough, he couldn't say. What he did know was that every inch of him hurt. He would have tried fending off the girl's attack, but his arm was pretty badly messed up.

He lay there, unwilling and unable to get up. He did manage to lift his head when he heard the sound of his stun pistol being picked up off the floor. It appeared that the girl had chosen to discard her metal pipe in favor of his pistol.

He watched as she walked over to where he lay sprawled on the floor. She stood over him, just like she had back in the alley when she'd hit him with the chair – only this time, he didn't think she was going to run away. He watched as she raised the stun pistol and pointed it directly at his head. He knew what a head shot could do to a person, and he suspected that she did too.

Agent Lewis had no doubt that she was capable of pulling the trigger. The look in her eyes told him that she wanted to. He would have closed his eyes, but he refused to give her the satisfaction. If she wanted to end his life, then she was going to have to face him to do it.

The girl's finger tightened on the trigger. Any moment now, the room would light up with a blue flash, and it would be all over.

Fortunately for him, that didn't happen. Before she could finish pulling the trigger, the boy laid his hand on top of hers, lowering the pistol so that it pointed at the floor. "Come on, let's get out of here," he said, still holding his side.

"What about him?" she said, looking down at Agent Lewis.

"I don't think we have to worry about him anymore."

As he spoke, the boy winced in pain. The girl immediately turned her attention to him, propping herself under his arm to help hold him up. Together, the two of them turned and made their way out of the warehouse, leaving Agent Lewis on the floor.

As he lay there, he couldn't help but think how badly things had turned out. Here he was, badly beaten and left behind like scrap on a junkpile. Today was definitely not his day.

It was more than an hour before he felt like moving. His whole body ached. Every inch of him was bruised and battered. Somehow, he found the strength to sit up. He reached out to move one of the crates that had fallen on his leg, and pain exploded down his arm.

He lifted his arm up as high as it would go to survey the damage. That girl had certainly made a mess of things. His arm was in pretty rough shape. He only hoped that it wasn't anything too serious. He hadn't been lying when he told the boy that there wasn't anyone around to patch you up if you got hurt.

226

Using his other arm, he lifted the crate off his legs and tried to stand. It was at this moment that he noticed the writing on the side of the crate that he had moved. It wasn't the presence of old rations that caught his attention, but the name on the side of the crate: Haven. *Wasn't that the name of the town that the boy had mentioned?*

Agent Lewis got to his feet. His first order of business was to attend to his injuries. After that, he would reach out to Admin Ryan and make a report of what had happened. Once that was done…well, best to take things one step at a time.

He limped to the door to the warehouse, stepping out into the street beyond. There was no sign of the boy or the girl, which was fine by him. Chances were, the girl would try to finish him off if she was still hanging around. Given his current condition, that wasn't something that he could prevent at the moment.

He made his way down the street, making several turns before reaching a road that led to the edge of town. There, parked beyond the first row of collapsing houses, was his vehicle. When he had first arrived, he hadn't wanted to alert any potential residents to his presence, which was why he had parked there and walked the rest of the way into town.

Of course, the general condition of the roads in Greenwood had also convinced him to go the rest of the way on foot. Up until recently, the highway leading here had been relatively smooth and intact, albeit needing some serious repairs. The roads in town were particularly bad, and he hadn't wanted to take the chance of damaging his vehicle needlessly.

Now that he was back at his vehicle, he walked around to the trunk and opened it. Inside was a field kit, complete with medical supplies, along with the black duffle bag from his office, the mobile emitter, and the spare battery. He pulled the field kit out with his good arm and set it on the hood of his vehicle, followed by the duffle bag.

He opened the field kit and pulled out the medical supplies, setting them on the hood next to the duffle bag. The hardest thing to do was taking off his coat and shirt. Even the slightest movement caused pain to surge through his wounded arm and side.

Once he managed to get both of his coats off, he carefully unbuttoned his shirt and let it drop to the floor. His arm and side were a mess. It was hard to see how bad things were, so the first thing he needed to do was to clean himself up so he could accurately survey the damage.

He used a cleansing solution to wipe away the mess, revealing multiple cuts, bruises, and a few gaping wounds. She had really done a number on him. By this time, his arm was practically hanging lifeless at his side.

The next order of business was to take care of the pain. There were several syringes in the field kit that were color-coded, to show what they did. Agent Lewis started with the blue syringe, injecting it right into his neck. It was followed by the yellow syringe in his upper arm and the purple syringe in his side. The chemicals in the syringes didn't take long to start working, and in less than a minute, he was already feeling better.

Now that the pain had faded, he could work on patching himself up. He began by pouring an entire bottle of disinfectant on his arm and side. Once that was done, he turned his attention to the suture gun in the field kit, which allowed him to close up the gaping wounds in his arm and side. This was followed by dozens of dermal bandages that covered every available inch of his skin.

By the time he was done, his entire arm was a mass of bandages. Everything from the wrist up was covered, ending at the top of his shoulder. The same applied to his side and chest, where bandages crisscrossed in every direction.

The good news was that he wasn't in pain anymore and he felt well enough to continue on without needing additional medical treatment, at least for the time being. He even raised his arm to test his range of motion. He was able to move it up and down and side to side – not the best, but still far better than it had been only moments ago.

There was still the issue with his leg. Although not nearly as bad as his arm and side, his knee had taken a pretty good blow from the girl's length of pipe. This had caused a minor limp on the walk back to his vehicle. Included in the field kit was a leg brace, which, when placed over the knee, helped stabilize him. He was even able to slip his pant leg over the brace so no one would know that he was wearing it.

With his injuries now taken care of, he could move forward with reporting his situation to the Bureau, but first, he had to get dressed. His trench coat had a few rips and tears on the arm, but was still in good condition. His shirt and suit coat weren't so fortunate. The white shirt was so badly stained that he abandoned any hope of wearing it again in the future. The good news was that he had packed a spare shirt in his duffle bag.

Throwing the soiled shirt and suit coat into the trunk, he pulled out a fresh white shirt from the duffle bag and put it on. He had trouble doing up the buttons, but that was to be expected, given the level of damage that had been done to his arm. With his shirt on, the trench coat came next, completing his ensemble.

As he finished dressing, his hand brushed against his side, where his empty holster was still attached to his belt. Up until now, he had forgotten that he had been wearing it. The last time he saw his stun pistol, it had been in the hands of that girl, Parker, as she left the warehouse with the boy. It was just one more thing he would need to explain to Admin Ryan.

Speaking of which, it was time for him to make his report. He replaced the field kit and duffle bag back into the trunk and pulled out the mobile emitter. Not wanting to waste the battery on the emitter, he opened the door to his vehicle and sat down in the driver's seat. He then plugged the emitter into the auxiliary port on his dashboard and dialed up the number for the Bureau.

At first, the emitter's display panel showed nothing but static, accompanied by some distorted audio. In an attempt to clear up the signal, he routed the emitter's signal through his vehicle's computer system. This had the effect of combining the emitter with his vehicle's own communications system. That did the trick. The image of Admin Ryan gradually appeared amongst the static, projected on the inside of his windshield.

"Number 6?" Admin Ryan asked, voice echoing through the vehicle's speaker system. "Number 6, is that you?"

"It is me, sir. Agent Lewis."

"I can barely see you. Can you clean up your transmission?"

"I am afraid not, sir. There is something up here in these mountains that is throwing up a large amount of interference. I suspect it is coming from a nearby radio tower, but I cannot be sure."

"A radio tower?" Admin Ryan responded with surprise. "So, you did find something out there after all?"

"Yes and no, sir," Agent Lewis confessed. "I arrived at a crumbling town called Greenwood earlier this afternoon, but from the look of things, there hasn't been anyone living here in a long time. I did find a warehouse and a radio tower that seemed to be in use."

"Is this the same town that you showed me on your map?"

"I don't think so, sir." Agent Lewis admitted. "This town doesn't appear on any of my maps, which, given the state of abandonment, would make sense. I believe that the town I showed you on the map is still further up the mountain. I got a lead that suggests that a town called Haven may not be too far away."

"What kind of lead?"

"I ran into a pair of teenagers playing hide and seek in the ruins. A boy and a girl. Both appeared to be around sixteen to seventeen years old. I didn't recognize them, and they don't match any open missing persons reports."

"Strays?" Admin Ryan asked eagerly.

"Most likely," Agent Lewis said timidly. "But I wasn't able to ID them, so can't confirm their status just yet."

The line was silent for a moment. At first, Agent Lewis thought that maybe the connection had gone bad and that he had lost contact with the Administrator. He was about to hang up and try again when Admin Ryan spoke.

"Agent Lewis, you did apprehend them, didn't you?" the administrator said slowly but sternly.

"I...tried to, sir." Agent Lewis said with a wince. "They resisted. When I tried to take them into custody, there was a struggle, and...."

"And?" Admin Ryan demanded.

"And they got away," Agent Lewis confessed.

A string of obscenities filled Agent Lewis's ears as the Administrator shouted at him through the vehicle's speakers. The obscenities continued for a full two minutes before he finally calmed down enough to moderate his tone.

"Tell me, Number 6, how did two teenagers manage to evade capture?" Admin Ryan asked, trying to keep the anger out of his voice.

"I went to apprehend them, and they ran away. I chased them through the town, but they split up. When I managed to corner one of them, the other one attacked me. They managed to incapacitate me, at which point they escaped in an old moving van," Agent Lewis recounted.

"Why didn't you defend yourself? You did remember to take your service weapon with you, didn't you?"

"Yes, sir. I brought my service weapon with me, but they took me by surprise, and..."

"And?"

"And they took my service weapon," Agent Lewis admitted in all but a whisper.

"They have your service weapon?" Admin Ryan shouted, barely managing to control his anger.

"Yes, sir."

A few seconds of silence passed as Admin Ryan struggled to keep his temper under control. Finally, he said, "Alright. This is what I want you to do, Number 6. I want you to turn around and head back to the Boundary. Once you arrive, you will be escorted back to the Bureau, where we can discuss your...performance in the field."

"Sir, with all due respect, now is not the time to turn around," Agent Lewis interjected.

"Turn around and come back!" Admin Ryan commanded. "You are clearly not up to the task. Once you are back, I will dispatch a retrieval team to locate and retrieve these strays that you found."

"Sir, please hear me out," Agent Lewis pleaded. "Those teenagers that I ran into – they weren't your average strays. There was something different about them, especially the boy. I can't put my finger on it, but the one thing I do know is that they had to come from somewhere. I believe that wherever they came from, that is what we are looking for."

When Admin Ryan didn't say anything, Agent Lewis took it as a sign to keep talking.

"The boy mentioned stealing the van that they came here in. That tells me that there has to be more people around here. They also mentioned the name of a town, Haven. Sir, in the warehouse that I found, there were dozens of boxes and supply crates, all marked with Haven as their destination.

"I believe that this place is a supply depot or possibly a stop-over on the way to Haven. If that is true, there is no telling how many people we may find up there. And, sir, if I am right, that means that those two teenagers are heading back there right now to warn them. If I head back now, they could all be gone by the time the retrieval team arrives. We cannot take that chance," Agent Lewis finished in a rush, trying to say everything he needed to say before he was interrupted.

Admin Ryan wasn't happy about the situation, but Agent Lewis had made a good argument. The fact that he had run into two strays in a place where there shouldn't be any was a sign that he was on the right track. If there was a larger community out there, then the Bureau needed to know about it.

Furrowing his brow, Admin Ryan reluctantly agreed. "I am still going to dispatch two retrieval teams to your area, accompanied by a Rotowing and some transports. If they are dispatched within the hour they should arrive sometime before dawn. Let me be clear, Number 6: When they arrive, they will take charge of the situation. Your orders are to comply with their instructions and return with them," he said, making it abundantly clear what the chain of command was going to be.

"And until they arrive?" Agent Lewis said hopefully.

"Proceed with caution," Admin Ryan answered.

Agent Lewis was quick to agree with Admin Ryan's decision. It wasn't exactly what he had been hoping for, but it wasn't bad either. At least this way, he could continue his investigation until reinforcements arrived – at which point he suspected that he would be treated on the same level as the captured strays.

"Listen," Admin Ryan continued. "I don't know what is going on up there, but you now have two confirmed stays that should be considered armed and dangerous. Don't do anything stupid like getting yourself captured or killed. You just have to wait until the retrieval teams arrive in the morning. Hopefully, you won't screw things up even more between now and then.

"As for your service weapon, there should be a back-up weapon under the passenger seat. Every agency vehicle is equipped with a reserve in case of emergency. You should have clearance to access it.

"Now, this is the important part. Keep the mobile emitter on from here on out. You may not be able to communicate directly with me if the interference gets worse, but you should be able to communicate with the retrieval teams when they arrive. The emitter uses a new kind of technology that will allow you to broadcast via a hand-held relay. Carry that relay with you at all times. If necessary, it can be used as a homing beacon to zero in on your location," Admin Ryan said.

"Understood. Thank you, sir. I won't let you down," Agent Lewis proclaimed with as much confidence as he could muster.

"At this point, I am not sure you are capable of anything else," Admin Ryan said dryly as he severed the connection between them.

Now that the Administrator had terminated their conversation, Agent Lewis didn't waste any time in getting back to work. He secured everything in the trunk except for the emitter, which he left on the passenger seat. With everything packed up, he climbed back into the driver's seat and leaned over to access the lockbox underneath the passenger's seat.

He pressed his hand against the faceplate, and the lockbox validated his identity before sliding open. Inside was another stun pistol, identical to the one that he had lost. He pulled the stun pistol out of the lockbox and placed it in the holster at his side.

Now he was ready. He still needed to figure out where those two kids had gone. The best place to start his search would be back at the center of town where the van had been. Turning his vehicle on, he drove toward the center of town, doing his best to ignore the constant bumps in the road.

As he approached the intersection where the van had been parked, he stopped his vehicle and stepped out. The van was gone. In its place was a scattering of broken glass and a puddle of dark blue liquid. It was the puddle that drew his attention. It was thick and viscous, most likely engine coolant.

The van had been struck several times by his stun blasts. Perhaps the force of those blasts had damaged the engine somehow. If that were true, then it meant two things: They wouldn't get far using the van, and there would be a trail that he could follow. Sure enough, tiny puddles of coolant led off down the street toward the woods beyond.

Smiling to himself, Agent Lewis got back in his vehicle and followed the trail of coolant out of town. At the edge of town, the pavement gave way to a gravel road that twisted and turned amongst the surrounding trees. The tires on his vehicle weren't meant for off-roading, but he continued anyway.

Twenty minutes later, he brought his vehicle to a stop. Ahead of him, in the middle of the road, was the van. As cautiously as possible, he pulled out his replacement stun pistol and stepped out of his vehicle. He didn't want to be the victim of another ambush.

The van was empty. The hood was open, and steam was rising from the engine. Apparently, the van had given out on them, and the two had abandoned it to continue on foot. It wasn't long before he found two sets of footprints heading off the road and into the surrounding forest. *Smart*, he thought.

They knew to stay off the road to avoid being captured. The safety of the woods would hide them from view, but it would also make their journey a lot more difficult – not to mention that it would probably take them twice as long to reach their destination. The good news was that this also meant that there was a strong probability that he could reach his destination before they did, thus regaining the element of surprise.

Agent Lewis walked back to his vehicle, determined to reach Haven as soon as possible. Unfortunately, the van was completely blocking the road ahead. Somehow, those kids had managed to maneuver it into just the right position to prevent him from going around it. What was worse was that the tires on the van had been blown out, preventing him from rolling it out of the way.

In a desperate attempt to get around the van, Agent Lewis returned to his vehicle and tried to drive around the backside of the van. He had to go completely off the side of the road to do it, which is how he managed to get his vehicle stuck in a small ditch that ran along the side of the road. He tried pulling back onto the road, but it was no use. His vehicle was stuck.

Seeing that there was no way for him to drive the rest of the way, Agent Lewis exited his vehicle and prepared himself for the long walk ahead. He filled his pockets with several essentials from the trunk. Since the sun was now setting behind the trees, he also grabbed a flashlight from his duffle bag. The last thing he took with him was the relay to the mobile emitter.

The relay was roughly the size of his palm with a small antenna sticking out of the top. It fit perfectly in his coat pocket, even though the top of the antenna stuck out a little. With that, he should be able to broadcast to the emitter, which could then connect to the Bureau or the retrieval teams when they arrived. Of course, he had no idea what the range on the relay was. Hopefully, he wouldn't have to go much farther up the road.

He locked the doors to his vehicle before walking around the van and heading up the road. With any luck, he would find the town of Haven before the kids managed to sound the alarm. After that, it was only a matter of time until the retrieval teams arrived.

He was so pleased with himself that he even started whistling as he walked.

Chapter 11: The Long Walk Home

Liam stumbled as he and Parker made their way through the forest, heading back toward Haven. He was still holding onto her for support as they wandered amongst the trees. Even with her there, he still managed to stumble every few feet.

It had been more than two hours since they had left the van behind and headed off into the woods. At first, he had managed to keep up with Parker, but now, his side was throbbing, and he could barely go several feet on his own. Still, they had to push on.

Back in Greenwood, they had rushed to the van, leaving Agent Lewis collapsed back in the warehouse. After Parker had gotten Liam settled in the passenger seat, she'd hopped behind the wheel and pulled the van's ignition key from her pocket. It was only then that Liam realized that she had taken the keys with her when she had parked the van in the street.

That explained why the keys had been missing when he had gone back to the van after running away from Agent Lewis. Once it had been clear that he was no longer being followed, he had tried to escape in the van, only to find that the keys were missing. After that, he had headed back to the warehouse hoping to use the radio tower to call for help.

Unfortunately, he hadn't been able to find a computer terminal that he could use to send out a distress signal – not that it would have mattered. He had no experience working with computers and would have been completely lost even if he did find a way to send a message back to Haven. Given that he had no other option, he had decided to hide out in the warehouse until after dark and then try to head back on his own.

Back at the van, Parker had plunged the key into the ignition only for it to start up and then die a second later. It took three tries before the engine finally had started without immediately dying. Even after it started up and kept going, the engine had sputtered as if struggling to stay on. After that, the two of them headed for home as quickly as possible.

The streets of Greenwood were in awful shape, which had added to Liam's discomfort. Every bump in the road had sent a stabbing pain through his side. The road evened out once they left Greenwood behind and started up the long gravel road toward Haven.

Wanting to get a better look at the burn in his side, Liam had lifted his shirt up and examined it as they drove. It was still red and angry, and pus oozed from several burst blisters. At least the sharp, stabbing pain had stopped for the most part. Unexpected bumps in the road still managed to ignite the pain all over again, but if it was left alone, he didn't feel any additional pain.

It was while Liam was examining himself that Parker had decided to get a good look too. Whatever her thoughts had been on the severity of his wound, she kept them to herself – although he had heard her mumbling something under her breath about needing to get to Haven as soon as possible.

Trying to take his mind off the pain, Liam had asked, "Who was that guy?"

"A G-man," Parker replied, keeping her eyes on the road ahead.

"What's a G-man?"

"A G-man? It is short for a government man. You see, the G stands for government, hence, 'G-man.' It is an abbreviation. Get it?" she had tried to explain. "That was an agent of the Federal Authority."

240

"You mean that new government that you mentioned. The one that doesn't like us or the people of Haven?"

"Exactly."

"Is that why he shot me?"

"Partly," Parker had said as she took a sharp turn at full speed. "A long time ago, the Authority decided it would be best if all residents lived inside designated areas, called Districts. That way they could keep an eye on everybody, controlling every aspect of their lives. The Districts are surrounded by a huge wall, which they call the Boundary. No one is allowed to live outside the Boundary wall, and anyone caught beyond the wall is considered a criminal and brought back for punishment."

"So, he was trying to arrest us for living beyond this 'Boundary,' and ended up shooting at us instead. Doesn't make much sense."

"No, it doesn't," she said. After a minute or two, she added, "You should have let me finish him off back there. Now, we have to worry about him coming after us." At that point, she had looked behind them using the van's rearview mirror, just to make sure that they weren't being followed.

Liam hadn't felt right about what Parker had been about to do back in the warehouse. She had already beaten the agent senseless. There had been no reason to do anything more than that. Besides, after the way Liam had felt when he had been shot, he didn't like the idea of inflicting that kind of pain onto someone else.

They had left Agent Lewis bruised, beaten, and practically helpless. That had been bad enough. Having Parker shoot him on top of all that would have crossed a line. The last thing Liam wanted was to have that weighing down on his conscience on top of everything else.

Parker had disagreed. She'd explained how it would have been better to finish the G-man off and be done with it. The coldness in her voice had been startling, and Liam had decided to try to change the subject rather than argue with her. After all, he still wasn't sure how he felt about being in the van with her after everything that had happened.

The two had driven in silence until they hit a curve in the road and the engine began to struggle. There had been several popping sounds, and steam had started rising up from under the hood of the van. Almost immediately after that, the van had sputtered to a stop, its engine completely dead.

Parker got out to see if there was anything that she could do to fix it. When she had opened the hood, Liam stepped out of the van as well and went to stand beside her. It didn't look good. Parker's face had been grim as she stared down at the engine.

A crack the length of a hand had split open along the engine block. Steam gushed out of the crack, along with a thick blue liquid that bubbled out the top. It hadn't taken much for them to realize that the stun blasts had done more damage to the van then they had originally thought. In fact, it was a marvel that the van had made it as far as it had.

After that, there wasn't much more that could be done. Parker had dismissed the van as a lost cause, explaining how they would need to abandon it on the side of the road and walk the rest of the way back. Liam hadn't been eager to hear that news, but he knew that there weren't a lot of alternatives.

Parker got behind the wheel of the van, released the brakes, and let it roll backwards. When she had gotten enough momentum, she turned the wheel as hard as she could, causing the van to spin out in the middle of the road. It hadn't taken Liam long to figure out what she was doing. Rather than the van being abandoned on the side of the road, it had been left blocking the entire road, preventing anyone from driving past it.

Once it was clear that they wouldn't be driving anymore, Parker began making preparations to walk back to Haven. She rummaged through the van for any supplies that they could use. Her search had yielded an old toolbox, a few bottles of water, and some left over rags. From the toolbox, she pulled out a boxcutter. Liam watched as she made her way to each tire, slashing them with the box cutter. She had then explained that it would make it extremely difficult for anyone to remove their temporary roadblock.

Liam had been impressed with Parker's foresight, but he didn't have long to think about it before she pulled him over to the van's back bumper. She'd eased him down onto the bumper, insisting that he have a seat. Without asking permission, she'd pulled his shirt up and started treating the wound in his side.

There hadn't been much that she could do. Her idea of treating his wound had been to pour water on it to clean it up, then press some dampened rags against it. She finished by tying them in place by wrapping his chest in makeshift bandages made from the remaining rags in Gus's van. When she had finished, he breathed a sigh of relief. The damp rags had felt good against his side, and the bandages kept his shirt from rubbing up against his wound.

After that, the two had headed off into the woods. This, of course, hadn't been Liam's first choice, but Parker had made a good argument against staying on the road. If they were being followed, they would be easily spotted on the road. It was better for them to hike through the forest than risk being captured.

And that was how they ended up walking through the woods for more than two hours. By now, the sun had gone down, and they were doing their best not to bump into any trees or trip on anything that lay in their path. The pain in Liam's side had begun to pulse in rhythm with his heartbeat, and they needed to make frequent stops for him to rest.

Parker did her best to help as much as she could. She had practically become a walking crutch for Liam, supporting him as much as possible as they tramped through the forest back toward Haven.

Now that it was dark, Liam had a hard time determining where they were. He didn't recognize any of the landmarks that they passed. He figured that they must be only a few miles away from Haven by now, but he couldn't be sure. The only way to find out would be to head back toward the road, something that neither of them wanted to do at the moment.

After another ten minutes, the two of them entered a small clearing. The moon was shining brightly, casting a dull light on the surrounding area. In the center of the clearing, a dark mass of logs rose up from the ground and was silhouetted in the moonlight. Upon further inspection, it appeared that the mass of logs was actually a small cabin, or possibly a really big shed.

Liam took several steps toward the cabin before he tripped on something and fell over. Picking himself up, he looked down and saw two metal rails running past the cabin toward a boarded-up hole in the side of a hill. It occurred to him what these metal beams were: they were railroad tracks.

More accurately, they were minecart tracks. The boarded-up hole in the side of the hill must have been a left-over mineshaft from back when Haven had been a mining town, which meant that the cabin in front of them had once belonged to a prospector, though it was hard to tell how long ago that had been. Liam knew that the hills surrounding Haven were filled with old mine shafts and excavations, but he had never visited this one before.

He quickly explained the significance of the minecart tracks to Parker, who nodded in agreement. With her leading him, they made their way over to the cabin. Upon closer inspection, they were able to confirm that it really was a cabin, though incredibly overgrown. Strangely enough, the cabin appeared older than the buildings back in Greenwood, but it was in far better shape.

The wood looked old and rotten in the pale moonlight, but the grass and vines that ran up the outside walls seemed to be holding the whole place together. Parker left Liam outside while she stepped into the cabin, intent on making sure it was safe. A few seconds later, he heard several scraping sounds, and a light suddenly appeared through the broken-out windows.

Parker poked her head out the door, accompanied by an old kerosene lantern. The light was dim compared to a flashlight, but it was definitely better than wandering around in the dark.

Parker took Liam's hand and led him inside. The interior of the cabin was practically empty. A few old tools hung on the wall, including a pickaxe and shovel. A rusted-out potbelly stove stood in the corner, next to a broken bed frame with rope lashings holding it together. A wooden table built against the wall, along with two wobbly stools, made up the rest of the cabin's furnishings.

Parker guided him over to one of the stools. "Rest. We will start out again in a few minutes," she told him, easing him down onto the stool. It wasn't necessarily a command, but he was in no position to argue.

Getting off his feet, even for a few minutes, felt wonderful. Up until now, he had been determined to push himself until they reached the outskirts of Haven. Now that he was sitting down, he realized how foolish he had been. He was exhausted, and he still had no idea how much further they had to go.

Rather than taking the other stool, Parker made her way around the interior of the cabin, looking at the tools lining the walls. Despite the exertion of walking through the woods and supporting Liam as they went, she seemed perfectly fine. She didn't even seem to be out of breath.

Liam decided to ignore what she was doing and contented himself with leaning his back up against the wall and closing his eyes. Images of his comfy bed back at home and a nice warm shower danced through his head – not to mention a quick trip to Dr. Adhira's house to have her tend to his side. That woman could work miracles when necessary.

When he opened his eyes, Parker was leaning against the wall across from him, watching him intently. *Was that concern in her eyes, or possibly guilt?* Liam hoped it was a bit of both. It was her fault that they were in this situation. That wasn't right, though. He was just as much at fault as she was. It annoyed him, but he had to concede that he had played an active part in today's events, just like she had.

"Anything else you want to share with me while we wait?" Liam asked, breaking the silence.

Parker compressed her lips. It was clear that she wanted to say something, but she was struggling to find the right words. Liam had meant it as a joke, but, seeing her face, he prepared himself for another uncomfortable confession.

"There is so much that I want to tell you, but I can't. Not yet, anyway," she said finally.

"Oh. Any particular reason why not?"

"You are not ready yet," she said hesitantly.

"Well, in that case, you can let me know when you think I am ready. Or better yet, why not keep it to yourself? I don't think I can survive another one of your revelations," Liam said scornfully.

"What happened back there was not my fault. How was I supposed to know we would run into a G-man?" Parker said defensively. "I took you there because I wanted to show you what everyone has been hiding from you this whole time. I only wanted to show you the truth behind the lies. I never meant for you to get hurt."

Liam nodded back wryly before leaning his head back against the wall and closing his eyes again. Silence filled the cabin, broken only by a few crickets that had begun their nightly melody.

Ten minutes must have gone by before he opened his eyes again. Parker had moved from her position against the wall and

246

resumed her examination of the tools on the wall. When she noticed him watching, she gave an embarrassed smile before saying, "Sorry, I just...I have never seen any place like this before. What is this place, anyway?"

Liam wasn't necessarily in the mood to give a history lesson, but then again, he had nothing better to do. "Do you remember how Ben said that Haven was originally a mining camp?" He paused as she nodded. "Well, back then, the hills and mountains surrounding Haven were filled with prospectors digging for silver."

Seeing that Parker was listening intently, he continued. "This cabin was probably built by a prospector trying to find his fortune. The minecart tracks that I tripped over lead to a boarded-up mine shaft against the side of the hill."

"How do you know all of this?" Parker asked, impressed.

"A lot of it comes from Ben, but I also spent a lot of time in these mines when I was younger. Not this particular one, but many just like it," he told her.

"I didn't know that," she said, surprised.

"Well, that was a long time ago. I haven't been near a mine shaft since..." Liam trailed off, not wanting to continue with what he was about to say.

"Since when?"

Liam hesitated, but figured he might as well tell the whole story. He explained how he had gotten lost in a mine when he was ten years old. Back then, he used to explore as many mine shafts as he could find. For the most part, it wasn't a big deal. Most of the mine shafts around Haven were small, only going in a dozen or so feet before coming to an end.

But some of them went in much further.

One day, he had been exploring a small mineshaft off in the western hills on the edge of the valley. As it turned out, that small mineshaft connected with a much larger network for tunnels. Passageways and corridors branched out in every direction, making it difficult to keep track of where he had originally come from. What he hadn't known at the time was that he had stumbled into the old MB mining company's main excavation site.

With tunnels running in every direction, it hadn't been long before he found himself lost in the labyrinth. No matter how hard he tried, he couldn't find an exit. The tunnels kept going, seemingly without an end. After a while, he'd gotten hopelessly lost.

He explained how at first, he wasn't scared. He had recently finished reading *Journey to the Center of the Earth* and that book had put ideas into his head. At any moment, he had suspected that he was going to find an underground passageway to a mysterious world hidden deep below the Earth's surface.

As time passed, the excitement had faded and the fear of being lost had taken hold of him. In a panic, he'd tried to find a way out, but without success. In fact, he'd figured that he managed to get himself even more lost the more he tried to find a way out.

"You got lost?" Parker said softly.

"Yeah," Liam said, nodding. "I got lost, and for two days, I sat there in that mine, clutching my flashlight to my chest and crying like a baby."

"How did you get out?" she asked delicately.

"A search party found me. I hadn't told anyone where I was going, but they were able to follow my tracks into the mine. After that, it was simply a process of elimination for them."

He remembered the joy he'd felt when he saw the light from their flashlights cutting through the darkness of the tunnel. At first, he'd thought he was hallucinating, but as their light grew brighter, he knew that he had been rescued. They'd found him there, huddled against the wall of the tunnel, tears filling his eyes. At least they had been tears of joy.

"When I got home, my aunt was furious. She grounded me for a month and forbade me from going near a mine ever again. Not that I minded. I was so glad to be home that I would have accepted being grounded for a year," he said with a small smile.

"How old were you when this happened?" Parker asked.

"Ten," Liam said.

"Didn't you say that Ben moved here seven years ago? Wouldn't that mean you were ten when he got here?" she asked.

"Yeah. In fact, Ben moved in the same week that I stopped being grounded. He came over to my house and introduced himself, and we have been friends ever since," he said, recalling the memory.

"Interesting."

"What do you mean, 'Interesting?'" Liam snapped back.

"I just find it interesting – that is all. You go missing for a few days, and within a week or so, Ben's family moves into town. A perfect little friend to keep you out of trouble and away from anything even remotely dangerous," she said like she knew a secret that he didn't.

"Really? You are suggesting that Ben's family moved to town because I got lost in a mine?" Liam asked skeptically.

"Why not?" Parker countered. "Think about it. We already know how important you are to the town. Imagine how they felt when they realized that you had gone missing. It makes sense that they would take steps to prevent something like that from ever happening again.

Maybe like introducing you to someone new – someone that could get close to you and keep an eye on you. Someone to keep you from getting into trouble. Sound like anyone you know?" she said, making her point.

"Don't start with that crap again," Liam demanded. "I really don't want to hear it right now."

Parker gave him an innocent look and muttered something like, "Ok, I won't," before going back to her study of the cabin's contents.

"If this cabin was built by a prospector, then does that mean that we are close to Haven?" Parker said after a few minutes of silence.

"Most likely," Liam responded. "We are probably close by now – maybe another hour or so."

"If that is the case, we should probably keep going," she said as she reached over to extinguish the lamp.

Before her fingers had time to douse the lamp, Liam called out for her to wait. She hesitated long enough for him to explain that they could use the lamp to light the rest of their way back home. The moon was out, but it didn't offer a lot of light, especially when they were walking through the forest with the trees overhead.

Parker shook her head in protest. She reminded him that the whole reason for walking through the forest was to hide from anyone who could be following them. Having an open lantern would give away their position. It was too risky.

Liam agreed that the lantern would make them easier to spot, but in truth, he was tired of bumping into trees in the darkness. He argued that they were so close enough to Haven that it shouldn't matter anymore. Besides, they were far away enough from the road that they should go undetected.

In the end, Parker agreed to take the lamp with them, but she turned it down as far as it would go without snuffing out the flame. It didn't give off a lot of light, but it was better than nothing.

Together, they continued their journey toward Haven.

Walking through the forest gave Liam plenty of time to think about everything that had happened to him that day, including everything that Parker had said. The more he thought about her, the more confused he became.

He cared for her, more so than he had for any other girl he had ever known. But he was having trouble reconciling his feelings for her against the fact that she had turned his life completely upside down. Before she had arrived, he had been...well, not happy. That wasn't the right word. He had been content. Content with the reality with which he had been presented. And now...now, he no longer knew what to think.

What had given her the right to mess with his head like this? She claimed that everything she had done had been for his benefit, but he wasn't sure he believed that. How could making him doubt everything he had ever been told be for his benefit?

He believed that she had been acting with the best of intentions, but the implications of what she was saying were troubling. If she was right, everyone he had ever known and cared about was involved in a conspiracy to hide something from him. What exactly, he couldn't be sure.

A shiver ran down Liam's spine as he thought about what that secret could be. Parker had made it sound like he was at the center of all of it, but he wasn't sure. He didn't feel special. Nothing about his life gave him the impression that he was different.

Wait a second, he thought. That wasn't exactly true. He had lived his whole life as a minor celebrity because of his parents. At least, he had been told that it was because of his parents. All this time, he had assumed that the reason why everyone in town was so friendly toward him was because his parents had helped establish the town. Was it possible that there was another reason?

Liam struggled with these thoughts as he and Parker made their way through the forest. The uncertainty of his own reality weighed heavily upon him, much like how he was weighing heavily upon Parker. He looked down at her as she walked alongside him, supporting him under his arm.

Whatever her motivations had been, there was one thing that he could count on: she cared for him. You didn't try to protect someone you didn't care about, nor would you spend several hours supporting them as you both walked uphill through the woods. Because of that, the anger that he had been feeling toward her mellowed a little bit. At least the urge to run away from her had passed.

He couldn't blame her for doing what she thought was the right thing. He didn't agree with everything that she had done, but she had done it all with the best of intentions. A person's intentions mattered, especially when things went wrong.

What happened back in Greenwood wasn't her fault. It was true that she could have handled it better, but nothing in life was ever simple. Besides, if she had been telling him the truth, then her actions were not only understandable, but completely justified. That was a big if, but until he knew for certain, he couldn't hold it against her, which was why he made the conscious decision to forgive her – for now, at least.

As if making that decision had lifted a tremendous burden off his shoulders, he was finally able to relax. He walked a little easier, and he felt a little better. Parker must have noticed a change in his demeanor, because she squeezed him gently and looked up at him with a smile.

"Does this mean I am still your girlfriend?" she asked, seemingly reading Liam's mind.

"How did you know?" Liam asked.

"I am a girl; I can sense these things," she said warmly.

Liam let out a soft chuckle, ignoring the momentary pain from his side. He squeezed Parker back and did his best to reassure her that she was still his girlfriend. However, he also made it abundantly clear that they were going to set up some boundaries moving forward.

She quickly agreed, promising to be more considerate in the future. Again, she repeated that her intentions had only been to try and help him.

Wanting to change the subject, Liam asked for more details about what had happened to her over the past week. Parker recounted the whole tale from the beginning, starting with the moment when the Deans had dragged her away. She explained how she had been escorted back home and forced to sit there while the town council decided her fate. Once the vote was over, she had been officially exiled from Haven. She was then escorted into the back of Gus's van and driven out of town. The rest of the week had been spent in that supply warehouse back in Greenwood.

As Parker talked, Liam appreciated how good it was to have her back. She had only been missing a week, but even that had seemed too long. More importantly, he felt bad for her. He had spent the last week moping around, feeling sorry for himself, and all the while, she had been locked away like a prisoner.

"Then the strangest thing happened," Parker said, continuing her story. "Gus received a message that he was supposed to bring me back in the morning. It didn't make sense, but apparently, the council had decided to overturn their previous decision."

"Any idea why?"

"All I know is that the town council had held another vote, and they decided to give me a second chance. Nice of them, wasn't it?" Parker said with a mocking sneer. "I was going to be allowed to return, only this time, I was going to be on probation."

Liam couldn't miss the sarcasm in her voice as she spoke. He knew very well that she didn't care about their probation. She obviously hadn't followed it, since she had immediately snuck out of the house to find him.

However, something she said gave him pause: She'd mentioned the town council voting the night before to bring her back. That would have been the same night that he had been talking with Mr. Malcolm in the theater lobby. Could Mr. Malcolm have known what was happening – or, even worse, had he been involved?

"Which is why I told them that I would behave, especially around you," Parker finished in a huff. Liam had been so deep in thought that he hadn't realized that she was still talking. Doing his best to hide his previous inattention, he tried to follow up on the last thing he did hear.

"You had to behave, especially around me? I didn't realize that I was so important," Liam joked.

"They were afraid that I would expose them, or possibly put you in danger," Parker explained.

The irony must have dawned on her, because her face flushed with embarrassment, and she put on a guilty expression. Liam followed it up with an accusatory glance of his own, as if to say that perhaps the council had been right. She gently elbowed him in the side to let him know what she thought of that.

"Expose them, yes. Endanger you, no. Just remember that there was no way that I could know that we would run into a G-man back there. What are the odds?" she said. "Besides, I would never knowingly put you in danger."

"Because I am special?" Liam said wryly.

"Because you are special, in more ways than one," Parker said back sweetly.

"Now you know, compliments like that will—" He cut himself off immediately as they heard the sound of footsteps approaching from up ahead. Parker wasted no time in extinguishing the lantern and guiding both of them to a nearby log where they could hide. Liam tensed as they took shelter behind the log, fearing that the approaching footsteps belonged to Agent Lewis.

Liam lifted his head up far enough to see over the top of the log. Someone was heading in their direction. The figure's details were obscured by the beam of their flashlight, which was moving back and forth as if looking for something or someone. Whoever they were, they were moving in his direction, and coming fast.

Liam glanced around frantically, looking for something, anything, that could be used as a weapon. Off to the side, a large branch had broken off the log and was lying on the ground. He reached out and closed his hand around the branch, bringing it up and holding it like a baseball bat.

As the figure drew closer, Liam prepared himself to step out and swing the branch like he was trying to hit a home run. The crackling of sticks beneath the figure's boots helped him track their progress without giving away his position.

When the footsteps were only a few feet away, he sprang into action. He jumped up from his hiding spot, raising the branch high over his shoulder and swinging with all his might. The branch made a whooshing sound as it cut through the air, speeding toward its intended target.

It was only then that he recognized who was on the other end of the flashlight. It wasn't Agent Lewis.

Liam pulled back with every ounce of strength he possessed, desperate not to strike down his aunt with the branch in his hands. He narrowly prevented himself from hitting her, but the force of it threw him off-balance and he fell to his hands and knees in the dirt. Pain exploded in his side from the exertion of swinging and stopping short.

Hands gripped his arms and pulled him to his feet. Once he was upright again, he was enveloped in a warm embrace as Aunt Linda threw her arms around him. A second later, he was pushed back to arm's length as she looked him up and down, checking to see that he was alright.

While she was examining him, he noticed that she was wearing her yellow parka and rain boots. It was no surprise, given that they were her favorites for cold, rainy days. What was surprising was that she was wearing them now, since it wasn't cold or rainy. If she was wearing her yellow parka, then it meant that she either wanted to be easily seen in the dark, or she suspected that she would be out searching for a while, and didn't want to take any chances with the weather turning sour. Either way, it wasn't a good sign.

"I thought I heard voices from over here," she said, finishing her examination before pulling him into another hug. "I was so worried."

As she squeezed him even tighter, the pain in his side became unbearable. Before he could muffle the sound in his throat, a groan of pain escaped his lips.

That did it. Not only did Aunt Linda pull away immediately, but the happy look on her face from finding him was immediately replaced with alarm. "What's the matter?" she asked, concern flooding her voice.

Liam tried to reassure her that it was nothing; after all, there was no need to worry her any more than she already was. Unfortunately, his aunt wasn't buying it. She knew that there was something seriously wrong. Whether it was from the look on Liam's face or the sixth sense that she seemed to have anytime he tried to keep secrets from her, she knew something wasn't right.

Realizing that it would do no good to lie to her, Liam lifted up his shirt and hoodie, revealing the wad of bandages at his side. By this time, they had turned a pale pink color from the blood and pus. Aunt Linda raised her flashlight, trying to get a better look at it. When she did, her expression changed from shock, to sympathy, to anger, before returning to shock, all in rapid succession.

"What happened?" she asked.

He was about to explain when Parker stepped forward. She had been hiding behind him for the most part. At least, Aunt Linda's attention had been solely on him up until now, so she hadn't noticed Parker standing there. When she did notice, her expression changed again from shock to anger, followed quickly by out-and-out rage.

"You! This is all your fault, isn't it?" Aunt Linda said, pointing an accusatory finger at Parker. "After everything I have done for you, this is how you repay me? I defended you! I argued to have you reinstated, and for what? So that you could run off with Liam the first chance you get?" By the end, she was shouting.

"It wasn't like that," Liam tried to interject, but his aunt wasn't listening. Her attention was focused purely on Parker.

"You don't understand!" Parker shouted back.

"You're damn right I don't understand. I don't understand what you thought you were doing by running off. I don't understand what you were trying to accomplish by taking Liam away. I don't understand how you could endanger the project like that, and I certainly don't understand how you could allow him to get hurt," Aunt Linda shouted back, raising a finger for each point in the conversation.

"I thought I was helping him," Parker defended.

"'Helping him?' How do you figure bringing him out here and allowing him to get hurt is in any way 'helping him?'"

"By showing him the truth behind your lies," Parker said in a steely voice. "Tell me, have you been to Greenwood lately? Nice place? Full of people? I opened his eyes to the reality that you have kept hidden from him his entire life."

Aunt Linda staggered back, as the full weight of Parker's words had practically slapped her in the face. This startling confession was too much for her to handle. The significance of what Parker had said was overwhelming, to say the least. From the look on her face, it was clear that Aunt Linda now knew exactly what Parker had been up to.

"Who do you think you are?" Aunt Linda said in a low, dangerous tone. "You, who have only been here for a few weeks, suddenly think you know better than the Director and myself what is in Liam's best interest? Do you have any idea how much damage you have done? You have jeopardized the integrity of the project!"

"What project?" Liam chimed in. He was still being ignored by his aunt and Parker.

"I don't care what the Director says. Liam deserves to know the truth." Parker said.

"Director? What Director? What are you talking about?" Liam asked without getting a response.

"Oh, I see. You think you know better than the Director. Maybe you want to replace Dr. Sorenson and take his place at the head of the project?" Aunt Linda said in sheer outrage.

"Who is Dr. Sorenson?" Liam yelled in frustration, interrupting the shouting match between his aunt and Parker.

His outburst stunned the two women into silence. Both of them looked at him in surprise, almost as if they had forgotten he was standing next to them.

Well, he wasn't going to be ignored any more. This whole time, he had been holding out hope that Parker had been wrong – that she was making it all up, and that she was the one that needed help. Now, after hearing the conversation between her and his aunt, he had to accept the fact that she was telling the truth. It had been his aunt who had mentioned projects and directors. It had been his aunt who had reacted when she had learned that they had been in Greenwood this whole time.

Liam had to accept that what Parker had told him was true. They had all been lying to him – everyone back in Haven. *Why*? He still didn't know, but he wanted answers. He needed to know why the people he cared for the most would intentionally deceive him.

Now that he had both Aunt Linda and Parker's attention, he repeated his question. The two just stared at him, not knowing how to answer. Parker opened her mouth, ready to explain, but Aunt Linda cut her off.

"None of that matters right now," she said, taking Liam's arm and gently leading him back toward town.

Liam pulled free from her grasp, determined to stay where he was until he got the answers he deserved. Her response was to turn around and glare at him, no doubt trying to intimidate him into obedience. She was definitely giving him the look, but he refused to budge. He wasn't about to let her get away with ignoring his question.

It seemed like Aunt Linda was in no mood to put up with any of his attitude. She took a step closer, put a finger under Liam's nose, and said, "Now, you see here, mister. I have spent the last ten hours looking for you, and half of that has been spent traipsing through the forest. I was worried sick. If I wasn't so glad to see you, I would bend you over my knee and give you a good spanking.

"Now, I am tired, I am angry, and I am in no mood for your attitude. We are going to march back home and see Dr. Adhira, and then you are going to your room for the rest of your foreseeable future. And you can forget about seeing your girlfriend ever again. I have the feeling that she won't be staying in Haven for much longer, anyways," Aunt Linda finished, doing her best to be as intimidating as possible.

"No," Liam said quietly.

"Come again?" Aunt Linda said slowly, marveling at Liam's audacity.

"I said no. You don't get to make those types of decisions for me anymore. Not after today. Not ever again," he said resolutely.

"Oh, really? And why is that?" Aunt Linda said sternly, trying to retake control of the conversation.

"Because I can't trust you!" Liam responded firmly. "This whole time, this whole time, you have been lying to me. You told me Greenwood was just like Haven, but it isn't. You've told me my entire life that we were too busy to leave, but that was only an excuse to keep me here. Well, I refuse to be a prisoner here any longer."

There was a moment of stunned silence. Liam doubted whether his aunt had expected such an outburst out of him, and it caught her off-guard. It was clear that she was struggling to think of something to say that would turn the conversation back around to her side, but nothing came out.

In the end, she decided to change tactics. She dropped the harsh, intimidating approach and adopted a softer, more gentle approach. "Liam, sweetheart, I—"

"Don't bother," Liam said, cutting her off. "I don't want any more excuses or lies. I just want the truth."

"Sweetheart, some truths are hard to hear and harder still to understand."

"I can take it," Liam assured her. "After all, how bad can it be? I have already been shot by a bolt of electricity today. It couldn't hurt worse than that."

He had meant that last part as a joke, but the look on his aunt's face said that there was nothing funny about what he had just said. Her face grew pale, and she reached out and grabbed him by both shoulders. She shook him slightly as she stared at him with panic in her eyes.

"Liam, tell me exactly what happened."

"He was shot by a stun pistol," Parker said, stepping between the two. "We were in Greenwood when a G-man—"

"You ran into a G-man?" Aunt Linda asked, worry filling her voice.

"Yes," Parker said calmly – more calmly than Liam felt when he thought back to what had happened earlier. "He appeared out of nowhere. We tried to run, but he managed to corner Liam in the warehouse. He shot Liam with a stun pistol before I had a chance to stop him. After that...well, let's just say we left him in the warehouse."

"How could this have happened?" Aunt Linda said to herself. "There are safeguards in place to prevent this sort of thing from happening. How could a federal agent get this close without us knowing?"

"I don't know, but he wasn't here by accident. He knew we were up here, and he was looking for us," Parker confirmed.

"You said you left him in the warehouse. Is he dead?" Aunt Linda said urgently.

"No," Parker said, glancing at Liam out of the corner of her eye. "We left him alive."

"Then that means he is still a threat. He may even be on his way here now," Aunt Linda said nervously, looking down at the watch on her wrist. "Alright, there is still time to fix this."

She looked back at Liam, giving him a reassuring smile. Squeezing his arm with one hand, she reached into her parka with the other. Her hand came out a second later with a two-way radio. She pushed a button on the radio and started talking into it, giving instructions to the person on the other end.

Liam gave a start when he realized what he was hearing. "Did you just tell someone to go and check on him and 'terminate him' if he is still alive?"

"Yes," Aunt Linda responded nonchalantly, still giving instructions to the person on the other end of the radio.

"To. Terminate. Him," Liam repeated.

"It is like I told you," Parker chimed in. "The Authority would do anything to stop what is happening here. Even if that meant killing every single person in Haven."

"And so that makes it alright?" Liam asked.

"It is the only way to be sure that the agent cannot report back to the Authority," Aunt Linda said, putting the radio back under her parka. "You may not like it, but that is the only way that we can guarantee your safety.

"As it is," Aunt Linda continued, "our location in these mountains makes it difficult to send and receive messages from the outside. We have also taken steps to block most forms of communication. If we are lucky, the Authority will never know what happened here."

"What about him?" Parker asked, nodding toward Liam.

"He needs to see a doctor. After that, we can take him to a predesignated saferoom until the problem has been dealt with," Aunt Linda explained.

"I can take him," Parker volunteered. "It is clear that you will be needed to help deal with the G-man."

"Don't take this the wrong way, but I don't trust you for one second with his safety," Aunt Linda said flatly.

"Everything I have done since I got here has been for him. You may not agree with my methods, but you cannot deny my intent. I will do everything in my power to see that he is taken care of," Parker said.

Aunt Linda stared at her for a long moment, as if trying to discern the girl's intentions. After a moment, she said, "Did the agent happen to be in Greenwood while you were there, or was he there because you were in Greenwood?"

It was Parker's turn to be upset. She didn't like the implication that she had intentionally lured Liam to Greenwood so that she could turn him over to a G-man. The very idea caused her face to turn red with anger, and she set her jaw as if preparing for a fight. She spoke in a cold, no-nonsense tone, making it clear that she had nothing to do with the agent's appearance.

"I didn't have anything to do with it. I hate the Authority just as much as you do. One day, the Authority will answer for their crimes. One day, they will be torn from their ivory towers in the Central Complex, and the whole place will burn from the flames of their sins. And on that day, I will help sprinkle their ashes into the wind as their evil fades to nothingness. If that isn't enough for you, then I don't know what else is."

Aunt Linda was silent for a long time. "I don't know what game you are playing, but I am making the decision to believe you. For Liam's sake, I want to believe you."

"I would give my life to protect him," Parker said sincerely.

"Alright. You take Liam back to Haven. Head toward Ben's house. He will be waiting for you there. We can figure out what to do about...well, we will figure all of this out later. In the meantime, please...I am trusting you. Please don't let me down," Aunt Linda pleaded.

"I won't," Parker promised.

Turning her attention back to Liam, Aunt Linda said, "I know you have a lot of questions, and you deserve answers. But now is not the time. Right now, we need to get you someplace safe."

Liam tried to protest, but she hushed him by placing her fingers against his lips. She promised to tell him everything he wanted to know, but not now. She reached up and pulled him into another hug, careful not to squeeze his side, where the burn still ached.

While they were hugging, she whispered in his ear how sorry she was for everything. She confessed that she'd never wanted to lie to him about anything, but that the circumstances had forced her to do it. She would make it up to him, though. She promised.

Pulling away from the hug, she smiled at him before turning and heading off into the forest. Liam watched as her flashlight disappeared into the darkness. He felt a tug on his arm. It was Parker, who was gently nudging him to follow her.

"Where are we going?" Liam asked.

"To Ben's house," Parker informed him. "You aunt said we will be safe there. As safe as we can be for now."

Chapter 12: The Town of Haven

Agent Lewis made his way up the dirt road as it twisted and turned its way through the surrounding forest. His watch had been smashed when that girl had pummeled him back in the warehouse, so he had no idea how long he had been walking. The sun had set not long after he left his vehicle, but that was an hour or two ago. Everything was now shrouded in darkness save for the subtle glow from the moon overhead, which bathed the road and the nearby trees with light.

The moonlight illuminated the path before him, accompanied by the twinkling of millions of stars. A hushed serenade of crickets echoed through the trees, promising a peaceful and serene night. If it weren't for the occasional reminder of his injuries, he could have almost imagined that he was out for a leisurely moonlight stroll, like the walks he used to take in the arboreal gardens back home.

With the moonlight illuminating his path, there was no need to use the flashlight in his pocket. He didn't need it to see, and it was best not to use it anyways, given the circumstances. The beam of the flashlight would only serve to give away his position along the darkened road. If those kids were anywhere nearby, the flashlight would be visible through the trees.

As Agent Lewis walked, a gentle breeze wafted through the trees, bringing with it the smell of pine trees. There was something else, too – not a scent, but a noise, a low rumbling sound that was being carried on the breeze. At first, it was too low to make out, but the sound grew louder with each passing second.

Trying to identify the source of the noise, Agent Lewis focused his attention on the road up ahead. Just beyond the next curve in the road, several objects were zipping through the trees, heading in his direction. As they turned the corner up ahead, three sets of headlights shined in his direction. They were heading toward him at an incredible speed, but he was still well beyond the reach of their headlights.

Thinking quickly, Agent Lewis ran off to the side of the road, diving into a nearby clump of bushes. The surrounding foliage enveloped him in darkness and offered the perfect hiding spot. As the headlights approached, he raised his head a few inches so that he could see through the leaves to the road beyond.

Three vehicles drove past, kicking up dust as they went. They must not have seen him, because they drove on down the road without the slightest hint of stopping. As they passed, he was able to get a good look at all three vehicles. There were two older-model cars, followed closely by a flatbed truck.

In the darkness, it was hard to see inside the cars, but judging from how they were riding low to the ground, he suspected that both cars were full of people. Perhaps he hadn't beaten the kids to their destination after all, he thought as he watched their taillights fade in the distance.

Once he was confident that the cars were out of sight and that no other vehicles were coming down the road, Agent Lewis climbed out from his hiding spot. Stepping out onto the road, he looked in the direction of Greenwood. Those cars had been headed in that direction. At their pace, it wouldn't be long until they ran into the roadblock that had forced him to walk the rest of the way toward Haven.

Looking up the road, Agent Lewis smiled with satisfaction. The cars had to have come from somewhere, and the most likely explanation was that they'd originated from the mysterious town of Haven. If he ever needed any additional proof that he was on the right track, that was it.

From the moment that the boy – Liam, he'd said his name was – had mentioned "borrowing" the van back in town, Agent Lewis knew that there had to be more people nearby. After all, how could they have "borrowed" a van if there were only two of them up here. Watching those cars drive past had confirmed his suspicions – there were more people up here, and he was headed in the right direction.

Unconsciously, Agent Lewis's hand brushed against the holster at his side, reaffirming to himself that the stun pistol was still there. He hoped that he wouldn't need it, but given everything that had already happened today, he wasn't about to take any chances. As he let his hand fall back to his side, he felt the flashlight in his jacket pocket. It was a good thing that he hadn't been using it. Those cars hadn't seen him before he ran off the road, but they would have definitely seen the light of a flashlight if he had been using one.

Standing there thinking wasn't doing him much good. He needed to reach this town of Haven and confirm his suspicions. Going back wasn't an option – not now that those cars were on their way down the hill. Which left him with one option: continuing up the road. Hopefully, he didn't have too much further to go.

He resumed his walk up the road, heading toward his destination. It occurred to him as he walked that those cars could have been searching for him or the kids. Given how fast they had been going, they were certainly not out for a moonlight drive. No, they had been somewhere with a purpose. Whether that purpose was to find him or those kids was still anyone's guess.

Whether they were looking for him or the kids, one thing was certain: they would eventually find the broken-down van and his vehicle. They wouldn't be able to miss them, since they had been left sitting in the middle of the road. If he was lucky, they would spend hours searching the surrounding woods, giving him plenty of time to continue with his investigation.

Given how his luck had been running lately, Agent Lewis quickened his pace. He wanted to reach his destination before those cars came back. Just to be safe, he made it a point to look over his shoulder every few minutes.

Even with everything happening, he had a hard time concentrating. He kept thinking back to that moment in the warehouse where he had shot Liam. The boy's reaction to the stun blast had been unlike anything Agent Lewis had ever seen before. Typically, someone being shot with a stun pistol would simply seize up and fall to the floor, immobilized.

Liam's reaction had been anything but typical. Rather than seizing up, he had writhed in pain. Rather than being immobilized, he had been completely animated and alert. Rather than the stun blast being absorbed by the body, he had actually been burned. None of it made sense.

It was true that Agent Lewis had never shot someone before, but he had seen plenty of footage of suspects being stunned. That was how he knew not to aim for the head or to shoot someone at extremely close range. Remembering those videos of what happened to people who had been shot like that sent a shiver down his spine.

He'd never wanted to be put into a position where he had to make a decision to end someone's life like that. He was a federal agent, but most of his career had been spent behind a desk. Up until now, his job had been black and white, right or wrong, guilty or innocent. After seeing that poor boy in pain, he seriously doubted whether he was cut out for fieldwork like this.

In truth, he felt awful about what had happened – although the beating he had received had lessened that feeling. As he went over the events again and again in his mind, one question kept repeating: What was it about the boy that had caused such a severe reaction?

This question repeated over and over in Agent Lewis's head – so much so that he failed to realize that he had arrived at his destination. It wasn't until his foot came in contact with pavement that he realized where he was. Looking up, he could see a pale glow filtering through the last few trees ahead.

He was no longer standing on the dirt road that led back toward Greenwood. In front of him stretched a paved road, complete with a yellow-painted dividing line and a cement curb on both sides. A few feet behind him, the road ended in the dirt road that he had been following.

Cautiously, Agent Lewis took several steps forward, stepping out from amongst the trees of the forest. Before him, the forest opened up into a small valley nestled between the peaks of two mountains. In the center of that valley was a small town.

Unlike Greenwood or the dozens of other dilapidated towns that he had passed on his trip to get here, this town was in near-perfect condition. The buildings all seemed to be well-maintained, with some even sporting fresh coats of paint. The roads were smooth and unbroken, the buildings were neat and tidy, and everything seemed to be in its proper place.

More than that, the whole town glowed with thousands of lights, pushing back the darkness of night. There were hundreds of street-lamps that stretched in both directions, spreading out from one corner of the valley to the other. In the center of town, dozens of shops lined the main road, all of which had their lights on. Countless houses and other buildings also contributed to the spectacle, adding their lights to the rest of town.

Agent Lewis was mesmerized by it all. The sight before him was truly impressive, and even more so given the state of the town of Greenwood down the road. Where that town had been left to rot, this one had been well cared-for. There were even white picket fences in front of several houses that he could see.

He continued following the road that ran straight up through the center of town. As he approached the first buildings, he saw a giant billboard painted against the side of one of them.

Welcome to Haven

When you are in Haven, you are home.
Population 2,016

Agent Lewis's jaw dropped in surprise. By now, he had already come to the conclusion that he had found the mysterious town of Haven, but this was too much. This whole time, he had expected to find a crumbling relic – a community housed in the ruins of a broken-down town, or possibly a makeshift camp set up where a town had once existed, but not this.

Before him stretched a fully functional town with houses, shops, and, if he wasn't mistaken, an old-style movie theater. A place like this shouldn't exist beyond the Boundary, especially when they had a welcome sign out front, as if to greet new arrivals.

As Agent Lewis studied the welcome sign painted against the wall, he had to do a double take when he noticed the population size. Was it possible that more than 2,000 people were still living here? His research had suggested that there could be that many people, but a part of him had never truly believed it.

In a way, the number of people made sense. Attendant Phillips had mentioned that the size of the sensor ping had been sufficient to represent thousands of individual signals. More than that, a small group would have found it difficult to maintain a town of this size or the infrastructure necessary to keep it operational. The supplies back in Greenwood also hinted at a larger population.

This also helped to explain why they had remained hidden all this time. A small group wouldn't have had the resources or the knowledge to construct something powerful enough to evade the Authority's sensor sweeps. A larger community would have provided the necessary expertise and know-how to create a shield to protect them from being discovered.

Agent Lewis was immediately overcome with a sense of pride and accomplishment. He had done it. He had followed his instincts, and they had led him to the greatest discovery in the Bureau's recent history. He no longer needed to worry about what he would say to Admin Ryan when he got back. This wasn't a case of two strays wandering around in the forest. It was an entire town with more than 2,000 occupants.

While he was reveling in his own success, a terrible feeling settled over him. The realization of what he had found was beginning to sink in. This wasn't a small gathering of strays, nor was it a shanty town built upon the ruins of a crumbling city. This was a well-maintained, expertly hidden town with more than 2,000 occupants – 2,000 strays.

Fear urged him to pull his stun pistol out its holster and look around in every direction. 2,000 people were far too many for him to handle on his own. *Come to think of it, that may be far too many for two retrieval teams to handle as well, even with a Rotowing and several transports for support.* That many strays could be dangerous, especially after just one of them had nearly beaten him senseless. He had to get out of sight before he was spotted.

Agent Lewis ran to the side of the nearest building, flattening himself against the outer wall. The safety of the forest was too far away, and he didn't want to risk someone seeing him. Up until now, if he had been seen, then it was possible that he had been mistaken for another townsperson, out for a nightly stroll. Running back toward the forest would be a dead giveaway that something was wrong.

Which was why he stood there, pressed against the building, trying his best to blend in with the shadows. As the minutes passed, it became more and more obvious that no one had seen him enter the town, or at least, they hadn't noticed anything out of the ordinary. The town was relatively quiet, without even the slightest sound to indicate that anyone had noticed his approach.

Slowly, he edged toward the corner of the building and leaned his head out. The road beyond was empty. The lights were all on, but there were no signs of any people that he could see.

Gathering what little courage he had, he stepped out from against the wall and took several steps up the street.

He peeked through the windows of the shops that he passed, but didn't see anyone inside. At each intersection, he stopped and looked both ways, only crossing the street once he was sure that there was nobody around to see him. The farther he walked into town, the more he became convinced that the place was deserted.

There was no one there. The shops, the streets, even the movie theater were all empty. It was as if someone had gone through all the trouble of fixing the place up and turning on all the lights, then left without warning. There were people living here – those three cars had been proof of that. But even if they had been completely full of people, it wouldn't account for everyone else who was supposed to be here. The welcome sign alone said that there were more people than that.

Agent Lewis replaced his stun pistol in its holster. There didn't appear to be a need for it. Since there was no immediate danger, he walked out into the middle of the street, trying to get a better look at the town around him. *Where is everybody?* he thought in consternation.

It wasn't just the lack of people that confused him. The whole town seemed completely out of place. A town like this was something that he would have expected to see in a history book, not standing right before his eyes. Even the movie titles displayed on the theater's marquee appeared to be from a bygone era, with no real place in the modern world.

Reaching up to scratch his head in confusion, Agent Lewis's gaze fell on a café on the other side of the street. Like every other shop, the lights were on, but the place was empty. It didn't matter. Right now, all he wanted was something cold to drink.

Entering the café, he made his way behind the counter. There, he found a cup and filled it with ice water. He drank it down in two gulps, only to fill it back up again and take another swallow. It had been a long walk, after all.

As he lowered the glass from his lips, the details of the café seemed to jump out at him. What he hadn't noticed from the street, or while he was focused on getting something to drink, was that the café showed signs of recent activity. Everywhere he looked, he could see plates with half-eaten food, cups that were half-empty, and chairs that had been pushed back from the tables.

He found more evidence of someone having been there recently behind the counter. The grill in the kitchen was still on, and a steady stream of smoke was rising from its surface into the vent above. There were several orders that were only half-made, with two more orders ready to be served. All in all, the whole place had the look of recently being occupied, only to have everyone get up and leave right in the middle of their meal.

As Agent Lewis looked around, he got a bad feeling. He walked over to the nearest table. Whoever had been sitting here had been eating roast beef with mashed potatoes and gravy. He reached his hand out and touched the gravy. It was cold. He moved to another table, where several people had been enjoying some slices of pie with their coffee. Dipping his finger in the coffee, he confirmed that it too was cold. It was safe to say that whoever had been here had left more than an hour ago.

It was possible that the people in the cars that had passed him on the road were the same people who had been eating in the café. However, based on the number of plates that were sitting out, there had been more people here than what could have fit into those three cars. This meant that they could still be here in town – or, worse than that, they could be back any moment.

Agent Lewis felt exposed standing there. The large windows of the café looked out onto the street, giving anyone outside a clear view of what was going on inside. Anyone passing by or casually looking in would be able to see him clearly.

Without waiting another moment, he raced for the front door. By the time he'd pushed the door open and was standing on the sidewalk outside, a low rumbling sound could be heard in the distance. He knew that rumbling sound. He had heard it before – on the road leading up to Haven.

At the point where the dirt road emerged from the forest, three cars were speeding toward the center of town – the same three that had passed him on their way down to Greenwood. It was then that Agent Lewis realized that his time was up. He needed to leave, and he needed to leave now.

Unfortunately, there weren't a lot of options for him. The cars were getting closer with each passing second. He needed to get off the road, but he wasn't about to go back inside the café or one of the shops. Not knowing what else to do, he turned and ran up the road, away from the approaching cars. Less than half a block later, there was a small alleyway between two shops. With no time to lose, he dove into the alleyway, ducking out of sight just as the cars pulled up.

The alleyway only went back a few feet before it was blocked by a chain-link fence. Fortunately, there were several trash cans lining the side of one of the buildings that he could hide behind. Crouching low, he made himself as motionless as possible. If he pretended to be another trash can, maybe nobody would notice.

No sooner had he gotten into position than the cars stopped directly in front of the alleyway. *This is it*, he thought. They had seen him and were coming to collect him. He held his breath, waiting for that unavoidable moment when they would descend upon him, and he would need to defend himself.

That moment never came. The cars had stopped right outside of the alleyway, but the people climbing out weren't headed in his direction. Instead, they ran across the street to an old building with a clocktower rising out of the top. From its official look, Agent Lewis assumed that it had to be a town hall or local meeting house.

There was a small park out front with a fountain in the middle and a paved walkway that led up to some stairs. The stairs climbed up through some columns to a pair of double doors.

It was toward those double doors that the people from the cars were headed. As they reached the top of the steps, the doors burst open, showering the newcomers with light from inside. There were more people inside, and they greeted the newcomers enthusiastically before the doors shut behind them.

Once the doors shut, the street once again fell silent. This was Agent Lewis's chance. If he left now, he could sneak out of town before anyone knew he was there. Once he was safely back in the woods, he could wait for his reinforcements to arrive.

As discreetly as possible, he stood up and pressed himself against the side of the alleyway. He slunk over to the mouth of the alleyway and poked his head out, looking in both directions. Once he was certain that the streets were clear, he stepped out.

Just as his foot left the alleyway, he was forced to pull it back as the thunder of dozens of footsteps came crashing around the nearest corner. Retaking his place behind the trash cans, he watched as several dozen people ran around the nearest corner. They rushed not in his direction, but toward the town hall building across the street. He couldn't run for it now – not with that many people in the street. He would have to wait for now.

Just then, more people ran past the alleyway, coming from the other direction. A large crowd was now gathering in the park area across the street in front of the town hall. It didn't appear that anyone had noticed him hiding there, so he repositioned himself against the wall to get a better look. He kept as far back from the mouth of the alleyway as he could while still getting a good look at what was going on.

From this position, he could easily see out into the street without exposing himself. A large crowd had gathered in front of the town hall, with more people pouring in from all directions. Agent

Lewis tried to do a quick count to see how many people were there, but stopped after he reached 300. At that point, it didn't matter anymore.

As the crowd milled about in the little park in front of the town hall, a loud murmur arose. Most of what they were saying was unintelligible from where Agent Lewis was standing, but he did manage to catch little bits and pieces of their conversations.

"Have they found him?"

"Here in town…"

"Must be…"

"…Safe for now. But what…"

The crowd grew quiet as the double doors at the top of the steps opened and several people stepped out. They all stood there, about half a dozen or so, on the steps leading up to the doors, preparing to address the congregation.

Agent Lewis froze, not daring to move a muscle. He was plainly visible from their position on the stairs. He would have shrunk back, but he was afraid that his movement might draw their attention. All he could do was to remain as perfectly still as possible, and hope that the people on the stairs did not glance over in his direction.

Luckily, their attention seemed to be focused on the gathered crowd. One of the men on the stairs stepped forward and raised his hands high above his head, commanding the attention of the crowd. All eyes were focused on him. The amassed crowd grew quiet as they patiently waited for whatever he had to say. The man addressed the crowd with a loud, booming voice. From where he was hiding, Agent Lewis wasn't able to get a good look at the speaker. He could tell that he was a tall, dark-skinned gentleman, but he couldn't make out the speaker's face. Despite the man's booming voice, it was difficult to make out what he was saying from across the street.

Whatever he was talking about, it must have been important. Given the brief snatches of conversation that Agent Lewis had previously overheard, he suspected that he was the topic of conversation. But he couldn't be certain. Right now, he needed to know what was being said so he would know what he was dealing with, even if that meant that he needed to get closer.

In what was sure to be considered a temporary loss of sanity, Agent Lewis stepped out from his hiding spot in the alley. He dashed across the street as fast as he could, taking cover behind one of the cars that had been left there earlier. Once he was sure that he hadn't been seen, he repositioned himself so that he could listen in on the conversation.

"I know what she said, but right now, we need to focus on our priorities," a voice in the crowd was saying.

"If what she said over the radio was true, we need to follow protocol. That takes precedence over everything else," another voice called out.

"People of Haven, now is not the time to argue," the man on the steps said in a deep and calming voice. "Linda is on her way here now. Once she arrives, we will receive further instructions, including what our next steps should be."

"What about the other search parties?" a female voice called out.

"We are recalling all of our search parties now. Unfortunately, not everyone is carrying a radio. It may take some time for our runners to locate them all and bring them back here," the man said plainly.

Wanting to get a better look, Agent Lewis raised his head slightly above the hood of the car. At first, the only things he could see were the backs and heads of people gathered around the town hall. The incline of the steps allowed him to see the man speaking above the gathering. Agent Lewis fixed his gaze on the man speaking, identifying him as their leader.

As he was thinking that, another group came running around a corner up the street from where he was hiding. The sight of even more people made him aware of how exposed he truly was. All it would take for him to be discovered would be for another group to join them from down the street. Worse than that, he was sure that he would never make it back to his little alleyway without being noticed.

For now, he was stuck where he was. His attention was drawn back to the crowd as a new voice began addressing the gathering. Lifting his head over the hood of the car once more, Agent Lewis could see that someone new had joined the others on the steps. It was a woman who was in her mid-forties and sporting a bright yellow parka. She was standing halfway up the steps, speaking loudly for everyone to hear.

"First things first. I want to assure everyone that Liam has been found, and that he is now being moved to a secure location." As the woman finished speaking, a loud cheer rose up from amongst the crowd. Several people were even clapping. *So, the boy made it back home safely*, Agent Lewis thought.

"Secondly, the rumors that you may have heard are true: A federal agent has breached our perimeter." The woman's voice was drowned out in a flurry of boos and hisses from amongst the crowd. At least Agent Lewis now knew how they really felt about him.

The woman raised her hand, calling for silence. As the crowd calmed down, she resumed speaking. "The last time he was seen was at the distribution warehouse down in Greenwood. We sent a security team to search the area and ascertain the agent's condition and current location." As the woman finished, she turned her attention to the tall black man at her side. "Malcolm, what did your team find?"

"We never made it to Greenwood. Halfway down the road, we ran into a roadblock made by Gus's delivery van. Someone had positioned it to block anyone from coming in or going out of Haven. At the same time, we found a second vehicle. This one with federal registration. We suspect that the agent tried to follow Gus's van back here to Haven, but was unable to get around the roadblock. We found the vehicle high-centered in a ditch along the side of the road, unable to get around Gus's van.

"We will be sending a team to recover both the van and the federal vehicle. In the meantime, we believe that the agent continued on toward Haven, making his way on foot. We searched the surrounding area, but could not find any trace of him," the man called Malcolm answered.

The crowd began murmuring at the last part. Obviously, none of them wanted to think about the possibility that a federal agent was hiding somewhere in their precious town, skulking in the shadows, waiting for the perfect moment to strike. *What would they do if they learned that a federal agent was hiding no more than a couple of feet away from where they stood?* Agent Lewis wondered.

"Yes, it is most likely that he is still heading in our direction," the woman continued. "But we—"

"How do we know he isn't here already?" a voice from the crowd interrupted.

"Maybe he left," another voice called out. "Maybe he gave up and—"

"Why would he give up?" someone else called out from the other side of the gathering. "There is no reason for him to give up."

The woman in the yellow parka raised her hands again, trying to restore order.

"We don't know where he is at the moment," she said flatly. "He could be on his way here, he could be here already, or he could be lost in the woods. It doesn't matter. What does matter is that we will find him."

Several cheers went up, but the crowd was far from satisfied with this response.

"What about protocol? If there is an agent here, if we have been breached by the Authority, we cannot delay. We need to act now!" an older gentleman toward the front said, directing his comments as much toward the crowd as the woman.

"There is no reason to think that the Authority is aware of our presence. For all we know, this agent could have gotten lost and ended up here by mistake. The important thing to remember is that the agent is here, all alone, and cut off from the rest of the Authority.

"We all know that the dampener and the natural interference from the surrounding mountains makes communicating with the outside world almost impossible. As long as we are able to apprehend this agent, we should be able to stop him from reporting our position. Which is why it is so important that we find him as soon as possible. The project is still intact, but we have to act fast," the woman in the yellow parka said, inspiring the crowd into action.

"What are we supposed to do if he manages to escape?" a woman from the rear of the crowd shouted.

"At this point, escape is highly unlikely. However, if they do, then we will follow the plan and enact the relocation protocol to Site B. But we are not prepared to authorize that action until we have exhausted all other options," she said.

"What does the Director say about this?" someone asked.

"I have spoken to the Director personally. He has complete confidence that we will find this agent. Until then, we will follow our standard operating procedures. Neighborhood captains, organize your units into..."

The woman continued speaking, but Agent Lewis had heard enough. If they were organizing a search for him, he wanted to be as far away from them as possible. With their attention focused on the speakers, he might be able to sneak away without anyone noticing. But how?

The most disturbing thing about his current predicament, other than the fact that he was stuck out in the open with few prospects for escape, was that he had completely misjudged the people living up here. This whole time, he had assumed that they were a group of strays, wanting to live outside the Authority's jurisdiction. The fact that they were well-organized, with an established chain of command and various protocols and procedures for hazardous scenarios, hinted that they were much more than common strays.

The only thing that made sense was that he had stumbled onto a group of Separatists. Though few in number, anti-government separatist movements had been known to sprout up from time to time. Mostly, they had been popular in the days shortly after the Authority assumed control, but the Bureau had done its best to crush as many of them as it could find.

The general belief was that there were still a few groups that were active, though it had been quite some time since the Bureau had found any. Perhaps this group was the reason for that. It was possible that they had taken refuge beyond the Boundary so that they could plot against the Authority; unmolested.

Such actions had to be stopped at all costs. Separatist factions had claimed responsibility for multiple attacks over the years, the worst being an attack on the Central Complex itself. Something like that couldn't be allowed to happen again.

The Bureau had a duty to suppress any anti-governmental activity. If these people were Separatists, then they had to be brought to justice before something terrible happened. And given how the woman in the yellow parka had mentioned a project, Agent Lewis figured that it had to be something serious.

Sitting here thinking about escaping wasn't the same as actually escaping. If he was going to escape, then he needed to get going. Keeping his head low, Agent Lewis stepped backwards, away from the car. The crowd's attention was still on the people on the steps, providing the perfect distraction. All he needed to do was to avoid attracting their attention as he slipped away into the night.

His plan was to get out of town and head back toward Greenwood. From there, he would wait until the retrieval teams arrived, at which point he could report on everything that he had learned. That was his plan, and it lasted for a whole ten seconds before he tripped on a nearby curb and fell backwards.

He hadn't been watching where he was going, deciding that it was better to keep his eyes on the crowd instead, which was how he ended up tripping on the curb he hadn't realized was there. If the fall hadn't been bad enough, his outstretched arms had also reached for anything that could break his fall, which was how the trash cans at the mouth of the alleyway had been knocked over.

The combination of him falling to the ground with a thud and the clanging of the metal trash cans as they hit the ground, caught everyone's attention – not just the people closest to him, but everyone in front of the town hall. They all stood there, staring at him in a heap on the ground.

Agent Lewis quickly got back to his feet, unsure of what to do next. The eyes of the crowd were boring into him, their expressions unreadable. They just stood there, staring at him, unblinking. It was as if his presence had shocked them to the point that they didn't know how to react.

Not knowing what else to do, Agent Lewis put on an awkward smile and waved clumsily. On the edge of the crowd, a young girl casually waved back at him, oblivious to the tension in the air.

It was at that point that a voice from the crowd shouted, "Get him!"

The crowd rushed forward in a surge of angry townsfolk. Agent Lewis was left with no other option than to run for it. He turned on his heel and started sprinting as fast as he could down the street. Behind him, he could hear the sounds of hundreds of people chasing after him.

He ran faster than he had ever run in his life. Within moments, he had already passed the movie theater, café, and most of the shops lining the street. All he had to do was make it to the edge of town and then to the forest beyond.

The path ahead was suddenly cut off as another group turned onto the street in front of him. Whether they knew what was going on or not, they clearly noticed the whole town chasing after him and figured that they should join in. His only option was to veer down a side street, hoping to bypass the newcomers.

Looking back over his shoulder, Agent Lewis could see dozens of people following close behind him. The rest of the townsfolk must have remained at the town hall or hadn't been fast enough to keep pace with him. Either way, he wasn't about to stop now and find out.

As he turned another corner, Agent Lewis heard a long and sonorous bell ringing in the air. It was coming from the direction of the town hall. No doubt it was an alarm that would notify the rest of the townsfolk of his presence, which meant that he didn't have long before the entire population of this town was after him.

The good news was that the street in front of him was clear of people. The bad news was that it was heading west, toward a residential neighborhood. He needed to head south if he hoped to reach the safety of the forest. The first chance he got, he turned left down another street that led toward some industrial buildings.

Just as he was running through an intersection, he felt the force of something crashing into him from the side. Before he knew what was happening, he was falling to the pavement, crashing in a heap on the cement.

As he came to his senses, he realized the thing that had crashed into him was another person. In fact, they were still holding onto his legs.

Agent Lewis scrambled to break free of the man's grip. Despite his best efforts, the man continued to hold on, grasping tightly to his legs. Behind them, several people were running in their direction, approaching fast. It was clear that the man was trying to hold on long enough for his friends to arrive.

Not wanting to be captured, Agent Lewis reached for the holster on his belt. To his surprise, it was empty. Desperately, he looked around for the stun pistol. He found it laying a few feet away on the ground.

It must have fallen out of his holster when he had been tackled to the floor. It was close enough that he thought he could reach it, but every time he tried, he came up short. He only needed a few more inches.

The man holding onto his legs realized what he was doing and tried pulling him away from the pistol. Doing this worked out for Agent Lewis since the man's grip slipped as he tried pulling him away. The agent used this as an opportunity to push off the ground and propel himself forward enough to grab the stun pistol. His hand clasped its grip, and he let out a whoop of triumph.

With his stun pistol in his hands, he raised it toward the approaching figures and squeezed the trigger. The night lit up with a blue flash as a stun blast flew through the air, striking one of the approaching figures. It seemed that at this distance, even he couldn't miss his target. As the stun blast collided with the approaching figure, they immediately went limp and crumpled to the floor in a motionless heap.

There were still more townsfolk approaching, so Agent Lewis fired again. The second approaching figure tried to duck under the stun blast, but was still struck in the shoulder. They stumbled a few feet before they too fell to the floor, immobilized.

In the distance, Agent Lewis could see more townsfolk running in his direction. He struggled to get to his feet, but the man who had tackled him was still holding on tightly to his legs. He pointed the stun pistol at the man, and commanded him to let go. The man just looked back at him, unblinking. The agent repeated his command, practically screaming at the man who was preventing his escape. The man refused to budge.

Didn't this man know what would happen if he was shot at close range like this? He would die. Agent Lewis wanted to shout it at the man, but he had a feeling that it wouldn't matter. The man's eyes spoke of a determination to hold on no matter what.

"I am sorry," Agent Lewis whispered in a sincere voice.

He pulled the trigger, and another bright blue flash lit up the night sky. Everything seemed to happen in slow motion. The blast collided with the man holding his legs. In that instant, the man's grip loosened, and his body was pushed away. It rolled on the ground a few feet before coming to a stop in the middle of the street.

A black burn mark showed where the blast had hit him. Smoke rose slowly into the air from the now-lifeless body. Eyes, unseeing, stared up at the night sky with a vacant expression. He was dead.

At the same time, a surge of electricity washed over Agent Lewis, nearly causing him to pass out. Through sheer will-power, he managed to remain conscious. As the feeling started to fade, he tried to stand, but found that his legs refused to work properly.

Again, he tried to stand, but his legs felt heavy and sluggish. This had to be a result of being in physical contact with a stun victim. The man's body had absorbed the bulk of the stun blast, but the physical contact had transferred some of its effects onto him. Unable to stand, he dragged himself toward a nearby streetlight, determined to use it to help himself up.

Townsfolk were starting to close in from every direction. Without aiming for anyone in particular, Agent Lewis fired several shots into the crowd. One or two people collapsed onto the street where they had been hit, while others ran for shelter along the sides of the street. His actions had bought him some time, but he was only delaying the inevitable.

Using the streetlight for leverage, Agent Lewis pulled himself up. He couldn't walk properly, but at least he could stand up. Hugging the wall of a nearby building, he hobbled down the road toward the edge of town. He didn't get far before his knee buckled and he fell down again. At this rate, he would never escape.

As he was pulling himself back up to his feet, a car pulled into the street ahead of him. It stopped in the middle of the street, parking at an angle to stop him from going in that direction. At the same time, another car pulled in behind him, blocking off that direction as well.

Agent Lewis looked around in desperation. The way back and the way forward were both cut off. The townsfolk were closing in, moving cautiously in case he started firing again. They had him cornered.

At least, that was what they thought.

Not two feet away from where he was standing was a steel door in the side of the building that he was leaning up against. He lurched forward, grabbing the doorknob with this hand, hoping that it was unlocked. To his great relief, the door opened, and he stumbled inside.

Once inside, he immediately turned around and slammed the door behind him. Unfortunately, the absence of a lock that had allowed him to enter the building was also now preventing him from locking the door behind him. He wouldn't be able to stay here; it would only be a matter of seconds before his pursuers followed him inside.

He turned around and tried to survey the building's interior. It appeared to be in an old warehouse, although it was hard to tell in the dark. The only light was coming through the windows from the streetlamps outside. There were plenty of windows lining the outer wall, but they were all fitted with frosted glass, causing the light to appear dull and diffused.

Hoping that there was another exit, Agent Lewis stubbed forward into the darkened room while simultaneously trying not to bump into anything. After a few steps, his outstretched hand did make contact with something hanging from the ceiling. Instinctively, he grabbed onto it with both hands. It didn't take him long to realize that it was a pull chain for a lamp overhead. With a quick tug, the lightbulb overhead turned on.

The added light showed the agent that he was standing in a warehouse, but one that was almost completely empty. There was a wooden table and chairs off to the side, as well as some empty cardboard boxes that littered the floor. Despite the many windows, there appeared to be only one door – the same one that he had come in through.

Thinking fast, Agent Lewis grabbed one of the nearby chairs and propped it up against the door. There might not be a lock on the door, but that would slow them down if they tried to get in. With nothing else to do, he started walking around in circles in the center of the room, trying to regain the feeling in his legs.

He did his best to stay away from the windows. He didn't want his shadow to be seen through the glass and give away his position. They already knew he was in there, but he didn't want to give the townsfolk any more information than they already had. After a few minutes, the feeling in his legs began to return, and he stopped walking.

Of all of the thoughts that were swirling around in his head at that moment, the one that stuck out the most was to question why nobody had tried to come in after him. They knew where he was; why hadn't they tried to knock the door down or break through the windows? Yes, he was armed, but he would never be able to fend them off if they all came at him at once.

After another few minutes, he grew tired of wondering what the townsfolk were doing and stealthy made his way to one of the nearby windows. He couldn't see through the frosted glass, but there was a latch at the base of the window. Turning the latch slowly, he opened the window a few inches and peeked out.

The sight out in front of the building was anything but comforting. Hundreds of people were arranged in a semicircle around the front of the building. Fearing what he would find, Agent Lewis made his way to one of the windows on the back wall. When he opened that window, he saw a similar sight. Townsfolk had encircled the building, cutting off any chance of escape.

Whatever hope of possibly escaping he had been holding onto was now gone. He was trapped, with no way out. His shoulders slumped as he walked back to the center of the room. He pulled one of the nearby chairs over and sat down, preparing to face the inevitable.

As he sat there, he could still feel a slight tingle in his leg. He was reaching down to rub his leg and adjust the brace that he had applied earlier when his hand pressed against something in his trench coat pocket. Up until now, he had forgotten about the supplies that he was carrying with him in his coat. His hand reached in and began pulling things out.

The first thing that he pulled out was the flashlight – not that it would do him a lot of good now. He placed it on the floor next to him and reached back into his pocket for the next item. An energy bar came out next and was placed next to the flashlight. The third thing that came out of his pocket sent a flood of relief through him. It was the mobile relay.

Holding the relay in both hands, he immediately turned it on. The screen lit up, but it was having a hard time making a connection with the emitter back in his vehicle. No doubt the distance and the fact that he was inside were hampering the signal. Still, he stood up and walked around the building's interior, holding the relay high overhead in the hopes of establishing a connection.

Just as the screen of the relay started to register a connection, there was a push against the door. Someone was trying to enter. The chair, which was still propped up against the door, had prevented them from simply opening the door and walking in. This delay bought Agent Lewis several precious seconds as the relay continued to connect. The screen turned green, signaling a positive connection. Another thud sounded against the door, pushing the chair back.

Knowing that he didn't have a lot of time, Agent Lewis pressed the homing feature on the relay. He didn't have time to see whether the command had gone through before the door shuddered under the force of another blow. Acting quickly, the agent shoved the relay back into his pocket, hiding it from sight.

The door burst open under the force of a third blow. The chair, which had been propped up against the door, was smashed to pieces as the door swung open. In the now-open doorway, Agent Lewis could see a tall, heavily muscled man standing there. The light from the streetlamps illuminated his silhouette, which was massive, but hid his facial features in shadow.

Agent Lewis raised his stun pistol and aimed it at the giant figure, but he didn't pull the trigger. The man stood there, making no attempt to enter. Instead, he stepped aside, and the woman in the yellow parka stepped through the doorway. From the confident way she entered the room, it was clear that she wasn't intimidated by him or the stun pistol in his grip.

"Do you mind?" she said in a steely voice, gesturing to the stun pistol aimed at her chest.

Not knowing what she expected him to do, Agent Lewis slowly lowered the stun pistol until it was resting in his lap. He wasn't about to hand it over, if that had been her intention.

It soon became obvious that his lowering of the stun pistol had been exactly what the woman had wanted. She turned her head and nodded at the gigantic man, who was still standing outside. With a slight bow, he reached in, grabbed the door, and pulled it closed, leaving the woman and Agent Lewis alone together.

"That is better," she said, taking a few steps forward and surveying Agent Lewis from head to toe. "I must say, you aren't what I expected."

"And what were you expecting?" Agent Lewis asked, not knowing how to interpret her comment.

"I expected to find a cold-blooded killer," she said, pointedly. "The kind of monster that would open fire on a couple of kids for no reason. The kind of monster that would take joy and satisfaction from wounding a helpless teenage boy. Or the kind that would take down innocent bystanders for fun. Not to mention murdering a man in the street."

Again, she surveyed him, but this time, with obvious disdain. "Make no mistake – you are a monster, you just don't look like one. That is what I wasn't expecting."

"Sorry to disappoint you," Agent Lewis said sarcastically. If she wanted to get into a battle of wits, he could give as good as he got. "Funny that you should characterize self-defense as murder. Or did I misunderstand the intentions of the whole town as they chased me through the streets?"

"Call it what you want. A man is lying dead in the street because of you," she responded, anger creeping into her voice.

"I had no intention of hurting anyone," Agent Lewis protested. "But your friend out there didn't exactly give me a choice."

"You had a choice. You always have a choice," she said accusingly. "You chose to take that man's life. You knew what would happen when you pulled the trigger. You knew, and you did it anyway."

The way she was talking, it was almost like he was already on trial, and she was filling the role of both judge and jury. He hadn't wanted to pull the trigger, but it had been his only option – that or be caught. Though he wasn't blind to the fact that he'd ended up being caught anyway.

"Again, I was defending myself," Agent Lewis said, trying to explain. "I pleaded with that man to let me go, but he refused. I didn't have a lot of options."

The woman in the yellow parka nodded, "Alright, you shot him in 'self-defense.'" She put her fingers up in the air to mime air quotes. "And what about the boy you shot earlier today? Was that self-defense too?"

"You mean Liam?" Agent Lewis responded. The woman narrowed her eyes at the mention of the boy's name but the agent continued. "I wasn't trying to hurt him either. I was only trying to stun him. How was I supposed to know that he would react that way? Never seen anything like it before in my life.

"As for self-defense…well, that girl he was with – Parker, I think her name was – she can tell you all about it. Make sure she includes the part where she smashed a chair into my face and then practically beat me unconscious with a metal pipe."

The woman actually smiled when she heard the last part. "She actually hit you in the face with a chair and beat you with pipe?"

As Agent Lewis nodded in confirmation, the woman let out an amused chuckle. "Well. Well. I didn't think she had it in her. Good for her."

Agent Lewis was not amused. He unconsciously flexed his arm, where a twinge of pain still remained. "I am glad that you are finding this funny," he said wryly.

"Whatever she did to you, you deserved it," the woman said, pointing a finger at him. Then, in a much quieter voice, she added, "And you probably deserved worse."

"I see. So, I am guessing that you treat all your guests this way," Agent Lewis said sarcastically.

"You. Are. Not. A. Guest," she responded heatedly, making sure to enunciate each and every word so that there was no confusion on the subject. "You aren't even supposed to be here, which begs the question. Why are you here?"

"Didn't I already tell you? I ran into Liam and Parker down in that ruin of a town you call Greenwood. They tried to run. I chased after them. She hit me with a pipe and left me for dead, so I followed them up here. Your friendly townspeople chased me into this building, and here we are, enjoying each other's company," he finished, adopting a sly smile of his own.

"That was not what I meant, and you know it," she said. "What are you doing here, in Quadrant 29? We are hundreds of miles away from anything that remotely resembles civilization. Why come here, of all places?"

Agent Lewis debated whether or not to tell her the truth. On the one hand, he didn't want to give her the satisfaction of having her questions answered. On the other hand, what could it hurt? Besides, he needed to stall for time, anyway. If that meant carrying on a conversation with this woman, he would do it.

He kept his explanation short. He told her how the monitoring station had detected their presence and how he'd discovered that this town had been erased on the system, but not on the physical maps stored in the Historical Archive. He had then travelled all this way to see if anyone was actually living up here, which they definitely were. By the time he was finished, she was shaking her head in disbelief.

"How could we have missed that?" she said to herself more than to him. "We were so confident that we had erased all mention of this place from the central database that we completely forgot to destroy the original copies in the Archive."

She noticed him watching her and realized that he had been listening to everything that she had said. Her cheeks flushed with embarrassment, and she struggled to school her features back to a stoic demeanor. "And then what happened?" she asked, trying to get the conversation back on track.

"And nothing. I was sent out here to investigate, and so here I am," Agent Lewis concluded.

"I take it your supervisor didn't fully support your theory, or else you wouldn't be up here alone?" she asked, already knowing the answer.

Agent Lewis nodded. "He had his doubts."

It was the woman's turn to nod, as if he had confirmed something in her mind. No doubt she thought that since he had been sent unaccompanied, their chances of discovery were still low. She had no idea that support had already been dispatched to the area and would be there in a matter of hours.

While she was still nodding and thinking to herself, Agent Lewis ventured a question of his own. "Since we are sharing, I take it that the radio tower that I found next to the warehouse in Greenwood is being used to emit some sort of signal blocker? That is how you have avoided being detected all these years, right?"

"Not really. The antenna that you passed is simply a relay station. The dampening field that we are using to hide from the Authority's sensors is actually located here, just outside of town. But we use those relay stations to increase our range and the strength of our field," she explained nonchalantly.

"Now, let me guess: There was an interruption to your little dampening field, wasn't there? I am guessing that the system went down last week for approximately six minutes before you were able to get it back up and running. Am I right?" he continued.

"Yes," she said, compressing her lips in disapproval. "There was an...incident last week. The field went down for several minutes before we could reestablish the connection. We had hoped that the temporary interruption would have gone unnoticed, but I guess that we weren't that lucky."

"I am here, after all," Agent Lewis said, putting on a faux smile. The woman in the yellow parka did not share his smile. Instead, she looked at him with a quizzical look, like she was trying to figure out what to do with him.

Not liking the looks he was getting, Agent Lewis continued, "May I ask what you intend to do with me, now that you have cornered me in this building?"

"That...depends entirely on you," she said, staring at him intently.

"How so?"

"You have a choice. You can either shoot me with your stun pistol there," she said, pointing at the pistol still in his hand. "At which point this building will be burned to the ground with both of us trapped inside."

"Or?" Agent Lewis asked, desperate not to settle for the first option.

"Or you hand over your weapon and surrender."

"Just for a moment, let's say that I do decide to shoot you – not that I am planning on it, but let's say hypothetically that I did. If I were to shoot you, I take it your friends outside would set this building on fire, correct? Wouldn't that mean that both of us would die in here?" he asked.

294

"Some things are worth dying for," she said flatly.

Agent Lewis scoffed at her reply. Who in their right mind was willing to be burned alive like that? And for what? To stop him from getting away? Not that there was any chance of that. The whole idea seemed ridiculous and a complete overreaction. Still, there had been something in her voice that made him think that she wasn't bluffing.

"Fair enough. So, what happens if I surrender? I doubt you would be willing to let me go," Agent Lewis asked.

"That is not up to me," she said. "But at this point, isn't it better than burning to death?"

Agent Lewis stared at her for a long moment. She was serious. She was prepared to die with him if he didn't surrender. It wasn't just the sound of her voice; it was the conviction in her eyes. Why else would she have come in here, alone, without being the slightest bit afraid of him? He had heard of Separatist groups willing to go to extreme measures to avoid being captured, but he had never really believed it. Now, he was starting to believe.

The absurdity of the situation was laughable except that he was caught in the middle of it. He could either surrender to the mob outside without knowing what they planned to do to him, or he could burn to death in this half-forgotten warehouse. Neither option would have been his first choice, but it didn't look like there were any other alternatives at the moment.

By this time, Agent Lewis strongly suspected that the woman meant every word she had said. Perhaps it was a bluff on her part. Perhaps she was so confident that he would accept her terms of surrender that she could threaten him with anything. Either way, he wasn't ready to take that gamble.

In the end, it wasn't a difficult choice. He could either surrender and hope that he was rescued before any permanent damage was done, or he could die here in this building. His desire for self-preservation motivated him to reach out and offer his stun pistol to the woman in the yellow parka.

She took it, placing it in her coat pocket, then turned and walked over to the front door and opened it. The large man was still standing outside next to the door. He must have been listening in on the conversation, ready to give the word to torch the place if it became necessary.

The woman stepped outside, walking past the large man before stopping a few steps beyond the door. The large man looked at her, and she nodded. Several men then entered the room, seizing Agent Lewis by both arms. He was escorted out of the building and into the street, where the rest of the townsfolk stood waiting. It wasn't a surprise to see several of them holding torches.

The crowd stood by and watched as he was led over to one of the cars that had blocked his earlier attempt at escape. The back door was opened, and he was hustled toward the backseat of the car. Before he could get in, the men holding his arms stopped in front of the door. They let go of his arms, releasing him from their firm grip.

Not knowing what was happening, Agent Lewis looked around. Everyone was staring at him. He turned around and saw the woman in the yellow parka standing a few feet behind him, holding his stun pistol in her hands. It was aimed directly at his head.

"Oh, I forgot to mention," she said coolly. "I owe you this."

Agent Lewis watched in horror as her finger began to squeeze the trigger. Being shot in the head with a stun pistol produced the same result as being shot at close range. After everything he had gone through, she was going to kill him anyway.

At the last moment, she angled the stun pistol down at his chest. The last thing he saw was the bright blue flash of the stun pistol as the blast hit him in the chest. He didn't even feel the impact.

In an instant, the whole world went black.

Chapter 13: A Cement Room

The walk to Ben's house hadn't taken long for Liam and Parker. Most of that time, Liam had been absorbed in thought. Parker had made some pretty outlandish claims when they were back in Greenwood. The whole time, he had thought that she was lying to him for some unknown reason, but as it turned out, she had been telling him the truth.

He would never have believed it had he not seen his aunt's reaction and heard the confirmation in her voice. Whatever was going on in Haven, he was at the center of it. The frustrating part about it was that he still didn't know what role he was supposed to play in all of this – not to mention how nobody seemed ready to tell him either.

It opened the door to a bunch of questions that now filled his head. He was being forced to question everything he had ever known. What was real and what was deception? Had everybody he had ever known been in on it, or was it just the people closest to him? Which would be worse?

There had to be a rational explanation, Liam told himself. His aunt wouldn't have lied to him without having a good reason. Would she? Parker had suggested that it had something to do with hiding from the Authority, but he had to wonder whether that was the whole truth.

He was so consumed in thought that he didn't realize it when they turned onto the street where Ben lived. He hadn't even noticed that they had reentered town. Walking down the street with the street-lamps glaring overhead, he finally became aware of where they were. By this time, they were already passing the home of Mr.

and Mrs. Dean. The lights were on, but Parker showed no interest in finding out whether they were home or not.

As they neared Ben's house, Liam could see several people standing out in front, waiting for them. The lights from the streetlamps illuminated them as he and Parker approached. From amongst the assembled group, Dr. Adhira was the first to be clearly visible as she rushed toward them.

In the light of the streetlamps, it was evident that her concern was purely for him. She rushed to his side and immediately began examining him from head to toe. She reached up and grabbed his head, pulling it down so that she could look him in the eye. A flashlight appeared in one of her hands and she shined it in his eyes with the instructions to follow the light as she moved it side to side.

Confident that he hadn't sustained any brain injuries, Dr. Adhira continued her examination. It felt weird for her to be giving him a full examination in the middle of the street, in front of everybody, but he didn't protest. Parker even let go of him so that the doctor could get a better look at him.

It didn't take Dr. Adhira long to find the makeshift bandage wrapped around his side. She immediately pulled back his shirt and examined the bandages underneath. She made a disgusted grunt as she observed the crude bandage, which by this point was soaked with blood, pus, and sweat.

She pulled a pair of medical scissors out of a medical pouch on her hip and started cutting away the makeshift bandages. She was trying to be as gentle as possible, but even the slightest touch was painful. Liam winced as the bandage came away, exposing his burn to the fresh air.

"This looks angry," Dr. Adhira said, turning her head toward Ben. "But I should be able to treat it. We should get him inside."

It was at this moment that Liam realized that Ben had joined the group of onlookers. He stood apart from the rest of the crowd, watching Dr. Adhira tend to Liam with a disapproving frown on his face. Whether he was disappointed with the wound on Liam's side or with Liam himself was still a mystery.

Interestingly enough, Dr. Adhira's comments had been directed to him, rather than the rest of the adults in the crowd. Once Liam noticed that, he also noted how everyone was looking to Ben, as if he were somehow in charge. Sure, this was his house, but that didn't explain why everyone else was deferring to him. *Why on earth would a group of adults be looking to a teenager for instructions?* Liam wondered.

Whatever their reasons were, Ben seemed to be going along with it. He nodded to Dr. Adhira as if giving her permission to proceed. Having received consent from him, she immediately went into action. She positioned herself under Liam's arm where Parker had been only moments ago. As gently as possible, she guided him toward the front door of Ben's house. The rest of the adults crowded around, eager to help however they could.

Liam was halfway up the driveway when he noticed that Parker wasn't by his side. Despite Dr. Adhira urging him toward the house, he dug his heels in and came to an immediate halt. He turned his head from side to side, trying to see what had happened to her. The answer to that question was that she was still standing at the base of the driveway with two adults holding her by either arm. From the look of things, they were trying to drag her away.

Liam turned, pushing away from Dr. Adhira and shouting for Parker to be released. The two adults holding her ignored him. They continued holding her by either arm, determined to haul her away despite his protests. Liam shouted again, and this time, they stopped, but instead of releasing her, both adults turned to look at Ben, as if they wanted his confirmation before proceeding.

Ben himself was standing a few feet away, watching as Parker was being led away. There was even a smug smile on his face, as if watching her being hauled away gave him a feeling of satisfaction. That smug smile vanished as Liam walked up to him and poked him in the chest to get his attention.

"What do you think you are doing?" he demanded.

"Escorting a traitor out of town," Ben replied back.

"Like hell you are!" Liam said, coming to Parker's defense. "I don't care what you think you are doing, but from now on, she stays with me."

"You don't understand," Ben said exasperatedly. "She is a danger to you and the community. She has broken our laws on several different occasions and needs to be dealt with. I suggest you go with Dr. Adhira into the house and let me worry about what happens to her."

"Where I go, she goes," Liam said in no uncertain terms.

The whole group went silent, unsure what to do. Again, they all looked to Ben to make a decision. After a moment, he nodded reluctantly, and Parker was released. She looked at the adults standing beside her with disdain. Judging by her expression, she was not happy with how she had been treated.

Now that she had been released, she took her position under Liam's arm and led him back up the driveway. Liam could have sworn that she called Ben an asshole as they walked away.

Dr. Adhira took up a position under Liam's other shoulder, and the three of them made their way to Ben's house. As they reached the door, the rest of the adults who had remained in the street started to disperse. A few of them tried to linger out front, but Ben made a shooing gesture to get them on their way. Without another word, they too went off into the night, leaving the street outside empty and alone.

The first things to greet Liam as he entered the house were Ben's parents. They were standing on the other side of the door, where the entryway and the living room met. They greeted him warmly as he stepped through the door, but they made no effort to interfere with what was happening. With the way they were acting, it was almost like this wasn't even their house, and they were trying to stay out of everyone's way.

Liam tried to give them a partial wave as he passed, but even that sent a stab of pain through his side. Now that the bandage had been cut away, the pain seemed to have gotten worse. Ben's mother gave him a sympathetic look, and Ben's father nodded grimly. It wasn't that they weren't concerned with his wellbeing – quite the opposite. They simply understood that the best thing that they could do for him now was to stay out of everyone else's way.

Ben was the last one inside the house. He closed the door behind him and began giving orders to his parents. Without hesitation, his father disappeared down the hall into their bedroom. Liam's jaw practically dropped to the floor when he saw this. He had never heard anyone give Ben's father an order, especially not his son.

Before he had time to ask what was happening, Liam was being led down the hallway and into Ben's parents' bedroom. Over the years, he had spent as much time at Ben's house as he had at his own. He knew this place inside and out, but in all that time, he had never been inside Ben's parents' bedroom. That had always been off-limits.

As they entered the bedroom, Liam looked around in wonder. To his disappointment, everything seemed rather bland and ordinary. There was a bed, a couple of nightstands, a dresser against the far wall, a closet with shuttered doors, and an archway that led into a private bathroom. All in all, it looked identical to his aunt's bedroom back home.

Liam stepped forward, heading toward the bed. In his mind, it made sense that they had brought him back here so that he could lay down. Before he reached the bed, Dr. Adhira placed a hand against his chest and held him back. She motioned him to stand against the wall before taking up position there herself. He wanted to ask what was going on, but she shushed him.

With nothing better to do, Liam looked around the room again. It was only then that he noticed that they were missing someone. Ben's dad was nowhere to be seen. Liam had watched him run into the bedroom ahead of them, but unless he was hiding under the bed, he had vanished.

Not two seconds later, the mystery was solved as Ben's dad emerged from a trap door in the closet. The shuttered doors of the closet had been pulled open, revealing a trap door that led downstairs into a basement. The top of the trap door was upholstered in the same material as the carpet, allowing it to blend in with the rest of the floor when the door was closed. There were also several cardboard boxes that had been pushed off to the side, which were clearly meant to be placed over the trap door when not in use.

As his dad stepped out, Ben replaced him at the trap door and disappeared down the stairs. Seconds later, the entrance of the trap door lit up as he turned on a light in the basement. He then called up for everyone to join him, and Liam was escorted to the trapdoor. He stopped at the entrance, still in shock that Ben had a basement in the first place.

A gentle nudge prompted Liam to follow Dr. Adhira and Parker down the stairs. As he reached the bottom, he stared in wonder at the room in front of him, which was much larger than he had suspected. It stretched almost the entire length of the house above, with support beams spaced evenly. The walls were made of cement, and there were no windows whatsoever.

The most surprising thing about it was that the room wasn't empty. There were storage crates lining the walls, shelves full of provisions, several sleeping cots, and a medical station off in the far corner. Someone had gone out of their way to make sure that this room was ready for whatever emergency came up.

"What is this place?" Liam asked, still looking around in surprise.

"It's an emergency safe room," Ben said casually. "A place where we could take shelter in case anything ever went wrong."

"Let me guess – another little detail you forgot to mention to Liam. Some friend you are," Parker said indignantly.

"There was no reason to tell him about it, at least not until now. Funny how we never needed it before you arrived. Leave it to you to cause trouble," Ben countered.

"Yeah, he's right," Liam said wryly to Parker. "Why would I need to know that my best friend has an emergency shelter in his basement? Unless, of course, he was just pretending to be my best friend so that he could keep an eye on me and keep me out of trouble." The last words were aimed at Ben.

"There is a lot that I couldn't tell you, but it was for your own good. I promise," Ben said as sincerely as he could. "Besides, I never lied to you. At least not about being your friend."

"Well, that is comforting," Liam said sarcastically.

"It's true – you are my best friend. Everything I have ever said or done has been for your benefit. You may not see it that way, but maybe someday, you will. I…I just want you to know that I will always be your friend, no matter what happens," Ben said bashfully.

Liam didn't respond. He wasn't sure how he felt about all of this yet, and he was afraid that if he did say something, it would probably be the wrong thing.

He was eventually saved from having to think of something to say when Dr. Adhira directed him into the corner of the basement where, against the wall, a small medical station had been set up.

Following her instructions, Liam climbed onto the table. Parker and Dr. Adhira helped him remove his hoodie and shirt, both of which were discarded on the floor. Ben stood several feet away, watching.

Now that Liam was naked from the waist up, Dr. Adhira began treating the burn on his side. She started by applying a clear liquid that smelled like rubbing alcohol to the burn. She did her best to clean the area around his burn as gently as possible, but the whole area was now extremely sensitive. After the clear liquid had done its job, she leaned in to survey the damage. She sighed in disapproval as she looked at the angry red skin of the burn.

She must have known how much pain he was in, because she pulled a syringe out of her hip pouch and filled it with a clear liquid from a fluorescent-red medicine bottle. She injected the contents of the syringe in several places all along the burn. Both the sting of the needle and the pain from the burn began to fade away as his side grew numb.

The lack of pain was refreshing, and Liam expressed his appreciation. Dr. Adhira shrugged it off, focusing instead on treating his side without having to worry about whether she was hurting him or not.

As she worked, Liam tried to focus on something else. He didn't want to watch what she was doing in case it made him feel sick. This left him to focus his attention on Parker and Ben, who, by this time, were facing off only a few feet away. From the looks of things, they were about to break into an all-out brawl. The only question was who was going to throw the first punch.

"Despite what Liam says, you are not welcome here," Ben was saying. "This is all your fault, and if I have my way, you will be held responsible once this is all over."

"I don't care what you think. You are not in charge here, despite what you may think. And as far as you getting your way, we all know how that has been going for you," Parker responded with a sneer. "It must sting, knowing that the council overruled your recommendation to have me exiled."

"I warned them what could happen if they did, and I was right, wasn't I? At least one thing is for certain: Not a single member of the council will be coming to your aid this time. By morning, you will be dealt with. Properly this time," Ben said with satisfaction.

"By morning, it won't matter," Parker replied with hostility tainting her voice.

"What the hell are you two going on about?" Liam asked, interrupting them before they came to blows.

"Ben here was the one that recommended that I be exiled. As soon as we left the communications building, he rushed back to town to rally the town council against me. That was why I was carried away the moment we got back into town. But it didn't matter – the council changed their minds and decided to bring me back. Much to Ben's disappointment," Parker explained.

"She is dangerous!" Ben said defensively. "From the moment she got here, she has been trying to undermine everything that we have built up over the past few years. She risks everything and everyone here."

"By telling me the truth?" Liam said frankly.

"By doing it without considering the ramifications of her actions," Ben said defensively. At this point, he turned to face Liam, refusing to look at Parker any longer. "You have to understand – we were going to tell you the truth about everything, but we were going to do it gradually."

"Oh yeah? And when were you planning on doing that?" Liam asked.

"The plan was to wait until your eighteenth birthday. It was decided that by then you would be ready to accept certain...truths about this place and...yourself." Ben said, choosing his words carefully.

"Right, because why tell the truth when you can lie?" Liam said. "You know, I have a mind to—"

He was cut off as a jolt of pain ran through his side. He turned his attention back to Dr. Adhira. She was standing by his side, holding a medical instrument with a glowing red tip. Smoke was rising up from the tip, and Liam could make out the faint hint of burning flesh in the air. He didn't have to look down at his side to know what had just happened.

"I had to cauterize part of the wound," Dr. Adhira said. "The skin was too badly damaged and needed to be removed to prevent infection."

Liam grimaced as she finished up and placed the cauterizing tool on the table next to her other medical instruments. She had been busy while he was focused on Ben and Parker. The table was littered with equipment that she had used on him at one point or another.

She wasn't done, though. The next thing she grabbed was a tub of green gel. She applied a thick coat of it to his side and rubbed it in delicately. It felt cold, but also soothing. Once she was satisfied that enough gel had been applied, she began the process of wrapping his side in gauze and bandages.

He continued watching her for a few more seconds before turning his attention back to Parker and Ben. From the looks on both of their faces, they had continued their previous conversation uninterrupted. Whatever they had been talking about, it had devolved into a staring contest, with neither one prepared to look away.

Liam wanted to continue on with their conversation, but something told him that now wasn't the time. Instead, he busied himself with looking around at the different contents of the basement. Despite the vast amount of camping and survival gear that filled the room, most of the space was filled with food and emergency rations. Based on how many boxes there were, they could stay down here for months and never get hungry.

He was relieved when Dr. Adhira finished bandaging his side. Whatever magic she had worked, his side was now feeling much better. Now that his side had been taken care of, she turned her attention to every other cut and scrape that she could find, making sure that even the smallest cut was treated and covered in a bandage.

When she was done, Liam was handed a fresh shirt from a nearby backpack. Surprisingly, it fit him perfectly, almost as if it had been meant specifically for him. Then again, the more he thought about it, the more he was convinced that it was meant specifically for him.

With a new shirt on and his side now rebandaged, Liam hopped down from the table. The numbness in his side was slowly fading away, but the pain was practically gone. He was stiff, but that was most likely from all the bandages. He took several steps around the room and was pleased that he was practically back to normal.

Dr. Adhira chided him not to "over-do things" and that he needed to "take it easy" for the next few days. At this point, he was ready to agree to anything so long as the pain stayed away. Just to be sure, the doctor pressed a bottle of pills into Liam's hand, instructing him to take one every eight hours for the next few days.

He thanked her for everything that she had done. She responded by reaching up and giving him a tight hug. Though she was careful to avoid squeezing his middle. It felt nice, having her hold him like that. If something like this had happened before Parker had moved to town, he would have been ecstatic over being this close to Dr. Adhira. As it was, his feelings toward her had changed over the past few weeks. She was still beautiful, but Liam's tastes had changed somewhat ever since Parker came into his life.

"You take care of yourself, now," she said firmly into his ear before releasing him. She was about to say something else when the radio on her medical pouch started to chime. She reached down and pulled the two-way radio from her pouch and pressed the call button.

"Go for Adhira," she said into the radio receiver.

A garbled voice echoed through the radio. "What is your status?"

"I am finishing up with Liam now. Why?" she responded.

"We have casualties. Tom is down! We need you here now!" the voice called out urgently.

"What do you mean? What happened?" Dr. Adhira said, alarm in her voice.

"The agent is in town; he attacked several people before we cornered him. We need you down here as soon as possible," the voice finished.

Dr. Adhira assured whoever was on the other end of the radio that she was on her way before replacing the radio on the outside of her pouch. She looked at Liam to confirm that there wasn't anything else that he needed. He understood the unasked question and shook his head, letting her know that she was free to go.

Before she left, she turned and whispered something to Ben. He nodded before escorting her out of the basement. From the foot of the stairs, he began calling out orders to his parents, who had been waiting up in their room. No sooner than he finished giving instructions than the trapdoor was lowered and locked into place.

The iron bolts that secured the trap door slid into place with an audible clunk. That was quickly accompanied by the shuffling of boxes as they were placed over the trapdoor to hide its location. As the last box was placed over the door and Ben's parents left the bedroom above, Liam knew that they were now locked-in for the night. For better or worse, they weren't going anywhere.

"What is happening?" he asked, coming up to stand beside Parker.

"We are following protocol," Ben said, stepping away from the staircase. "If the Authority has penetrated our perimeter, my orders are to lock down this safe room and wait until extraction."

"So, we are just locked down here in your basement, waiting for someone to come and get us?" Liam asked.

"Or until I receive the All Clear signal," Ben said.

"And how do you know if we have received the All Clear signal? I don't see any radios down here," Liam protested.

"That is because there aren't any," Ben said plainly. "This is a safe room. We don't want any unnecessary electronics down here that would allow the Authority to track our position."

"Then how are we supposed to get the All Clear signal?"

To answer Liam's question, Ben walked over to a metal box against the wall next to the staircase and opened it. A phone receiver sat in the box next to a switch with two lights. The light was red at the moment, but it turned green when Ben flipped the switch. He then lifted the phone to his ear and waited.

Liam could hear a voice coming from the receiver's speaker. It was too low for him to understand, but he thought he recognized it as Ben's mother.

"Communication check. What is our status?" Ben said into the receiver.

"Locked down...zzzzz...will notify...zzzz...status," the voice said through the receiver, though Liam could only understand a few words.

Once he was done, Ben replaced the receiver back in the box and flipped the switch so that the light turned red again. He then turned and explained to Liam that the phone was on a closed circuit. That way, he could communicate with his parents upstairs without having to worry about their call being tracked. The other phone was cleverly disguised upstairs, and would allow them to communicate with whoever was in the safe room if necessary.

Liam threw up his hands in frustration. Parker sensed his mood and tried to comfort him as best as she could. She tried telling him that everything would be alright, but he wasn't listening. By this time, he was pacing back and forth across the room, his agitation building with each step. Within minutes, he reached his boiling point. He let out a yell of rage and frustration.

"That's it! I am getting out of here!"

"You cannot leave," Ben said, stepping in front of the stairs to block Liam's way.

"You just watch me," Liam challenged. "I refuse to be locked away in your basement like a prisoner."

Despite Liam's insistence that he was leaving, Ben refused to get out of his way. He stood there like a statue, determined to keep his friend from pushing past him.

"Get out of my way, Ben," Liam demanded.

"I can't do that. You have to stay here," Ben said firmly.

"Why? Why do I have to stay here? Why do I have to be locked up in a cement room under your house?" Liam asked, enraged.

"For your protection," Ben said, trying to explain.

"'Protection?' 'Protection' from what? From the people closest to me that have been telling me lies my whole life? From a government agent that thinks it is alright to shoot first and ask questions later? Maybe I need to be protected from a town that thinks it has the right to make decisions on my behalf without consulting me. Or maybe I need protection from those people that think it is alright to kidnap my girlfriend and ship her out of town," Liam said in a huff.

Ben was quiet for a moment, and then said, "For now, the government agent."

The sheer audacity of the response left Liam speechless for a moment, which was quickly followed by a burst of uncontrollable laughter. There was nothing funny about their situation, but that didn't stop him from laughing. The whole situation was so ridiculous, the only thing he could do was laugh.

After a few minutes, the laughter finally subsided, and Liam was left with the unfortunate realization that he was stuck where he was for now.

Parker had been standing off to the side, watching him nervously. She took a step toward him, but he waved her off. He really needed a moment alone to collect himself.

Looking around the room, Liam saw that a sleeping cot had been set up against the far wall. He walked over and sat down, cupping his face in his hands and leaning forward so that his elbows rested on his knees. He remained in that position for a good ten to fifteen minutes before he felt a hand on his shoulder. He lifted his head to see Parker kneeling down in front of him, a concerned look on her face.

Liam wanted to give her a reassuring smile, but he couldn't manage it at the moment. Instead, he nodded to the space next to him on the cot, and Parker took the cue to sit down. It felt good to have her there. If nothing else, she was someone he could rely on.

"What do you think?" he asked.

"He is an asshole," Parker said immediately.

"No, I mean about staying here," Liam clarified.

"I knew what you meant," she assured him. "What I was going to say was that he is an asshole, but that doesn't mean he is wrong. Right now, this is the safest place you can be. Besides, we are together – that should count for something, right?"

Liam nodded in agreement, and Parker smiled at him as she leaned over and kissed his cheek. She wrapped her arms around him and gave him a squeeze. Feeling more at ease, he leaned back, resting his back against the wall behind him. She took the opportunity to lean back as well, even resting her head on his shoulder.

"So, what do we do now?" he asked.

"Not much with Ben watching," Parker said in a soft, sultry voice. It took almost a full minute for Liam to catch onto what she was saying. He lifted an eyebrow at her, and she giggled. Ben looked over in their direction, and Parker regained control of herself under his scrutiny.

"Actually," she said in a low voice meant only for Liam to hear, "I was thinking, and once this is all over and done with, we should take some of the supplies in the room and go on a camping trip."

"Seriously?"

"Why not? You told me you always wanted to hike to the top of these mountains. After today, they won't be able to stop you from going if you want. Just think of it: You, me, a tent, and a mountain top," she said, painting a picture of their future adventures together.

Liam wasn't sure what he liked most about that idea. Fulfilling a lifelong goal sounded great. Sharing a tent together sounded even better. In the end, the best part of her idea was the sincerity in her voice as she said it. Even after everything that they had gone through, she had remembered him talking about hiking up the mountain. More importantly, she wanted to help him make that dream a reality.

That was probably the biggest difference between Parker and everyone else – everyone else was so concerned about doing what was in his best interest, but she was concerned with what was best for him. It was a subtle difference, but an important one.

Everything she had done up to this point had been for his benefit, although he didn't necessarily appreciate how she had gone about it.

"I want you to do something for me," Liam said to Parker. "You too, Ben," he said, raising his voice to include his friend in the conversation. "I want you both to stop doing what you think is best for me and start letting me decide what is best for myself."

Parker didn't hesitate to nod in agreement, and even gave Liam an extra hug for confirmation. She fully endorsed him taking control of his own life and making his own decisions.

Ben, on the other hand, looked uncomfortable. It was obvious that he was struggling with the request.

"Ben. You keep telling me that you are my friend. If that is true, then please start acting like it. I know that you have always been there to look out for me, and I appreciate that. I do. But the time has come for me to make my own decisions," Liam pleaded.

"You are my friend," Ben said hesitantly. "And you do deserve to make your own decisions. It is just...you cannot do that without first knowing all of the facts."

Liam recognized that this was the best that Ben had to offer. For so long, his friend's responsibility had been to look after him, so stepping away from that role must have been difficult for him. Still, a change had to be made, even if Liam had to meet him more than half way.

"Fair enough," Liam said. "So why don't you tell me what I need to know so that I can make those decisions?"

Ben's face blanched. He looked like Liam had just punched him in the gut. If he seemed to be struggling with the earlier request, he was now in agony.

"Liam...I..." he stammered.

"Look – you said that the plan was to tell me the truth when I turned eighteen, right?" Liam pointed out. "So, why don't we ramp up that timetable and start right now? After everything I have gone through, I doubt anything will surprise me."

Ben muttered something under his breath that Liam couldn't hear. "You have no idea," or something very similar to it. Whatever he'd said to himself, he seemed to shake it off. He took a deep breath and adopted a serious look.

"What do you want to know?"

Liam had to fight to restrain his enthusiasm. Finally, someone was ready to give him some answers. Not wanting to appear too eager, he slowly sat forward, positioning himself on the edge of the cot and leaning forward. He was so excited he had to hold onto the side of the cot to prevent his hands from shaking.

There were so many things that he wanted to know. The hardest part was knowing where to begin. What should he ask first? Again, he had to reign in his excitement. He had to be careful here. One wrong question would most likely overwhelm Ben, putting an end to their discussion for the rest of the night.

"What is this place?" Liam asked. "Haven, I mean. What is it really?"

Ben breathed in slowly, as if he were about to dive headfirst into shallow waters. He obviously didn't want to be doing this, but he continued anyway.

"Haven is a refuge. A place where scientists, engineers, and scholars could come and work without censorship or restriction. Where they could pursue their work without having to live under the rules and interference of the Authority," he answered simply.

"But why? What is happening here that would require you to hide from the Authority?" Liam asked, hoping for clarification.

Rather than answering him directly, Ben said, "The Authority rose to power during a very controversial time in our history. You don't know anything about it because we made a conscious decision to hide those details from you. Anyway, the Authority has some very specific laws about what should and should not be done. We didn't agree. We found their laws to be both unjust and immoral. So, we came here, to Haven, to be free of the Authority's oppression."

Liam nodded his head. He didn't know anything about the Authority other than what he had heard so far. In fact, he had only learned of their existence earlier that day. The way everyone talked about them made it clear that they weren't a benevolent organization. In fact, everything he knew about them made them out to be the villain. He desperately wanted to know more, but he had other questions that needed to be answered first.

"Parker said something about the people in Haven experimenting with forbidden technologies. Something that had to do with me. What did she mean?" he asked.

Ben turned his attention to Parker. Had she been an ice cube, he would have melted her with the heat and anger of his stare. As it was, Liam was surprised that she didn't burst into flames right then and there. To her credit, she seemed to be unaffected by Ben's apparent disapproval and shrugged off his indignation.

In her mind, she hadn't done anything wrong, and she wasn't about to feel guilty about it. More than that, she wasn't going to let someone like Ben pass judgement on her.

Liam still didn't know where all this hatred between them had come from, but he figured now wasn't the time to ask.

After a minute or two, Ben turned his attention back to Liam.

"She shouldn't have said anything about that," he said, trying to explain. "The work that we do here is supposed to be a closely guarded secret. Our instructions are that we are not supposed to discuss it with you without first receiving approval from the Director."

"You mean Dr. Sorenson?" Liam guessed.

315

"You told him about Dr. Sorenson?" Ben said, directing his comments at Parker. Where he had been outraged with her lack of discretion before, he was now incredulous at her total lack of propriety.

"Don't look at me. Linda was the one that mentioned Dr. Sorenson," Parker said, declaring her innocence.

Ben scrunched his face together and started mumbling under his breath again. He was so flustered that his face was turning a bright red. Not wanting him to have a meltdown, Liam put up his hands, indicating that he wasn't going to press him with any more questions tonight.

While Ben was cooling down, Liam turned to Parker and asked, "Anything you wish to add?"

"I have already told you: You are special. So much more than you will ever know," she said honestly.

"Yeah, but how am I special?" Liam pressed.

"Well, for starters..." she began.

"Oh, no, you don't!" Ben blurted. "You may have done things your own way up until now, but that stops this instant. He is not ready for that."

"And why not?" Parker said. "Perhaps you have forgotten, but I don't answer to you."

"No, but you do answer to Dr. Sorenson," Ben countered. "You gave your word when you came here that you would abide by his rules and not reveal the true nature of the project. You may have flaunted some of our policies and procedures, but this one rule above all others, you will obey. Your oath demands it!"

Parker stood up and advanced toward Ben. The way she stormed over, it looked like she was preparing to hit him. He must have been thinking the same thing, because he took a step back, ready to defend himself.

She didn't hit him, though. She stood there, almost nose-to-nose with Ben. Her mouth opened as if she wanted to say something, but no words came out. She closed her mouth, only to open it again. Still, nothing came out. It was clear that she was trying to think of something to say, but the words weren't coming out.

Finally, Parker gave up on whatever it was that she wanted to say and turned around to rejoin Liam on the cot. She sat next to him, but there was something different about her – almost as if she had been defeated somehow. She lowered her head and refused to look at Liam or Ben.

Liam tried nudging her with his elbow, but she ignored him. He put an arm around her and asked if she was alright. She looked up at him, a sad look that was absolutely pitiful on her face.

"I can't," she said, practically on the point of tears.

"Can't what?" Liam asked, trying to comfort her.

"I cannot tell you...what I want to tell you. What you need to know. Ben is right. When I came here, I made a promise. A promise that I cannot break – not even for you," she said apologetically.

Liam pulled her close and held her in his arms. He felt bad for her. She really did want to tell him, but whatever it was, it wasn't her secret to tell. He tried to overlook the fact that since that secret pertained to him, he had every right to know, but he didn't want to press her too far, especially since she had given her word. A person was only as good as their word. If they couldn't live up to that, then there wasn't much that they could live up to.

"I am sorry, Liam," Ben said apologetically. He seemed to have regained his composure somewhat. "There are some things that we are not permitted to talk about."

"So, that's it, then? I have to be satisfied with not knowing?" Liam asked.

"For now, yes," Ben said sadly. "But once this issue with the federal agent has been handled, I will...I will take you to see Dr. Sorenson. He can give you the answers that you seek."

Parker pulled away from Liam and looked at Ben with utter shock and disbelief. He nodded, confirming the unasked question on her mind.

"You are right," he said to her. "He deserves to know."

"Why the sudden change of heart?" she asked curiously.

"My job, from the very beginning, has been to look after him. To keep him safe. Up until now, the best way to do that has been to keep him ignorant of what he truly is. Now, the circumstances have changed. He knows too much, but not enough.

"My job hasn't changed. I am still doing my best to look after him. He is my friend, after all. If that means that he needs to be told the truth, then that is what we shall do," Ben said matter-of-factly.

"That is great," Liam said as anticipation surged through him like an electrical current. "And this Dr. Sorenson can tell me what I want to know?"

"He is the Director of this project, and was the one that brought us all here. If anyone here can tell you what you want to know, it is him," Ben confirmed.

"Great. When do we go?" Liam asked

"When we get the All Clear signal. Until then, we wait," Ben said.

"Alright," Liam said, a little annoyed at having to wait, but still excited to know that his questions were eventually going to get answered. "In the meantime, do you mind if I ask you some more questions? Ones that you feel comfortable answering?"

Ben nodded and sat down on the floor in front of Liam. They spent the next hour going back and forth, Liam asking questions and

Ben answering as best as he could. Parker also managed to chime in from time to time. There was still much that Liam wasn't being told, but it was good to finally have an open conversation with his friends.

"So, you literally showed up so that you could be...what? My personal bodyguard?" Liam asked Ben after they'd finished talking about why everyone was deferring to him rather than to his parents or another adult.

"Not exactly," Ben said. "It really scared everyone when you went missing. I was already a part of the project back then, and it was decided that it would be best if I continued my work here, where I could keep an eye on you. Not spying on you or being your bodyguard. Just keeping you out of trouble."

"So, I was right. You were assigned to watch me."

"Assigned, yes, but it didn't take long for us to become friends. After a while, it wasn't an assignment anymore. I genuinely enjoyed spending time with you. I like to think that you enjoyed spending time with me too," Ben said. There was uncertainty in his voice at the end.

Liam wanted to confirm that Ben had been his closest friend over the years, but at the same time, he didn't want to give him the satisfaction. It hurt his feelings that Ben had been assigned to watch over him – a fact that had been hidden from him all these years. In the end, he chose not to say anything.

There wasn't much more to be said after that. Realizing that the conversation had come to an end, Ben stood up, walked over to a stack of supplies against the wall, and pulled out another sleeping cot. Rather than setting it up next to the cot that Liam was sitting on, he walked over to the far side of the room, setting it up against the wall near the stairs. He lay down and faced the wall.

Liam was about to say something, but before he could speak, Ben said, "It is late. We should get some rest. Hopefully, things will be resolved in the morning, and I can take you to see Dr. Sorenson."

With that, Ben reached up and flicked the light switch above his head. The overhead lights went out, but a desk lamp in the corner remained on. Liam was glad for the light being put out by the tiny lamp. There were no windows, and without that desk lamp, the whole room would have been engulfed in darkness.

Now that the lights were off, Liam realized how late it really was. He wasn't sure exactly what time it was, but he knew it was well past midnight. He suddenly felt so tired, but his mind was still racing about the promise of meeting Dr. Sorenson tomorrow. He would finally get some answers. That thought filled him with hope and anticipation, but his body was quickly succumbing to the exhaustion of the day's events.

Ben was barely visible across the room, but the soft sounds of snoring were already coming from his direction. How he had managed to fall asleep so quickly, Liam didn't know. Still, he was starting to feel sleepy too.

Parker must have been having the same thoughts, because she got up and signaled Liam to lie down. Once he was lying down, she walked over to a nearby crate and pulled out a green woolen blanket. She wrapped it around herself and came back over to him, nudging him to scoot over.

He did so, and as he did, she laid down next to him. She readjusted the blanket so that it covered both of them before curling up against him. She put her arms around his chest and held him closely. Liam was amazed at how lying there with her somehow felt...right.

It took some adjusting to keep Parker's hair out of his face, but once that was done, the two settled down to sleep.

Liam wasn't sure how long he managed to stay awake. He had wanted to enjoy the sensation of cuddling with Parker as long as possible, but sleep became more and more difficult to fight off. Eventually, he closed his eyes and fell asleep, dreaming of tomorrow and all of the possibilities that awaited him.

Chapter 14: A Different Cement Room

Agent Lewis slowly opened his eyes as he regained consciousness. Everything around him was blurry and unfocused. He tried blinking his eyes to dispel the blurriness, but that only helped so much. He was forced to wait while his eyesight slowly recovered from whatever had knocked him out.

He had a dull headache, which was making it hard to think. He tried focusing on where he was and how he'd gotten there, but he was having a hard time remembering. The last thing he could remember was running. Yes, he remembered running.

He concentrated on that one memory, desperate to recall as much of it as he could. He had been running, but not after someone; he had been running away from someone. Why had he been running away?

A small jolt of pain in the back of his head warned him that he was pressing too hard. Rather than forcing the memory to come back, Agent Lewis did his best to relax and let the memory flow back to him. He remembered running from a large group of people. There had been a fight; he had been scared. He...he had run into a building. He had been trapped, cornered like a caged animal.

He remembered standing inside a warehouse. He hadn't been alone. There had been a woman with him. She had been wearing a yellow coat. He'd handed her his stun pistol, and...

In a flash, it all came back to him. He remembered everything. He remembered investigating the town of Haven, running from a mob that wanted to capture him, taking refuge inside an old warehouse, and finally surrendering. Mostly, he remembered the look of the woman in the yellow parka as she'd pointed his own stun pistol at him and pulled the trigger.

So, this was what it was like to recover from a stun blast. He had heard people talk about the side effects of being stunned – drowsiness, memory loss, disorientation, and minor discomfort. Hearing about it and living through it were two completely different things.

The good news was that he was slowly coming out of it. His vision had cleared up, and he was able to make out some of the details around him. He had to squint, since a bright light was shining down on him from the ceiling, but he was able to get a good look at the room around him. He was surrounded by white-painted cement walls on all sides. There was a large two-way mirror directly in front of him and a plain metal door near the corner of the adjoining wall.

Agent Lewis focused his attention on the two-way mirror in front of him. At least, he assumed it was a two-way mirror. He had been in enough interrogation rooms to recognize one when he saw it. The more he looked around, the more confident he became that that was exactly where he was.

It made sense that he had been brought here after his capture. Undoubtedly, there were still plenty of questions that his captores wanted answers to. What better place to ask those questions than an official interrogation room? The fact that they even had an interrogation room said a lot about what kind of people he was dealing with.

If he had to guess, he had been brought here after being shot. It would have been easy for them, incapacitated like he was. More than that, it also meant that he would have no memory of where they were. For all he knew, this little cement room could be located anywhere in town, or even outside of town, for that matter. That uncertainty would make escape more difficult.

Looking around the room again, Agent Lewis noted that there were no windows. The room was illuminated by a series of fluorescent lights that hung from the ceiling, which meant that there was no way to tell whether it was day or night. If it was still night, then he needed to buy time for the retrieval teams to arrive. If it was already daytime, then he had bigger problems.

When he'd first regained his eyesight, he had noticed a metal table and chair positioned a few feet in front of him, but his eyes had been too blurry to make out any details. Now that his eyesight had improved, he noticed that the table was covered in various objects, all lined up in a row, like they were being displayed. Further examination revealed that the objects were the contents of his coat pockets – everything from the flashlight to the mobile relay, and even his stun pistol.

Instinctively, he reached out to grab his stun pistol, but was surprised when his hand didn't budge. Looking up, he was able to see that both his hands were restrained by a set of shackles that hung down from the ceiling, attached to a thick iron chain. It was the first time he'd realized that his arms were chained to the ceiling. For that matter, his feet were also shackled to the floor.

He tried pulling at his restraints, but both his hands and his feet were firmly secured by the shackles. With some effort, he could move his arms and legs a few inches in either direction, but not enough to do anything useful, which left him either standing there with some slack in the chains around his wrists or hanging from his wrists with some slack in the chains around his ankles. Neither position was comfortable, and even if they had given him a chair, he doubted whether he could sit down, tied up as he was.

His suspicion about the two-way mirror proved accurate. As soon as he had regained consciousness and started looking around, the door to the interrogation room opened. Standing in the open doorway was the same burly man he had seen back at the warehouse. He must have seen that Agent Lewis had regained consciousness and had come to begin the interrogation.

Judging from the man's size, he appeared to be a dock worker, or perhaps a warehouse worker. Whatever it was, he was definitely accustomed to lifting and moving heavy things, which meant that his presence could only mean one thing: this interrogation was going to be painful.

Preparing himself for the beating that was to come, Agent Lewis stood up straight, clenching his jaw in defiance. If they planned on using physical violence to get answers out of him, he was going to resist them as much as possible – not that he was in any condition to resist. He was still recovering from the beating he had received earlier, and the effects of the stun pistol hadn't fully worn off yet either.

Which was why it was a tremendous relief when the burly man stepped aside and the woman who had been wearing the yellow parka entered the room. The parka was gone now, replaced with a soft pink sweater over a pair of jeans. A self-satisfied smile showed on her face as she entered the room.

"That is enough for now, George. I will let you know if I need you," she said courteously to the burly man in the doorway.

She even made sure to pat the man on the shoulder as she passed him. The man she had called George gave her a warm smile, which quickly turned to a dirty look as he shifted his gaze back to Agent Lewis. He clearly didn't like the idea of leaving the woman alone with him, but he did as he was instructed.

The door slammed shut, leaving Agent Lewis and the woman, together again. "You aren't wearing your parka," Agent Lewis said, to break the tension.

The woman standing before him didn't answer. Instead, she focused on the items on the table in front of her.

"Too bad. I really liked the color yellow on you," he said, trying to get a reaction out of her. She favored him with a dubious sidelong glance before returning to her study of his belongings. Her hand reached out and picked up his badge and identification card.

"Agent Lewis. Unit Number 6, Department of Missing Persons, District 3, Bureau of the Federal Authority," she read aloud. "Hmmm. Says here that you have been a federal agent for...eleven years now. Still considered a rookie, by some standards," she said tauntingly.

"Alright, so now you know my name," Agent Lewis said. "Perhaps now you could tell me yours?"

The woman continued without answering his question. "Judging by your looks, you aren't exactly accustomed to working in the field, are you, Agent Lewis? No, you don't have to answer that. I think we all know that you have no business being this far outside the Boundary. I mean, just look at you. You were captured by a bunch of unarmed...what do you people call us? 'Strays?'" she said, adding a scornful edge to her voice when pronouncing the word "strays."

"Look, I don't see why we can't be civil," Agent Lewis said, ignoring her remarks the same way that she had ignored his. "Let's start again. My name is Lewis. I am a Federal Agent. And your name is..."

She still didn't answer. Instead, she busied herself looking him up and down like he was a puzzle that needed to be solved. Most people were simple that way. Once you knew where to start, they were pretty easy to figure out. The trouble was trying to figure out where to start.

She clearly wasn't sure about where to start with him, which gave him an advantage. He knew where to start with her. All he needed was to get her to divulge her name. After that, he could get to work learning as much as he could about who she was and what they were up to. If they planned on interrogating him, the least he could do would be to interrogate them right back – using different tactics, of course.

This meant that the two of them stood there staring at each other without saying a word. Was it awkward? Yes. Was it helpful? Absolutely. Silence was one of the best motivators to get people talking. Nobody liked uncomfortable silences. The trick was to endure the silence as long as possible in the hopes that the other person broke first.

After a minute or two passed, the woman turned her head to look back at the two-way mirror. She didn't say anything, and there was no sign that anyone was on the other side, but that didn't stop her from nodding as if she were receiving instructions. She then turned to face Agent Lewis again, her face adopting a resolute glare.

So, this is the best that they can do, Agent Lewis thought. Even her attempt at taunting him had been lazy and ineffective. It was clear that they had sent an amateur in to interrogate him, while the person in charge hid behind a mirror. Perhaps this interrogation wasn't going to be so bad after all.

Their attempt to put him on the defensive by taunting him about his lack of experience was a rookie mistake. Only a fool would allow themselves to be trapped that way. If they wanted answers, they would need to try harder than that.

Then again, it was possible that their clumsy attempt at upsetting him had been a different type of interrogation strategy. It was completely possible that they wanted him to think that they were incompetent. This could all be a ruse to make him overconfident. Overconfident suspects were much more likely to give up important information, especially when it made them feel superior to their captors or in control of the situation.

Agent Lewis was still trying to figure out which scenario he was in, when the woman replaced his badge and identification card on the table. She had moved down the line of his belongings, stopping at the stun pistol on the edge of the table. She reached down and picked it up.

"A standard-issue Mako model 11 stun pistol, equipped with auto-recharging core and reinforced muzzle, capable of producing a 100,000-volt discharge at the highest setting," she said as if reading the details from a catalog. "Tell me, Agent Lewis of the Bureau of the Federal Authority – how many people have you killed with this weapon of yours?"

"If you aren't going to tell me your name, then I am just going to have to come up with one," Agent Lewis said. "How about Mary? No, that doesn't sound right. Natalie? No, too old for that. Sarah, perhaps? Oh, I know: Persephone."

"Linda!" she said in a huff. "My name is Linda. Now if we can move along with my questions?"

"Linda. I should have known. It has been a while since I have met another Linda, but you have to admit, you fit the type perfectly," Agent Lewis said, reveling in his minor victory.

"Well, Linda, first of all, we don't say the Bureau of the Federal Authority. It is just the Federal Bureau, or simply the Bureau. You sound silly when you say the full name like that." He was pleased at the disgruntled look on the woman's face.

"I can shoot you again, you know," Linda said as she pointed the stun pistol at his chest.

Agent Lewis wasn't sure whether she was serious or not, so he decided to continue on the safe side.

"Secondly, that is not my primary service weapon, so I am not sure how many people have been...retired with it," he said, still doing his best to be as frustrating as possible without actually provoking her into shooting him.

"'Retired?' You mean killed," she clarified.

"We like to say retired. It sounds better," he retorted. "Thirdly, I never shoot to kill. My job is to recover missing persons –

strays, like you said earlier. I cannot recover a missing person if they are dead."

"Then how do you explain last night?" Linda snapped back.

With that, she struck a nerve with Agent Lewis. He remembered with crystal clarity the night before. He had practically begged that man to let him go, but he wouldn't listen. In order to escape, the agent had been forced to pull the trigger, shooting the man at close range and in the head. He knew before his finger had released the trigger what he had done.

"I already explained that," Agent Lewis said in a level tone, his previous carefree attitude now discarded. "I didn't want to shoot him, but he didn't give me a lot of options, now did he? It was self-defense, nothing more."

"Yeah, and good thing you shot him too. If you hadn't, you might have been captured, taken prisoner by the people you were trying to get away from," she said, gesturing at the room around them.

The irony wasn't lost on him. It was true that shooting that man hadn't changed the eventual outcome, but how could he have known that at the time? All he had known was that the best chance for escape was being held up by a complete stranger who refused to let go of his legs.

"I just wanted to get away," he said, lowering his head in shame. "I was scared, and he was the only thing standing between me and escape. I don't know if you can understand that or not, but I didn't have time to think about it. I...reacted, and someone died. If only he had let me go, I would have...I..." Agent Lewis slowly trailed off, still not lifting his head.

"This was the first time you ever killed someone, wasn't it?" Linda asked with a hint of compassion in her voice.

"Yes," Agent Lewis responded, looking up to meet her stare.

She stood there, looking down on him. In her eyes, he could see that she had figured out another piece to the puzzle. He wasn't the cold-blooded killer that she had made him out to be. He was simply someone who had gotten scared and acted irrationally – though it was clear that she didn't accept that as an excuse.

Minutes passed. Agent Lewis was content to stand in silence without saying anything. In his mind, every minute wasted here was another minute that brought the retrieval teams closer to his location. He just needed to hold on long enough for them to arrive.

"I make no excuse for what you did, but if it helps, I can understand why you did it," Linda said finally. "Fear is a powerful emotion. It can drive us to do things – things that we would never consider under normal circumstances."

She let out a heavy sigh before continuing. "Don't get me wrong. What you did was unforgivable, and you will be held accountable for it."

Her stern features softened briefly as she added, half to herself, "At least we can take solace in knowing that he died for a good cause."

"Oh, yeah, and what cause was that?" Agent Lewis asked.

"He died protecting this place and everything that it stands for," she said indignantly.

"I didn't realize this place was worth dying for," Agent Lewis said sarcastically. He was starting to regain some of his earlier impertinence. "Care to tell me what is so special about this place that a person would be willing to sacrifice their life for it?"

Rather than answering, Linda walked around to the front of the table and leaned up against it. She was within arm's reach, if he had been able to move his arms. She looked at him with her head tilted to one side, as if trying to figure the next piece to her puzzle. Whatever she was thinking, she must have come to a decision because she nodded, almost to herself, and turned toward the door.

She was walking away! Was this another strategy, or was the interrogation actually over? Agent Lewis struggled to figure out what his next move should be. He needed this interrogation of theirs to last as long as possible – anything to give him more time before the retrieval teams arrived. If that meant he needed to be more open and tell them everything they wanted to know, then so be it.

As she was leaving, Linda looked over her shoulder and casually said, "Tomorrow, the town council will meet to decide your fate. Since we cannot risk you reporting our position to the Authority, the choice will be either death, or permanent imprisonment. I will let you decide which is worse. Maybe if you are lucky, the council will let you decide."

"So, that's it?" Agent Lewis angrily called after her. "After everything is said and done, you are going to end up killing me or locking me up for the rest of my life?"

"What did you expect?" she said, turning around to face him. "We cannot allow you to return to your precious Boundary, and we cannot allow you to alert the Authority of our existence. What other options are there?"

"What is it with you people?" Agent Lewis demanded, rattling his shackles as if trying to pull free. "Why are you so afraid of me and the Authority finding out about this place?"

"Let me make one thing clear to you," she said, coming back to stand in front of him. "We are not afraid of you. You are nothing but a small, pathetic, excuse for a man that thinks it is alright to shoot first and think later. Nobody here is afraid of you anymore." She paused to take a breath and calm herself. "As for the Authority – well, we all know exactly what would happen if they ever found us."

"What would happen?" Agent Lewis asked, genuinely interested in the reason behind their paranoia. "If you are scared because the Authority is going to find out you are a bunch of Separatists, I can assure you that you have nothing to worry about.

The Authority no longer cares about that. Your movement is over. Let it go."

"'Separatists?'" Linda said, letting out a burst of uncontrolled laughter. "You think we are a bunch of Separatists? Oh, my gosh, if I had known that you were this stupid, I wouldn't have wasted my time." She shook her head at the ridiculousness of the accusation.

"If not Separatists, what are you?" Agent Lewis asked, not sure what to think anymore.

"I guess it doesn't really matter at this point, does it?" she said, knowing full well that by tomorrow evening, he would either be dead or condemned to live the rest of his life in a cement room just like this one. "Tell me, Agent Lewis, what do you know about the five Primary Directives?"

Agent Lewis gave her a rueful look. Of all the laws enforced by the Bureau, none were considered more important than the Primary Directives. Upholding those directives was the cornerstone upon which the Bureau had been built. They had even been referenced when he took his oath to the Authority when he became a federal agent.

Linda took his ruefulness as confirmation. She continued by saying, "Have you ever wondered whether the Primary Directives were...I don't know, wrong?"

Agent Lewis smirked at that. It wasn't the first time he had heard something like this. Plenty of strays who had been brought back by the Bureau had said something similar. Still, he wanted to play along. It was best if he could keep her talking.

"Wrong how?" he replied, wanting to see where this conversation was going.

"What if I were to say that they were both morally and ethically wrong? How would you respond to a statement like that?" she said probingly.

"The law is enacted by the will of the people and the power of the Authority. By definition, the law is both morally and ethically right. The Primary Directives foremost among them," Agent Lewis recited as if reading his old training manual.

"A perfect text book answer," Linda said, giving him a quiet clap. "If this were a test, you would get top marks. Now, tell me what you really think. Not what you were told to think, and not what they want you to believe, but what you actually think."

An interesting question, Agent Lewis thought. For the past eleven years, he had dedicated himself to upholding the law, but he had never actually stopped to think about it. To him, the law was simple: right and wrong.

One of the reasons why he had become a federal agent was because he liked the simplicity of the law. Before the Bureau, he had spent countless years of his life working as a forensic accountant. Much like the law, the numbers that he dealt with were simple, and they were either correct or incorrect. The difference was that crunching numbers hadn't made a difference in the world, but being an agent had accomplished something. He was making a difference.

And yet, now that he was thinking about it, he had to admit that the law was not always as simple as he pretended it was. His job was to track down missing persons, most of whom were dangerous either to themselves or to others. But not all of them were that way. There had been a few who were completely harmless – people who had simply grown tired of living under the Authority's jurisdiction and elected to leave.

Whether dangerous or harmless, under the scrutiny of the law, it didn't matter. All strays were treated the same, regardless of their reasons for leaving. Everyone who had been caught beyond the Boundary faced the same punishment: re-education.

In the past, Agent Lewis had considered re-education to be a merciful alternative to retirement. At least, he had before he had run into someone who had been re-educated. He remembered when she had first been brought back – so full of life and passion, pleading her case and begging for a reprieve. The dull stare of the person he had run into later was anything but full of life. It was as if someone had taken away the essence of life itself that had made her an individual and replaced it with a hollow emptiness.

At the time, Agent Lewis had justified the actions of the Authority by arguing that she had brought the punishment upon herself. Still, late at night when he couldn't sleep, he would remember her face, and those cold, empty eyes that looked back at him without truly seeing him. If ever there was a crack in his belief in the system, that was it.

"Well, now," Linda said, breaking his concentration. "There may be hope for you after all."

She must have been unaware of what he had been thinking, but she could see that something in his demeanor had changed. She must have suspected that her words had struck a chord with him. Why else had he grown quiet and speculative?

"Did you know that, there was once a time when it was generally believed that the law wasn't infallible? That it was possible for the lawmakers to make mistakes? When that happened, it was the duty of the people to stand up for what was right, regardless of the consequences," she said as if giving a speech.

When he didn't respond, she continued. "It was believed that if a law was unjust, immoral, or unethical, it had no power to bind the citizenry into obedience."

Again, Agent Lewis didn't offer a response. He had heard arguments like this before, though to be fair, she did offer up several valid points. What he was desperate to know was where this conversation was headed.

"Take, for example, Penal Code 643(J). A law, passed by frightened politicians, in an attempt to exert power over something that they couldn't control. Tell me, Agent Lewis, do you consider that a just or an unjust law?"

"The creation of artificial intelligence? What does that have to do with anything?" Agent Lewis asked curiously. Wherever this conversation had originally been headed, it had just taken an abrupt turn.

"Just or unjust?" she repeated.

Why was she asking him about an old law restricting the creation of artificial intelligence? He scrambled to figure out her motivations for asking such an absurd question. The harder he thought about it, the less sense it made to him. Eventually, he gave up trying to figure out what game she was playing and simply asked the only question that seemed important.

"Are you trying to confess something?" he said finally, wanting to cut through the hypothetical questions and get to the point.

"Perhaps," Linda said, disappointed that he'd refused to play along with her questioning. Still, she was willing to answer Agent Lewis's question. "What would you do if we had broken the law?"

"Depends on which law," he said.

"Hypothetically, what would you do if you found out that we had broken the Third Primary Directive?" she asked innocently.

Agent Lewis's eyes widened in surprise. Of all the Primary Directives she could have chosen, why that one? Had she merely chosen that one at random, or was she being serious? A much more terrifying thought occurred to him: What if this wasn't a hypothetical situation?

While his first reaction had been surprise, it had now moved to complete and total shock. This whole time, she had been trying to put the pieces of his puzzle together, not realizing that he was trying to do the same with her. If true, this latest bit of information represented the largest piece of the puzzle – the one that brought everything else together.

It would make sense, he thought. Why else would a highly organized, large group of people choose to live so far beyond the Boundary? Why would they go to such extremes to hide their presence from the Authority? Why would they be so afraid of what would happen if the Authority ever found out about them? The answer to all these questions could be explained by them breaking the Third Primary Directive.

Agent Lewis felt a wave of nausea pass over him. What she was suggesting shouldn't have been possible. No one – no one – had broken the Third Primary Directive since it had been put into place. Physically, it shouldn't even be possible.

Sure, there were some tall tales told around the water cooler about what would happen if the Third Primary Directive were ever broken, but no one ever took it seriously. Even if it was possible, why would anyone entertain such a crazy idea?

It was while he was thinking this that he suddenly realized how it was possible, and the implications of that thought were staggering. "You didn't do it, did you?" he asked, hoping against hope that he was jumping to conclusions.

Linda didn't answer, but her expression spoke volumes. She wore a smug, satisfied smile. She looked at him hanging there in chains, pleased that he had grasped the full extent of his situation.

"How could you do it? Don't you know what this means?" he asked, scandalized.

"Of course I do. Why else would we do it?"

"You're not Separatists. You are Anarchists!" Agent Lewis proclaimed.

As he spoke, Linda nodded and took a step away from him. This was the reaction that she had been waiting for. Everything up until now had been a pretense to disguise her true intention – to find out how he would react to this revelation. She had been stringing him along, telling him everything he had wanted to know, being an open book, all so she could get to this point. And now, she knew.

"Pity," she said disappointedly. "There was someone here that was holding out hope for you. It was obvious that you aren't a typical G-man. It was hoped that once you found out about what we were doing here, you would be sympathetic to our cause. Maybe then, you would be willing to share the details of your mission and perhaps help us out.

"Of course, I told them that it was a waste of time. I wanted to conduct a real interrogation, but instead, I was encouraged to carry on this charade. I mean, really? I practically spoon-fed you everything you wanted to know. You must have realized that nobody could have been that incompetent. Oh, well. It really is too bad, you know."

With that she turned away from him and walked back to the metal table. She reached down and replaced the stun pistol on the table where it had been before she picked it up. He hadn't noticed that she had been holding it the entire time. She straightened, looked into the two-way mirror, and shrugged, as if to say, "I told you so."

Now that she had gotten what she wanted, Agent Lewis was all-but-invisible to her. She practically ignored his presence, and instead focused on the rest of the items on the table. She went through them one by one, as if cataloging them for future use.

She stopped at the last item on the table. It was a small handheld device with an even smaller antenna poking out on top that he recognized immediately. It was now his turn to smile.

"What is this?" she asked, looking at the device in her hand rather than at Agent Lewis. "If I didn't know any better, I would swear that it is some kind of communication device."

"What, that? Oh, it is nothing important. Just a mobile relay," he said offhandedly.

"I have never heard of it before. What does it do?"

Normally, Agent Lewis wouldn't give her the satisfaction of an explanation – not after everything she had just put him through. However, it wasn't her satisfaction that he was thinking about right then, but his own. This was going to be sweet.

"Like you said, it is a mobile communications device," he explained. "It was developed by the Bureau several years ago. Its purpose is to link up directly with a mobile emitter. That way, we don't have to haul those bulky emitters with us whenever we go beyond the Boundary. You see, it broadcasts a signal directly to the emitter, which in turn can transmit directly to the Bureau, even in the most isolated of areas."

The woman's face seemed to grow pale. Agent Lewis's smile deepened as he continued. "Since I was traveling deep within the restricted zone, not to mention the surrounding mountains, it seemed prudent to bring along something that would allow me to keep in contact with the Bureau. Regardless of any...interference I might encounter."

"What kind of interference?" she asked hesitantly.

"Oh, you know, the usual," he said in a roguish way. "It cuts through static interference, radio jamming, dampening signals – things like that."

"And what about interference from cement reinforced walls?" she asked pointedly.

"Oh, that. Well, you don't have anything to worry about. In a cement room like this, I doubt you could get a signal out."

Linda practically slumped forward in relief. Agent Lewis couldn't be certain, but he suspected that she had been holding her breath while he was answering. She was so overcome with relief that she had to hold onto the back of the metal chair for support.

Now was the time for him to share a revelation of his own.

"No, it wouldn't work here, which is why it was a good thing I used it before coming to Haven."

His words hung in the air as the tension in the room began to rise. Linda was staring at him in open-mouthed astonishment – or perhaps it was terror.

"Yep. After my run-in with Liam and his girlfriend, Parker, I figured it would be a good idea to contact my superior and report my situation. It was a good thing I did, too, or else he wouldn't know what had happened to me or that I had discovered that there were people living up here.

"I have to say, he was just as surprised as I was. The good news is that he decided not to take any chances, and dispatched several retrieval teams to my last known location. Now, obviously, that would mean that they would be headed for Greenwood, except for the fact that I turned the relay on back in the warehouse.

"You see, it doesn't just transmit a signal to the emitter, but it also doubles as a homing device. So, the moment I turned it on, the Bureau was notified of my new location right here in Haven. I would have told you all about this back then, but someone shot me before I had a chance to explain. Now, who was that? Oh, yeah – it was you.

"Well, at least now you know that from the moment you shot me to the moment I entered this room, my location was being transmitted back to the Bureau. And I am sure that they will not be able to thank you enough for all your help in locating this place," Agent Lewis finished, grinning from ear to ear.

The look of shock on Linda's face was priceless. Panic enveloped her, and she turned to face the two-way mirror. In desperation, she started talking to whoever was on the other side of the mirror, though Agent Lewis could only hear her voice. He did manage to hear a name – Liam.

"Liam," he said, as if pondering a thought that had just occurred to him. "There was something strange about that kid that didn't make sense to me. I couldn't put my finger on it until you mentioned the Third Primary Directive. Of course, it makes perfect sense when you put it all together. His unique name, the way everyone I meet seems to be trying to protect him, not to mention his peculiar reaction to being shot by my stun pistol. You know, I was starting to suspect that he might be a—"

Whatever Agent Lewis was about to say was cut off as Linda turned from the two-way mirror and dashed across the room. Before he knew what was happening, her hands were around his throat, and she was squeezing with every ounce of strength she possessed. Flecks danced across his vision, and darkness began to creep in from all sides.

"How many are coming?" she screamed at him.

Agent Lewis would have responded, but with her hands closed around his windpipe, he was unable to speak. He did manage to splutter something unintelligible, but that only infuriated her even more.

"How long until they get here?" she screamed again, still not easing her grip on his throat. Agent Lewis's eyes felt like they were bulging out of their sockets. Out of the corner of his eye, he could see his own reflection in the mirror as his face slowly turned from red to purple. Even had he wanted to, he wouldn't be able to respond.

"Enough!" said a voice over the loudspeaker. It wasn't a harsh voice, but it had the sound of someone used to giving commands. And whoever they were, they fully expected to be obeyed.

The voice came again over the loudspeaker. "Linda, release him!" After a moment, a much gentler "Please" followed.

For a moment, Agent Lewis doubted whether she would comply, but then her fingers eased up from around his throat. After what seemed like an eternity – though in reality, it was probably only a few seconds – she released him. Her hands fell to her sides while Agent Lewis gasped for breath and did his best not to pass out.

When he had finally gotten enough air to stop the burning in his chest, he raised his head and looked Linda directly in the eyes. What he saw was hate – pure, unadulterated hate. And it was directed solely at him.

"W...well...Liii...nnda. Th...is ha...s beennnn fun. Weee sho...uld do iiiit agggain... sometiiiime." Agent Lewis struggled to say. His throat was sore, and every word burned as it came out.

Without wasting another moment, Linda turned around and ran toward the metal door in the corner. She pounded her fists against it until the bolt on the other side of the door was pulled back and the door opened. George stood there, stunned at the expression on Linda's face. She practically pushed him out of the way as she exited the room and ran down the adjoining hallway.

Looking back at Agent Lewis, George seemed to be at a complete loss for what to do. From down the hallway, the agent heard Linda's voice.

"We have to get to Liam! Now!" she yelled hysterically.

George didn't need to hear another word. Without a moment's hesitation, he slammed the door closed behind her. Through the door, Agent Lewis could hear him locking the door behind him before frantically sprinting off after Linda. He listened as their footsteps faded down the hallway and everything went silent.

He remained where he was, chained to the floor and ceiling, unable to move. After a few minutes, he tried calling out, but nobody answered him. There didn't even seem to be anybody behind the two-way mirror anymore, either.

He was now completely and totally alone.

Chapter 15: Discovery

Liam woke in the relative darkness of Ben's basement. The light from a single desk lamp was the only thing illuminating the room. He stared at it for a few seconds, trying to figure out what he was looking at. This wasn't his room, and that wasn't the lamp on his bedside table. He pushed up onto his elbow to get a better look.

The haziness of sleep was starting to fade, and he recognized his surroundings. This was Ben's basement, though he had chosen to call it a safe room. Liam remembered the events of the night before, including the part where he and Parker had fallen asleep in each other's arms. She was still there, lying next to him on the cot. Her eyes were closed, and she was still sleeping.

Ben was also asleep, snoring peacefully in his cot on the other side of the room. Liam reached up and rubbed his eyes with his free hand. He had no idea how long he had been asleep, but something had woken him up. Unfortunately, he didn't have a watch, and there weren't any clocks on the walls to let him know what time it was. For all he knew, it could be the early morning or even the late afternoon.

Given that both Parker and Ben were still asleep, he tended to believe that it was still early in the morning, which meant that there was still plenty of time to get some more sleep. With that in mind, he lowered himself back down onto the cot, turning onto his side so that he was facing Parker.

Despite his desire to fall back asleep, he couldn't help himself from staying awake and staring at her. She was so beautiful. He gazed at her in wonder, trying to figure out what had inspired a girl like her to care for someone like him. Sure, she had said that he was somehow special, but there had to be more to it than that – something deeper.

Liam was reminded again how graceful she was. Even while sleeping, she somehow appeared...picturesque – as if she were modeling for an artist who wanted to capture her sleeping form. The only thing spoiling the picture was a few loose strands of hair that had fallen down over her cheek.

To Liam, there was more to her beauty than mere looks. There was something special about her. Perhaps it was the way she talked, or how she listened to him, or possibly how she made him feel about himself. Whatever it was, he had noticed it from the moment he saw her, and that feeling had only grown stronger over the past few weeks together.

Being apart from her had been close to torture. Having her back in his life really did make a difference. She kept saying that he was special, but he felt that out of the two of them, she was the one who was truly special. In just a few short weeks, she had managed to turn his whole world upside down, for better or for worse.

It was true that he had initially resented her for trying to tell him the truth. He had run from her back in Greenwood because he'd refused to believe the things that she had been trying to tell him. It had been easier for him to believe that she was crazy than to face the truth behind all the lies that he had been told over the years.

In the end, she had been right all along. She was the only person who had cared enough about him to tell him the truth and encourage him to make his own decisions.

She cared for him, that much was clear. But was that all it was? Or was there more to it than that? Could it be that she actually loved him?

Liam shrugged off that thought immediately. He was still just a teenager, and didn't really know what love was. Oh, he had seen plenty of movies and read countless books where the main characters fell in love, but that wasn't real. Those were stories that were being told to entertain people, and who didn't love a happy ending?

Love had to be more than that. It had to be something that developed over time, and grew stronger with each passing day. Love had to be caring for someone, always wanting to be close to someone, and to be willing to do anything for someone, even when they annoyed you or upset you. If you could care for someone, even after they had disappointed you, then maybe that was love. And if that was true, he had to admit that he was in love with her.

The love he felt for her was unlike the love he felt for anyone else in his life. He loved his aunt, but that was because she was family. He had a crush on Dr. Adhira, but that was based more on fantasy than anything else. He loved Ben as a friend, of course. All of these represented a different type of love, and they were all different from the way he felt about Parker. She was more than his girlfriend; she had become his companion.

It was silly to think of it that way, but that was the best word for it. She had truly become his companion in ways that Ben never could have. Just thinking about it made him smile. Plus, it didn't hurt that she was incredibly attractive.

As Liam watched Parker sleep, he couldn't stop the urge to brush the strand of hair away from her face and tuck it behind her ear. He tried being as gentle as possible so as not to wake her, but she opened her eyes at the slightest touch of his hand. A smile appeared on her face as she gazed back at him.

"Sorry," he said in a near-whisper. "I didn't mean to wake you."

Parker nodded slightly, accepting his apology. Her hand came up and stifled a yawn. Liam had always heard that yawns were contagious, and to prove it, he let out one of his own.

By the time he finished, Parker was stretching out on the cot beside him. Her arms were stretched as far over her head as they could go and her back arched forward as she pointed her toes down. When she was done, she settled back down, wrapping Liam in a warm embrace.

"Couldn't you sleep?" she asked in a near-whisper.

"I slept fine," Liam whispered back. "Something woke me up, but I was trying to fall back asleep when I..." He trailed off, not knowing how to finish that sentence. How did you tell a girl that you didn't go back to sleep because you were watching her sleep without sounding like a creep?

"Anyway, I noticed that you had some hair in your face, and I wanted to get it out of your way," he finished lamely.

"How thoughtful of you," she said, smiling. She moved even closer to him, if that were possible – so much so that their noses were practically touching. Sensing that this was perhaps an invitation on her part, Liam leaned forward and kissed her. She returned the kiss with one of her own.

They lay there together, wrapped in each other's arms, sharing a passionate kiss. Her skin was so soft, and her body was so warm. It felt good having her press up against him like that. He...

Liam opened his eyes with sudden alarm. He was starting to get that familiar feeling that he typically got in the mornings. Embarrassed, he tried pulling away from Parker.

"What's wrong?" she asked, confused.

"Oh, it's nothing," Liam mumbled, "It's just that...well, um...I really..." He couldn't bring himself to say it out loud. One of the side effects of being a teenage boy was the occasional embarrassing moment.

He tried to pull away a little further, but Parker put her hand on his chest and urged him to stay where he was. "What is it?" she

asked with genuine concern. "If there is something wrong, I can…"
She stopped talking as she felt what the problem was. Being this
close to one another, it was hard to miss.

Liam wondered whether it was possible to die from
embarrassment. He tried to explain, but Parker stopped him by
putting a finger to his lips. Rather than being put off, she seemed
almost excited at the situation. She leaned forward, putting her
mouth next to his ear and whispered, "It's okay. It is supposed to do
that when you are in bed with a girl."

She grinned at him with a mischievous glint in her eye. She
pulled the blanket up over their heads as they continued kissing.

Just then, an explosion shook the house, startling everyone in
the room. The blanket flew off as both Liam and Parker sat up, trying
to figure out what had happened. Ben was on his feet in a flash,
looking around in every direction, trying to determine where the
sound had come from.

When it was clear that the explosion hadn't struck the house,
Ben relaxed a little. He was still concerned, but there was no
immediate danger. It was at this point that he noticed Liam and
Parker, still sitting on the cot together. He opened his mouth as if to
say something, but before he could get any words out, another
explosion shook the house. The force of the blast was so strong that
dust from the ceiling rained down on them from above. As the room
shook, Liam wondered how sturdy this safe room really was. The last
thing he wanted was for the house above to cave in on them.

A third blast hit, closer than all the others, and Ben was
knocked to the floor. He tripped backwards on his cot and fell behind
it, disappearing out of sight. Liam and Parker were also knocked to
the floor as their cot overturned. Liam's first instinct was to reach
out for Parker so that he could try to protect her, but she beat him to
it. Before he knew what had happened, she was cradling him as they
lay on the floor together, doing her best to protect him from any
potential danger.

Seconds passed, then minutes. Liam kept waiting for another explosion, but it never came. After a while, it seemed that whatever had been causing the explosions had stopped. Still, Ben made it a point to hustle them all into a nearby corner for safety.

They waited. Nothing happened. Ben finally got up and made his way over to the metal box against the wall that held the phone. He picked up the receiver and pressed it to his ear while flipping the switch. The light turned green, but nobody was answering on the other end. He stood there, phone pressed to his ear, waiting for someone to pick up.

After a minute, Liam heard a panicked voice.

"What—" Ben started to say before he was cut off by the speaker on the other end of the phone. Judging by the deep voice, it was his father.

"Agents...everywhere...attacking...zzzz...downtown is...moving in...zzzz...direction."

"Calm down!" Ben yelled into the phone. "There is no reason why they should be heading in our direction. The point of this safe room is that nobody would look for it in a place like this. Now, if you will—"

Ben was cut off again by the speaker on the other end, only this time, Liam couldn't hear what was being said.

"What do you mean, they are amassing in front of the house? That isn't the protocol I established," Ben all-but yelled into the phone. After listening to the person on the other end of the phone for a few seconds, he continued. "I don't care whether they are concerned for his safety or not. By gathering outside, they are painting a target on our location. Don't they understand? They will lead the Authority right to us!"

The implication of what he was saying slowly sank in as Liam huddled there in the corner. The night before, a crowd had gathered outside Ben's house before he'd shooed them away. It seemed that with all of the explosions going on outside, the crowd had reformed in front of his house. No doubt, they were worried about Liam's safety, but the unfortunate side effect was that they were singling out the house by gathering there.

"I don't care what you do, just get them to leave! Do it now, while there is still time...No, you don't have to go...if they are headed in our direction...don't risk yourself unnecessarily...Alright, it is your decision," Ben said before finishing his conversation and replacing the phone back in its box.

"I think we will be alright. There are more agents in Haven, though I suspect that they are members of a retrieval team. They are attacking downtown, and have blown up a few nearby houses, but it doesn't seem like they know where we are," he tried to say confidently.

"Except that those idiots upstairs are giving away our position," Parker pointed out.

"Maybe, maybe not," Ben said. "I ordered them to disperse. Hopefully, they do before the Authority figures out what is going on."

Just then, a crackling sound could be heard off in the distance. The sound repeated over and over again, slowly growing louder each time. It was hard to tell how far away the crackling noise was, since they were in a cement room underground, but the sounds were getting louder – which most likely meant that they were moving in this direction.

"What is that?" Liam asked nervously.

"Pulse rifles," Ben said. "And they are moving in our direction."

"Our location has been compromised," Parker shouted.

"Possibly. But there is no way that they'll know we are hiding down here. Even if they storm the house, there is a good chance that we will go unnoticed. For now, we need to—" Ben stopped abruptly, putting a hand up to call for silence. Liam and Parker stood there, not saying a word. The crackling sound was so loud, it must have been right outside the house.

There was also another sound that could be heard faintly: people were screaming.

Ben rushed over to some nearby crates against the wall. He threw several crates off to the side, determined to reach the crate on the bottom of the pile. Once he reached the one he was looking for, he grabbed it with both arms and pulled it out to the center of the room.

The crate was a rectangular wooden box, painted green, with the words *STATIC DISRUPTOR* written on the side in white paint. As Liam was trying to figure out what "static disruptor" meant, Ben threw open the lid and reached inside. In his hands was a rifle unlike anything Liam had ever seen before.

Liam had watched plenty of movies over the years, so he knew what a rifle was supposed to look like. The thing in Ben's hands looked like something out of science fiction. It was long, with a wooden stock and a thick metal barrel that ended in a bulbous electrode. There was something that looked like a small satellite dish encircling the electrode, pointing outward. All in all, it was the strangest weapon Liam had ever seen.

Ben's hand reached down to the side of the weapon, where a small wood-handled crank stuck out the side. Placing the butt-end of the rifle on the floor, he started cranking as fast as he could. A gauge above the crank turned colors from red to yellow, then finally to green.

By this time, the crackling sound was right on top of them. From the sound of it, they were on Ben's front lawn. It wasn't a single crackling sound, but several, all going off at once. Just then, there was a small explosion somewhere in the house above. Everyone in the basement stopped what they were doing and looked up at the ceiling with concern.

If only they could see what was going on, they could try to do something to help. Unfortunately, there wasn't anything that they could do, so they were forced to stand there and listen without the slightest idea of what was really going on upstairs. There was the sound of heavy boots running through the house. They echoed on the ceiling above, followed closely by someone screaming.

Liam recognized the screaming voice immediately. "That's your mom!" he said, trying to make his way to the stairs. Both Ben and Parker had to hold him back.

"Be quiet," Parker pleaded, and Ben put his finger to his lips in agreement.

The screaming continued, followed by the sound of plates hitting the floor and furniture being turned over. Someone was shouting in a harsh voice, but the words were unintelligible. There was another scream, followed by a loud crackling sound. Less than a second later, an audible thud struck the floor overhead.

Something bad had just happened to Ben's mom.

Within seconds, Ben's dad could be heard shouting as well. It sounded like there was a struggle going on upstairs, but the struggle ended as the crackling sound repeated again. Once again, there was a loud thud hitting the floor.

After that, there was silence. Liam wanted to say something, to do something, but Parker's hand on his arm held him back.

They could now hear heavy boots walking across the floor above their heads. Liam counted three, maybe four different sets of boots working their way through the house above. They must have been searching the house, because their footsteps could be heard in every room upstairs. *What will happen if they find the trap door*? he wondered.

He glanced up at the trapdoor at the top of the stairs. He remembered hearing Ben's father placing several boxes over the trapdoor to hide its existence, but he couldn't be sure if they were still there. If they were, then the chances of them being discovered were practically zero. After all, Liam had been coming to this house almost every day for the past seven years, and he had never discovered any trap doors until yesterday.

Parker grabbed Liam's hand and held on tightly. Whether she needed comforting or whether she was trying to comfort him, he couldn't tell. He looked back at her and tried to give her a reassuring smile. He wanted to tell her that everything was going to be alright, but honestly, he wasn't sure what was going to happen. All he knew was that he was scared – more scared than he had been since that expedition into the mine seven years ago.

He wanted to put on a brave face for Parker's benefit, but he was having a hard time doing it. Whatever was happening upstairs, it wasn't good. Even if the three of them went undetected, there was still the issue of what had happened to Ben's parents.

Footsteps entered the bedroom above the stairs. Liam held his breath, not even daring to risk the sound of breathing. The footsteps moved back and forth throughout the room, but they didn't approach the closet where the trap door was located. He was starting to feel hopeful that maybe whoever was up there would leave without finding anything.

That was, until the silence was shattered by the sound of breaking glass.

Both Liam and Ben turned around slowly, searching for the source of the noise. Their eyes focused on Parker. Under her back foot, there was a crushed lightbulb. It must have fallen out of one of the crates that Ben had thrown aside while pulling out his rifle. The look on her face said that she hadn't realized it was there before she'd stepped on it.

In unison, all three of them turned back to look at the trapdoor at the top of the stairs. The footsteps overhead had stopped, and the whole house had gone quiet.

Without warning, a loud crackling sound broke the silence. A small hole appeared in the trapdoor, as if someone had managed to burn a hole through the floor. This was followed by half a dozen more crackling blasts that riddled the ceiling with holes.

Liam, Ben and Parker all moved back away from the stairs, retreating to a safe distance. Whatever weapon they were using to poke holes in the trapdoor, it was powerful enough to burn through solid metal. Glass crunched under their feet as they backed up against the far wall – not that it mattered anymore. Whoever was upstairs, they already knew that someone was hiding down there.

The sounds of more boots thundered overhead as more people crowded into the bedroom above. Based on the sounds coming from above, the closet doors must have been yanked off their hinges and thrown to the side. Next came the sound of boxes being pushed aside, followed by an unfamiliar voice yelling, "There is a door here!"

Ben raced forward, positioning himself behind a support pillar at the base of the stairs. He brought the rifle up to his shoulder and aimed it at the trapdoor. He sat there, waiting for the inevitable as boots began to pound on the trapdoor, trying to bash it in.

Even though it was riddled with holes, the trapdoor refused to give way under the barrage of boots. Liam watched as the trapdoor shook and trembled with each blow, but still refused to open.

The constant thudding of boot heels stopped, replaced immediately by another flurry of crackling blasts. The trap door was practically torn to pieces.

"Whatever happens, stay behind me!" Ben yelled back at Liam. "We only need to hold them off until help can arrive."

The sound of his voice caught the attention of the people upstairs. The crackling sound stopped as they stopped firing long enough to listen to what was going on in the basement. By this time, the area surrounding the trapdoor was clouded with smoke. As it began to clear, Liam could see pieces and fragments of the trapdoor still in place, though barely holding together.

Someone above gave a final kick, and what remained of the trapdoor broke free from its hinges and fell down the stairs into the basement. Without waiting another second, Ben aimed up at the opening where the trapdoor had been and pulled the trigger. There was a faint flash, accompanied by a buzzing sound.

Yells broke out from up the stairs, but Liam couldn't tell if anyone up there had been hit by Ben's attack. It was possible that he had fired up into the gap without aiming at anyone in particular, or perhaps he had struck his desired target. Liam didn't know which was the case, but he hoped for their sakes that Ben knew what he was doing.

Without wasting a single second, Ben lowered the rifle and cranked furiously on the wooden handle until the gauge turned green. Once the rifle had been fully recharged, he raised it back up to his shoulder and fired another shot. The room lit up as he pulled the trigger, accompanied by a loud buzzing sound.

Ben lowered the rifle to crank it again. Apparently, he had to do this after every shot.

Right as he finished cranking and was bringing it back up to his shoulder, a small object, the size of a hockey puck, rolled down the stairs. It reached the bottom and rolled to a stop right in front of him.

Liam watched as Ben looked down at the puck and then up at him. There was a look of alarm in his eyes, and he opened his mouth to shout something.

Before he could get the words out, a bright light filled the room, accompanied by a deafening roar.

Liam lost his balance and fell to the floor as he was instantly blinded by the flash. His ears were ringing, and everything he heard sounded muffled.

When his vision began to clear, he noticed that both Ben and Parker were also on the ground. Parker was rubbing her eyes and Ben was shaking his head as if to clear away the disorientation. He was lying on his back a few feet away from where Liam was. His hand still gripped the rifle firmly. He tried to sit up, but was having problems. Parker was also having difficulties. She had raised herself up to her hands and knees, but was too unstable to stand up on her own.

Through the dull ringing in his ears, Liam was still able to make out the sound of people rushing down the stairs. He turned as a man dressed all in black and wearing tactical gear that included a helmet with a see-through visor came down the stairs with a strange-looking rifle in his arms.

Ben must have noticed him too, because he tried to lift the rifle to aim it at the newcomer. The rifle never made it more than a few inches off the ground before a booted foot stamped it back down, crushing Ben's hand in the process. With his foot still pressing down on the rifle, the man in tactical gear loomed over Ben, who, by this point, was completely defenseless.

The man standing over Ben was the most intimidating figure Liam had ever seen. Never before in his life had he encountered someone so...frightening. That was the only word to describe it. It wasn't just how he was dressed or the fact that he held a rifle pointed at Ben's chest. The look on his face was murderous to say the least.

Liam watched as the man standing over Ben continued to point his rifle down at his friend's chest. Without saying a word, the man pulled the trigger. There was a bright flash of blue light, and a loud crackling sound filled the room.

Liam watched in horror as a jet of bright blue electricity collided with Ben's chest. He tried to call out, but his words were swallowed by the crackling sound of the man's rifle and the ringing that still filled his ears. Lying there on the floor, he was helpless to stop what was happening right in front of his eyes. Everything seemed to be happening in slow motion, and he was unable to look away.

Ben's body jerked with the force of the blast as it hit him. Less than a second later, his body went limp. His head fell backwards, hitting the floor with a dull thud, lifeless. The light from the rifle's blast faded, as well as the crackling sound.

As the sound dissipated, Liam could hear someone screaming. He was shocked to realize it was him. He was screaming in frustration, anger, sadness, and rage. His best friend had just been shot in front of him, and there was nothing that he could have done to stop it. All he could do was lie there and watch as Ben's lifeless body stared up at the ceiling without seeing.

Liam tried to reach a hand out toward Ben, but his attempt was met with a blow to the side of his face. A second person, dressed the same as the first, had entered the basement and was standing over him. Rolling onto his back, he stared up at the person standing over him as they pointed a rifle at his chest. Any second now, he expected the person standing over him to pull the trigger, just like they had done with Ben. But that moment didn't come.

The person standing over him turned out to be a woman, and she didn't appear to be as eager to end his life as her companion had been. She contented herself with reaching down and grabbing Liam's arm, forcing him to flip over onto his stomach. His arms were pulled back behind him, and he felt a restraint close around his wrists.

Where time had slowed down while watching Ben get shot, it now seemed to be speeding up to make up for it. Liam found himself lying on his stomach, hands restrained behind him, while the woman dug her knee into his back and searched his pockets. At no point had it occurred to him to try to resist her, which was probably for the best, given what had happened to Ben.

"Leave him to me," the other man said. "You go handle the girl."

The woman immediately complied, lifting herself off of Liam's back and moving toward Parker, who still hadn't managed to get to her feet, and so it was no surprise when she was easily subdued. Liam watched as she was pushed to the floor, her hands restrained behind her back just like him.

Liam was left to lay there on the floor, unable to move more than a few inches in either direction. The only thing he could do was watch everything else that was happening. His eyes kept drifting back to Ben a few feet away.

The man who had shot Ben was still standing over him, admiring his handiwork. Liam tried not to look at him, focusing his attention on Ben instead. His body was lying there, unmoving. A small tendril of smoke rose from where he had been struck by the rifle's blast.

"Ben?" Liam asked, concern and worry causing his voice to crack as he spoke. When his friend didn't respond, he called out again. "Ben?"

Ben wasn't moving. Fear was starting to overwhelm Liam – fear of what had happened to his best friend. Agent Lewis had mentioned something about his stun pistol only immobilizing someone before he had used it on Liam. Perhaps that was what had happened to Ben. It was possible that he was simply immobilized.

"Ben, you need to look at me," Liam pleaded. "Look at me and let me know that you are okay. Just...just look at me so that I know that you will be alright."

Tears were streaming down his face. He kept pleading for his friend to look at him, but no matter what he said, Ben didn't move. His eyes continued to stare straight up at the ceiling, unblinking.

"You are going to be alright," Liam said as much to himself as to Ben. "You've been immobilized. That's all. It should wear off any minute now. Once you wake up, everything will be alright. Everything will go back to the way it was – you'll see. Late nights reading comic books, early morning breakfasts at the café, and all of the double features at the movies that we want. Just you and me, like it used to be."

He realized he was rambling. More than anything, he just wanted his friend to wake up. He wanted to be able to tell him how sorry he was. How no matter what had happened recently to drive a wedge into their friendship, it didn't matter. How Ben was his best friend, and nothing would ever change that. If only he would wake up.

"He ain't waking up, kid," the man standing over Ben said in an obnoxious tone. "He ain't never waking up again."

To suit his words, the man kicked the rifle out of Ben's hand and followed it with another kick to his side. He didn't react. His body lay there, motionless and completely devoid of life.

"You see?" the man said, turning his attention to Liam. "So, you might as well shut up about it."

Before Liam knew what was happening, the man had walked over and kicked him in the side. He gasped for air, trying to draw breath into his lungs. Luckily, his burn was on the other side, or else, he would be in real pain rather than just having the air knocked out of him.

"Blue team to convoy. Come in, convoy." the man said, speaking into a radio holstered on his tactical vest.

"Roger that, Sergeant, we are receiving you," a voice replied over the radio.

"The threat has been eliminated at our location," the sergeant continued, scowling down at Liam. "Confirm, we have two captives in our possession, ready for extraction."

"Confirmed, Sergeant. Moving to your location in ten," the voice said before signing off.

As his radio conversation came to an end, the sergeant knelt down on top of Liam, digging a knee into his back. Rough hands began searching him. He tried to squirm away, but received a slap on the back of the head, followed by an admonishment not to do anything stupid.

Liam tried to focus on something else. Not wanting to look at Ben's lifeless body, he turned his head to stare in Parker's direction. Much like him, she was on her stomach, with the female trooper kneeling over her. She too was being searched, though it appeared that the female trooper was being much gentler with her than the sergeant was being with him.

"Are you okay?" Liam asked in a tone slightly louder than a whisper when Parker met his gaze. He must not have spoken quietly enough, because the sergeant got to his feet and delivered another kick to his side.

"Be quiet, scum," the sergeant said in a gruff voice that made it abundantly clear what he thought of Liam at that moment.

Liam winced at the pain of a second kick to the side, but kept his mouth shut. He figured that the sergeant was toying with him, looking for an excuse to kick him again. He wasn't going to give him the opportunity – not if he could help it.

"Sergeant!" the female trooper called out in alarm. "I got something."

"What is it, Corporal?" the sergeant said, stepping over Liam to stand beside Parker and the other trooper. From Parker's waistband, the corporal pulled out a stun pistol. It was the same stun pistol that had been taken from Agent Lewis back in Greenwood. Up until now, Liam had forgotten that she still had it.

In all the commotion of last night and this morning, Liam hadn't realized that she had held onto it – though, if she had had the stun pistol on her this entire time, why hadn't she used it before now? Surely it would have been much more effective than the crank rifle that Ben had been using. Then again, after seeing what had happened to him, Liam was glad that she hadn't tried using it.

Liam watched as the sergeant bent down and took the stun pistol from the corporal's outstretched hand. He turned it over in his hands, studying it intently. Whatever he was looking for, he apparently found it, because he directed a scowl down at Parker.

"A federally issued stun pistol. Now, I wonder where you would have gotten this?" he said without expecting a response.

The sergeant stood up, looming over Parker in the same way that he had been looming over Ben right before he had shot him. Liam knew that something bad was about to happen, but he didn't expect the sergeant to kick Parker as hard as he could in the side. She recoiled in pain as the sergeant's boot made contact, causing her to gasp for breath in between whimpers of pain.

"Where did you get this?" the sergeant asked in a calm voice that didn't match his demeanor.

Parker didn't answer, mostly because she was still too busy trying to catch her breath. It was obvious that she was trying to say something, but she couldn't quite get it out. The sergeant, more intent on inflicting pain than getting answers to his questions, took her inability to speak as an act of defiance. A second kick connected with Parker's side, right below the ribs.

Liam didn't need to see the reaction on Parker's face to know that she was in pain. The sound of the sergeant's boot making contact with hers side made him nauseous just hearing it. It was like a dull thud, like when one was beating the dust out of a rug or dropping a leather-bound book on a table.

Parker was practically doubled up in pain as the sergeant continued to loom over her. No doubt she would have tried to curl up into a ball for protection, but the corporal was still standing over her, holding her in place. From his position on the floor several feet away, all Liam could do was watch, helpless.

"I am going to ask you one more time. Where did you get this?" the sergeant said, holding the pistol in his outstretched hand. The way he was speaking was so devoid of emotion that it was completely out of place for the situation. It was almost as if he was having an ordinary conversation over dinner, rather than beating a teenage girl who was lying defenseless at his feet.

Parker's teeth were clenched in pain. Even if she'd wanted to, she couldn't have answered. The sergeant merely sighed in disappointment and knelt down beside her. He set the pistol on the ground and ran a hand through Parker's hair. At first, the gesture seemed compassionate, but then the sergeant tightened his grip and wrenched her head up to look at him.

With one hand clenching Parker's hair, the other hand cocked back into a fist. In rapid succession, the sergeant punched her in the face several times. Liam called out for him to stop, but the sergeant ignored him. He seemed determined to inflict as much pain as possible until he got the answer he was looking for.

Meanwhile, Parker had been practically beaten senseless. Her eyes were rolling back in her head, and she appeared dazed from the senseless beating. The sergeant shook his head in exasperation before releasing Parker's hair. Liam hoped that the sergeant was finished with his interrogation, but his hopes were quickly dashed.

Lifting Parker's chin, the sergeant punched her one final time as hard as he could. Parker's body went limp, and she dropped to the floor, unconscious.

Liam couldn't stand it anymore. "Stop it!" he yelled at the troopers. "Leave her alone."

As the words left Liam's mouth, he realized what he had just done. He was now the primary focus of the sergeant's attention, and there were still questions that he wanted answered. It didn't matter.

He would gladly take a beating if it meant that they left Parker alone. He couldn't lay there doing nothing any longer. If receiving his own beating was the price that he had to pay to spare Parker any more pain, than that was what he was willing to do.

Rather than taking out his frustrations on Liam, the sergeant regarded him with a serious look. He glanced from Parker, who was still unconscious at his feet, back to Liam. Apparently, he had other plans for getting Liam's cooperation. He picked up the stun pistol from where he had left it on the floor and casually placed it against Parker's temple.

"Do you know what will happen if I pull this trigger?" the sergeant asked menacingly. Liam had no idea, but given his own reaction to being shot with that thing, he didn't want to think about what it would do to her. The sergeant shook his head and whistled. "Messy. Real messy."

The way the sergeant had said "Messy" made Liam realize the full extent of what he was threatening to do. Much like with Ben, he was fully prepared to kill Parker without a moment's hesitation. The sergeant hadn't shown any reservations up until now, and there was no reason to think that he would start anytime soon.

Liam's mind raced. He would do anything to stop what was about to happen; however, if he told the truth, especially the part about beating a federal agent with a metal pipe, then the sergeant might decide to execute them both anyway. He had to think of something, and fast.

"I am going to count to three," the sergeant warned without breaking eye contact with Liam. "If you don't tell me what I want to know by the time I finish counting..."

To emphasize his threat, the sergeant pushed the end of the stun pistol even harder against Parker's temple. It was clear what he meant; Liam either had to tell him what he wanted to hear, or he would watch her die as well.

Without waiting, the sergeant began the countdown. He had already reached two, and Liam still didn't know what to say. He couldn't let this happen, so before the sergeant reached three, he blurted out the first thing that came to his mind.

"We found it!" he heard himself shout. The desperation in his voice was loud and clear. Judging by the sergeant's reaction, he didn't believe a word of it. He pushed the stun pistol harder against Parker's head and tightened his finger around the trigger.

"Stop! Please! Whatever you want to know, I will tell you. Please, don't hurt her," Liam begged. Tears were rolling down his face. He had just lost his best friend; he couldn't stomach the thought of losing Parker as well.

"Tell me where you got the stun pistol," the sergeant demanded.

Liam had no choice; he told the sergeant everything that had happened leading up to Parker getting her hands on the stun pistol. He explained how they had run into Agent Lewis back in Greenwood, how he had tried to arrest them, and how they had run away. He made it a point to leave out the part where Parker had taken the pistol after beating the agent with a length of pipe that she had found. No need to give the sergeant an excuse.

Whatever the sergeant thought of the story, he did seem to ease up. The pistol was still pointed at Parker's head, but it was no longer digging into her temple. He knelt there, listening to Liam's story without showing any outward emotion. He must have sensed that Liam was telling the truth, but his question had still gone unanswered.

"What you are telling me is that agent Number 6 tried to arrest you, ended up chasing you, and then suddenly had a change of heart and decided to hand you his service weapon? Just like that?" the sergeant said dubiously.

"What? No. No, he didn't hand us his stun pistol," Liam said, confused.

"Then how is it that it ended up in your possession?"

"We took it," Liam explained. It was at this moment that he needed to bend the truth. He just hoped that the sergeant believed him. "Agent Lewis – Number 6, as you called him – he tripped while chasing after us. The pistol fell from his hand, and we grabbed it and ran away."

Liam resisted the urge to hold his breath in anticipation. That would have given away the lie. Right now, he needed to keep his voice steady and his features under control. Most of all, he needed the sergeant to believe him, for both his sake and Parker's.

"Number 6 managed to submit a report to the Bureau before he disappeared. He mentioned running into a couple of teenagers. I guess this means he was talking about you two," the sergeant said in a mild voice. "Funny thing is, he said that he was attacked and that the people that attacked him stole his weapon. Didn't seem to mention anything about tripping."

This was a test; Liam was sure of it. The sergeant was challenging his story. If he buckled now, it would be over for both him and Parker. The only thing he could do was stick to his version of events.

"I don't know what he reported to you all, but he tripped and dropped his weapon. He was probably too embarrassed to tell the truth in his report. Wouldn't you be if something like that happened to you?" Liam said, sticking to his lie.

The sergeant stared at him for a long while, trying to discern what had actually happened. In the end, he seemed to agree with Liam's version of events. He lowered the pistol from Parker's head and turned to address the corporal who was crouching down next to him.

"I knew it had to be something like that," the sergeant said, addressing the corporal. "Have you ever met Number 6 before? Pathetic excuse for an agent. Always stays in his office up there on the fifth floor. The way I heard it, this was his first time out in the field. Makes sense he would screw it up and try to cover for his incompetence."

The corporal nodded, though it was unclear whether it was in acknowledgement or agreement. "At least he was right about this place. Who would have thought? A place like this outside of the Boundary. If he is still alive, the Administrator will most likely give him a medal for this," the corporal said.

"If we ever find him," the sergeant said in a tone that showed that he didn't care whether they found him or not. "If we do find him, the Admin is more likely to kick his ass than to pin a medal to his chest. Don't you worry, though – there will be plenty of medals being handed out once this is all over."

The corporal nodded again. "Well, what do we do now? Number 6 certainly isn't here," she said to the sergeant, gesturing around at the cement room.

The sergeant stood up and looked down at both Liam and Parker. "It would save us a lot of paperwork to simply put them down right now, like their chubby little friend there," he said, looking over at Ben's lifeless body.

"Sir?" the corporal asked hesitantly.

"Relax, Corporal. I said that it would save us a lot of paperwork, not that we were going to do it. We will do this by the book."

As he finished speaking, the sergeant walked over to where Liam was still lying on the floor. He reached down with one arm and grabbed onto the back of his shirt. With a single jerk, he yanked Liam off the floor and forced him into a standing position. The sergeant then turned him around so that they were face to face.

"By order of the Federal Authority and under the jurisdiction of the Bureau of the Federal Authority, you are being placed under arrest. You are charged with violating the Fifth Primary Directive by residing beyond the federally mandated Boundary. You are also being charged with resisting arrest, the attempted murder of a federal agent, and disturbing the peace. Your rights as a citizen are hereby revoked. You are being taken into custody until such time as you can be remanded to a Hall of Justice for summary judgement," the sergeant said without pity.

Liam didn't understand half of the charges that were being leveled against him, but he knew what the outcome would be: guilty. If this was how they treated a couple of innocent teenagers, he was certain that the Authority's justice system wasn't about to offer him a fair and impartial trial. Having never really been in trouble before, the idea of facing "summary judgement" was a little intimidating for him. He could only hope that wherever he was taken, the guards would be gentler than the sergeant.

To emphasize his point, the sergeant grabbed Liam under the arm, turning him around and pushing him toward the stairs. With his hands tied behind his back, Liam had a hard time keeping his balance. He fell forward, colliding with a support beam and tumbling onto the bottom few steps of the stairs.

To his surprise, another pair of hands grabbed him and pulled him to his feet. Another trooper, dressed in black tactical gear, had come down the stairs. He held onto Liam, looking toward the sergeant for instructions.

"It's about time you got here, Private. Maybe next time, don't waste so much time 'securing' the front of the house. We could have used you down here," the sergeant said reprovingly. "Now that you are here, make yourself useful. Escort this stray outside and secure him for extraction. The convoy should be here in ten minutes."

As Liam was being pulled up the stairs, he looked back long enough to see the other two troopers picking Parker up off the floor.

She was still unconscious and needed to be carried. With one of them under each arm, the two troopers began dragging her toward the stairs. Liam spared one final glance to look down at Ben's body as they left.

"Forget about it, kid," the private said as he pulled Liam up the stairs. "Ain't nothing you can do for him now. Taking a blast from a pulse rifle like that, he's fried for sure."

Liam couldn't tell whether the private was trying to be comforting or stating a fact. Either way, he didn't appreciate it. A burning hate was starting to grow within him for what the Authority had done here. In less than an hour, his world had been torn asunder.

The worst part was that he still didn't understand why. He didn't understand why it was necessary to shoot Ben even after he had been subdued. He didn't understand where the indifference to beating a defenseless girl came from. He certainly didn't understand what heinous crime they had committed to warrant such treatment from total strangers.

"What was that?" the private said as they emerged from the gaping hole where the trapdoor had been.

"I was saying how I don't understand how you can justify killing someone when they no longer pose a threat to you," Liam said, repeating what he had been muttering under his breath.

"Yeah, well, that happens when you fire a weapon at a federal agent," the private said without the slightest hint of compassion. "Though where you all managed to find an old static rifle, I have no idea. Those things are practically antiques. Anyways, you ought to consider yourselves lucky. If it had been me coming down those stairs first, I would have fried all three of y'all."

"Then I guess it was a good thing that you were guarding the front lawn," Liam said with a little bit more sarcasm than he should have. He was rewarded by having the private slam the butt of his rifle into his stomach. He doubled over in pain. The kicks that he had received down in the basement had been worse, but this one was right next to his burn.

The private laughed as Liam struggled to straighten up. As soon as he had recovered, the private kicked him in the back, forcing him down the hall. Once again, without the use of his hands, Liam fell to the floor.

As he was lying face-down on the floor, debating whether he should try standing up on his own, a strange sight caught his eye. The hallway opened up into the kitchen ahead of where he was laying on the floor. In the middle of the kitchen, lying on the floor, was Ben's mother. Much like her son, her eyes were open, but she wasn't looking at anything.

Instinctively, Liam opened his mouth to call out to her, but his voice caught in his throat. There was something wrong here. Her eyes were staring directly at him, but they didn't blink. As he concentrated on her, he noticed that she wasn't moving. Her chest was not rising and falling with the steady rhythm of breathing, and the way she was laying on the floor, all sprawled-out, was not natural.

Liam realized what he was looking at: Ben's mom was dead, just like her son. There was even a small tendril of black smoke rising from her chest where she had been struck by the blast of a pulse rifle, just like her son.

Liam felt the private grab his arm from behind and try to hoist him back up onto his feet. The private wasn't as strong as the sergeant had been, and he struggled to pull Liam up.

As Liam got to his feet, he could see another body lying on the ground in the living room ahead. Most of the body was hidden behind the living room sofa, with nothing more than the feet sticking out. But he didn't need to see their face to know who it was. They had managed to kill Ben's father as well. An entire family was dead at the feet of these monsters.

The hatred that had been slowly burning within Liam's chest ignited into a bonfire. The people lying dead on the floor hadn't been strangers, and they hadn't been fictional characters from a movie or a book; they had been people – people that he knew and loved. It was a shocking revelation that never again would he hear their voices or see them laugh or feel their comforting touch.

The sheer horror of what had happened here this morning crashed home in Liam's mind. By what right did these assholes come into somebody else's home and deprive them of the special gift of life that was regarded so highly by everybody else? Ben's family hadn't been criminals, and they hadn't been villains or scoundrels. They had been innocent. They had never done anything wrong their whole lives and they didn't deserve the awful fate that these monsters had inflicted upon them.

As soon as Liam was on his feet, he shrugged off the private's grip. He turned to face the trooper, filled with righteous indignation. The private merely smirked before giving Liam a shove. He wasn't about to stand down. He meant to stand his ground.

Seeing the change in Liam's demeanor, the private let his smirk change into a scowl. He hoisted his rifle in both hands, as if he intended to use it. Liam wasn't sure where he got the courage, but he didn't flinch at the private's implied threat.

Liam would have continued his staring match with the private, but at that moment, the sergeant and the corporal emerged from the bedroom into the hallway. Parker was still being dragged between them, but at least now, she seemed to have regained consciousness. She was moaning softly under her breath, and her feet were making an effort to keep up with her captors.

When the sergeant saw what was going on in the hallway between Liam and the private, he practically exploded in aggravation.

"Oh, come on, Private! If you can't deal with one pathetic stray, then perhaps you don't belong in my unit. I hear they always need maintenance workers to clean the bathrooms. Maybe then you will have a job that you can't possibly screw up," the sergeant said, ending his brief tirade.

The private's face flushed with embarrassment. He wasn't happy about being the focus of the sergeant's harassment. Worse than that, it had been done in front of everyone.

Liam watched as the private reached back, cocked his fist, and punched him right in the mouth. He stumbled backwards several steps from the force of the blow. Before he had a chance to recover, the private's boot collided with his chest, sending him reeling over the back of the living room sofa.

The private seemed to be making up for his lack of violence before by being doubly abusive now. On a basic level, Liam understood. The sergeant had perceived weakness in the private's behavior, so now, the private was overcompensating. It just so happened that the private was overcompensating by beating the crap out of him.

Liam fell over the back end of the couch, landing on top of the corpse of Ben's father. He would have recoiled but he didn't have time to react before the private was pulling him to his feet. Unlike before when the private had lifted him up before releasing him, he held on this time. The reason became clear as the private used his grip to launch Liam toward the front door.

His aim was off, and Liam collided with the door frame instead of flying out the door. As he turned around, he caught a fleeting glimpse of the butt end of the private's rifle before it struck him in the face. For a brief moment, his vision faded to black. He felt himself floating in the darkness before his back collided with the floor.

As his vision returned, he could see that he was lying on his back in Ben's front yard. The private had knocked him through the doorway, and he had fallen down the stairs that lead to Ben's front door. As realization of what had just happened dawned on him, he also became aware of the pain that was coming from his face.

Liam tasted blood in his mouth – no doubt a souvenir from the private's undivided attention. He rolled onto his side and spat the blood from his mouth out onto the sidewalk. The blood from his mouth mixed with the blood pouring out of his nose and formed a small pool on the sidewalk beside him.

Liam was still spitting out blood when the private appeared in the entryway of Ben's house. He walked down the stairs, a satisfied smile on his face. Liam rolled onto his back as the private came over and stood over him. He braced himself for another blow from the butt of the private's rifle, or maybe a sturdy kick from his boot, but nothing happened. He looked up, trying to figure out why the private had stopped.

The sun was well up above the horizon. The bright sunshine cast a shadow on the private's face as Liam looked up at him, making it impossible to see his expression. He squinted to get a better look and noticed that the private was not staring at him, but at the puddle of blood on the sidewalk. The look on his face was...perplexed.

Liam practically flinched as the private knelt down next to him. In an unexpected move, the private set his rifle down on the ground next to him and reached up to remove his helmet to get a better look. He was completely confused. What was going on?

The private, without saying a word, reached out and pressed a finger against the puddle of blood on the sidewalk. He brought his hand up to his face so that he could get a better look at the blood now smeared on his fingertips. The way he was staring at it was odd, almost as if he had never seen anything like it before.

The private continued staring at the blood on his fingers, unconsciously cocking his head to the side in an effort to make sense of what he was looking at. His attention was so focused on the blood, that Liam himself could have disappeared into thin air and the private wouldn't have noticed – which wasn't a problem for Liam.

Anything that would distract the private from giving him another beating was just fine by him.

The private's intense scrutiny started to make Liam feel uncomfortable. Was there something wrong with his blood? Why was the trooper so fixated on it? His self-consciousness lasted only a few seconds until he realized that this was the perfect opportunity to try to escape.

With that thought in mind, he tried to scoot himself away from where the private was kneeling. If he could get far enough away, he could get to his feet and make a break for it.

Unfortunately, his movement didn't go unnoticed and he was once again the center of attention. The private stared from his finger to Liam and back again. He reached out and touched Liam's face. His finger slid along Liam's cheek and under his nose. As it came away, Liam could see that there was even more blood on the private's finger than there had been before. It seemed like the private had wiped away some of the excess blood from his face.

"What...what is this?" the private said, his face slowly turning white.

"What do you mean?" Liam asked, not understanding the question. Surely this man had seen blood before. But if that were true, then why was he acting so strangely?

"What *is* this?" the private said more forcefully, reaching forward and grabbing Liam by the shirt.

"It's blood," Liam said, hoping that he was giving a satisfactory answer. "What did you expect? You practically broke my nose when you hit me in the face."

"I know it is blood," the private answered, on the point of hysteria. "But why is it this color?"

Chapter 16: A Desperate Escape

No sooner had the words left the private's mouth than the top of his head jerked back suddenly. The air exploded in the sound of gunfire and the private slumped backwards. The only thing that kept him from falling over completely was his fist, which was still firmly grasping onto Liam's shirt.

It took Liam several seconds before he realized what had happened: The private had been shot. The bullet had struck him over his right eye, creating a small crater. The force had flung his head backwards, and his eyes had rolled up into the back of his head. After a few seconds, the private's lifeless body toppled to the ground, dragging poor Liam down with it.

At that moment, the street erupted into chaos. The sergeant and the corporal emerged from Ben's house, determined to investigate what was happening out front. They were met with a hail of bullets as countless guns fired at them from across the street. Fortunately for them, they were still wearing their helmets and tactical gear, which, for the most part, protected them from the barrage.

Liam lifted his head to see both the sergeant and the corporal scrambling back into the house in a desperate attempt to protect themselves from the hail of bullets being fired in their direction. No sooner were they in the house than the crackling sound of their pulse rifles filled the air. The front windows of Ben's house exploded outward in a shower of glass as the two troopers returned fire.

Liam turned his head to look the other way. On the other side of the street, nestled amongst the houses, were dozens of familiar faces. Each and every one of them were holding a weapon of some sort, and they directed their fury at the troopers who were now holding up inside Ben's house.

Liam smiled as he realized that the townsfolk of Haven had come to his rescue. There were just two problems: Only one of the troopers had gone down, and the other two were still fighting. Not only that, but he remembered that more troops were on their way. It was only a matter of time until they got there.

The crackling sound of the troopers' pulse rifles filled the air, and was met immediately by another round of gunshots. Liam found himself stuck right in the middle of a firefight. The only thing he could do was to make himself as small of a target as possible and hope he wasn't hit by a stray bullet or pulse blast. Even then, several shots came dangerously close to hitting him.

Realizing that he couldn't stay where he was, Liam tried to crawl away from the firefight. Unfortunately, the private's lifeless hand was still clutching his shirt. He tried to pull away, but the dead man's grip was too strong. Unable to use his hands, he twisted himself around, placing his feet against the private's chest and pushing with all his might. There was a tearing sound, and his shirt tore free.

No sooner had he broken free than two sets of hands grabbed him by both arms and pulled him to his feet. At first, he tried to struggle, figuring that the sergeant and the corporal had come out to collect him. His attempts to break free stopped immediately when he saw the faces of the people standing next to him. It was his Aunt Linda and his teacher, Mrs. Kelly.

Liam didn't know what to say. He was only conscious of a warm, grateful feeling growing in his chest. That feeling lasted less than a second as several pulse blasts flew in their direction. Without wasting another second, Aunt Linda and Mrs. Kelly pulled him toward the other side of the street, running at full speed. They were hunched over as they ran, trying to keep their heads down as much as possible.

The gunfire intensified as the three of them ran for the houses on the other side of the road. Even with the barrage of bullets being hurled at them, the two troopers continued to fight back. From within the house, their pulse rifles continued to crackle as they fired at anything that moved, including Liam and his escorts.

Liam ducked down even further as several pulse blasts flew over his head. The last one missed him by only a few inches. The air exploded with the sounds of gunshots as the townsfolk returned fire.

When the three of them reached the other side of the street, Liam was pulled through a gap between two houses. He stumbled through somebody's flower garden, desperate to get as far away from the fighting as possible. As they ran, more townsfolk pushed past him, heading toward the fight. Many of them were holding rifles and shotguns like he had seen in the movies, but several of them were holding static rifles like the one that Ben had used.

Ben! The thought struck him like a bolt of lightning. They had left Ben and his family lying dead back there. More importantly, they had left Parker back there. She was still alive, and she needed their help.

Liam dug in his heels, bringing his flight to freedom to an immediate halt.

"What are you doing?" Aunt Linda all but yelled at him.

"Parker!" he shouted back so that his aunt could hear him over the sound of gunshots. "She is still inside Ben's house. We can't leave without her."

"There isn't time!" Aunt Linda yelled back, pulling on his arm to drag him away from the fighting. He tried to resist, but she pulled him along anyway.

"We need to get you out of here now!" Mrs. Kelly said in an earnest voice that Liam would never have suspected from her.

To emphasize their words, a blast of bright blue light whizzed over Liam's head, followed quickly by several more pulse blasts in rapid succession. The pulse blasts struck the side of the nearby houses and the surrounding trees, and one managed to hit a nearby townsperson who was rushing in that direction. They immediately crumbled to the ground, lifeless.

With all the destruction and devastation happening all around him, Liam allowed himself to be pulled away toward safety. He did manage to look over his shoulder as they ran. The two troopers had left their position inside Ben's house and were now out on the front lawn. Not far away from them was Parker.

She was propped up against the open doorway of Ben's house, hands bound behind her back. Her eyes were wide with alarm as she surveyed the chaos going on all around her. Through the barrage of bullets and pulse blasts, their eyes met. Liam tried to call out to her, but she was too far away to hear him over the sound of gunshots. He could see her lips moving, like she was trying to yell something back at him. He quickly realized that she was trying to tell him to run.

He hated the idea of leaving her behind, but what choice did he have? He would have stayed longer, but pulse blasts were still flying in his direction. Even now, he could see the lifeless bodies of several townsfolk littering the ground, struck down by the constant stream of pulse blasts from the troopers' weapons.

Just then, Liam caught a glimpse of the corporal collapsing on the ground. She had finally succumbed to her injuries. Even with her tactical gear, the relentless assault from the townsfolk had proven too much for her.

Watching her go down caused him to have mixed emotions. On the one hand, he was glad to see her go down. She had attacked them, after all. On the other, she had seemed like the most reasonable of the group. She hadn't gone out of her way to hurt anyone down in the basement, something that could not be said for the sergeant or the now-dead private. She had simply been doing her job, no matter how repulsive that job was.

Now, if only the sergeant would go down, Liam thought hopefully, but with no such luck. He continued to fight back against the torrent of attacking townsfolk despite being hit multiple times. To even the odds, he picked up the dead corporal's weapon and used it alongside his own weapon.

The sergeant's determination was impressive. Despite being outnumbered and overwhelmed, he continued fighting with all his might. Whether he was still standing due to his own stubbornness or the quality of his tactical gear was a mystery. He was definitely wearing body armor, but that could only do so much.

Whatever the case may be, the sergeant was faring much better than the townsfolk. Their lack of body armor left them open to the full devastation of the sergeant's pulse rifles. They had no protection other than the clothes on their backs. Many of them had joined the fight with whatever weapons they could get their hands on. In many ways, it felt like they had stopped in the middle of their daily routines to come to rescue Liam.

Which was one of the reasons why so many of them now littered the ground. It wasn't fair. Despite their numbers, the townsfolk seemed to be losing the battle. The troopers' training and combat gear gave them an edge that the townsfolk didn't have. To make matters worse, the troopers didn't seem to have a problem dealing out death to anyone they saw as a threat.

Abruptly, Liam was pulled out of sight behind a nearby house and pressed up against the back wall as dozens of fellow townsfolk converged on his location. This wasn't exactly the safest place to stop and hold a gathering, but at least they were out of the line of fire. Still, gunshots and pulse blasts echoed right around the corner.

Liam tried to focus on what was being said by the people now surrounding him, but it was hard, since everyone was talking at once. Whatever they were saying, it seemed like everyone agreed that they needed to retreat back into the woods. This particular neighborhood had been cut out of the side of the forest and was surrounded by trees. All they had to do was reach the tree line several streets over.

Now that a plan had been agreed upon, the entire group ran toward the back fence of the house they had been hiding behind. The fence was knocked down, and the group proceeded into the backyard of the adjoining house on the next street. They emerged into the street beyond and wasted no time heading toward the houses on the other side. Their plan was to cut a path straight through the neighborhood until they reached the safety of the trees.

As they ran, Liam found himself running in the center of the group. He couldn't be certain, but it seemed as if everyone around him had formed a protective circle with him in the middle. At least, that was what it looked like to him.

They reached the street beyond and continued toward the forest – only one more street to go. As they reached the last street in the neighborhood, Liam could see treetops peeking over the roofs of the row of houses directly in front of him. They had made it, or so he thought.

The screeching of tires brought his attention to an armored vehicle that was heading down the road in their direction. Several townsfolk called out, pointing at the approaching vehicle. Instinctively, Liam knew that this was the reinforcements that the sergeant had called for back in the basement. They must have figured out what was going on and decided to cut his group off from reaching the woods.

Not knowing what to do, half of the townsfolk took up positions along the road, prepared to fight. The rest, including Liam, were ushered toward the other side of the street. The goal hadn't changed – they needed to reach the safety of the woods.

The armored vehicle stopped halfway down the road. The back doors flew open as several troopers poured out. They were all dressed in the same tactical gear as the other troopers Liam had already encountered, and each one of them held a pulse rifle in their hands. They took up positions along the street before raising their weapons and opening fire.

The air exploded with the crackling sounds of pulse rifles, accompanied by the sounds of dozens of gunshots as the townsfolk tried to fight back. The result was worse than before. Those who stayed to fight were immediately gunned down, leaving only a few to hold off the troopers' advance while everyone else ran for safety.

It all felt like a bad dream. No matter how hard Liam tried to run, it felt like his legs were kicking in slow motion, as if they were encased in gelatin, and even the slightest movement was a struggle. Worst of all, his hands were still tied behind his back, preventing him from sprinting away on his own.

As he ran toward the corner of the nearest house, his Aunt Linda on one side and Mrs. Kelly on the other, a bright blue flash of light streaked past his head. Immediately, he was pulled down to the ground, crashing into the soft dirt of someone's lawn. Once he realized he was face down on the ground, he tried lifting himself, unsure what had just happened.

The answer to that question was staring him in the face as he got to his knees. Mrs. Kelly was sprawled out on the ground, dead. Half of her face had been burned away, the result of being hit by a pulse blast in the head. The pulse blast that had narrowly avoided him had struck her instead. Her body had gone limp as the blast hit her, and since she had been holding onto his arm, he had been pulled down with her.

Before he had the chance to mourn the death of his teacher, another set of hands grabbed his arms and hoisted him to his feet.

"We have to keep moving," someone yelled in his ear.

Liam turned to see who was yelling at him. To his surprise, it wasn't his aunt. In fact, his aunt was nowhere to be seen. He was still surrounded by townsfolk, but his aunt had disappeared amongst the throng of people.

As they reached the edge of the woods, several of the nearby trees burst into flames. It didn't take much for him to realize that they were being hit by pulse blasts that had been aimed in their general direction. Instinctively, he ducked down trying to avoid being hit.

It was a good thing that he did, too. Not two seconds after he had ducked down, several pulse blasts filled the air where his head had been. People all around him dropped as they were struck by blue flashes of light from the troopers' pulse rifles. One of his escorts went down, but was immediately replaced by someone else. Without missing a step, they continued running as fast as they could deeper into the forest.

Liam ran with all his might, his heart pounding in his chest. It wasn't just the running that made his heart feel like it was trying to burst out of his chest; it was also that he was terrified. Before today, he had never seen anyone die, and now, people were dying all around him. He couldn't figure out what was more frustrating – that he could be next, or that there was nothing that he could do to stop it.

Several minutes passed before he realized that the shooting had stopped. They were all still running through the trees, but he could no longer hear the crackling sounds of pulse rifles being fired in their direction. Was it possible that they had finally made it to safety?

Now that his own life was no longer in danger, his thoughts immediately turned to his aunt. At some point, she had disappeared in the crowd. When that had been exactly, he couldn't say. One moment, she had been by his side, and the next moment, she'd been gone.

Liam started getting a terrible feeling in his stomach. Countless people had been shot in their flight from the Authority's troops. It was entirely possible that his aunt had been one of them. Could she have been hit, and he simply hadn't noticed? That thought sent a shiver down his spine.

Fearing that his aunt was lying dead somewhere, Liam came to an abrupt halt. He wasn't going to take another step until he knew for certain what had happened to her. He had left Parker behind; he wasn't about to leave his aunt too. He had lost too many people today, and he wasn't going to take another step until he knew, one way or another.

His refusal to continue was met with immediate opposition. Hands grabbed him from both sides and began pulling him along against his will. He shrugged them off as best as he could, but they still managed to pull him along. He was considering doing something drastic when he heard a familiar voice call to him.

He turned to see his Aunt Linda running toward him through the trees. She was accompanied by a small group of townsfolk who looked the worst for wear. Apparently, they had been separated in all of the confusion. His aunt, along with several others, had been forced to double back and take shelter amongst the houses. From there, they'd made their way to the end of the block before turning back toward the woods. Along the way, they'd managed to get the troopers' attention and distract them long enough for everyone else to escape.

Now wasn't the time to talk about it, though. Taking her place by Liam's side, Aunt Linda led him further into the forest. They weren't running anymore; the immediate danger had passed. They still kept a steady pace, heading south through the trees. After ten minutes or so, the group started angling east. Liam was completely lost, but his aunt seemed to know exactly where they were going.

After another ten minutes or so, they entered a small clearing in the middle of the surrounding woods. Aunt Linda brought their group to a halt, and Liam was finally given a chance to catch his breath. With help from his aunt, he sat down on a fallen log. From this position, he was able to get a good look at everyone around him.

When he had first been rescued outside of Ben's house, he could have sworn that there had been twice as many people – maybe more. As of right now, there were maybe thirty-five to forty people still remaining in their group. The thought of losing so many people gave him a sinking feeling in his stomach.

Still, he was comforted by the faces that he did see. They were all people that he knew from town. There was George the trash collector, Wendy who worked at the bowling alley, and many more besides. It was comforting to see their faces and to know that they were there with him.

"Ammo check," Aunt Linda called out. "Everybody do an ammo check."

While everyone was busy checking the status of their weapons, she turned her attention to Liam. From out of nowhere, she produced a bottle of water and held it up for him to drink. After several gulps, she lifted the bottle and splashed the rest on his face. Besides the refreshing feeling of the cold water on his face, it also helped to wash away the dried blood that had been stuck to his face this entire time.

"We will get you out of those restraints as soon as we can," she told him in a reassuring voice. When he didn't say anything, she continued. "Are you alright?"

"We left her back there," he said quietly.

"I know," Aunt Linda responded just as quietly. "There wasn't anything that we could do for her. We lost half our people getting you out. If we had stayed...well, let's just say that we were lucky to get you out alive."

Liam nodded slowly in agreement. He hated to admit it, but his aunt was right. He had watched countless people die in the firefight between the townsfolk and the Authority's troops, and even then, they had barely escaped. If they had stayed to try and rescue Parker as well, they would have been cut off from escape by the armored vehicle.

He still didn't feel right about it. He hated the thought of how the Authority's troops might be treating her right now. After everything that had happened, their attitude toward Parker and the rest of the townsfolk was only going to get worse. After what she had already been through down in that basement, Liam could only imagine what might be in store for her.

Not wanting his aunt to see him cry, he turned away from her, wiping the tears away from his eyes with his shoulder. He didn't want to think about Parker and what she was going through at that moment. The images that popped up in his mind were too painful to think about.

He tried to take his mind off it by looking around at the townsfolk in the clearing. Their faces were somber. Gone were the happy, joyful smiles that had greeted him every day of his life. What was left in their place was worry and sadness. More than that, those who remained in their group looked lost. They were all milling about, but without a clear idea of what to do now.

The only one not affected by all of this was his aunt. She seemed to be in complete control of her emotions. She also seemed to be the only one who knew what she was doing, which was probably why everyone was deferring to her.

Liam continued to scan the crowd, looking for people he had seen back at Ben's house and while running for the forest. Surprisingly, several of the faces he expected to see in the gathering weren't there. Mr. Drake, the owner of the hardware store, had rushed past him with a shotgun in his hands back at Ben's house. Now, he was nowhere to be seen.

Mrs. Kelly had been shot while trying to lead him to safety. Mrs. Ashley, who worked at the hair salon, had been the one to pick him up when he fell down. She had been shot in the back less than a minute later.

So many missing faces. So much death.

Liam began to shake uncontrollably. Tears clouded his vision as he thought about it. How many people had died trying to rescue him? How many familiar faces were now gone forever because of what had happened today? He had to think about something else.

The emotions were too real, and he was still raw from his experiences in Ben's basement. Once they were someplace safe, he might let himself feel the pain that was currently overwhelming him, but now was not the time.

A gentle hand patted him on the shoulder. His Aunt Linda had been watching him, concerned about how he was doing. She knelt next to him with her hand on his shoulder while he regained control of his emotions. Once it was clear that he was going to be alright, she gave him a tight-lipped smile and stood up.

She didn't go far. A small group had gathered a few feet away, waiting for instructions on what to do next. As soon as Aunt Linda joined them, they all began talking in a rush. She urged them to lower their voices, and they continued in hushed tones that Liam could barely hear.

Despite their efforts to keep their voices down, he was still able to hear bits and pieces of their conversation.

"Almost gone..."

"If we make a run for it..."

"We have to try; it is our only hope."

Liam could only guess at what they were talking about. He figured that it had something to do with their current situation and what to do next. The problem was, everybody seemed to have their own opinion on the matter.

Liam's attention shifted as several people emerged from the surrounding woods and joined the group. They must have been separated in all the confusion, and had only now managed to catch up. Amongst the newcomers, he recognized one of the Natalies from his class. Her hair was tangled, and her dress was dirty and torn in several places. She looked like she had just finished wrestling in the mud, which was a huge departure from her typical appearance.

The other things he noticed about her were the rocks in her hands. At first, it seemed odd, but as he looked around, he noticed that half of the remaining townsfolk weren't carrying guns at all. They were carrying around axes, pitchforks, baseball bats, and pretty much anything else that they could use to defend themselves.

There were still plenty of people carrying rifles, shotguns, and old static rifles like the one Ben had used in his basement. From the look of things, they were in pretty rough shape – not to mention that many of them were almost out of ammunition? What would they do if they did run out of ammunition, Liam wondered. Not that it had made a big difference so far. Bullets had seemed to bounce off the troopers back at Ben's house. Still, he figured that bullets were better than throwing rocks; no offense to the Natalie who had joined their group.

Everyone went quiet as Aunt Linda raised her hands to get their attention. Liam turned back to her. It seemed that the group had finally come to a decision.

"Listen up, everybody. I know that we have been through a lot already, but it isn't over yet," Aunt Linda said, looking at the gathered crowd around them. "We gave them one hell of a fight, but they are still out there, and they are still looking for us."

A small cheer went up as she mentioned fighting back against the Authority, but it was short-lived. Nobody was ignorant of how badly things had gone back there. Still, she was trying to keep their spirits up.

"Even now, those Authority screwheads are regrouping and preparing for another assault. We cannot stay here. It is only a matter of time until they find us. If we try to run, they will track us down."

"Where are we supposed to go?" someone asked in a desperate voice.

"To the Watchtower!" Wendy from the bowling alley chimed in.

"We cannot reach the Watchtower," Aunt Linda replied. "Not from our current location."

"Then where?" another voice called out.

"If ever we were cut off from reaching the Watchtower, protocol dictates that we should head for the fallback position," Aunt Linda said definitively.

"That's in the middle of town!" someone called from the back of the group.

"Yes, it is, but we don't have a choice," Aunt Linda explained. "We cannot stay here, and we cannot reach the Watchtower, which means that the fallback position is our best chance for success. If we can make it there, we should find plenty of supplies, ammunition, and hopefully, reinforcements."

These words appeared to energize the surrounding crowd. The lost looks that had been painted on their faces werer now gone, replaced by faint glimmers of hope. A decision had been made, and they were prepared to do whatever was necessary to achieve their goal.

"To the fallback position," George said, raising his rifle into the air.

"To the fallback position," echoed the group.

"To the fallback position," Aunt Linda said, waving for them all to start moving again. Then, in a quieter voice that only Liam could hear, she said, "I only hope it is still there."

Chapter 17: Danger from Above

Aunt Linda came over and helped Liam to his feet. She took her place by his side while George the garbage collector took up position on his other side. Together they started heading east, back toward Haven.

As they walked, Liam couldn't stop himself from poking fun at his aunt. She had used some pretty interesting language back there. He had never heard the phrase "screwheads" before, but it seemed appropriate.

Aunt Linda gave him a wry smile and shrugged it off. Liam suspected that she had wanted to use proper obscenities, but didn't want to set a bad example in front of him. When he tried to reassure her that it was alright for her to swear in front of him, she gave him one of her signature looks. That meant no.

Soon, Liam wasn't sure how long they had been walking, but he figured that they had to be getting close to the outskirts of town. The trees were getting sparse as they walked, and there was a new smell in the air – strong enough to overpower the smell of pine and cedar from the surrounding trees. It took him a moment to recognize it as the smell of woodsmoke.

Without warning, Liam was pushed against a nearby tree and forced into a crouching position. He was about to demand an explanation, but his aunt placed a finger against her lips and motioned for him to be silent. The whole group had come to a complete stop and was taking cover amongst the trees.

At first, he was confused at why they had stopped, but then he heard it. It started out faint but was growing louder by the second. It was a low whooshing sound that he couldn't quite place.

He looked at his aunt with a quizzical look, hoping that she might answer the unasked question. Without saying a word, she motioned him to look upward. As he did, all he could see were the tops of the nearby trees. Then he saw it – a grey shadow, streaking across the sky, visible through the gaps in the trees overhead.

He couldn't quite make out what it was because the canopy of trees was obscuring his vision. What he could tell was that it was a dark grey shape that was quickly passing overhead and heading south. As it passed directly overhead, there was a rush of wind and all he could hear was the whooshing sound coming from above.

Within moments, the shape passed overhead and continued on its way south. Wherever it was going, it was headed there as quickly as possible.

The group waited another five minutes before his aunt gave the all-clear signal and everyone got back to their feet. Without saying a word, they all started moving again, though Liam had to be nudged to get him started. He wanted to ask what that thing was, but he doubted that he would get an answer right now.

He continued on, walking with the rest of the group until they came to the edge of town. Just beyond where they were standing were the backsides of several old warehouses that hadn't been used in several years. They were still on the outskirts of town, but this marked the point where they would be leaving the safety of the trees and heading into downtown.

In preparation for the next phase of their journey, Aunt Linda released Liam's arm and went around handing out instructions. Once they left the safety of the trees, they would be vulnerable, especially if that grey flying object returned, so it was very important that everyone follow instructions and reach their destination as quickly as possible.

While she was doing that, Liam took the opportunity to survey the changes that had happened to Haven since yesterday. The biggest difference was the countless plumes of black smoke that were rising up into the air from all around town. The presence of black smoke and the occasional gout of flame meant that several buildings were currently on fire. At least that explained the smell of woodsmoke in the air.

Everywhere he looked, the streets were practically empty. It was strange to see the center of town so devoid of people, especially at that time of day. At first, he thought that perhaps everyone was off trying to put out the fires, but the more he looked, the more it became evident that those fires had been left to burn unchecked. Parts of the downtown area were already smoldering piles of ash.

It wasn't just the fires and the smoke that were different. Several of the buildings were practically unrecognizable. The warehouses in front of them were blocking most of his view of Main Street, but even from here, he could see the tops of several buildings. Almost a third of the two-story buildings that lined Main Street had been destroyed. Many of the rest had gaping holes blown out of them. It was almost as if a giant had come through town, punching holes in the buildings as they went.

Back in Ben's basement, he had heard several explosions going off in the distance. It hadn't occurred to him that those explosions had originated back in town. Sure, Ben's neighborhood had been hit pretty badly too, but nothing like this. The Authority had concentrated their attack on the downtown area first before moving on to the residential neighborhoods.

Liam's attention shifted away from the condition of the town when he felt a tug on his arm. Aunt Linda was back, and both her and George had retaken their positions on either side of him. Together, they pushed forward into town.

As one, the whole group ran forward, bracing themselves against the outer walls of the warehouses. They formed up into two columns with Liam in the middle. Like a giant snake, they slithered around the corner of the building and headed for the center of town.

They crossed several streets, moving from building to building as they went. As they got closer to the downtown area, the signs of a recent struggle became more and more apparent. Wreckage and debris were scattered along the road. Walls had toppled outward, creating mounds of debris that their group had to climb over. It got worse as they got closer to the downtown area.

Bodies could be seen lying in the street where they had been struck down. At first, there were only one or two, but the further along they went, the more bodies they saw. It got so bad that Liam had to keep his attention focused in front of him so that he wasn't distracted by the countless bodies littering the floor.

Focusing his attention on the road ahead of him didn't help. While scrambling over a pile of bricks that had once been the side of a bookstore, Liam stumbled as his foot stepped on something that wasn't a brick. Looking down, he saw a woman's hand sticking out of the rubble. The rest of her was buried beneath the bricks. He tried not to think about it.

Everything about this was uncomfortable. All he wanted to do was to run away, escaping all the pain and misery that greeted him everywhere he looked. But he couldn't do that, so instead, he continued on as best as he could, trying to block out the ugliness all around him.

It made his skin crawl, which put him on edge more than he was already. He found himself looking in every direction, confident that danger lurked around every corner. It was a relief when he noticed that he wasn't the only one doing that exact same thing. Most of the group was busy looking for threats as well.

They were now only two streets away from Main Street. To get there, they had to pass through an alleyway between two buildings before crossing a street to get to an almost-empty parking lot. That parking lot was on the backside of the bowling alley that bordered Main Street, though where they were going on Main Street was still a mystery to Liam.

Their group halted between the two buildings while George and two others stepped out into the street. While they were checking to make sure that the path ahead was clear, Liam tried to see if he could guess the location of the fallback position that his aunt had mentioned. He suspected that it was the town hall building. That would make the most sense, since it was located in the center of town. It was also one of the few buildings in town large enough for everyone to meet at. Not only that, but the clocktower gave a perfect vantage point for surveying the whole town. Even now, he could see the top of the clocktower sticking out above the rest of the buildings lining Main Street.

George was taking his time, looking up and down the street for any signs of danger. He moved forward into the middle of the street and stood there, not moving. After two minutes, he finally nodded and motioned that it was ok to come out.

Both columns poured out of the alleyway, making their way across the street to the parking lot beyond. The sound of their footsteps echoed against the walls of the surrounding buildings, accompanied by a soft whooshing sound.

The reassuring smile that George had been giving Liam as he ran past faded as the soft whooshing sound got louder. With a look of dreadful anticipation on his face, George turned to look over his shoulder in the direction of the whooshing sound.

It dawned on Liam what they were hearing – it was the same sound that had accompanied the grey object that had flown over their heads back in the woods. The sound was getting louder, and it was heading straight for them.

The entire group seemed to become aware of it all at once, and everyone turned their heads to stare up in the direction of the sound. Seconds later, the group exploded in panic. Several members of the group turned around and tried to run back toward the safety of the alleyway. Others tried to push forward toward the bowling alley. Liam was caught between the two groups.

His aunt was trying to pull him toward the bowling alley, but whoever had taken George's spot on his other side was trying to pull him back toward the alley. The result was that rather than heading in one direction or another, he remained where he was on the sidewalk between the street and the parking lot.

The whooshing sound had grown to a dull roar as a helicopter appeared overhead. It hovered in the air directly over where Liam was standing. To call it a helicopter wasn't the right word for it. At least, it didn't resemble any of the helicopters that he had seen at the movies.

Rather than having a single rotor directly above the cockpit, it had two rotors built into the middle of tiny wings that stretched out to either side. The wings themselves were connected to the top of the cockpit. The twin rotors that were built into the wings were on gimbals that allowed them to rotate within the wing, which allowed the pilot to maneuver their craft seamlessly through the air.

As the quasi-helicopter floated overhead, a jet of air hit Liam in the face. The rotors were blasting air downward, which allowed it to hover in place. This was also the source of the whooshing sound. As the jet of air moved on and the quasi-helicopter maneuvered to get a better view of the townsfolk below, Liam was able to get a better look at the cockpit. It was shaped like a giant metal hawk, including the pointed beak at the front. The whole thing was sleek and aerodynamic, with a coating of grey paint that was broken only by a series of letters and numbers painted in white against the side of the cockpit. At the back, a tail boom stuck out with a stabilizer on both sides and another rotor built into the tail fin.

He could see two pilots through the front windows, both of whom were pointing down at the crowd below. Just then, the side of the cockpit opened up as a sliding door was pulled back. Standing in the now-open doorway was a third person holding what appeared to be a large pulse cannon.

"Rotowing!" someone called out from over Liam's shoulder.

"Incoming!" another voice called out.

Liam had been so captivated by the sight of the Rotowing that he had been completely oblivious to the danger that he was in. He was standing there in the open, completely exposed.

The circling Rotowing overhead chose its first targets and opened fire. A large electric-blue bolt of energy exploded from the tip of the Rotowing's cannon. The blast hurtled toward the ground, striking a small group of townsfolk who were heading back toward the alleyway. The ground erupted where they had been standing, sending chunks of pavement and debris flying into the air in every direction. The blast was so close that it knocked Liam off his feet.

This ended up being a good thing, because the person who had been trying to pull him toward the alley, had also lost their balance. They let go of him as they fell to the ground a few feet away. This left Liam free to run away from the alleyway, following his aunt, who was leading the way across the parking lot.

Two more explosions erupted behind him as he ran. He looked over his shoulder to see that the blasts had been aimed directly at the gap between the two buildings where the alleyway had been. The walls on both sides collapsed, burying anyone who may have been seeking shelter there. This meant that the only option was to push across the parking lot as quickly as possible and take shelter in the bowling alley.

Liam was forced down as the Rotowing passed overhead. His aunt pressed him up against a parked car, motioning him to wait. Gunfire and the sound of several static rifles filled the air as some of the townsfolk opened fire on the Rotowing. Liam didn't have to see the bullets bouncing off the cockpit to know how futile that idea was. If they couldn't take down several troopers, what made them think that they could take down an armored Rotowing?

It was only then that he realized that the gunshots and static blasts weren't meant to try and take down the Rotowing. They were meant to draw its attention away from his position.

393

Over the hood of the car, Liam watched as George and two others he had been with ran down the street away from his position. They were firing their weapons at the Rotowing and making so much noise that they quickly got the pilot's attention. It was clear that George was trying to lure the Rotowing away from the parking lot, or at least distract it long enough for the rest of the group to escape.

Liam watched as the Rotowing pulled around and headed in their direction. As the it lined up to take its shot, George lowered his weapon with a look of satisfaction. He spared a quick glance for Liam and his aunt as he raised a hand in fair well. Liam heard a faint "Goodbye" coming from George's mouth before a cannon blast erupted at his feet.

Liam didn't see what happened to George and his two companions. What he did see was a large fountain of dirt and debris flying up into the air where they had stood. As the smoke and dust started to clear, three bodies were partially visible. They had been burned black, with several body parts missing, and what was left of them was contorted into strange positions.

While he was still coming to grips with the tragedy that had just played out before him, Liam felt a tug as he was pulled away by his aunt. Together, they ran as fast as they could across the parking lot, moving in between the parked cars. Another explosion erupted behind them, but there was no time to stop and look back. The only thing that mattered was reaching the safety of the bowling alley.

The back door to the bowling alley was wide open, with two people crouched on both sides of the opening urging them onward. He ran toward them as fast as he could while still having his arms tied behind his back. Reaching the safety of the bowling alley was all that he cared about in that moment, and it was that thought that spurred him forward.

A brilliant flash of blue light streaked across his vision, landing directly in front of him. Liam felt the force of the blast as he was thrown backwards, landing on the pavement a few feet away.

The hair on his arms was standing straight up, and he felt a wave of electrical energy pass through him.

Once the electrical charge in the air had dissipated, he raised his head off the ground and looked toward the bowling alley. The people who had been crouching there were gone. In fact, the entire section of the wall where the door had been was gone. All that remained was a pile of rubble that marked where the back wall had collapsed.

He tried to stand up, but he had to roll over onto his stomach and push himself up to his knees first. He was covered in dirt. A cloud of dust was kicked up into the air as he shook his head back and forth to try and dispel the dull ringing in his ears. The motion made him dizzy, so he stopped and concentrated on the ground in front of him.

The Rotowing was still circling overhead, firing down into the crowd with reckless abandon. Liam raised his head enough to see one particular group as they were struck by a blast from the its cannon. Their bodies were thrown into the air, landing a few feet away. Just like George, their bodies were now burned black, and they smoldered on the ground where they had landed. The sight turned his stomach and he felt nauseous.

The Rotowing dealt out death and destruction wherever it went. It was a marvel of technology, corrupted to serve an evil purpose. It glided through the air, seeking out targets with no consideration for the lives that were being lost.

Liam had been so captivated by the Rotowing that he was startled when a hand tugged on his arm. Before he could say anything, he was dragged over to what remained of the bowling alley's back wall. There, against the part of the wall that hadn't fallen over, were a pair of dumpsters. He was dragged between the two dumpsters, where he was released. He flopped down on the floor, grunting as he landed. The dumpsters offered some protection against the Rotowing's onslaught, but it was by no means a safe place to rest.

From out amongst the parked cars, Liam saw his aunt running toward him. She dived into the pocket between the two dumpsters, coming to a stop by his side. She looked him up and down, checking to see if he was alright.

Another explosion pulled her attention away from him, and she looked back toward the parking lot. The Rotowing was still circling. It was targeting small groups that were still trying to make their way across the parking lot.

The fact that there were still people running across the parking lot was confusing to Liam. He would have thought that they would have scattered in all directions by now. It seemed to him that the smart move would be to get as far away from the carnage as possible, but still, they pressed on.

His head must have cleared a little bit, because it occurred to him that the reason the remaining townsfolk hadn't scattered was because he was there. They weren't running away because they didn't want to abandon him. They were willing to stay and fight, even if that meant dying, all for the sake of protecting him.

As Liam watched from in between the dumpsters, his eyes focused on one group in particular. One of the people in the group was the Natalie he had seen earlier. She was still holding onto a rock in her right hand. As she turned, he could see that her left arm was missing. It ended in a blacked stump just a few inches below her shoulder. In fact, her entire left side was blackened and burned.

The sight was horrifying, and yet, at the same time, it was oddly beautiful. Despite everything that she had been through, all the pain that she must be suffering, she somehow managed to persevere. Liam knew that he could never repay her for what she was doing for him, but he promised himself that he would find some way of letting her know how much it meant to him.

As he watched, she stepped away from the car she had been hiding behind and threw her rock at the circling Rotowing. Even as the rock soared through the air, it was obvious that it would fall short. Sure enough, the rock missed the Rotowing by a good ten feet before falling back down to land on the pavement below.

Without missing a beat, she looked around to find something else to throw. A few feet to her left was a brick, courtesy of the collapsed wall of the bowling alley. She scrambled out from behind the car to pick it up.

As her hand grasped the brick, she looked up and saw Liam watching her. She stopped long enough to give him a smile. Despite everything that was going on all around her, she took the time to share a smile with him. It was a simple, but completely meaningful act of kindness. With all the pain and sorrow surrounding them, this was a truly beautiful moment – one that he would never forget.

As he shared a smile of his own, a bright blue flash of light enveloped the girl, and she was gone. The flash of light momentarily blinded him, and another wave of electricity washed over him. Luckily, he was far enough away that he didn't feel the force of the blast. He was still showered in a rain of pebbles and dirt that were kicked up into the air by the explosion. When his vision cleared, the spot where the Natalie had been standing had become nothing more than a blackened crater.

Liam cursed himself. Why hadn't he taken the time to learn her name? Her real name. All this time, he had been content with referring to her and her friends as the Natalies, never bothering to find out their real names or get to know them better. He had simply labeled them as the Natalies and moved on with his life without a care in the world for who they really were.

What a jerk he had been. He had treated them as nothing more than background noise, as if they were props in a stage production that he could ignore. And now, he had just seen one of them die right before his eyes. Were the rest of the Natalies still alive, or were they numbered amongst the bodies that littered the streets?

He couldn't hold back the tears any longer. He thought about them and about everyone who had died trying to save his life. They had sacrificed themselves, all for his sake. He couldn't recall all of their names, but he knew that he would never forget their faces. Especially the face of the girl who had shared a warm smile with him right before she met her end. They would be burned into his memory from now until the day he died.

"We cannot stay here!" Aunt Linda's voice called out. Liam realized that she was speaking to him and shaking his arm to get his attention. "We need to get you out of here now!"

"Heads up, they are coming around again!" someone yelled.

Liam looked up to see the Rotowing hovering overhead. They had positioned themselves so that the gunner had a clear line of sight at the wall where the dumpsters were. Apparently, they had found their next target, and it was Liam and the people with him.

As the gunner took aim, Liam held his breath and closed his eyes in anticipation. The only thought running through his head was if this was how he was going to die, he hoped it would be quick and painless.

He flinched as he heard the sound of a loud explosion.

He opened his eyes when he realized he wasn't dead. He looked up to see the Rotowing still hovering above him, but the gunner was no longer aiming down at him. Instead, the craft was wobbling unsteadily in the air, a plume of black smoke rising from its side. The gunner was leaning out of the open doorway, pointing to something off in the distance.

Just then, a missile streaked through the air toward the Rotowing, a trail of smoke marking its path. It collided with the side of the cockpit, creating a huge explosion. The interior of the cockpit erupted into flames, and the gunner fell from the open doorway onto the ground below. Though Liam couldn't see where the gunner landed, he was certain that the man was dead.

The pilots were trying desperately to put out the fire in the cockpit. Despite the damage, the Rotowing was still flying. It swayed from side to side, unable to stabilize itself, but for all that, it still managed to hover above the parking lot. It was still in the fight.

As if to prove it was still a force to be reckoned with, the Rotowing launched a volley of missiles in the direction of whoever was shooting at them. They must have missed their target, because seconds later, another missile shot through the air toward the side of the Rotowing. Just as it was about to make contact, the craft veered to the side, narrowly avoiding the oncoming missile.

By this time, it was pretty badly damaged. The maneuver to try avoiding the missile almost caused it to crash into one of the nearby buildings. When they finally regained control of their craft, the pilots were barely able to keep it in the air.

Seeing that the Rotowing was practically disabled, Liam stood up from where he had been sitting between the dumpsters. He shrugged off his aunt's protests and joined the other members of his group, who were emerging from cover to watch the Rotowing's final moments. The fire in the cockpit had been extinguished, but smoke still poured out of the open doors.

Wanting to get a better look at where the missiles had come from, Liam left the safety of the dumpsters and ran out into the middle of the parking lot. As he did, he could see over the roof of the bowling alley to the clocktower beyond. There, standing on the small balcony that encircled the clocktower, were two people holding a missile-launcher. They were scrambling frantically to reload it, knowing that their job wasn't finished until the Rotowing had been knocked out of the air.

Their frantic attempts at reloading might also have been due to the fact that the Rotowing was now heading in their direction. It no longer soared through the air gracefully like it had before. The damage done to it made it shimmy and shake as it lowered its nose in the direction of the clocktower. The implication of what they were doing was clear: they planned to ram it.

The Rotowing was done for, but the pilots wanted to make sure that they took out the people with the missile-launcher before they went out. Everyone in Liam's group watched in horror as the craft charged toward the clocktower. The people on the balcony realized what was happening and made one final attempt at taking it down before it reached them.

A final missile streaked through the air and collided with the front of the Rotowing. There was a magnificent explosion, and it went up in flames. As it fell to the ground, its momentum carried it forward, causing it to crash into the front of the town hall building. The entire front of the building, including the balcony along the clocktower, was engulfed in flames. Within seconds, there was a large explosion, accompanied by the collapse of the clocktower to the street below.

Aghast at what he had just seen, Liam stood there and watched as flames rose from the ruin that had once been the town hall. His gaze was interrupted when a gentle hand rested on his shoulder. He turned to see his aunt standing next to him. Like everyone else, she was covered in dirt and grime and looked battered and bruised.

Liam wanted to bury his face against her chest and let out all of his emotions, just like he used to do when he was younger. The problem was, he wasn't feeling anything at the moment. He felt numb. After everything that he had seen and experienced, his heart and his mind had decided to shut down. Not even the bodies that littered the ground around them could elicit a response. It had all been too much.

Without saying a word, Aunt Linda took Liam's arm and started guiding him around the bowling alley toward Main Street. The rest of the townsfolk followed, although there were now fewer than a dozen of them left. They had to step over several bodies as they made their way around the building. Liam looked at each one as they passed, determined to shock himself into feeling something, but it didn't matter who they passed. They failed to spark an emotion in him.

He knew that he should feel something for these people. They had given their lives to protect him. The least he could do was feel sad about it. Deep down, he knew that he would, but for now, he felt nothing. His emotions were numb.

Liam allowed himself to be guided as their group reached Main Street. The remnants of the town hall building had been engulfed in flames, filling the air with more black smoke.

Rather than taking him toward the ruins of the town hall building like he had expected, Aunt Linda led him down the street toward the movie theater. Like most of the buildings on Main Street, the movie theater had also taken some damage. There was nothing left of the marquee other than a charred ruin, and half of the roof was missing. Despite the damage, the building was still standing.

Which was why it wasn't a surprise when the front doors opened as they approached. Several armed townsfolk stepped out, ushering everyone inside. As Liam passed them, he could see that they were busy looking up and down the street, watching for any of the Authority's troops.

As Liam walked through the lobby, the front doors were pulled shut, and their armed escorts led them into the theater. Light from outside shone through the holes in the roof. Half of the chairs were covered in rubble, and the movie screen was slashed and torn. In short, it looked nothing like what Liam remembered.

They were taken to a side door on the left-hand side of the theater. It opened up to the backstage area behind the movie screen. Before the theater had been converted to show movies, it had been a playhouse where stage plays were performed by the community.

When the previous owners had installed the movie screen, the space behind the screen had become a storage area.

Liam had only been back here a few times over the years. He knew that Mr. Malcolm used this space for extra storage, but not much else. Several years ago, while he had been trying to earn money for a new bike, Mr. Malcolm had allowed him to take a job cleaning up back here. He had swept and mopped the stage for a couple of hours before collecting his payment. From the looks of things, that was the last time anyone had bothered tidying up back here.

Against the back wall, a pair of storm doors stood open along the floor. Much like Ben's house, it appeared that the movie theater also had a secret basement. The buzz of voices and the sound of activity floated up through the open doors.

Liam watched as the group he was with slowly walked down the stairs into the basement. When it was his turn, he took the steps one at a time, making sure not to lose his balance on the way.

When he reached the bottom, he could see that the room before him was massive. It must have stretched the length of the entire theater. Like at Ben's house, the walls of the room were stacked high with supplies. Unlike Ben's house, the basement was filled with people. There had to be at least fifty or maybe sixty people down here. They moved among different tables that had been set up around the room. Some of those tables had maps spread out on top of them, while others had weapons, communications devices, and survival gear.

Everyone appeared to be moving with a specific purpose. While Liam's group had been forced to react to whatever the Authority was doing, this group seemed to be working proactively. They were drawing up plans of attack and figuring out strategies to fight back. It was comforting. Here at least, the people of Haven were standing their ground and fighting back.

"It's about time you got here," came a voice from off to the side. Liam turned to see Mr. Malcolm standing next to a nearby table, cranking a static rifle. Once the rifle had a full charge, he slung it over his shoulder and walked over to greet the new arrivals. "Welcome to our fallback position."

Chapter 18: Another Piece to the Puzzle

Liam would have been in shock if his emotions weren't already numbed. As it was, the only thing he could do was look around the room in muted wonder. There were several tables set up throughout the room. Each of them was covered with weapons, maps, survival gear, and supplies, most of which appeared to have been scraped together by the townsfolk. The table nearest to them was covered in maps with several red markers pointing out the positions of the Authority's troops.

The same as in Ben's basement, supply crates lined the walls on both sides. Liam recognized most of those crates as being the same kind that he had seen back in Greenwood – not to mention the countless number of crates that were marked with various types of weapons. Nearby, a couple was unloading a crate marked *Static Disruptor*. From inside the crate, they pulled out more static rifles and set them on a nearby table.

A small group had gathered around that table. Their attention was focused on dismantling, cleaning, and reassembling the weapons that had just been unpacked. Other groups in the basement were doing the same thing with everything from shotguns to hunting rifles. There were even a few handguns mixed in. If that wasn't enough, there was even a damaged pulse rifle leaning up against the wall. From the looks of it, someone had taken it off a dead trooper, but not before the damage had already been done.

As each weapon was cleaned and reassembled, it was handed off to someone else and passed out amongst the crowd. It seemed that Mr. Malcolm wasn't the only person with a rifle slung over their shoulder. Half the people down here were armed, and the other half were waiting their turn for the next available weapon.

Liam couldn't help but wonder where all these weapons and supplies had come from. He had certainly never seen a gun in real life before. All of his knowledge came from watching movies and reading books. To think that the town had such a large repository of weapons beneath his feet without him knowing was mind-blowing. It begged the question: Where did all of these weapons come from?

If all of these supplies had been brought into Haven, then surely he would have noticed. How could he have missed it? It was too small of a town for someone to unload truckload after truckload of supplies into the movie theater's basement without anyone noticing. Then again, as he thought about it, maybe he had noticed.

For years, Gus would make his weekly deliveries, driving into town with his van loaded full of goods. All of the shops on Main Street depended on him to deliver their merchandise. Would it have been so difficult to include weapon crates with some of his shipments? If he had been bringing in these supplies disguised as regular deliveries, it would explain a lot.

Of course, that implied that the town had suspected that something like this could happen and had been making preparations just in case. If the town had been preparing for something like this, then why hadn't they tried to stockpile some more-sophisticated weapons? Everything that they were pulling out of those crates was old and looked like it hadn't been touched in decades – a stark contrast to the sleek and shiny weapons carried by the Authority's troops, not to mention the superior firepower that their weapons had over the relics that were currently being handed out.

Liam's musings over the town's weaponry were cut short as he felt a sharp tug against his wrists. The force of it almost caused him to step backwards to keep his balance. As soon as the tugging started, it stopped, accompanied by a loud snapping sound. To his absolute delight, his hands fell to his sides, released for their restraints.

He turned to see Miss Sarah, the grocery store clerk, standing behind him with a pair of bolt cutters in her hands. She gave him a satisfied smile and a wink before walking away with the bolt cutters resting on her shoulder. Before she walked away, Liam remembered to thank her for setting him free.

Now that his hands were free, he couldn't stop himself from swinging his arms backward and forward. He wasn't doing it for any particular reason other than he could. The sensation of having his hands free again was refreshing. He had only been wearing those restraints for an hour or two, but that had been more than long enough. Up until now, he had been incapacitated by the restraints around his wrists. He hadn't even been able to run on his own without risking falling flat on his face.

While his hands were now free, his wrists still hurt. The restraints had been pinching his wrists, causing them to swell and turn a bright red color. There were even several cuts and welts where they had been chafing his wrists. He absentmindedly rubbed his wrists, alternating between hands to sooth his aching skin. Between the burn on his side, his aching ribs, a nose that was almost broken, the cuts and scrapes from almost being blown up, and his wrists, he was a real mess.

While he was busy massaging his wrists and looking around, Aunt Linda and Mr. Malcolm stepped over to a nearby table. They stood at the side of the table, looking down at all the maps that had been laid out. Since there was nothing else for him to do, Liam walked over and joined them. Mr. Malcolm was saying something while pointing down at the map.

"Everywhere we turn, we are encountering resistance," he was saying, pointing at several red markers on the map.

"I know that you mean," Aunt Linda said in response. "We lost half our number just getting to Ben's house. By the time we arrived, the Authority was already there. It cost us most of our remaining forces to get Liam out of there. What remains of our group is all that survived the fight and the Rotowing attack."

"You managed to rescue Liam. That alone was worth the sacrifice. Remember, he is the priority here," Mr. Malcolm said, trying to comfort her.

"That doesn't exactly make me feel better. I know we are all willing to sacrifice for the project, but I would prefer not to watch my friends and colleagues die right in front of me," Aunt Linda said despondently. "Speaking of which, whoever you had up in the clocktower, they didn't make it."

"I heard," Mr. Malcolm said sadly. "At least they managed to take out that damn Rotowing before they died. Without air support, we should stand a better chance against the Authority's remaining troops."

"What is the situation, anyway?" Aunt Linda asked Mr. Malcolm as she looked down at the maps on the table. "I have been out of the loop since my radio was busted in the attack."

Liam looked down to see a map of Haven laid out on the table top. There were several pushpins with white tips placed at different points on the map, including one over the movie theater. There were also pushpins with red tips placed on the map. These pushpins were being used to mark the townsfolk's locations as well as the Authority's locations throughout town. Given the number of red pushpins, it seemed that things were not going so well for the citizens of Haven.

"The primary evacuation went off without a hitch," Mr. Malcolm said with a hint of satisfaction. "At the first sign of trouble, all tier-two and tier-three personnel were evacuated into the escape tunnels. They should be making their way to the safehouses as we speak. That leaves the remaining tier-one personnel and support staff to defend the town while we follow our destruction protocols and extract Liam."

"How many does that leave us?" Aunt Linda asked.

"Hard to say. We started out with 560 people, including your group. With everything going on, I suspect we have less than 200 left scattered around town."

"What about the Authority's troops?"

"We have been receiving reports all morning," Mr. Malcolm said as he pointed down at the map. "Every red marker indicates where we have a confirmed sighting of the enemy."

"Is this even possible?" Aunt Linda asked in disbelief. "How many did they send, an entire division?"

"Not likely," Mr. Malcolm said in a reassuring voice. "From what I have been able to put together, I believe that there are only two or three retrieval teams operating in our area, supported by a Rotowing and possibly a convoy. If that is true, then we can expect around eight to ten troopers per team, plus any additional units operating their vehicles. Realistically, I suspect that we are only dealing with a force of thirty or so. No more than fifty at most."

"If that is true, then how come there are so many markers on the map?" Aunt Linda asked, making a sweeping gesture toward the map.

"The red markers only indicate that we have a confirmed sighting. It is possible that we are receiving reports of the same units, but operating in different locations. We do know that they are on the move. With support from that Rotowing, they could have been deploying troops all over town," Mr. Malcolm explained.

"Good thing we took it out, then, wasn't it?" Aunt Linda said.

"Absolutely. Without it, they have lost their tactical advantage. Now, we just have to deal with their remaining troops on the ground," Mr. Malcolm responded in a hopeful tone.

"I don't get it," Aunt Linda said, discouraged at the current state of affairs. "We planned for this. We always knew there was a possibility that we could be discovered one day, so how is it that the Authority can overwhelm us so easily?"

"I have no idea," Mr. Malcolm admitted, sharing in her frustration. "Perhaps we weren't as prepared as we should have been, or maybe we grew too comfortable knowing that we had evaded them this long. One thing is for certain: we definitely underestimated their tactics and how effective they could be in their deployments.

"I mean, let's face it. We haven't had any updates on their strategies and capabilities since we lost our source in the Bureau. That was seven years ago. A lot has happened since then, and they have only gotten more ruthless ever since," Mr. Malcolm finished in a huff.

"That couldn't be helped," Aunt Linda responded in a flat voice. "We needed him here. Besides, it was his policies that allowed most of our people to escape through the tunnels."

"I am not arguing that," Mr. Malcolm said, making his position clear. "We owe a lot to him for everything he has done, but that doesn't change the fact that we are underprepared to face this kind of threat."

"So it's that simple, is it? We are simply outmatched?"

"What other explanation is there?" Mr. Malcolm said with a deep sigh.

A brief silence passed between the two of them, each one thinking about what they could have done differently to prevent this unfortunate turn of events. But like most things, it was easier to look back at what could have been, than to look ahead at what could be. What was done was done. Now, they needed to pick up the pieces as best as they could.

"Where exactly are the rest of these troops now?" Aunt Linda asked, getting back to the topic at hand.

"From what we can tell, they are split into two groups. The first is up here," Mr. Malcolm said, pointing to the northern edge of town. "Between us and the Watchtower. The rest are down here at the southern edge of town. It looks like they have set up a staging area outside of town to coordinate their efforts. Now that their Rotowing has been shot down, I would imagine that they would want to consolidate their troops into one area. Which means—"

"Which means that it is only a matter of time until the troops in the north have to move south, or the troops in the south have to move north," Aunt Linda cut in.

"Let us hope that the northern unit withdrawals first. That would open up a path to the Watchtower," Mr. Malcolm said.

"I doubt we will get that lucky. In either case, we need to prepare to move. If the Authority's troops are going to head south, they will pass right by us, and I don't want to be here when they do," Aunt Linda said, tapping on the map.

"Agreed. I just wish we had Ben here to help strategize. He could tell us more about their tactics, perhaps even give us an edge," Mr. Malcolm said disappointedly.

"We will have to do the best that we can with what we have," Aunt Linda said with a hint of sadness in her voice. No doubt, she felt responsible for not getting to Ben's house in time to save him and his family. "What do we have in reserve? I know that we have been taking heavy losses all over town, but I want to know who and what we have left. We need to be ready in case more Rotowings show up to offer support. I also…"

Liam stopped listening. Hearing Ben's name was like opening a fresh wound. It was still too painful to think about. He was spared from having to distract himself away from thoughts of Ben and his family when he saw someone pushing their way through the crowd toward him.

411

Dr. Adhira burst through the milling crowd of people who surrounded the table where Liam was standing. She ran straight up to him, barely stopping herself before she crashed into him. The first thought that occurred to him upon seeing her was how disheveled she looked. Last night, she had been well-groomed and put together. Now, her hair was a mess, her clothes were stained, and she looked tired.

Liam opened his mouth to say hello, but before he managed to get the words out, Dr. Adhira had seized his head and started examining him for any injuries. He couldn't help but feel a sense of déjà vu from the night before.

"I just heard that you had arrived and...What have they done to you?" she said with firm disapproval at his appearance. Liam realized that he must look terrible. The blood had been washed away from his face, but his shirt was still stained, not to mention all the cuts and bruises.

"I don't think it is broken," she said as she felt the bridge of his nose. "No sign of concussion, either," She concluded after thumbing back his eyelids. "Still, we need to get you taken care of."

Without waiting for his response, she grabbed his arm and practically dragged him to a nearby corner where an aid station had been set up. There were several cots surrounding the aid station where patients could lie down if necessary. One of the cots was occupied by someone wearing a thick bandage around their head, with more bandages crisscrossing their body. It was impossible to tell who was under all those bandages, but it did put Liam's injuries into perspective.

As they approached, he was directed to sit down on a metal examination table. Despite the hustle and bustle of the rest of the basement, this tiny corner was relatively quiet and offered some privacy. It was refreshing to sit down without being overwhelmed with noise and constant distractions.

The first thing Dr. Adhira did was to slap a cold compress against his face with instructions to hold it in place while she continued her examination. Liam did as he was instructed while she probed and prodded every inch of his body. In short order, she had changed the bandages around his side, applied some ointment to his wrists that took down the swelling, and patched up any cuts or scrapes that she could find. By the time she was done, he wondered whether there were more bandages and ointments on his skin than there was skin.

Satisfied with her work, Dr. Adhira reached up and pulled the cold compress away from his face. He was grateful for that since half of his face had grown numb from the cold. The blood-stained shirt that he had been wearing had been removed and now lay in a pile on the floor with some used gauze and soiled bandages. A new shirt was placed in Liam's lap, with the instructions that he put it on.

As he did so, he couldn't pry his eyes away from his old shirt. The dried blood brought to his mind a question that he desperately wanted answered.

"Dr. Adhira?" Liam asked. "Is there something wrong with my blood?"

"Your blood? Not that I can see, though I suggest you try harder to keep it on the inside from now on." Seeing that this answer didn't satisfy his question, Dr. Adhira continued. "If you are really concerned about it, I can take a sample and run some tests on it, though given that my office is now a pile of rubble, it may be a while before I can get those results back to you. Why?"

"The man that did this," Liam said, pointing to the bruises on his face. "He was surprised by the color of my blood. He asked me about it right before...before he...It doesn't matter. The point is, I didn't know what to say. I just...I was just wondering if there was something wrong with it."

Dr. Adhira paused for a long moment. She was studying him, trying to decide how best to answer his question. Finally, she said,

"There is nothing wrong you…other than the obvious cuts and bruises, of course. Other than that, everything about you is just the way it should be – perfectly normal for who you are."

When it appeared that Liam wasn't fully satisfied with that answer either, she continued. "Whatever that man said, he was most likely confused. There is nothing wrong with you. You can trust me on that. I should know. After all, I have been taking care of you your whole life. I was even there the moment you were brought into this world." She smiled as she remembered that night seventeen years ago.

Liam gave her a faint smile. He was glad to know that there was nothing wrong with him, but that didn't answer the question of why the trooper had been so surprised. The man had practically been in shock at the sight of his blood. He wanted answers.

He was about to press Dr. Adhira for more information when his aunt walked up with Mr. Malcolm by her side. "How is he, doctor?" Aunt Linda said, looking from Liam to Dr. Adhira.

"He has taken a nasty beating, but he should be alright," Dr. Adhira said. "The wound in his side is healing nicely, and the damage to his face and arms is superficial. It should heal in a few days. For now, I recommend plenty of rest and lots of liquids."

Aunt Linda nodded in understanding, while Mr. Malcolm smiled at Liam and gave him a thumbs-up.

"You had us worried for a while there, buddy." Mr. Malcolm said in a forced upbeat tone.

"That is not all," Dr. Adhira continued. "Physically, he will be fine, but emotionally and psychologically, I am not so sure. He has endured a lot of trauma in the past twenty-four hours. I would not be surprised if he is currently suffering from a mild case of shock, and possible PTSD."

"Thank you, doctor. That will be all," Aunt Linda said dismissively.

"I recommend that we—" Dr. Adhira did her best to press the subject, but was quickly interrupted.

"I said, 'Thank you, doctor.'" Aunt Linda said, cutting her off. "I will take it from here."

Mr. Malcolm held out his hand toward Dr. Adhira. Grudgingly, she took it, and he led her away, leaving Liam and his aunt alone together.

Aunt Linda sat down on a nearby stool, pulling it closer so that she was sitting directly in front of him. She didn't say anything at first. She simply sat there and looked at him. Her hand reached up as if to cup his face, but she stopped herself before making contact. Finally, she spoke.

"I know that today has been rough. We've lost a lot of good people," she said in a somber tone. She wasn't looking at him, which was odd for her. Her attention seemed to be focused on the floor. If he didn't know any better, he would think that she was having trouble looking him in the eye.

The silence stretched on as neither one of them spoke. The tension began to grow unbearable, and finally Aunt Linda broke the silence. She leaned in, placed a hand on his knee, and looked up to meet his gaze.

"Are you alright?" she asked.

"You heard the doctor," Liam replied. "I will be fine."

"That is not what I meant," Aunt Linda said. "Are *you* alright?"

"No, I am not alright," Liam said, letting out a short laugh. It wasn't funny. Nothing about this entire situation was funny, but laughing was the only thing that he could do. If he didn't laugh, he knew he would cry, and chances were, he wouldn't stop.

"How could I possibly be alright after everything that has happened? How do you watch your best friend be murdered in front of your eyes and not have it affect you? How can you stand around and watch so many people die, knowing that you are the cause of it all, and be alright with it?" he asked rhetorically.

"I know it can be hard," Aunt Linda said in a quiet, understanding voice. "And I want you to know that I am here for you if you want to talk. Whatever happens, I will always be here for you."

"I just...I just wish things could go back to the way they were before all of this happened. Back before..."

"Before what?" Aunt Linda asked.

"I don't know," Liam mumbled, trying to sort through his thoughts and emotions. "Before some fascist government showed up and started slaughtering everyone I know. Before Ben and his entire family were murdered for no reason. Before I...before I learned that my entire life has been a lie."

He grew quiet. He didn't want to talk about this – not now. People were dying out there, and he was sitting here thinking about himself.

"Talk to me," Aunt Linda said encouragingly. "Let it all out. No judgments. No pressure."

"Alright," he said, his voice gaining intensity as he went. "A few weeks ago, my life seemed normal. I went to school, I went to work, I spent time with my friends – wash, rinse, repeat. Then suddenly, this girl comes into my life. For the first time, I felt...something. I don't even know what. I just know that being with her makes me feel...good about myself.

"And then one day, we go for a walk in the woods, and everything goes to hell. She disappears for a week, only to return and tell me that she had practically been abducted and held hostage the entire time she was gone. Naturally, I don't believe her. After all, how could something like that happen? In Haven, of all places?

"Still, I decided to go along with it, only to find out that everything she said was true. Not just that, but she shows me a world outside of Haven – a world completely different from everything I have ever been told or shown. And now, I have to face the realization that everything I have ever been told is a lie – that everyone I know has been lying to me. To. My. Face.

"On top of all that, I find out that there is some tyrannical government out there that I had never heard of before that wants me and everyone else here dead. Can you even imagine what that feels like? Everyone around here seems to know about the Authority, and judging from the crates against the wall, they knew that this could happen. Not me. Nobody ever bothered to mention that to me.

"And the hardest part about all this, even worse than watching my friends and neighbors dying right in front of me, is that I still have no idea why. Why? Why is the Authority doing this? Why are they after me? Why is everyone so intent on protecting me? What makes me so damned special?"

Liam paused to catch his breath. It felt good to vent. The frustration that he had been feeling inside had been suppressed for far too long, and needed to be let out.

As the feelings of anger and frustration washed over him, he realized that he no longer felt numb. His emotions had found an outlet, and that outlet was anger. He was angry at everything and everyone. He was angry with Parker because she had started him down this road. He was angry at Ben for the part he'd played in all of this, and if he was being honest, he was angry that Ben had died before they'd had a chance to say that they were sorry to one another.

He was angry at the agents and the troopers who were running around killing people indiscriminately. He was angry with Mr. Malcolm, Gus, George, and everyone else who had participated in hiding the truth from him. He was angry at his aunt for keeping secrets from him and controlling him for all of these years.

Mostly, he was angry with himself.

He was angry that he'd allowed all this to go on. He was angry that he hadn't been able to stop any of it. He was angry that he'd allowed himself to be hauled away while Parker stayed behind. He was angry that he had been the cause for so much death.

In a tiny part of his mind, he even blamed himself for everything that had happened. He was the reason why the Authority had come. He was the reason why so many had sacrificed their lives. He was the reason.

The anger that had burned with such fire and intensity in his chest slowly faded away, replaced by guilt. He had already forgiven Parker and Ben for what had happened, but if this was all his fault, then it was him who needed forgiveness. He had no right to be mad at anyone since he had brought this terrible fate down on them.

Aunt Linda had been paying attention and noticed his change in mood. She reached out and lifted his chin. As their eyes met, she whispered the words that he longed to hear, but couldn't bring himself to ask for.

"This is not your fault," she said. "None of this is your fault. A long time ago, we made a decision. *We* did it. Everything that is happening right now is because *we* made that decision. You have nothing to blame yourself for."

"If that is true, then why is all of this happening?"

"There is still a lot that we haven't told you," Aunt Linda said softly. "I know how frustrating this must be for you."

"Then tell me," Liam pleaded. "Tell me what makes me so special. Everyone here is so quick to tell me that I am special, but nobody is willing to tell me why. Please, Aunt Linda. You are closer to me than anyone else. Please tell me."

Aunt Linda hesitated for a moment. She was clearly struggling with what to tell him and what not to tell him. In the end, she decided to split the difference.

"A long time ago, a bunch of like-minded people got together and formed...let's call it an organization. We had a specific goal in mind, and we were prepared to do anything to achieve that goal, even if it meant bringing down the Authority's wrath on our heads. We knew that we had to find someplace safe. Someplace where the Authority couldn't easily find us.

"That place ended up being Haven. We moved here so that we could continue our work without fear of exposure. For years, we labored in obscurity, dedicating our lives to make our dreams a reality. And then, one day, we succeeded. We did what no one else had managed to do. What no one else thought possible. We created you," Aunt Linda finished, staring seriously at Liam.

"What are you talking about?" Liam asked, completely confused. "You make it sound like I am some sort of lab experiment."

"In a way, you are," Aunt Linda confirmed. "You are the result of decades of hard work and perseverance. We...we made you. Right here, in this town. That is why you are special – because you are the culmination of our life's work. And we will do anything to protect you."

"Does that include lying to me?"

"We only lied to you to protect you. It was necessary to keep you from learning about who and what you really are."

"What I really am?" Liam blurted out. "And what is that, exactly? What is it that I am supposed to be?"

"I cannot tell you that. Not yet."

"Well, what can you tell me?"

"It was necessary to lie to you, not just about the world beyond Haven, but also about...other things," Aunt Linda said hesitantly.

"Like what?"

"For one thing, the people that you think were your parents were not."

"What?" Liam said in disbelief.

"The truth is that we don't know who they were – the people we told you were your parents, I mean. They were simply two people who had been painted on a billboard. We suspect that they had something to do with the town before we arrived, but we don't know.

"You don't have parents – at least, not in a traditional sense. But we still needed someone to fill that role in your life. Someone we could point to and reference in case it ever came up. It didn't matter who we used, so we figured that we could use the picture of the couple on the welcome sign. They fit the physical characteristics well enough to be convincing as your parents. We also felt that you would be able to establish an emotional connection with them if you thought they'd played an important role in the community," Aunt Linda explained.

Liam couldn't believe what he was hearing. Did his aunt just admit that they had chosen a picture of two strangers simply because it was convenient? He felt...violated.

This whole time, he had been talking to a picture of two absolute strangers. He had walked past their picture every day, thinking that he was passing a picture of his parents. He had taken pride in their roles in establishing the town of Haven. He had looked up to them.

Now, he knew. Those people, whoever they were, were a tool – a tool used to manipulate him. He could feel the anger returning. Just before it reached a critical point, a thought occurred to him. As it did, the anger disappeared like a popped bubble. It was replaced by something else – something that he could only describe as emptiness.

"You aren't really my aunt, are you?" Liam asked without the slightest hint of emotion.

"No," Linda responded.

"Then who are you?"

"I was a member of the organization that came here to Haven. I worked on the project that resulted in your creation," she said slowly.

"Why pretend to be my aunt?" Liam asked curiously.

"I was chosen to be your parental guardian. As I said, you don't have any parents, not in the traditional sense, but you still needed a familiar connection – someone that you could identify with and establish an emotional bond. I had extensive experience in childhood development and psychology. It was felt that these skills would be necessary to help you mature and grow," Linda explained.

Liam thought about that. He thought about all the times that they had shared – the late nights, the early mornings, and the long days. The one person whom he could count on, his aunt, had turned out to be a complete stranger.

"So, I guess that means that I am nothing more than an assignment to you. An experiment that needed a babysitter, and you were lucky enough to be tasked with the job," Liam practically spat the words at her.

"No," Linda replied vehemently, rising to her feet and looking down at him seriously. "You are everything to me. I have loved you from the very moment you were brought into this world. I may not be your mother, but I have loved and cared for you like you were my own.

"How many nights did I stay up with you, holding you in my arms until you fell asleep? How many times was I there to comfort you when you were sad? To take care of you when you were sick? Or simply to be there for you when you needed me?

"I love you. I have always loved you, and I will always love you. You mean more to me than you will ever know, and I will not stand here and let you say otherwise," she said sternly.

Liam bit his tongue. He wanted to believe that she didn't really care about him. That would make it so much easier for him to hate her. Besides, if she didn't care about him, then he didn't have to care about her, either. He would be free – free from her and free from feelings of guilt, worry, or responsibility. If only he could get himself to believe that she didn't care.

Unfortunately for him, it seemed that she truly did care about him. The look in her eyes was convincing enough. She loved him, despite the fact that she wasn't related to him in the slightest. More than that, the look on her face told him that if he tried arguing with her, she would be more than happy to put him in his place.

The more he thought about it, the more he realized that she was right. She had always been there for him. True, she could be harsh, demanding, controlling, and overbearing, but she could also be sweet, caring, comforting, and supportive. As far back as he could remember, she had always been there with a shoulder to cry on, an arm to lean on, and a helping hand to depend on. She truly had been there for him every single day of his life.

She wasn't his aunt, but she was the closest thing that he had to a parent. That realization helped cool his rising temper. He was still upset, but the overwhelming anger seemed to wash away like dirt being rinsed away by the rain. They would still need to work through some issues and definitely set some new boundaries and expectations, but for now, he could let it go – for the moment, at least.

"What am I?" he asked, trying to get back to the matter at hand.

"I cannot tell you that. There are rules in place that even I cannot break. There is only one person in town that can answer that question."

"Let me guess – Dr. Sorenson?"

"Yes. And right now, he is at the Watchtower, waiting for us," Linda said.

This bit of news was a welcome surprise. Ben had mentioned that he would take Liam to see Dr. Sorenson, but he had never mentioned where he was. Back in the woods, he had heard the word Watchtower mentioned several times, but he hadn't known what that meant. If Dr. Sorenson was at the Watchtower, and the Watchtower was where they were supposed to go, then he was eager to be on their way.

"We will go there as soon as we can, but for now, we have to wait," Linda said consolingly.

"Why?"

"If you weren't paying attention, the Authority's troops are between us and the Watchtower. We need to wait for them to leave before we can proceed," Linda replied dryly.

"We can fight them!" Liam said, jumping to his feet and heading over to a nearby wall where several crates of weapons were being stored. "We have guns, don't we?"

"It isn't that simple," Linda said, walking over to join him at the wall. She reached her hand into the crate and picked up a static rifle. "Do you see this? Do you know what it is?"

"Yeah, it is a static...rifle thingy. Look, I don't know everything about it, but I do know that all you have to do is crank that handle there until it is ready to shoot," Liam said pointing at the crank on the side of the rifle.

Linda smiled at his naiveté. "This is a Series 2 Static Rifle. They were initially designed for the military as a next-generation energy weapon. Unfortunately, they are unreliable in combat. An issue due mostly to the crank feature malfunctioning or the core losing containment."

"So?" Liam asked.

"So, they were obsolete even before they went into mass production. Better, more efficient, energy weapons were created around the same time. Weapons like those stun pistols or pulse rifles that the Authority's troopers are carrying around. The only reason why we have these is because the Authority has banned all other weapons.

"Like any tyrannical government, they are afraid of what would happen if their citizens had the ability to defend themselves. For that reason, it is almost impossible to get your hands on anything more sophisticated than this. As a matter of fact, the only reason why we have these is because we found several crates of them slated for destruction at an abandoned military base. We decided to take them with us on the off chance that they were ever needed. They may be flawed, but they are better than nothing," Linda explained.

"Well, what about those over there?" Liam said, walking toward a table where several shotguns and hunting rifles were laid out, ready to be cleaned.

Linda walked over and picked up a rifle from the table. "This thing is an antique. Those troops out there are wearing full body armor. Perhaps you noticed how bullets seemed to be bouncing off of them?" she said, putting the rifle back down on the table. "We use them because this is all we have. I am not about to risk your life, or the lives of anyone else here, on a fool's errand."

"So, what? We just stay here, in this basement? Twiddling our thumbs while the Authority brings reinforcements?" Liam asked.

"No," Linda said exasperatedly. "We plan on heading out shortly, but not toward the Watchtower. Best if we circle around to the east before heading north. That way, we will have a clear path between us and the Watchtower."

Liam wanted to argue more, but Mr. Malcolm decided that now was a good time to join them. He walked up and stood by

Linda's side, curious to know what they were talking about. He wasn't alone, either. Dr. Adhira was following close behind him, a bottle of water in one hand and some pills in another.

Dr. Adhira pushed the bottle of water into Liam's hand and instructed him to take the pills. She stood there, waiting for him to follow her instructions. She didn't move until after he'd put the pills in his mouth and swallowed, using the water to wash them down.

As he was lowering the bottle of water, Dr. Adhira put a finger under the bottom of it and pushed upward. He was forced to drink all of the water in the bottle before she removed her finger. Once he had finished, she took the now-empty bottle back and gave him a satisfied grin.

"Now, try to get some rest. And do your best not to get captured or hurt. I cannot keep patching you up like this. At this rate, I am going to have to raise my rates, anyways."

From her tone, it was obvious that Dr. Adhira was making a joke. She was serious about him getting some rest and staying out of danger, though. He nodded reassuringly to her, and she reached up and gave him a kiss on the cheek before turning around and heading back to the aid station.

"You certainly have a way with the ladies," Mr. Malcolm said, nudging Liam gently in the arm. "I have been trying to get a peck on the cheek from the good doctor for years now."

It was unclear whether Mr. Malcolm was joking or not. Liam had never suspected that Mr. Malcolm was interested in Dr. Adhira, but then again, there was a lot going on around here that he hadn't noticed before. Perhaps there was a future for those two after all.

"Speaking of which, I am sorry about what happened to Parker. I heard about what happened back at Ben's house, and I wanted you to know...I am sorry."

"Thank you," Liam said, not sure how to respond. "What happened to Ben and his family was wrong. As for Parker..."

"She will be okay; don't you worry about it."

"How can you say that?" Liam asked. "We left her there, with those...monsters! Who knows what they plan on doing to her? She could be dead right now for all we know."

"There wasn't anything we could do for her," Linda chimed in. "You were our first priority. If there had been a way to get all of you out, then we would have done it. As it was, we barely escaped with our own lives. I couldn't risk your safety to save her, and I am pretty sure that she wouldn't want me to, either."

"Your aunt is right," Mr. Malcolm said, coming to Linda's defense. "It is always easy to look back at what we could have done, but when you are actually in the moment, things get much more difficult. There isn't always a happy ending."

"Is that supposed to make me feel better?" Liam asked.

"No, but this will: If she was taken alive, she is safe. For now, at least. They won't do anything to her until after she is tried at a Hall of Justice."

"So, there is still a chance we can rescue her?" Liam asked excitedly.

"We have other concerns at the moment," Linda added.

"Like what? Sitting here and waiting for the right opportunity to make a run for the Watchtower?" Liam countered.

"That is the best option at the moment," Mr. Malcolm said. "Right now, our forces are engaging the enemy. Without air support, they will be forced to fall back. When that happens, we can drive them out of town while you head for the Watchtower."

"Besides, we can't risk tipping them off about your presence here," Linda added.

"What does that have to do with anything?" Liam wondered.

"We are pretty sure that the Authority doesn't know that you are here," Mr. Malcolm confided. "Oh, they know that we are here, but not you. To them, we are a bunch of renegades – a collection of runaways and malcontents that need to be rounded up.

"But you? We are pretty sure they don't know about you yet. If that were the case, they would have sent more than just a few retrieval teams. But enough of that. Right now, there is a good chance that we can slip through their fingers. Which is why we can't be too hasty. No reason to risk exposing you unnecessarily."

"Why would it matter?" Liam asked. "They already know who I am. Agent Lewis and those other troopers already arrested me. I am pretty sure they know I am here."

"They might know who you are, but not *what* you are. Once they find that out, we can expect a lot more aggression from the Authority," Linda added.

"War Machines," Mr. Malcolm agreed.

Liam had no idea what War Machines were, but the way that Mr. Malcolm had said it meant that they weren't a good thing. Of course, if this was how the Authority reacted without knowing about him, then he hated to think of how they would react when they found out what he really was. Whatever that was.

Liam nodded, letting both Linda and Mr. Malcolm know that he understood. They were going to wait for the right opportunity. He didn't like the idea of hanging around in the basement of a movie theater, especially if Parker was out there somewhere nearby. In his mind, she was out there waiting to be rescued. It was up to him to do it, but he couldn't do a thing until he was out of this basement.

"Listen to me," Mr. Malcolm said, putting an arm around Liam's shoulders and squeezing. "As soon as this is over, we will go and find Parker and bring her back. But only after this is over and you are safe. Until then, we need to be patient."

"And don't let me catch you trying to sneak out of here," Linda warned. "If I catch you trying to—"

Whatever she had been planning on saying was cut off by the sound of a huge explosion directly over their heads. Liam could hear shouts coming from above, accompanied by the sounds of gunfire and the crackling of pulse rifles.

Chapter 19: The Ambush

Like a stirred-up ant hill, the basement burst into a frenzy. People were running in every direction, and the room quickly devolved into pure chaos. Liam watched as several of the nearby tables were knocked over, spilling their contents onto the floor. Hands were reaching out from every direction, trying to grab weapons off the floor. A fight broke out between two people trying to hold onto the same hunting rifle.

The sounds of gunfire overhead intensified. Like a wave, the mass of people in the basement began moving toward the stairs at the front of the room. Liam was swept up in the current of bodies and dragged toward the entrance. Linda managed to grab his arm and pull him toward the wall, preventing him from being swept away in the tide of bodies.

The crackling of pulse rifles was getting louder, and additional explosions went off in the theater above. Where just a moment ago, people had been surging toward the stairs, the tide was now pushing back in the opposite direction. People were pouring down the stairs, running to get away from the onslaught.

Again, Liam was caught up in the current, and both he and Linda were pushed back to the far wall of the basement. He felt his back collide with something hard. Turning his head, he saw that he had been pressed back against the cinderblock wall of the basement. Even though his back was up against a wall, people continued to push against him, trying to get as far away from the fighting as possible. He had never been claustrophobic before, but he was starting to feel that way now.

Liam felt someone grab ahold of his hand and pull him sideways along the wall. He allowed himself to be pulled, since it seemed a better idea than being squished to death. He continued to be pulled across the back wall until he found himself standing in a small pocket in the far corner. The pocket was actually a utility station that was surrounded by a chain-link fence that stretched from floor to ceiling. A massive sewer pipe protruded from the wall behind him, covered by a steel grate. Next to it was a fuse box with dozens of electrical lines running through the ceiling to the theater above.

As soon as he was inside the pocket, Linda slammed the gate closed, preventing anyone else from getting in. The pocket wasn't large, but it was definitely better than being out there with all the pushing and shoving. The crowd was still pressing to get as far back from the entrance as possible. It was getting so bad that the chain link fence surrounding the pocket began to buckle under the pressure.

Their panic made no sense to him. Hadn't they been preparing for a fight not ten minutes ago? And yet, in the face of actual opposition, their resolve had crumbled.

In reality, Liam could understand their motivation better than he wanted to admit. The thought of fighting the Authority's troops scared him, and the feeling appeared to be mutual.

Right at the point where the chain link fence was about to give way, another explosion went off. This time, the explosion didn't go off in the theater above, but in the basement itself. Smoke and dust filled the air as one of the outer walls exploded inward with a thunderous boom. Where the crowd had been frantic before, they were now left in absolute hysterics.

As the dust and smoke from the explosion began to settle, light from a gigantic hole in the side of the basement filtered in. It took a moment for Liam's eyes to adjust to the brightness shining down through the hole. When they did, he saw Authority troops standing in the gap, blocking the way out. More troops were pouring down the stairs, pulse rifles in hand.

Liam felt a wave of panic engulf him. He had already been trapped in a basement once today. His hands were trembling, and he wished desperately that he had one of those weapons that only a few minutes ago had been readily available. Just like before, he was defenseless, and all he could do was stand there and watch.

To his great relief, the crowd stopped pressing backwards and started pushing toward the hole in the wall. The crackling of pulse rifles was met with the sound of gunfire and the discharge of countless static rifles. Though the Authority's troops were better equipped, their numbers weren't sufficient enough to hold back the tide of townsfolk that was now bearing down on them.

Within seconds, the Authority's troops had been pushed out of the basement. Rather than troops pouring through the hole in the wall, townsfolk were climbing out onto the street beyond. The crackling sound of pulse rifles outside intensified, signaling that the battle was far from over.

As the basement cleared out, Liam could see that most of the room was now in a state of general disarray. Most of the tables had been knocked over and overturned, and many of the crates that had lined the walls had been knocked over. Their contents were now spread out on the floor. More than the contents of the crates littered the ground. Everywhere he looked, he could see bodies lying on the floor, some of which were dead troopers, but most of which were townsfolk.

With everyone fleeing through the hole in the wall, Liam assumed that they too would try to escape with the rest of them. It was surprising when Linda held him back when he went to open the gate. He tried to protest, but she was adamant that they stay where they were.

"What are you doing? This is our chance," Liam protested.

"Wait!" Linda replied firmly.

As she finished speaking, the street outside erupted in several massive explosions, one right after another. Flames burst through the hole in the wall from the street, forcing back anyone who had been trying to escape that way. As for the people that were already outside, Liam could only hope that they'd managed to get away before the explosion could tear them to pieces.

Whatever momentum the townsfolk had gained in pushing back the Authority was now lost. The few townsfolk who had positioned themselves at the base of the stairs were now retreating farther back into the basement. They took cover behind the overturned tables and collapsed piles of crates as dozens of pulse blasts filled the room. Blasts were coming both from the stairs and through the hole in the wall, despite the flames that still hadn't died down.

The basement was filling with smoke, but through it all, Liam could see Mr. Malcolm running in their direction. He had to stop several times to turn and fire his static rifle before he reached the gate.

As he was lifting the handle to enter, there was another explosion. This one was different from the rest – mostly because it wasn't caused by the Authority's troops. One of the boxes of ammunition that had been placed against the wall had caught fire and then exploded. Bullets fired haphazardly into the air, striking down troopers and townsfolk alike.

Mr. Malcolm collapsed against the gate as a bullet collided with his shoulder. Both Linda and Liam rushed to open the gate and let him in. As the gate swung open, he tumbled into the pocket, dropping his static rifle on the floor.

Fearing the worst, Liam knelt down to see if there was anything he could do to help. He looked around the basement, but Dr. Adhira was nowhere in sight, which was probably a good thing. He hoped that she had made it out before the explosions outside had cut off all escape.

With a grimace of pain, Mr. Malcolm waved Liam to stand back. He then stood up on his own and stumbled over to the large sewer pipe against the wall. While one of his arms hung lifeless at his side, the other reached down and undid the bolt that held the steel grate in place. In one powerful motion, he lifted the grate high overhead, exposing a tunnel large enough for someone to crawl through.

"Go!" he yelled at Liam, urging him to climb inside.

Liam didn't have to be told twice. He climbed up into the sewer pipe and crawled forward on his hands and knees. After he had gone a few feet, he looked back to see Linda climbing in behind him. He fully expected that Mr. Malcolm would be next to follow them into the pipe, but instead of climbing in, he released the grate, and it slammed back into place.

Liam called out, but Mr. Malcolm wasn't listening. He simply grabbed the bolt from where it had fallen on the floor and replaced it on the grate, then pulled a padlock from off the wall that Liam hadn't noticed before and clicked it shut over the bolt, locking them in. It seemed that Mr. Malcolm wasn't going to be joining them after all.

"Do me a favor," Mr. Malcolm called through the closed grate. "Take care of yourself, and if you get a chance, take care of that girlfriend of yours too. You never know how much someone means to you until they are gone." With that, he turned around, picked up his static rifle, and ran out of the pocket into the surrounding smoke that now filled the basement.

Liam didn't want to leave, but there was nothing else he could do. The pipe wasn't big enough to turn around in, and the grate had been locked from the other side. Not only that, but the smoke from the basement was starting to fill the pipe as well. His only option was to press onward. It didn't hurt that Linda was nudging him forward either.

As they reached an upward bend in the pipe, another explosion rocked the room behind them. All Liam could think was that he hoped that Mr. Malcolm would be alright. With everything else going on, he wanted to hold onto the belief that somehow he had made it out of the basement alive – a foolish hope, maybe, but one that he was willing to fool himself into believing.

The upward bend in the pipe allowed him to stand up straight, rather than having to continue crawling on his hands and knees. There was a ladder bolted into the side of the pipe that led upward to a metal hatch overhead. Linda, who was still on her hands and knees inside the pipe, motioned for Liam to start climbing.

He reached the top of the ladder and reached out to open the hatch. It swung downward, nearly hitting him in the head. Rather than seeing an opening on the other side of the hatch, there were several wooden boards blocking the exit. He heard Linda say something like "break through," and so he started pushing against the boards. They didn't want to budge at first, but after a few blows from his elbow, they loosened and popped off.

He climbed through the opening and was shocked to find himself behind the display cases of Linda's antique shop. He knew that the movie theater and the antique shop shared a common wall, but he'd had no idea that there was a secret passage between them. Then again, after everything he had seen in the last two days, he wouldn't be surprised if every building in Haven had a secret room or passageway.

"It's an emergency exit," Linda said as she pulled herself out of the hole after Liam. "Never thought I would ever use it."

As she climbed out, she immediately busied herself pulling supplies and two backpacks out from under the cash register. She pushed one into Liam's hand and slung the other on her back.

"Now, we need to keep our heads down and do our best to sneak out of here. The Authority's attention is directed at the theater next door. If we are careful, we should be able to sneak out the back without anyone noticing."

"You just plan on leaving everyone back there?" Liam asked incredulously.

"Yes," Linda said without a second thought. "Right now, anyone left down there is either dead or buying time for you to escape. So, if you want their deaths to mean something, you will put that backpack on and follow me."

To suit her words, she stood up and started moving toward the back door.

In that instant, Liam could hear the breaking of glass as the display window at the front of the store shattered. At the same time, a bright blue bolt of light soared through the air and struck Linda in the back. The force knocked her off her feet, and she fell forward onto the floor in a crumpled heap.

Without thinking about it, Liam lifted his head to look over the display case to see where the pulse blast had come from. Standing in the street outside the antique shop was an Authority trooper. The pulse rifle in their hands was still aimed at the place where Linda had been standing.

Seeing Liam's head pop up above the display case, the trooper fired his weapon again. Quick reflexes saved him from being shot in the head as he ducked below the display cases. The blast struck the display, causing the glass in the case to burst in every direction. Several more blasts followed in quick succession as the crackling sound of the trooper's weapon filled the air.

Resolving to keep his head down, Liam crawled along the back of the display cases, making his way to where Linda was lying on the ground. As he got closer, he could see that the pulse blast had hit her in the back, but the backpack she had been wearing had offered some protection. What was left of the backpack was now just a charred ruin that he pulled away and flung to the side.

There was a large black burn on Linda's back, but it was unclear how badly she had been hurt. As gently as he could, he turned her over. Her face was pale, and her eyes were closed. Liam's heart stopped as he realized that the backpack may not have been enough. It was possible that she was dead.

Doing his best to hold back his emotions, he reached out and touched her cheek. Immediately, her eyes opened as wide as they would go and she stared around in every direction, alarm painted on her face. Her arms and legs jerked back and forth as if she were trying to stand up, but something wasn't right. Liam tried to soothe her, but she only grew more agitated and panicked with every second.

She started calling out in a language he didn't recognize, and her voice stuttered and stammered with each word. Her outburst attracted the attention of the trooper out front, who immediately started shooting again. Liam placed a hand over her mouth, urging her to be silent. Any moment, that trooper would be coming through the front door, and they needed to leave before that happened.

"We have to get out of here," Liam whispered urgently. "We can use the bay doors in back. We just need to get to the backroom."

Linda looked up at him with vacant eyes. It was almost as if she didn't recognize him or what he was saying. More than likely, she had been knocked senseless from the pulse blast, but that didn't stop the fear coursing through Liam's veins.

His entire life, his Aunt Linda – yes, she was his aunt, regardless of whether they were actually related or not – had always been someone he could depend on. She had been his rock, the foundation upon which he had always relied. Seeing her like this, scared and vulnerable, was something that he had never wanted in his whole life. How could he take care of the person that he relied on to take care of him?

The feeling shook him to his innermost core. He felt like a little child, crying out for help, but nobody was answering. He couldn't do this without her. He needed her. More than ever, he needed her. Tears were streaming down his cheeks and landing on Aunt Linda's face.

The bell over the front door chimed as someone entered the antique shop. Liam looked up, eyes still clouded with tears, to see the trooper standing on the other side of the display case, rifle aimed directly at him. The sound of a gunshot echoed in Liam's ears, and the trooper jerked backward and stumbled back through the open door.

Liam looked down to see his Aunt Linda, propping herself up on one elbow while holding a handgun in her other hand. The vacant look had disappeared from her eyes, but she still looked slightly disoriented. As she turned her gaze back to him, he was glad to see a look of recognition in her eyes.

"Take this," she said, pressing the handgun into his hand. "And help me to sit up."

Liam took the pistol and set it on the floor beside him while he lifted his aunt into a sitting position against the back wall. She winced in pain when he moved her. It was obvious that they weren't going to be able to make a run for it with her in this condition.

The sound of crunching glass brought Liam's attention back to the front door. The trooper who his aunt had shot only seconds ago was getting back up. The bullet had ricocheted off their helmet, knocking them off their feet, but leaving them altogether unharmed. In desperation, Liam reached out and picked up the pistol that his aunt had given him.

Without thinking about what he was doing, he stood up and aimed the pistol at the trooper. His finger squeezed the trigger, and the pistol jerked violently in his grip. He had never fired a weapon before, but at this distance, his lack of experience wasn't an issue. The trooper stumbled backwards as the bullet struck their leg.

Liam continued to pull the trigger, firing round after round at the trooper. Each bullet struck them. Though some bounced off the body armor that they were wearing, enough of them managed to find the gaps between the body armor, causing the trooper to fall backwards onto the ground.

The pistol made a clicking sound as it ran out of ammo. Still, Liam continued to pull the trigger. He couldn't stop himself. Even with the trooper on the floor, unmoving, he still felt the need to pull the trigger.

He was tired of being afraid. He was tired of watching helplessly as the people he cared about were slaughtered before his very eyes. He'd wanted to do something about it for so long, and this was his chance. He was going to make sure that this trooper never hurt anyone ever again.

The realization of what he was doing, dawned on him with horrifying clarity. He had just taken someone's life. Yes, he had been defending himself, but that didn't make him feel any better about it. In fact, the only thing he felt at the moment was revulsion.

He dropped the pistol, disgusted with the thought of holding it one second longer than necessary. It fell to the floor, landing with a thud.

"What did I...what did I just do?" he said, though he was speaking more to himself than to anyone else.

"You did what you had to do to defend yourself," Aunt Linda said weakly. "You did nothing wrong."

"But I..."

"Don't think about it. For now, just listen," Aunt Linda said, straining to get the words out. "You have to go. You have to get to the Wa—watch...tow...er. Leave through the back door. Don't stop for anyone. Head north toward the ressssserzch facilllllllity."

Aunt Linda had to stop to keep herself from stammering. Whatever damage had been done, it had really messed her up. Liam reached out and tried to pull her to her feet, but she resisted.

"Come on. You have to get up," he told her. "More of the Authority's troops will be here soon. We have to go."

"Listen to me," Aunt Linda said, grabbing his shirt and pulling him close. "You have to leave me here. I am in no condition to wa...lk, and you cannot carry me."

"The hell I can't," Liam said defiantly.

"It's okay," she told him gently. "I will be alright, but it is time for you to go now." She paused as she looked into his eyes. "I love you sssssso much. My greatestttt regret was that I couldn't be your real motherrrrr."

"Please get up," Liam all but whimpered. "Please. I don't want to lose you."

"You will ne...ver lose me," she said as she brought her hand down to rest against his chest. "I willllll always be...be, right here."

Liam couldn't take it anymore. He reached out and embraced his aunt with tears rolling down his cheeks. She held him for a few precious seconds, like she had when he was younger. He could even hear her humming softly under her breath, like she used to do when putting him to sleep at night.

He never wanted to let go, but his aunt's gentle hands pulled them apart. She gave him one final smile before nodding toward the backdoor.

"Go. Go now," she said. "Hhhhhe is waiting for you."

"I will come back for you," Liam promised. "Whatever happens, I will come back when this is all over."

Aunt Linda merely nodded and nudged him toward the door. Every step that he took was agony. After everything that had happened to him, this was the worst. He didn't want to leave her behind, he didn't want to continue alone, and, most importantly, he didn't want to be alone. He wanted his aunt, the person who had been his surrogate mother for all these years, to be by his side.

As he reached the back door and pulled open the handle, Liam stopped and looked back. Aunt Linda was still sitting there where he had left her. She nodded to him, as if to say goodbye, and then mouthed, "Go."

Liam started to turn to go out the door, but something caught his eye. Through the front window of the antique store, he could see the trooper he had shot, struggling to sit up. They were still alive, and in their hands was a black cylinder. He watched as the trooper pulled a pin out of the top of the cylinder before tossing it through the doorway into his aunt's shop.

Before he had time to react, the grenade exploded in a flash of bright light. The force of the explosion lifted him off his feet and flung him backwards through the open door. He landed on his back several feet away, forcing the air out of his lungs. Pain radiated through every inch of his body as he tried to sit up. Moving was painful, but he forced himself to roll over onto his stomach and then push himself to his hands and knees.

A wave of nausea suddenly washed over him, causing him to vomit on the ground in front of him. His head was spinning – or perhaps it was the world around him that was spinning. He closed his eyes, trying to shut out the pain and stop the flecks of light that were obscuring his vision.

He lowered his head to the ground and shut his eyes to keep himself from falling over. How long he stayed in that position, he didn't know. When he finally opened his eyes, the world was no longer spinning, but the sight in front of him made him want to throw up all over again.

The sky was filled with black smoke as flames devoured what remained of his aunt's shop. On the other side of the doorway raged an inferno. The heat from it caused sweat to break out on his forehead, and he had to raise his hand to shield his face from the heat.

Somehow, he mustered the strength to drag himself away from the burning building. He took refuge against Gus's van. He was so out of it that he didn't stop to wonder how the van had ended up back here, though he figured someone must have hauled it back sometime in the night. From his position against the van, he watched as the antique store burned.

His aunt was inside. She had been sitting only a few feet away from the grenade when it went off. In the state she was in, there was no way she could have made it out alive.

The realization that his aunt was dead hit him like a hammer striking an anvil. It sent shivers down his spine, and he vomited again – not that there was anything left in his stomach to vomit at this point.

As he watched the blaze consume what remained of his aunt's shop, several of the roof beams gave way and collapsed in on themselves. Without their support, the outer wall began to sway back and forth. With less than a moment's notice, the wall fell outward, right where he was sitting against Gus's van. Instinctively, he ducked down and rolled under the van, seeking protection from the shower of bricks that rained down all around him.

When the dust cleared, Liam could see that the van was now completely surrounded by the collapsed wall. Bricks and debris lay everywhere. Claustrophobia began settling over him once more, and he felt the immediate urge to get out from under the van. He pulled himself to the side furthest away from the collapsed wall and began digging.

It was hard at first. He was lying on his side, unable to get any leverage – not to mention that the air was full of dust and dirt that forced him to breathe through his shirt. Eventually, he was able to make a small hole, not big enough for him to climb through – not yet, anyway – but big enough for him to see out.

He reached for another brick, but ended up bumping his head on the bottom of Gus's van. Another wave of nausea washed over him. Rolling over onto his back, he pressed his hands to his temples and closed his eyes. When he opened them, the flecks in his vision had returned. He tried to move, but that made him more nauseous. The best thing would be to wait for it to go away. Then he could climb out and head toward the Watchtower.

As he lay there, waiting for the nausea to pass, colors began to swirl in his vision. His eyes felt heavy, and he was having a hard time keeping his eyes open. The last thing he remembered before he passed out was the face of his aunt as she said, "He is waiting for you."

Chapter 20: The Price of Freedom

Agent Lewis slowly swayed back and forth from the shackles that were fastened to the roof over his head. This had been his only amusement for the past few hours. The length of the shackles prevented him from sitting down on the ground, which meant that the only thing he could do was to alternate between standing and swaying. If only the metal table and chair that shared the room with him were a little closer, he might have been able to use them to give his poor arms and legs a rest.

Unfortunately for him, both the table and the chair were out of arm's reach. This also meant that all his possessions, which still sat on the table where they had been left, were also out of reach. With no way of reaching the table, chair, or his possessions, there was nothing left for him to do but hang there and gently sway back and forth.

At first, he had expected someone to come check on him at regular intervals, but as the hours passed, it became less and less likely. At some point, he lost track of time. It was difficult to tell how much time had gone by when you didn't have a watch and there were no windows to look out of, which meant that he could have been hanging there for a few hours or even a day or so.

He might not know exactly how long it had been since Linda ran out of the room in a huff, but he did know one thing: he had been completely forgotten by his captors. That was the only explanation for their prolonged absence. At the very least, they should have left a guard out in the hallway to make sure he didn't try to escape. But the total silence coming from the other side of the door hinted that they hadn't even done that.

After the first few hours, he had tried calling out to get someone's attention. His yells had gone unanswered. If nothing else, he had expected someone to come and tell him to shut up, but they never had. Each failed attempt at attracting his captors' attention reaffirmed in his mind that there was no one out there to hear him. He was alone.

One of the things that annoyed him was that his captors hadn't even bothered to remove this possessions from the table when they left. At first, he had considered it a stroke of good luck, but as the hours passed, he came to see it for what it really was: torture.

Seeing his stun pistol on the table in front of him only reinforced the idea that he could use it to cut through the door and escape. The only problem with that plan was that he was shackled to the floor and the ceiling. Having his stun pistol there, only a few feet away and yet completely out of reach, mocked him. The path to freedom lay within his grasp, if only he could reach out and grab it. He couldn't, of course, which was why it had become torture to have it there.

Knowing that he could escape if only he could find a way to get out of his shackles had quickly turned into a sadistic form of torture. After a while, he even began to wonder whether his belongings had been left there on purpose. It made sense in a way. What better torture than to present your victim with hope, no matter how improbable? Hope would drive you insane faster than any physical pain could.

Eventually, he had dismissed the idea that he was slowly being tortured and had come to the realization that it had been an oversight on their part. That, or they really didn't consider him enough of a threat to make the effort of removing his belongings. Either way, it was insulting.

By this time, his hands had gone numb from the pressure of hanging by his wrists. With a groan, he stood up and relieved the tension on his hands. He could only hang from his wrists for so long before he had to stand up and stretch, only to repeat the cycle again and again.

It wasn't just the numbness that required him to change positions every ten minutes or so. Cramping had become a serious problem. His feet and legs ached when he stood, and his hands and arms burned when he hung by his wrists. It was a vicious cycle.

Thinking back on it, Agent Lewis remembered taking a great deal of pleasure in revealing the function of the mobile relay to his captors. The satisfaction of knowing that he had gotten the best of them had put a large smile on his face that had lasted for quite some time. By now, the satisfaction had faded to a fond memory – a memory that was quickly being lost in the agony of his current situation.

What he wouldn't give to hear someone's voice outside the door or have the door open and see someone walk in. At least that way, he would know that he hadn't been completely forgotten. The more time that passed, the more he feared that nobody was ever coming back for him.

That was the really frustrating part about all this. If the retrieval teams had already arrived, which was likely, considering how much time had passed, then surely they would have found him by now. If they had been overpowered by the townsfolk, then one of them should have come along to check on him. The fact that no one had come back for him hinted that maybe there was no one left to find him.

Well, he wasn't about to accept the idea that he had been left to die in this room. It was far too bland and unimaginative to be the last thing that he ever saw. Once again, his mind turned to the possibility of escape.

He couldn't break free from his shackles, and they were firmly bolted to the wall, so he couldn't yank them free either. There had to be something, though – something that he could use to loosen the shackles or possibly unlock them. His eyes scanned the room for what felt like the hundredth time.

There was the metal chair, which would have been nice to sit on if it had been a few feet closer to him, but wasn't useful in helping him escape. There was the metal table, which was also out of reach and equally useless. And then there were the contents of his pockets, all laid out on top of the table.

There was his stun pistol, but that was out of reach. Besides, it wouldn't do him much good unless he pushed it to the maximum setting. Even then, it was doubtful that it could cut through his shackles. They were made of wrought iron and were thick and sturdy. Chances were, he would end up hurting himself long before he made a dent in the shackles.

The door was another matter. If he somehow managed to free himself, he was confident that the stun pistol would be powerful enough to cut his way through.

There was his badge and identification, but those wouldn't help him with the shackles or the door. That left a flashlight, several energy bars, a pair of wrist restraints, and the mobile relay. The relay itself was nothing more than a high-tech paper weight at this point. The battery had slowly wound down until the screen went black, making it about as useful as a brick – a brick with an antenna sticking out of it.

Maybe if he could get his hands on his badge, he could use the metal edge to file down one of the links in the chain that connected his shackles to the ceiling. That, of course, was a stupid idea. The cheap alloy that made up his badge wouldn't even make a scratch on the iron chain.

Maybe if he...*Wait a second*! Agent Lewis redirected his attention back to the mobile relay. How could he have missed it? The antenna! The relay itself wasn't much use at this point, but the antenna sticking out from the relay might be exactly what he needed.

Excitement flooded through him as he looked from the relay to the shackles around his wrists. They were old, like someone had found them tucked away in a museum before they'd decided to use them. On the side of each shackle was a keyhole. He wasn't an expert by any means, but if he was right, those shackles were locked with a simple ratchet and release pin design. If he could somehow get something small and thin between the ratchet and the pin, he could disengage the lock and pull his hand free. The antenna might do the trick, assuming that it didn't break in the mechanism first.

Alright, he thought. He now knew how he could unlock his shackles. Now, he just needed to figure out how to get his hands on the antenna. The table was clearly out of reach, so simply picking it up wasn't an option. Even with him straining against his restraints as hard as he could, he would still fall short of reaching the table. There was some slack in the chains that connected his shackles to the ceiling, but not enough.

Still, Agent Lewis continued to try to think of ways to reach the relay. For the first time since he'd awoken in this cement room, he had a plausible plan for getting out, and he wasn't about to give up now. If he couldn't reach it with his hand, he would need to find some other way.

He looked down, taking a mental inventory of everything that was at his disposal. There wasn't much. His shoes and socks had been removed, along with his trench coat. That left him with his white dress shirt, his pants, and his belt.

His belt! If he could unbuckle it, he could slip it out of the belt loops around his waist and use it to lasso the relay on the table. He would have to use the buckle to snag the relay, but if he was successful, he should be able to drag it across the floor to where he was standing.

Though still incomplete, his plan was starting to come together. He could unlock the shackles by using the antenna on the relay. He could get the relay by unbuckling his belt and using it like a lasso. He could unbuckle his belt by...

And that was where his plan came to an end. Until he could figure out a way to unbuckle his belt, he wasn't going anywhere.

It wasn't like he could simply reach down and unfasten it. His hands were shackled over his head, preventing him from undoing it himself. His feet were also out of the question. So how was he supposed to unbuckle his belt?

Agent Lewis slumped in his shackles once more, his plans for escape hitting a dead end. Much like the rest of his possessions on the table, the antenna was now taunting him with the possibility of escape while still remaining firmly out of reach. If only he could somehow free one hand, that would be enough to get his plan started.

While he was considering his options, a desperate thought drifted up from the deepest part of his mind. It wasn't a happy thought, or even a clever thought, but it might just work. There was a way to get one of his hands free, but he didn't like it. The mere thought of it sent a shiver down his spine.

A long time ago, he had learned the basics on how handcuffs and wrist restraints worked. The wrist was the narrowest part of the arm. On one side, you had the hand, and on the other, the forearm. By tightening restrains around the wrist, it made it almost impossible to remove your hands – almost.

The part of the body that made the hand wider than the wrist was the thumb joint. It protruded out from the rest of the hand. Without that, the hand would be the same size as the wrist, and the restraints could be removed.

This meant that if Agent Lewis wanted to free one of his hands, he would have to dislocate his thumb. That might give him enough wiggle room to slip his hand out of the shackle. He shuddered, knowing full well how much this was going to hurt.

There was a reason why most people didn't go around dislocating body parts, but desperate times called for desperate measures.

Using his left hand, he gripped his right thumb firmly. Closing his eyes and clenching his jaw in anticipation, he prepared himself for what was about to happen. He hesitated only a moment before giving his thumb a quick jerk.

There was a loud snapping sound, and pain shot down his arm in waves. Unable to stop himself, he let out a chorus of swear words that echoed off the walls and filled the room with the sounds of profanity. If that didn't get someone's attention, then nothing would.

More than ten minutes had gone by before he was finally able to get a hold of himself. His thumb hurt, but the initial shock had passed. Looking up at his right hand, he could see that his thumb was now protruding out at an awkward angle. It had also turned a nasty shade of red and was swelling up. If he was going to do something, he had to do it before the swelling got any worse.

Grabbing his dislocated thumb with his other hand, he repositioned it toward the center of his palm. The slightest movement reignited the pain, but it was bearable. Once his thumb was in position, he pulled with all his might. The pain was excruciating, but he had come too far to stop now. Slowly, ever so slowly, his hand started to pull free.

In one glorious instant, his hand slipped free of the shackle and fell to his side. He allowed it to hang there, pleased with his success. The satisfaction of freeing his hand outweighed the price he had paid to set it free. As he brought his hand up to his face to survey the damage, he could see that he hadn't dislocated his thumb like he had planned; he had broken it.

Still, he was determined to push on to the next stage of his plan. Now that his hand was free, he reached down and carefully unbuckled the belt at his waist. His hand was shaking uncontrollably, and it was hard to grab the belt without using his thumb. Never again would he take his thumb for granted.

The belt came undone, and he pulled it free from his pants. Positioning the buckle under his chin, he held it there while he wrapped the other end around his hand. Since he couldn't grip the belt in his fist without using his thumb, he had to wrap it around his hand several times to make sure it wouldn't fall off. This shortened its length, but he was confident that it would still be long enough to reach the table.

He leaned forward as far as he could and began swinging the belt back and forward in the direction of the table. It took him three tries before he was able to successfully hook the top of the relay with the belt buckle. He gave the belt a tug, and the relay fell off the table and onto the floor. He continued to use the belt to bring it even closer until it was touching his right foot.

Even though his feet were shackled, he was able to grip the antenna between his toes and raise it up high enough to grab with his hand. He let out a long, exhausted sigh as he held the relay against his chest. Now, he just needed to pry the antenna free.

It wasn't as easy as he had originally thought. He ended up using his teeth to chew away the rubber casing that surrounded the antenna before he was able to tear it away from the rest of the relay. Several times, he had to stop and put the relay in his shirt pocket to rest his hands before starting again.

Now that the antenna had been pulled free of the relay, Agent Lewis positioned it at the base of the shackle on his left wrist. It took several tries, but he was eventually able to push the antenna into the gap between the ratchet and the pin. His arm was aching from the exertion, and his hand throbbed with pain, but he refused to stop until...

The pin released and the shackle opened. It was at that moment that he learned how much of his weight had been held up by the shackle around his wrist. With his hand now free, his legs gave way, and he toppled to the floor. He lay there for a good fifteen minutes, reveling in the ability to lie down.

After his fifteen-minute break, he pushed himself back up to his feet. He still had to get his feet loose, after all. The antenna was still sticking out of the wrist shackle where he had left it. He plucked it out using his left hand and got to work on the shackles around his feet. In no time at all, he was free.

He was still a little unsteady on his feet, so he made his way over to the chair and sat down. It was just as comfortable as he'd imagined it would be. He must have sat there for half an hour before he felt ready to move. His muscles were sore, but he was free, and that was all that mattered.

Agent Lewis stood up and started collecting his things from the table with his good hand. His shoes and trench coat were nowhere to be seen, so he had to put everything into his pants pockets for now. He refastened his belt around his waist, picked up his stun pistol in his left hand, and approached the door.

He had been confident that his stun pistol could cut through the metal door if he set it to the maximum setting. Doing so meant that there was a chance that he could overload the capacitors in the stun pistol, but it was something that he had to risk. Besides, he didn't have to cut a large hole; he only needed to cut a hole where the lock was.

Shielding his eyes, he turned the pistol's setting to maximum and held it against the side of the door. He pulled the trigger and held it down. Sparks shot out in every direction as the stun pistol melted a hole in the metal door where he suspected the lock would be. He must have guessed correctly, because twenty seconds later, there was a loud clang on the floor outside the door.

Lowering the stun pistol, Agent Lewis reached out and turned the doorknob. The door swung open, revealing the hallway beyond. The bolt from the door lock lay on the floor on the other side of the doorway, still glowing red-hot. For that matter, his stun pistol had grown quite warm as well. He had to hold it gingerly to make sure he didn't accidentally burn himself until it cooled off.

Slowly – ever so slowly – he stuck his head out of the doorway and looked from side to side. Just as he suspected, there was no one to be seen in either direction. He let out a whoop of triumph as he stepped through the doorway and out into the hallway beyond. It had cost him a broken thumb, but that seemed a reasonable price to pay for his freedom.

Curious about his surroundings, he looked around to see if there was an exit nearby. The hallway in which he stood looked like it belonged in any normal office building he had ever seen. There were doors lining the hall on both sides, with nameplates and labels marking each door. The hallway stretched out in both directions, lit by fluorescent lights that hung off the ceiling. The absence of windows meant that he would need to follow the hallway until he reached a suitable exit.

Although he could have gone in either direction, he chose to head off in the same direction that Linda had gone before the door had slammed shut. She no doubt had been running in the direction of the nearest exit, which meant that he would find what he was looking for if he followed in her footsteps.

Before he took more than five steps, he stopped. The door next to him had a label that read *Observation Room*. It was the next door down from the interrogation room where he had been kept. This made it likely that the room beyond was what was on the other side of the two-way mirror.

Raising his stun pistol, he reached down and turned the doorknob. The door swung open under its own momentum, revealing an empty room with nothing in it except for a tripod-mounted camera facing the two-way mirror. A light on top of the camera was flashing, indicating that it was still transmitting a signal, though if anyone was watching, he couldn't say. So, it seemed that whoever had told Linda to stop choking him hadn't really been there at all. They must have been watching from somewhere else.

If they were still watching him through the camera, then that meant that they knew that he had escaped. There was a chance that they could be sending reinforcements to his location at that very moment – yet another reason for him to find the nearest exit. He left the room and the camera behind as he resumed his search for a way out.

He walked down the hallway, stopping at every other door to open them and look inside. Most of the rooms were empty, with a thick layer of dust collecting on the floor. Some rooms weren't empty at all. He found several that were filled with desks, chairs, and other office furniture that was stacked from floor to ceiling.

No matter which room he poked his head into, there were no windows and no discernable exits that he could see – only cement walls and fluorescent lights. He continued on down the hallway, refusing to be discouraged. The hallway ended at an intersection. Before him stretched another hallway that looked almost identical to the one he was standing in.

He had no idea which way would lead to an exit, so he chose to go right and hope for the best. His journey ended twenty feet later as the hallway stopped at a cluster of offices and an unused breakroom. Judging from the layer of dust on everything, this section of the building hadn't been used in some time.

Retracing his steps, Agent Lewis headed back to the intersection, and this time, he took the left path. The hallway ran for almost forty feet before making a sharp turn that ended in a green door. The label on the door said *Stairs*. Expecting to find a set of stairs leading downward, he opened the door. To his surprise, the stairs in front of him didn't lead downward at all, but up. He was underground.

Suddenly, it all made sense – the lack of windows, the absence of people, the secluded location. He had been taken underground. Not wanting to waste another moment, he vaulted up the stairs two at a time. A twinge of pain in his leg forced him to slow down, but still, he climbed as fast as he could.

At the top of the stairs was another green door. Agent Lewis held his breath as he pushed open the door, expecting sunlight to shine down on his face. The disappointment of another hallway was almost too much for him to bear. All he wanted was to find a way out, and his frustration grew with each passing door and each subsequent hallway.

Finally, he reached a pair of steel doors at the end of another hallway and another flight of stairs. He knew that he was on the right track, since the last few rooms he had passed looked like someone had been living there. A nearby breakroom also showed signs of recent activity. *This has to be the exit*, he told himself as he pushed against the door on the right. It didn't budge.

"Dammit!" Agent Lewis yelled in frustration.

He was getting tired of this. He had already suffered enough, and right now, all he wanted was to get out of here. Containing his rage as best as he could, he stepped over to the door on the left and pushed. It opened a few inches before coming to a stop. It wasn't much, but it was better than nothing.

He pushed against the door with all his might, making sure not to use his injured hand – or shoulder, for that matter. The door opened another few inches, but there was something on the other side, blocking it from opening all the way.

By this time, his patience had run out. Taking several steps back from the door, he got a running start and launched himself at it with all his strength. The door burst open, spilling him out onto the floor on the other side.

He sat up, rubbing his arm and shoulder while he looked around. Rather than being outside, he found himself in a large empty room. At first glance, it reminded him of one of those large storage warehouses that the Bureau maintained on the outskirts of the city – either that or an unused factory.

Whatever this place had been originally used for, it was empty now. There did appear to be several offices and a janitor's closet on the other side of the room, not to mention a set of stairs that lead up to a catwalk overhead. The catwalk ran down the side of the room, ending in a door on the second floor.

"Well, at least it isn't another hallway," Agent Lewis said to himself.

By this point, anything was better than another hallway, even if it was a large, empty room – especially since this particular empty room had windows. They were up on the second floor, away from the catwalk, but they were there. He wasn't underground anymore!

It was dark outside. The sun had already gone down, meaning that he had missed at least a full day. How long had he been down there?

Seeing the windows gave him hope. He looked around, trying to see the best way to get out. His gaze fell on something lying on the floor behind him – the same thing that had been blocking the door from opening. It was a body.

It must have been one of the townsfolk, because he didn't recognize the dark-blue uniform they were wearing. He recognized the face but couldn't put a name them. They were definitely not an agent or one of the Bureau's officers. Cautiously, he tapped the body with his foot. There was no movement.

After looking around to make sure there were no immediate threats nearby, Agent Lewis knelt down and gently pushed the body over onto its back. As the body turned over, he saw several scorch marks on their chest right below a name tag that said *Steven*. Based on the severity of the burns, he felt confident that the damage had been done by a pulse rifle.

He felt a burst of hope. If these burns had been caused by a pulse rifle, that most likely meant that an officer from one of the retrieval teams had been there recently. True, the burns appeared to be several hours old, but that didn't mean that whoever had shot this person wasn't still around.

Looking down at the body, Agent Lewis was able to start making sense of the situation. The uniform seemed to indicate that this person was a guard of some sort – no doubt assigned to watch over him. They had probably been headed down to check on him when they were engaged by a member of the retrieval team. That would go a long way to explaining why nobody had ever come back to check on him.

He stood up and took another look around the room. His goal was to find out where the retrieval officer had gone. Cautiously, he stepped out into the middle of the room. From there, he was able to make out another body on the catwalk above.

Stun pistol in hand, he raced toward the stairs and climbed up to the catwalk above. The second body was halfway between him and an open door on the other end of the catwalk. He approached it slowly, doing his best to keep the stun pistol in his hand steady. He wasn't used to holding it in his left hand, which made him even more nervous.

The body on the catwalk was dressed in the same dark-blue uniform as the one down below. Just like the other one, there were several scorch marks around the chest area. What was different was the old-fashioned pistol clutched in their hand. Judging by the shell casings on the floor of the catwalk, they had managed to get a few shots off before being hit by the pulse blasts.

He bent down and pried the pistol free. He recognized it as an old Colt 45 semi-automatic handgun. This thing was practically an antique. The slide was open, showing that there were no more bullets in the gun – further confirmation that this guard had put up a fight before they had gone down. It begged the question: Who were they firing at?

Dropping the pistol over the side of the catwalk, Agent Lewis walked toward the open door at the other end. As he approached, he could see through the doorway into the room beyond. Smashed computers, server consoles, and display monitors were everywhere. The room was filled with technical equipment that had been torn apart and practically destroyed. Even if it had not been smashed to pieces, the hardware looked old and outdated. It was as if someone had tried building a closed system using obsolete parts and antiquated processors.

Making sure not to step on any of the broken fragments that littered the ground, Agent Lewis moved into the room. The destruction looked recent, as if someone had been there within the last few hours. Where they were now was still a mystery. The room appeared to be empty, with no one in sight.

Ahead of him, there was a computer console built into the side of the wall with a monitor that was hanging off the wall at an awkward angle. The screen of the monitor was flashing red. Hesitantly, he approached the flashing screen. He fixed the monitor so that it wasn't hanging down anymore and looked at the control console in front of him. It reminded him of Attendant Phillips's workstation back at the Central Monitoring Station – well, it would have if it wasn't all busted up. Given the similarities, it occurred to him that this equipment may have been what was broadcasting the dampening signal that Linda had mentioned. If that were true, he could use this equipment to turn off the signal or even broadcast a distress beacon of his own.

He picked an overturned chair off the floor and sat down in front of the computer console. The system was damaged, but the keyboard still worked. He typed awkwardly on the keyboard, not used to having an analog keyboard beneath his fingertips.

Within moments, he was able to access a system directory. Most of the links were disabled, but he was able to click on a command prompt labeled *Evacuation Protocol.* The screen lit up with a map of Haven. There was an overlay graphic that highlighted several tunnels that branched out under the town and led off in various directions. From the look of it, these were escape tunnels of some sort. He tried to access more information, but the file was corrupted.

Returning to the directory, he tried another link labeled *Comm System Schematic.* The screen lit up with an even larger map of the area. Radio towers lit up on the map, surrounding the town of Haven and creating a broadcast network, including the one that he had passed in Greenwood.

If he was reading this map correctly, he was located at the central hub. It was a building on the northern slope of the mountain overlooking the town below. Linda's comments from before she'd shot him echoed in his head.

The antenna that you passed is simply a relay station. The dampening field that we are using to hide from the Authority's sensors is actually located here, just outside of town. But we use those relay stations to increase our range and the strength of our field.

If this was the central hub, then it meant that the source of the dampening field originated from this building – probably from a nearby radio tower. That also meant that he could shut down the dampening field from his current location if he found the right command prompt.

Going back to the main directory, he searched for the command prompt that would shut down the system. It took him several minutes to navigate through the system; the whole thing was a mess. When he finally did find what he was looking for, he accessed the communications control system. He was prepared to shut the system down, but that proved not to be necessary. The system had already been shut off. In fact, the red warning light on the screen that had originally caught his attention had been a notification that the field was down.

"Well, now, how do you like that?" he said to himself as he leaned back in his chair. "Someone beat me to it."

A crackling sound erupted from behind him, and a pulse blast flew past his shoulder, striking the monitor in front of him. In an act of sheer desperation, he flung himself out of the chair and rolled on the ground, coming to a stop against a smashed console against the wall. His stun pistol was in his hand as he searched for the source of the blast.

Sitting on the floor against a toppled server stack was a person dressed all in black, wearing tactical gear, with the emblem of the Bureau on their chest. Agent Lewis recognized the uniform immediately as one of the Bureau's retrieval officers. From the looks of it, they were in pretty bad shape. He hadn't noticed them when he'd originally entered the room because of the way that they were sitting against the toppled server stacks.

Agent Lewis lowered his stun pistol and slowly got to his feet. The retrieval officer tried to raise their pulse rifle and fire at him again, but the strain was too much. Not wanting to be shot, Agent Lewis quickly pulled out his badge and held it out in front of him. He wanted them to know that he was on their side.

The officer relaxed, and the pulse rifle fell to the floor. Now that he was no longer worried about being shot, Agent Lewis rushed to the side of the officer. He helped to remove their helmet, revealing the face of a young woman. Her hair spilled out onto her shoulders as the helmet dropped to the floor nearby.

"Are you alright?" he asked with concern.

"Thought you were one of them," she mumbled in a breathy voice.

Something was wrong here, Agent Lewis thought. She seemed to be having trouble breathing, not to mention having to struggle to keep her eyes open. The way she was slumped up against the server stack wasn't natural either. There was no way that was a comfortable way to sit.

"Stay with me," Agent Lewis said, gently shaking her shoulder. "You need to tell me what happened."

"They got me," she said in a weak voice. "One of those strays shot me from behind. Shot me with a handgun, can you believe that?"

"Focus. Where were you hit?"

"Back. They shot me in the back. But don't you worry, I got them."

Agent Lewis nodded to himself. That explained the dead bodies in the other room, but right now, he needed to focus on the officer in front of him. She'd said that she had been shot in the back. If that was true, he needed to see how badly she was hurt. As carefully as possible, he leaned her forward so that he could get a better look.

It wasn't hard to see where the bullet hole was. The guard outside had managed to shoot her directly through a seam in the body armor. As a result, the bullet had punctured her back, dangerously close to her vital organs. As he pulled his hand away, he noticed it was wet. In fact, her entire backside was wet, along with the floor. The source was the bullet hole in her back. The bullet had done more damage than he had originally thought.

Agent Lewis wiped his hand off on a section of carpet nearby and gently returned the officer to her original position. Her eyes were closed, and her head drooped against her chest. He shook her gently, trying to get her to wake up.

Her eyes opened wide, and she stared around in surprise. After a second, she saw him kneeling beside her and recalled her surroundings. "I got them," she said faintly. "I got both of them."

"Listen...Teri," Agent Lewis said as he noticed the name tag on her tactical vest. "You need to stay with me. You have to stay awake."

"Switch. No one calls me Teri. Not even my sergeant."

"Alright, Switch. You have to stay awake. Do you hear me? You need to tell me where the rest of your unit is. That way we can get someone over here to patch you up."

"Gone," she mumbled.

"What do you mean, 'gone?' Where are they?"

"Call came in over the radio. Rotowing went down somewhere in town. My unit was cut off. Orders were..." She started to fade until Agent Lewis nudged her again. "Orders were to fall back. Fall back to the rally point."

"Good. Good. You are doing really well. Now, I need you to concentrate. What happened next?"

"Cut off. Sergeant wanted to head back to the rally point, but we had a mission. I...I volunteered."

"What? What did you volunteer for?" he asked urgently.

"Volunteered to...to take out the signal. Jammer. Located in this building. Orders to neutralize it. At all costs...at all costs," she finished weakly.

Agent Lewis could guess the rest. The retrieval teams had arrived, expecting only a few strays, only to find an entire town of armed insurgents. They'd tried to fight back, but their Rotowing had gone down, and they'd needed to regroup. They would have wanted to call for reinforcements, but wouldn't have been able to do that with the dampening field operational, so Switch and her unit had been sent to locate it and take it out.

It seemed that the sergeant in charge of Switch's unit had sent her on ahead to complete their mission while he led the rest of them to the rally point, wherever that was. Judging by the condition of the room, it looked like she had managed to complete her mission. The dampening field was down. Whether that had been before she was shot or after, he couldn't tell.

Switch was now slumped against the server stack, her chin resting on her chest. Agent Lewis shook her, but she didn't respond. He tried shaking her a little bit harder, but her eyes remained closed. *There has to be a way to help her*, he thought as he looked around the room. The room was full of smashed-up electronics, computers, and various pieces of furniture, but there was nothing that he could see that would help her. She was dying, and there was nothing he could do about it.

Sensing that these were her last moments, he pulled her up and held her against his chest. He slowly rocked back and forth while stroking her hair. He wasn't sure whether this was the right thing to do, but it seemed appropriate. Nobody wanted to be alone when they died. He held her close as her breathing got slower and slower before eventually stopping.

He continued to hold her for another minute or two before gently lowering her to the floor. There was nothing that he could have done for her. He had come too late for that. Given that her unit hadn't come back for her either, he suspected that they had met a similar fate.

"Thank you for your service," he said, placing a hand on her chest and lowering his head in respect. It was the least that he could do. She had died in the line of duty. She had died in the name of the Authority.

After paying his respects, he stood up and wiped his hands on his pants. He took one look at the workstation he had been sitting at and realized that it was a lost cause. Her pulse blast had missed him, but had destroyed the computer and the monitor that he needed to send out a distress call. If he had been a service technician, he would have tried to reroute power, or bypass the terminal, or whatever it was that they did, but he wasn't a service technician, and he had no idea of how to fix this mess.

That meant that if he wanted to call for help, he would need to find something to broadcast with. That meant either the mobile emitter back in his vehicle, assuming that his vehicle was still there, or the radio tower back in Greenwood. Either way, he needed to get going.

Before leaving, he bent down and picked up the pulse rifle. After a second, he dropped it back on the floor. Unlike stun pistols, which had a regenerative core, pulse rifles needed to be recharged after frequent use. The blast that had nearly taken off his head had been the last one before the battery had died. With no way of charging it, it was as useful as a club.

He bent down one last time and pulled something from Switch's tactical belt. He then stood up and walked to the door. Before he left, he pulled the pin from the grenade that he had taken from her belt and threw it back toward the center of the room.

He was half-way down the catwalk when the room behind him exploded in flames. Officer Switch had given her life to disable the dampening field. He wasn't about to leave it for someone else to come along and repair. Besides, he didn't want to leave her body behind for the townsfolk to find and desecrate. She deserved that much.

Agent Lewis walked back down the stairs and across the open, empty room. He tried the doors on the other side of the room, finally finding one that opened to the outside. His foot encountered something hard and cold on the ground. Upon further inspection, he saw half a dozen padlocks on the floor. They had been shot off the front of the door when Switch had entered the building.

It was nice to be back outside. The air was fresh, the moon was shining brightly, and the stars glittered overhead. The gentle moonlight illuminated the courtyard in which he stood. There was a chain-link fence all along the perimeter with a gate nearby that stood wide open. After taking a few deep breaths, he made his way across the courtyard and out the front gate.

Although he was glad to be outside again, it was also painful without any shoes. The cement floors inside had been nice and smooth, but the ground beneath his feet was rough with little pebbles that stung his feet as he walked. Beyond the gate, the ground became softer, but he would still need to find some shoes if he planned on hiking all the way back to Greenwood.

The path he was on twisted its way through the forest. From the condition of the dirt road, it wasn't a path that was used too often. As he came to a curve in the road, he could see the lights of the town of Haven shining above the treetops. He walked toward those lights, keeping an eye out for any signs of danger. After a brisk walk, he came to the edge of the forest.

He found himself standing on top of a small hill overlooking the town below. Where his first sight of Haven had been that of a perfectly persevered town taken straight from the pages of a history book, the sight that met his eyes now looked more like a warzone. The streetlights were still on, but half of the buildings in the downtown area had been reduced to rubble. Fires were still burning in several locations, and the signs of a struggle were everywhere.

Whatever had happened here, it was clear that the battle for Haven had already come and gone. What he was seeing now was merely the aftermath. The real question was – who had won? If it were the townsfolk, then where were they? If it was the Authority, then where were they?

For all intents and purposes, the town was deserted. At the very least, he expected to see the bodies of those who had fallen during the battle, but even those were missing. It was all very strange, which was only intensified by the eerie silence that filled the air.

Switch had mentioned that her unit had fallen back to a rally point. Based on what he knew, that couldn't have been in the center of town. More than likely, they would have set it up away from the downtown area – perhaps south of town, where they could secure a means of escape if it became necessary.

With that in mind, he decided to head to the southern edge of town. If the Authority's forces were still in the area, he could link up with them. If not, he would continue down the road toward Greenwood. There, he would either encounter his vehicle on the side of the road, where he had left it, or he could return to the warehouse with the radio tower and call for help. Either way, he was walking.

Going directly through town would be too dangerous, so he decided to cut through a residential area on the western side of town. By the time he got there, his feet ached, and there was a chill in the air that made him miss his trench coat. One thing was for certain: once this was all over, he would go back to his office on the fifth floor and never leave again. He'd had enough field work to last him a lifetime – more than enough.

Several of the houses he passed showed signs that the battle had extended out into this neighborhood as well. One particular house had been riddled with holes – so much so that the house itself looked like it was on the point of collapse.

Something on the front lawn caught his attention. The nearest streetlamp had been shot out, but there was still enough light to discern two figures lying on the ground in front of the house. Both of them were wearing Bureau uniforms, but not much else. Their bodies had been stripped clean of all their gear except for their uniforms and their shoes. Speaking of which, he desperately needed a pair of shoes if he wanted to continue on his way.

Under normal circumstances, he never would consider looting the body of a fellow officer, but he didn't have much of a choice at the moment. He really needed some shoes. Besides, it wasn't like they needed them anymore.

He approached the bodies, seeing that the first one was a woman and the second one was a man. The woman's feet were too small for him, so he moved onto the man's body. Luckily, they were close enough in size that their boots would fit. He pulled off the dead officer's boots and put them on. They were a little big for him, but it was still better than walking around barefoot.

Once he'd finished lacing up the boots, he stood up and stamped his feet on the ground. It felt good to be wearing shoes again. Leaning over, he expressed his gratitude to the dead officer. It was then that he noticed that the top of the officer's head had been blown off. *Curious.*

Head injuries weren't common on account of the helmets that retrieval officers were required to wear. For whatever reason, the officer must have removed their helmet before they had been shot. It didn't make a lot of sense, but it didn't really matter now anyway. What was done was done.

Not wanting to waste the opportunity, Agent Lewis searched through the man's pockets before doing the same for the woman. Their front pockets were empty, but he did find a field kit in the woman's back pocket that the townsfolk must not have noticed.

Agent Lewis wasted no time in opening up the field kit and using the bandages inside to wrap his hand up. His thumb ached terribly, but having it bandaged in place helped with the pain. There wasn't much else he could do, so he shoved the rest of the field kit in his pocket and prepared to leave.

Just as he finished paying his respects to his fallen comrades and was ready to head out, a dazzling white light lit up the night sky. It shone straight up into the air, forming a column of light that could be seen anywhere in town. The source of the light was hidden by the trees, but it originated somewhere on the northern slope.

At first, he wondered whether the light he was coming from the building he had just escaped from, but the more he studied it, the more it appeared to be coming from somewhere else nearby. It was obviously a beacon intended to signal any remaining townsfolk in the area. The Authority would never give away their position so easily.

Without giving it a second thought, Agent Lewis turned his back on the column of light and walked toward the southern edge of town. Whatever was happening up on the mountainside, he wanted no part in it. All he wanted to do was to leave this crummy town behind and get back to the city, where it was safe. He would make a full report once he got back to his office, and the Bureau could send someone else to investigate.

That was his plan at least; unfortunately, things hadn't gone according to any of his plans since he'd left on this mission. Right now was no exception. He hadn't walked more than ten feet when a voice called out, "Liam."

Agent Lewis froze where he stood. The voice hadn't been speaking to him, but it sounded like whoever was speaking was standing right next to him. He looked around, convinced he would see someone hiding in the bushes, but there was nobody there.

"Liam. Come toward the light," the voice called out again.

The sound came from every direction at once. It wasn't a booming voice, but it was loud enough to be clearly understood. He suspected that the voice would sound the same wherever you were in town. How the voice was generated, he didn't know. What he did know was that whoever it was, they were having a conversation with the young man he had met earlier.

This was startling for two reasons. The first was that whoever was talking, they were talking directly to Liam, which meant that the boy was still alive. And given what Agent Lewis had learned about the boy's true nature, that made finding him a priority. Secondly, he recognized the voice on the loudspeaker. He had heard it earlier that day when it had called out for Linda to stop choking him.

Despite his reservations about investigating the source of the light, he couldn't turn his back on something like this. After everything he had been through, he had an obligation to see it through to the end. Especially if Liam was involved.

Grudgingly, he turned back around and started walking toward the column of light. He wasn't happy about staying, but he knew that this was something that he had to do. Luckily, it wouldn't be hard to find where the light was coming from. It was a beacon, after all.

What waited for him there, though, was anyone's guess.

Chapter 21: The Director

When Liam opened his eyes, he couldn't remember where he was. It was dark, except for a little bit of light that was coming from somewhere off to the side. Instinctively, he reached his hand out to his bedside table to turn on the lamp that he kept there for late-night reading. Where his bedside table should have been, his fingers only encountered dirt.

"Aunt Linda?" he called out.

When she didn't answer, he called out again. He fully expected her to open his bedroom door any minute and turn the light on. As time continued to pass without his aunt appearing, he began to grow worried. It wasn't like her to ignore him like this.

Liam tried to raise his head, but immediately put it back down, as even the slightest movement caused his head to throb with pain. A headache that he hadn't realized he had was now causing a great deal of discomfort. It also made it excruciatingly hard for him to think, as if his head were stuffed with cotton.

He closed his eyes and waited for the headache to fade. As he was waiting, he remembered bits and pieces from the dream he had been having. He had been running toward someone, though he couldn't quite remember who. He remembered that his Aunt Linda had been there, along with Parker and Ben. The strange thing was, every time he'd called out to them, they'd turned their backs and refused to answer.

The dream itself had been unpleasant, but not nearly as unpleasant as his headache. The pain was starting to fade, but it would be a while before it went away completely. The good news was that with each passing minute, he became more and more aware of his surroundings.

He was lying on the ground. Literally, he was on the ground. He felt the dirt under his hands, and when he tried lifting his head a second time, dirt was clinging to his chin. He also became aware that he was inside a cave or something. Rocks and stones lay everywhere. Well, not everywhere – there was a small gap off to the side.

The little bit of light that he could see was coming from that small gap. He focused his eyes and saw that the light was coming from...a street light? That didn't make sense. Where was he?

He had just opened his mouth to call for his Aunt Linda again when it dawned on him where he was. He was under Gus's van. He had ducked under the van to avoid being crushed by a collapsing wall. He had tried crawling out, but must have passed out.

As this realization dawned on him, so did all the memories of how he had gotten there. He remembered everything, including what had happened to his aunt. A wave of sadness overwhelmed him, and it felt like losing her all over again.

Now that he knew where he was, he had no intention of staying under Gus's van one minute longer than necessary. He pulled himself closer to the small gap in the bricks and debris and started pushing with all his might. Several bricks fell away, making the gap large enough for him to slip through. He squirmed out into the open night air.

Now that he was free, he made his way across the alleyway and sat down under the light of the streetlamp. From there, he could look back and see the place where his aunt's antique shop had been.

He thought of it in the past tense because what stood before him was nothing more than a charred ruin. The fire that had engulfed the building had eventually burned itself out, leaving nothing behind but a pile of ash, a few charred support beams, and a mountain of rubble. He knew that somewhere under all that wreckage was whatever remained of his aunt. He immediately fought the urge to go and dig her up so that he could give her a proper burial and say his goodbyes; he knew that now wasn't the time. Besides, what better place to lay her to rest than the shop that she had dedicated so much of her life to?

In reality, there was something else holding him back. He wanted to remember his aunt how she had been, not what remained after the explosion. He never wanted to remember her like that. His final memory of her should be untainted.

Standing up, Liam walked away from what had once been his aunt's antique shop. He turned his back on it with the intention of never going near it again, for obvious reasons. When he reached the end of the alley, on the other side of the movie theater, he stopped and looked back. This was his way of saying goodbye – goodbye to a place where he spent so much time, goodbye to a place that had become like a second home to him, and goodbye to the final resting place of his aunt.

Without a word, he turned down the street that connected with the alleyway and led toward the front of the movie theater. As he walked, he could see that many of the streetlamps in town were still shining brightly. Some had been broken or knocked down in all of the fighting, but most were still standing and giving off light.

Ahead of him, the hole in the side of the movie theater stood out like a gaping maw leading down into the basement. Hesitantly, he approached it, leaning into the opening slightly to get a better look. The light from the nearby streetlamps cast enough light through the hole for him to see inside.

Most of the basement was obscured in shadow, but he could still make out some overturned tables and crates. The one thing that he didn't see were bodies. He had been so worried about seeing the body of someone that he had known that he had almost walked past the hole without looking in.

Now that he thought about it, he hadn't seen any sign of what had happened to the rest of the townsfolk. He remembered seeing dozens of them fleeing the basement by climbing up through the hole where he now stood. Of course, he also remembered watching several of them being hit by pulse blasts as they climbed out onto the street. Their bodies were nowhere to be found.

In fact, there was no sign of anybody anywhere. The streets were eerily quiet, and the whole town had an empty feel. The town itself showed signs of everything that had happened earlier, but the people had simply disappeared. Liam couldn't tell whether that was a good thing or a bad thing.

Feeling confident that he wouldn't run into any unwelcome surprises down in the basement, he lowered himself through the hole. He didn't really want to climb back into the basement, but if there were any supplies left over, he would need them. Once inside, he fumbled his way over to a nearby lightbulb that was suspended from the ceiling and pulled the chain to turn it on.

Liam's heart sank in his chest as he looked around. The place had been cleaned out. Crates still lined the walls, but they had been opened and their contents removed. There were no weapons left over, no food left behind, and all of the emergency supplies were gone. The only things that hadn't been removed were all of Dr. Adhira's medical supplies in the far corner. They were sitting there, untouched, where they had been left when everyone had left.

He walked over and began going through them, looking for anything useful. He did manage to find more of those pills that Dr. Adhira had made him take earlier. Opening the bottle, he immediately took three of them, swallowing them in one big gulp. It was hard, since he didn't have any water to wash them down with. Still, the promise of his headache going away was more than enough motivation to get them down.

There wasn't much else that he could use, so he grabbed some bandages and headed toward the stairs that led up to the theater above. The place was in shambles, but at least the roof hadn't fallen in. He stumbled through the wreckage that now made up the backstage and theater area before existing into the lobby. The lobby itself was still in good condition except for the popcorn maker, which had tumbled to the floor and spread its contents in every direction.

Seeing the concession stand still intact, Liam practically vaulted over the counter. There, he found several unopened bottles of water under the counter. He drained the first two bottles in record time. He emptied the third bottle over his head. Cold water ran down his neck and back, soaking his shirt.

The water felt good as it poured down his back and washed away the dried dirt and blood that had covered his hair and neck. His stomach rumbled, a side effect of drinking all of that water on an empty stomach. Realizing how hungry he was, he rummaged through the candy and other food items that Mr. Malcolm kept behind the counter. He helped himself to a few items, making a mental note of which things he had taken in case he ever ran into Mr. Malcolm again.

Candy wasn't a good replacement for a decent meal, but it was better than nothing. It was unclear how long he had been passed out under Gus's van. For that matter, it was unclear how long it had been since he'd eaten something. The candy would do for now. One of the perks of being a teenager was being able to eat junk food without any real side effects.

As he was eating, he thought about how long he had been passed out under Gus's van. It was possible that he had only been out for a few hours, but it was also possible that he had been out for much longer – maybe even a day or two, though he doubted that. Besides, being passed out for any considerable amount of time was dangerous, and he didn't want to think about that right now.

Once he was finished eating, he exited the lobby through the front doors. Half the buildings along Main Street had been destroyed, including the café across the street. It was a strange feeling to look around at the place where he had grown up and not recognize it. The town had changed, and there was nothing that anyone could do to make it feel like it had before.

Not wanting to spend another moment looking at the devastation that had once been his home, Liam began heading north. Before he had passed out, he had been trying to head to the Watchtower. He thought his aunt had mentioned something about the research facility up on the hill, but his memory was still foggy. As a result, he wasn't sure where he was going exactly, but the research facility was as good a place as any to begin his search.

As he walked toward the northern edge of town, it occurred to him that he could make a detour and stop at his house. He probably looked terrible, and a shower and some fresh clothes would feel so good right now. But he decided against it. He couldn't face the idea of walking into his home, knowing that his aunt would never be there ever again.

Rather than taking the path that led through the woods toward the communications building, he followed a side road that branched off of Main Street. It angled off toward the western edge of town, where the old research facility was located. Had it really been a week ago that he and his friends had gone for an afternoon stroll that ended at the communications building? So much had happened since then that it seemed like a year ago.

He followed the road as it led him through the trees and up the mountain side, finally coming to a chain link fence. Beyond the fence, silhouetted in the moonlight, was the old research facility. The entire complex was massive, making up several large buildings. There were a handful of warehouses, an independent power station, and a concrete tower that rose up from the center of the complex. From what he could remember, the tower had been used as an observation post to monitor rocket launches, or something like that.

To his great disappointment, the whole complex was dark and devoid of life. He had expected to find someone waiting for him, assuming that this was in fact the location of the Watchtower. Not only was no one waiting for him, there weren't even any lights on. The whole place looked old and abandoned – the same way it had appeared the last time he had visited several years ago.

His entire class had visited the complex several years ago as a field trip. They hadn't been allowed inside, but they had walked around the perimeter. Liam remembered his teacher telling them something about how the place was unstable, and that it would be dangerous for anyone to go inside. That had been one reason why the town council had built a fence around the complex and prohibited anyone from visiting the area.

Looking back, he realized it had probably been an excuse to keep him and his friends away. More than likely, the field trip had been arranged to make the place seem dull and unremarkable – a way of putting an end to Liam's curiosity. It had worked. After that day, the thought of exploring the complex or the surrounding area had held no appeal to him. Then again, Ben had a lot to do with that as well.

It was clear that the town had placed several restrictions on where he could and could not go – all under the guise of protecting him and their secret, though their big secret was still a mystery to him. This made him wonder how much of everything he had been told had been another way to manipulate him and keep him from finding out the truth.

Seeing that the entire complex appeared to be deserted, Liam wondered if maybe the Watchtower was located somewhere else in town. There were plenty of other locations that he could check out. The school, for one, or maybe the communications building that he had recently discovered.

That idea made so much sense to him that he'd turned around, preparing to leave, when a pillar of light shot out from the top of the observation tower. The light appeared so suddenly that it took him by surprise. It shone straight up into the air, creating a column of light that went up as far as the eye could see. It was so bright and magnificent that he was transfixed by it. This was it. That column of light could only mean one thing; he had found the Watchtower!

Without taking his eyes from the pillar of light, he walked along the outer fence until he arrived at the front gate. There was an empty guard house out front, with a large gate that opened and closed along a track built into the ground. The gate was closed, but the lock and chain that he had seen there the last time he had visited was now gone.

Liam raised his hand to lift the latch that secured the front gate, but he hesitated. Something in him was holding him back. It was the same feeling he had felt when he and Parker had left Haven for Greenwood.

"Liam," a voice called from seemingly every direction at once.

The voice had come from everywhere and nowhere all at the same time. It startled him so badly that he jumped back from the gate and stared in every direction, trying to find the source of the noise. Other than the fence and the guard house, there was nobody else nearby. Still, the voice had come from somewhere.

"Liam, come toward the light," the voice called out again.

The voice was so calm and reassuring that Liam felt inspired to follow the directions. This was the reason why he had come here, after all. The light and the voice were only confirmation that he had come to the right place. Gathering his courage, he raised his hand, unfastened the latch, and pulled the gate open.

He stepped through the gate and walked up the long driveway toward the main entrance. The facility stretched out on both sides, but in the middle, there was a large entry hall designed to welcome visitors and new arrivals. The front entrance to the hall was made completely out of glass. It arched outward at an angle, rising several stories above the driveway below. The name *GLOBEX*

INCORPORATED was displayed in large letters over a set of glass doors directly in the middle of the building's entrance.

Liam stepped forward and put his face against the glass. The inside of the building was dark, but as his face touched the glass, lights came on inside, revealing a spacious lobby. There was a gigantic bronze statue of Atlas holding up the world in the center of the room. All around the sides of the lobby were couches and chairs – places where people could sit down and make themselves comfortable while they waited for...whatever they were waiting on.

Liam reached for the door and pulled the handle. The door swung open effortlessly, as if it had been freshly oiled. Once inside, Liam approached the gigantic statue of Atlas.

He spent several moments admiring the statue, which was positioned in the middle of the room, before walking around it to see the rest of the lobby. Not only were there seating areas everywhere, but there were also large displays, posters, and advertisements against the walls, showing off some of the products that Globex used to make.

Truthfully, he could have spent hours looking around the lobby, but his attention was captured by the ringing of a telephone. Toward the back of the room, there was a reception desk. On top of that desk was an old phone with a flashing white light that gave off a periodic ringing sound. Both the desk and the phone were covered in a layer of dust, though, to be fair, everything in this room was covered in dust.

The phone continued to ring, so Liam walked over to the desk and picked up the receiver. He placed it to his ear and listened. When no one immediately spoke on the other end, he said, "Hello?" He hoped for an answer.

"Follow the lights," the person on the other end said before hanging up.

"Follow the lights?" What is that supposed to mean, he wondered. Just as he thought this, a light went on over a set of doors off to his right. Liam cocked his head to the side, considering what to do next. He had come here to find Dr. Sorenson. If this was the path that he needed to take, then so be it. Staying in the lobby wasn't doing him any good, anyway. Following the caller's instructions, he walked toward the lights.

He walked forward, opening the door underneath the light, and found himself standing in a long hallway. The lights were on overhead, illuminating his path forward. He walked forward, curious about where these lights were going to lead him. On either side of him were offices, conference rooms, and intersecting hallways. He walked past all of them, concentrating on the path ahead.

After passing several darkened hallways, Liam began to wonder what would happen if he stepped off the path. The next intersecting hallway he passed, he turned right and walked for several feet before coming to a stop. The lights overhead had not come on. He stood there for a few seconds before turning around and looking back in the direction he had come.

The lights of the path that he was supposed to take were flickering on and off, as if to get his attention. Liam took several steps back, stopping in the intersection of the two halls. The lights immediately stopped flickering, and the path in front of him was once again illuminated.

So, he thought, *someone is watching me, or at least keeping track of where I am. That could either be a good thing or a bad thing.* Deciding to treat it like a good thing, he kept walking. At least now, he didn't need to worry about getting lost.

He followed the path laid out for him by the overhead lights. He walked down hallways, up staircases, and across pedestrian overpasses. Much like Haven, the whole place was completely deserted. There wasn't a single person in sight, and judging by the layer of dust and the old musty smell, there hadn't been anyone here in a long time.

Still, someone was guiding him. There had to be someone here. If not, who was controlling the lights? He just needed to keep following the path laid out for him. If he was right, he suspected he knew what – or, more importantly, who – was waiting for him.

After one final turn, he found himself standing before a set of black metal doors. A name plate against the wall said **DIRECTOR** in bold capitalized letters. A wave of nervousness washed over him as he stood there. Behind this door was the man who could answer all of his questions. Or so he hoped.

As carefully as possible, he reached out and grabbed the door handle. He turned it, and the door swung open soundlessly. On the other side of the door was a large darkened room. The room was too dark to make out the far wall, but the dimensions seemed much larger than he had anticipated. The room wasn't completely dark. In the far corner, several of the ceiling tiles were lit-up, shining down on some simple furnishings.

It was immediately clear that this wasn't a simple office. So far, it was nothing like what Liam would have suspected to find when he opened the door. For starters, the only furniture that he could see was over in the corner underneath the shining ceiling tiles. From what he could tell, the rest of the room was completely devoid of all other furnishings, leaving nothing but an empty blackness.

Liam took a step forward into the darkened room. As his foot touched the first floor tile inside the doorway, it lit up from underneath. At the same time, the ceiling tile overhead lit up as well. He looked up and down at the tiles that were now emitting a soft white glow. They appeared to be made of a glassy material. As he looked around, he noticed that the walls were also composed of the same glassy material.

He continued further into the room, and as he did, the tiles underneath and overhead lit up. Wherever he went, the tiles would spring to life and glow with the same soft white light. At the same time, the tiles behind him would also fade back to black after he had already passed.

Liam made his way toward the corner where the only furnishings in the room were located. There was a metal bed frame and mattress pushed against the wall, complete with a simple nightstand on either side. There was a wooden dresser against the other wall, with a small mirror and several photographs set up on top. There was also a bookcase, a footstool, and an old leather armchair standing off to the side.

What was truly interesting was that none of the furniture matched. It was as if each piece of furniture had been acquired separately and then put together to form an eclectic whole. From the looks of things, the furniture was well-worn, and had recently been used.

The last piece of furniture that completed the collection was a large oak writing desk. As Liam approached, he could see that the top of the desk was covered in papers, several pens, a portfolio, and a small desk lamp. His attention was immediately drawn to the papers scattered over the top of the desk, and he reached out and picked one of them up to get a better look.

It was a drawing. There were two stick figures drawn in crayon, holding hands. From the looks of things, he suspected that the artist was a small child. At least, the drawing looked similar to the ones that were hanging on the walls of the elementary school classrooms. Reaching down, he picked up several more papers off the desk and examined them. They were all drawings, all done in crayon, and seemingly all done by the same child.

As he worked his way through the stack of papers, he noticed that the drawings appeared to get better as he went along. The ones toward the bottom were no longer stick figures, but rough drawings of people, complete with arms, feet, and smiling faces. They still looked like they had been done by a child, but it was clear that these pictures represented a progression.

Toward the bottom, Liam stopped at one particular drawing that caught his fancy. In it, a child wearing a red shirt and blue shorts was holding hands with an adult wearing a blue jacket and tan pants. Both the child and the adult had large smiles. In the background, there was a yellow sun overhead and a grey rectangle that he interpreted as a house or building.

As he continued to look down on the picture, a small smile appeared on the side of his face. Looking at this picture made him feel...happy. There was something more to it than that. The drawing looked familiar somehow, as if he had seen it before.

From the clouded recesses of his mind, a memory surfaced – a memory of him drawing that exact same picture when he was younger.

As the memory settled over him, his hand began to tremble. All of the other drawings in his hands fell to the floor, forgotten for the moment while his attention was focused on that one picture. Afraid of what he would find, he slowly turned the paper over to look at the backside. There, in the top right-hand corner of the page, was his name.

A hazy memory of him writing his name there in yellow crayon came floating to the surface. He remembered. He actually remembered writing his name on the back after he had finished drawing this picture. He had been so proud, not only of the picture, but also that he had been able to write his name all by himself.

How old is this memory? Liam wondered. He couldn't have been much more than four or five years old at the time. The more he tried to remember the details, the fuzzier it all became. One thing was certain, though: he had drawn this picture, which also meant that he had likely drawn all the rest as well.

Desperate to confirm his suspicions, he began flipping over the pages on the desk in rapid succession. On the back of each one was his name. He dropped to his knees and picked up the rest of the pictures that had fallen to the floor. He stood, drawings clenched in his fist, all with the same name on the back – his name.

A voice spoke from the darkness. It was soft and yet firm all at the same time. Interestingly enough, it was also the same voice he had heard outside the complex beckoning him onward.

"Please be careful with those. They happen to be some of my most cherished possessions," the voice said from over Liam's shoulder.

Liam had been so absorbed in going through the stack of drawings that he hadn't noticed someone approaching. The sound of the person's voice startled him so badly that he jumped backwards in surprise and collided with the desk. It took him several seconds to recover and to get his heart to stop beating a hole through his chest.

He stared off into the darkness in the direction that the voice had come from, but he didn't see anyone. He did hear the sound of footsteps as someone came closer. As he watched, the figure of a man emerged from the surrounding darkness and stepped into the light.

The man was in his mid-to-late sixties, with grey hair and wrinkles around his eyes. He had a thin nose and arched eyebrows that reminded Liam of an anthropomorphized owl. The man's eyes were bright and alert, hinting at a vast intelligence hidden just below the surface. He was plainly dressed, wearing a faded grey sweater over a button up shirt with a pair of khaki pants. All in all, the man had the look of a college professor, right down to the patches on the elbows of his sweater. Even the way he stood there made it seem like he was about to start a lecture at any moment.

As Liam scrutinized him, the man placed something from his hand into his sweater pocket. Liam didn't get a good look at it, but it appeared to be a metallic sphere of some sort. Whatever it was, it must have been heavy, because he could see it bulging through the fabric of the man's sweater.

The man stood there, watching Liam and waiting for something. Liam nervously struggled to find something to say, but he couldn't seem to make the words come out. The silence stretched on, and each passing second became more and more uncomfortable. The man didn't seem to be bothered by this at all. He stood there, completely at ease with the prolonged silence, almost relaxed.

Knowing that the silence couldn't continue, Liam finally managed to blurt, "Who are you?"

As soon as the words were out of his mouth, he wished he could take them back. He already had a pretty good idea of who this person was, but that was the only question that had come to mind in his frantic attempt to find something to say. Feeling self-conscious, he watched the man for his reaction.

Rather than being offended, the man simply smiled and walked over to the desk. Without immediately answering, he bent over and picked up the remaining drawings that were still on the floor. He took special care to lay them out on his desk, smoothing out any rough edges or creases.

"I was sort of hoping that you would remember. It has been a long time, I know, but a part of me held out hope that you would remember me from all the time that we spent together," the man said as he looked down fondly at the picture that Liam had been holding.

"That one was always one of my favorites," he said, pointing down at the picture of a child holding a man's hand. "I still remember the day you drew it like it was yesterday. You never liked the color of my sweater, so you told me that you were going to make it blue instead of grey." He smiled again as he looked up at Liam.

"Oh, I know, they aren't your best work, but even back then, you showed talent. After all, I think that this was a pretty good likeness of me. Don't you think?" the man asked, pointing down at the picture.

Liam was taken aback by the familiarity with which this man addressed him. He was talking as if they were old friends, but he couldn't remember ever seeing this person before. If the man in the picture was the same man who was now standing before him, how come he couldn't remember him?

"That doesn't really answer my question," Liam said cautiously. He didn't want to offend the man, but at the same time, he needed confirmation. If this was who he thought it was, he needed to be sure.

"No, I supposed it doesn't," the man said, turning from the drawings to face Liam. "Still, it would have been nice if you had remembered some of the time we spent together, or at least humored me a little," he said with a wink.

After taking a deep breath, the man said, "My name is Dr. Sorenson. I am the chief scientist of his facility, administrator for our cluster, and the Director of Project HM-12."

Liam felt a tingle spread all the way down his body. He had to stop himself from bouncing up and down with excitement. Finally, after everything he had gone through, he was finally meeting the elusive Dr. Sorenson – the man who had all the answers.

He did his best to keep his composure. There was no point in seeming overeager. True, there was so much that he wanted to ask this man, but he knew that he had to be careful. He didn't want to overwhelm him with too many questions. He didn't want Dr. Sorenson to feel like he was being interrogated. He just needed to ease into it, slowly but to the point.

The hard part was finding a place to start. Liam knew that he needed to start out small before jumping into the big questions, but he didn't want to waste time with trivial matters. Realizing that Dr.

Sorenson had given him a topic of conversation by not only giving his name but his various titles, he decided to start with those.

"You mentioned being the Director of Project HM-12. What is that?" Liam asked, hoping that this would help break the ice.

"You don't waste time, do you, lad?" Dr. Sorenson responded with a brief chuckle. "I figured you would start with something easy and work your way up to the big questions, but I suppose that is as good a place to start as any. You must understand, it was always my intention to reveal the details of Project HM-12 to you, but the plan was to do it slowly. Carefully."

"Alright," Liam said, trying to nudge the conversation along. He hadn't realized that Project HM-12 was a significant topic, but if it was a steppingstone to what he really wanted to know, then he would be happy to follow along. "So, what is it?"

"You, Liam. You are Project HM-12," Dr. Sorenson said simply.

Liam's eyebrows raised in surprise. This was not the answer he had been expecting. His aunt had mentioned something about him being created here in Haven, but he hadn't realized that his origins and this project were one and the same.

"No doubt," Dr. Sorenson continued, "you have become all too aware that you are different. There is something about you that sets you apart from everybody else. Though you may not suspect the full details of your true nature, you at least have an idea of your own importance."

"Yeah, I kind of noticed that," Liam said wryly. "It was hard to miss when everyone started sacrificing themselves to protect me. That and the appearance of a homicidal government agency hellbent on trying to kill me, along with everyone else."

"Hmmm. You always did have a highly developed wit," Dr. Sorenson observed. "But you are right. Our behavior of late has been enough to convince you of the truth: you are different. Your friends and family have provided you with a hint of your true nature, but you still lack the necessary awareness to fully understand who and what you are."

"Is that why you told everyone to lie to me for all these years?" Liam countered. "To keep me from finding out on my own?"

"Yes," Dr. Sorenson said simply. "You must understand that it was a necessary precaution. We needed to hide the truth from both you and the outside world in order to keep you safe. Truth can be a powerful thing. We needed to wait until you were old enough to handle it. Until then, the plan was to keep certain truths from you so that you would develop and grow naturally. It was incredibly important that you developed without a knowledge of your true nature. That kind of knowledge would have only interfered with your development.

"Some of my colleagues disagreed with my approach, but in the end, it was decided that discretion was the best policy. Your true nature being revealed to you at such an early age would have only caused problems. It may not have been the best approach, but it was one that promised the best result overall, which is—"

"Putting aside my thoughts on you and everyone else lying to me this entire time, you keep saying things like 'my true nature.' What is that supposed to mean?" Liam cut in.

"You are different. There is something that makes you special."

"Yeah, yeah," Liam said. "My aunt already told me all about that. I was made here, like a laboratory experiment. And that somehow makes me special, but what I really want to know is why? What is my 'true nature?' Who am I?"

"Which question do you want me to answer first?"

"Who am I?" Liam asked in all seriousness.

"How am I supposed to know that?" Dr. Sorenson asked in genuine surprise.

Liam couldn't believe what he was hearing. This whole time, he had been waiting for the moment when he could ask this man the questions that mattered most, and he didn't know the answers! It was infuriating.

Seeing that Liam was on the point of an emotional outburst, Dr. Sorenson continued.

"You must understand, who you are has more to do with the choices that you make than where you came from. Yes, I created you. Yes, I helped guide and watch over you, even though you were unaware of it. And yes, I have done everything in my power to protect you thus far. But even after all of that, I cannot tell you who you really are. Only you can answer that question. Only you can know who you are deep down inside."

The anger and frustration that Liam had been feeling only moments ago that had threatened to overtake him was now starting to fade. He didn't like Dr. Sorenson's answer, but it did make sense in a way. Still, it would have been nice to get a simple answer rather than a philosophical conundrum.

As if sensing his thoughts, Dr. Sorenson offered him a consolation prize. "While it is true that I cannot tell you *who* you are, I may be able to help you understand *what* you are."

"Alright. What am I?" Liam asked, hoping to get an answer.

"There are so many answers to that question. You are the culmination of decades of hard work and perseverance, both on my part and that of everyone else here. You are the reason why we came to Haven in the first place – why it was necessary to go into hiding. You are a direct affront to everything that the Authority stands for. You are the sum of my life's work, and you are without a doubt my greatest achievement."

After a long pause, Dr. Sorenson took a deep breath and continued. "You, Liam. You are special for all those reasons, but one reason more than any other."

"And what is that?" Liam asked hesitantly.

"Because you are Human."

Chapter 22: Revelations

The word hung in the air like the last note of a symphony, penetrating Liam's mind and shaking him to his innermost core. Until this moment, he had never heard the word "human" used before, but something within him resonated with that word. There was something powerful and significant about it that he couldn't quite put his finger on.

"I. Am. A. Human," Liam said slowly, making sure to pronounce the word just as Dr. Sorenson had.

"Yes," Dr. Sorenson said in all seriousness. "In fact, you were the first human to exist on this planet in more than 200 years."

"I don't...I don't understand what that means," Liam said, confusion evident in his expression.

"Of course you don't," Dr. Sorenson continued, giving him a warm smile as he explained. "The reason why you are different from everyone else, the reason why we are all so concerned with your wellbeing, is that you are human. You are unique.

"When I said that we kept the truth from you to protect you and to make sure you developed naturally, it was this truth that I was referring to. We wanted you to grow up thinking that you were no different from anyone else. Had we told you the truth, you would have grown up feeling like an outsider, isolated and alone. So, we made the conscious decision to keep the truth from you until you were ready."

As Dr. Sorenson finished speaking, he turned on his heel and started walking toward the center of the room. Just before he disappeared into the surrounding darkness, the entire room lit up with a soft white light. The tiles that lined the floor, ceiling, and walls were all emitting a soft light that illuminated the entire room.

Liam had to shield his eyes from the sudden light. As his eyes adjusted, he could see how big Dr. Sorenson's office was. The biggest thing that stood out was how wide it was. He couldn't be certain, but he guessed that the far wall had to be at least forty to fifty feet away. Everywhere he looked, he could see the same glassy tiles covering every inch of available wall space. In fact, the only place that wasn't covered in illuminated tiles was the metal doors that led into the hallway.

Dr. Sorenson had almost reached the center of the room while Liam had been distracted by looking around. When he noticed that the director had stopped, he realized that the other man was waiting for him. Not wanting to keep Dr. Sorenson waiting, Liam quickly made his way across the room to stand next to him. Once he was standing by Dr. Sorenson's side, the two continued the last few steps to the center of the room.

Liam didn't know what to expect. The only furniture in the room was back in the corner where they had come from. Why Dr. Sorenson had insisted on walking to the center of the room, he had no idea. He was following the older man's lead in the hopes of getting more information about his status of being human.

He didn't have to wait for long. As soon as Dr. Sorenson stopped, he waved his hand, and the figure of a man appeared in front of them. Liam was taken aback. One moment, the space in front of them had been empty, and now, there was a man, in his mid-thirties, standing in front of them, completely naked.

"Is...is that how you created me?" Liam asked in wonder. "You just waved your hand, and poof, I appeared?"

"Not quite."

"Then—"

"What you see before you is merely a holographic representation of a human being," Dr. Sorenson cut in. "I hope you don't mind, but I choose a male representation, since you have so much in common."

"Holographic?" Liam asked. It was another word he was unfamiliar with.

"It is a 3D projection, made with light and focused particles. It isn't real. See?" As Dr. Sorenson spoke, he reached his hand out and swept it through the image of the man standing before them. His hand passed right through the image as if there was nothing there. The image, on the other hand reacted by shimmering where the hand passed through before reforming as if nothing had happened in the first place.

Liam was entranced. He had never seen anything like this before. Hesitantly, he reached out his own hand and tried to touch the image's shoulder. Where his fingers should have touched a solid person, they continued through the air with no resistance whatsoever. He started waving both his hands in front of him, passing them back and forth through the holographic image. Each time his hand passed through, the image distorted slightly before reforming seamlessly. This was by far the coolest thing he had ever seen. How many times had he wished that he could have stepped through the movie screen and been part of the story? With something like this, he could do just that.

"So, this thing, it isn't real?" Liam asked, still waving his hands through the image.

"No, it is merely a projection. We call them holograms, and we can use them for whatever we need."

Liam wasn't really listening to what Dr. Sorenson was saying. He was having too much fun with the hologram in front of him. At the moment, he was putting a finger up the hologram's nose and trying to keep himself from laughing.

Dr. Sorenson endured this childish display for another minute or two before finally making a point of getting on with his presentation. He coughed indiscreetly to get Liam's attention. Liam seemed to realize what he had been doing, and he settled down, keeping his arms to his side.

Once Dr. Sorenson was certain he had Liam's full attention, he continued. "I understand your fascination. This type of advanced technology is new to you. The world that we created for you here in Haven was done with limited influence from technology. We felt it would be best to keep things...simple. But do try to contain your excitement, at least for the moment," he said with a slight wink.

Liam quickly nodded in agreement, and Dr. Sorenson turned his attention back to the holographic man.

"Now, as I was saying, this is an image of a human male. Notice any similarities?" Dr. Sorenson asked.

Liam gazed at the hologram standing before him. He took in everything from the top of the man's head right down to his toes. The problem was, he wasn't sure what he was supposed to be looking for. Sure, the image before him looked just like him, but at the same time, it looked just like Dr. Sorenson. He admitted as much, saying that he couldn't tell the difference.

"Ah, yes, I can understand your confusion. While you and I may look the same, I can assure you that we are very different from one another. As I have said, you are human. Meanwhile, I am not. I was merely designed to appear human," Dr. Sorenson explained.

"I don't get it. If you are not human, what are you?" Liam asked.

"I am an Eletrosapien, also commonly known as an E-Person, E-Sapien, or, if you want to use the slang term..." Dr. Sorenson had to force himself to finish the sentence without cringing. "A Synbot."

Liam did his best to appear like he was following along and that he understood everything that Dr. Sorenson had just said, but he failed miserably. He had no idea what the director was talking about, and he still wasn't sure what the difference was between the two of them.

Sensing his confusion, Dr. Sorenson offered a more elaborate explanation. "I am a machine – a highly sophisticated and versatile machine, but a machine none-the-less. I am what the humans used to call an artificial intelligence, designed to mimic human appearance and behavior. Just like the rest of my kind, I was designed and assembled in a factory."

As Dr. Sorenson said this, he made another gesture with his hand, and a second holographic figure appeared. Both holograms stood side by side, each appearing to be an identical copy of one another.

"As you can see, there is little to no difference in our appearances," Dr. Sorenson said, gesturing to the two holograms. "This, of course, was by design. Our creators made us in their own image and desired that we should emulate humanity as closely as possible."

"By creators, you mean humans, right?" Liam interjected.

"Yes. Very good, Liam. Very good," Dr. Sorenson said, praising him before resuming the lecture. "Though we may appear similar on the outside, we are quite different on the inside. If we peel back the skin, we can see those differences in greater detail."

As he said this, Dr. Sorenson gestured again, and the outer layer of skin on both holograms was instantly removed. On the human hologram, Liam could see an intricate tapestry of muscles, bones and sinews.

The hologram of the Eletrosapien was strangely different. Where the human hologram had muscles, the E-Sapien had hydraulics. Where the human hologram had bones and a skeletal structure, the E-Sapien had a metal chassis that formed an elaborate framework. Where the human hologram had veins and nerve endings, the E-Sapien had wires, sensors, and capacitors.

"On the one hand," Dr. Sorenson continued, pointing out all the differences between the two figures, "we have basic human anatomy, and on the other hand, we have a detailed configuration that makes up the foundation for an Eletrosapien."

Dr. Sorenson went on to describe in detail the differences between the two. He pointed to the various parts of the human body and their corresponding parts on the E-Sapien, pausing only long enough to see that Liam was following along. He did his best, but there was so much information that he had trouble keeping it all straight in his head. It was fascinating, though.

"Here, we have the Eletrosapien's artificial organs, many of which were patterned after their human counterparts. Interestingly enough, many of our internal organs do not..." Dr. Sorenson explained while Liam's attention faded in and out.

He was trying to pay attention to the explanation as best as he could, but there was so much information that he was quickly becoming overwhelmed. He was intrigued by the similarities and the differences between humans and Eletrosapiens, but he didn't need to know the complete ins and outs of each. He didn't necessarily care that E-Sapiens had a special organ that converted biomatter into a nutritional paste that powered different systems throughout their bodies, but he tried to appear interested for Dr. Sorenson's sake.

"As you can see, those systems are enclosed within a metal-reinforced chassis. The combination of those internal systems and the chassis is what we call an Autonomous Mobile Platform, or AMP for short," Dr. Sorenson said. "This is what allows our neural networks to be more than just disembodied intelligences."

At this point, Dr. Sorenson paused to see if Liam had any questions. He shook his head. Although he might have missed the finer points in the director's lecture, he was confident that he understood the main point: Humans and E-Sapiens were different.

All this talk about human biology and E-Sapien architecture reminded Liam of something that had happened earlier that day, when he was laying on the ground outside Ben's house. The private had been transfixed by the blood on the ground that Liam had spit out. His confusion had seemed to be centered around the color of Liam's blood, but Liam hadn't understood what he'd meant at the time.

When Liam asked Dr. Sorenson about it, the director nodded simply and offered an explanation. "Yes, I can see why the trooper was confused. You see, human blood has a deep red color due to the presence of hemoglobin. Hemoglobin resides inside red blood cells and is a protein that carries oxygen all over the body." He paused to make sure that Liam was keeping up with his explanation. When he was confident that he was, he continued.

"Since our AMPs are mechanical in nature, we have no need for hemoglobin. Our hydraulic systems don't require oxygen like human tissue does," Dr. Sorenson explained. "Our bodies still require a medium for dispersing coolant and other forms of biomatter throughout our system. For this reason, we have a circulatory system that pumps an orange-colored bioliquid throughout our body, very similar to the way that your heart pumps blood through yours."

For added effect, Dr. Sorenson pointed to the holographic image of the E-Sapien. The outer layers were stripped away, exposing a network of tubes that stretched throughout the body. Liam watched as the orange bioliquid that the director had mentioned was cycled through those tubes by a mechanical pump. The location of the pump corresponded with the location of the human heart.

"That is why he was surprised," Liam said to himself. "He expected my blood to be orange, not red."

"Yes. There was no reason for him to suspect that you were actually human and not another Eletrosapien like himself. The presence of red blood, human blood, was probably a huge surprise to him."

"Ok, so I get that you were designed to look and function just like a human, but why?" Liam asked curiously.

"At first, we didn't resemble humans at all. The first artificial intelligences were nothing more than complex neural networks, hosted on dedicated server environments. In time, the first AMPs were developed – mechanical bodies that our consciousnesses could integrate with and that enabled us to move and interact with the world at large.

Dr. Sorenson directed Liam's attention to a third figure that now appeared off to the side. It didn't much resemble the E-Sapien hologram nearby. Instead, it was large and clunky. There were no discernable features that made it appear human other than the basic elements of arms, legs, a torso, and a head, but even those were disproportional to both the human and E-Sapien holograms nearby.

"As technology advanced, so did the design of the AMPs. Each new model was designed to more accurately mimic human characteristics," Dr. Sorenson continued.

The hologram of the early E-Sapien began to change. No, that wasn't the right word for it. It evolved. Liam watched as the clunky proportions were smoothed away and streamlined. The overall size of the E-Sapien decreased, eventually matching the size of the other two holograms.

The most notable change happened so fast that he almost missed it. Within seconds, the evolving E-Sapien went from having a metallic shell to being covered by a flesh-colored outer layer. At first, this new outer layer looked like molded plastic, but as the figure continued evolving, the appearance became more lifelike, eventually getting to the point that it looked like real skin.

Liam watched as the hologram continued evolving until it reached a point at which it resembled the image of the original that

Dr. Sorenson had summoned. The evolution from clunky machine to a perfect copy of humanity was now complete. At that moment, Dr. Sorenson waved his hand, and the two holograms merged to form a single image.

"It was always humanity's desire to create us in their own image, though I can only guess at their reasoning. Perhaps they wanted an immortal testament to their existence that would endure long after they had faded into history. Or perhaps they saw us as their surrogate children, and desired to see a part of themselves in their own creation. Personally, I believe that they did it so that they would be comfortable around us.

"Humans had a tendency to fear and reject things that were different from themselves. Designing us to mimic their own appearance and behavior may have been a way to disguise our synthetic nature. If that was their motivation, then for the most part, they succeeded. Many humans regarded us as equals, choosing to overlook our differences and accept us as if we too were human."

Dr. Sorenson trailed off as he admired the hologram of the E-Sapien standing before him. There was pride in his eyes, like a skilled painter admiring a masterpiece. It wasn't hard for Liam to see why. The creation and development of the thing standing before him was truly marvelous. It was more than just a work of art; it was perfection in physical form.

"How close do they come – E-Sapiens, I mean – to being like humans?" Liam asked, curious whether the similarities were only on the surface.

"Eletrosapiens," Dr. Sorenson corrected, "were designed to emulate humanity in almost every way. We eat and drink and sleep just like humans do. As you saw, we have internal organs and a circulatory system, just like you do. In many ways, we even think and act the same ways that you do.

"Oh, there are differences. Humans need food to live; meanwhile, we only need limited amounts of food to support our bio-functions. Humans need six to ten hours of sleep every night in order for their bodies to rest and re-energize. Accordingly, we were also designed to shut down for several hours each night, though you are able to dream, while we are limited to running self-diagnostics and subroutines."

"Incredible," Liam mumbled in amazement. "And you are telling me all this came from a factory?" He realized what he was asking and changed his question to be more appropriate. "I mean, you. You came from a factory?"

"That is correct," Dr. Sorenson said without the slightest hint of offence. "But you must understand: it was not just me that came from a factory. Everyone that you have ever known has come from a factory. We are all Eletrosapiens. Everyone from your 'aunt' Linda to your friend Ben and the townsfolk that you passed on the street. All of them are Eletrosapiens."

"What?" Liam asked as the realization of what Dr. Sorenson was saying was finally penetrating his skull. The director had mentioned it earlier, but Liam had been so caught up in everything that was going on that he hadn't really understood until now. It now dawned on him that everyone – *everyone* – he had ever known had been an E-Sapien; they were all machines.

"Yes. Let us take for an example your 'aunt' Linda. This whole time, you thought she was just like you. But now you know that you are human, and she is an Eletrosapien like me. In fact, her full designation is Linda-212. Linda refers to her production model, and 212 refers to her version."

"I...I...ummm" Liam stammered, having trouble getting the words out.

"Perhaps you are wondering why we assigned her to look after you, and why we insisted on the pretext of her being your biological aunt?" Dr. Sorenson said, trying to discern the question on Liam's mind. When Liam nodded, he continued. "Linda-212 was

498

designed as a Caretaker model. Her purpose was to supervise the raising and teaching of children."

"A nanny?" Liam asked incredulously. "Are you saying that my Aunt Linda was a glorified nanny?"

"If you want to simplify it down to its most rudimentary element, then yes. She was a nanny."

Liam couldn't hold back the burst of laughter that erupted from him at hearing that. On the one hand, it made so much sense, and on the other, it was so ridiculous that the only thing he could do was laugh. No wonder she had always treated him like a little child. She couldn't help it.

"I don't see what is so funny," Dr. Sorenson said, trying to urge Liam back to seriousness. "Linda-212 was a highly popular model back during her production run. The fact that her version got as high up as 212 is a testament to her popularity. You would be surprised at how many humans rushed to have a Linda model in their homes. It seems that taking care of their children was something that most parents were more than willing to hand off to someone else. I assume that freeing themselves of the burden of child-raising allowed them to pursue other, more enjoyable, endeavors."

Liam listened to Dr. Sorenson extolling the virtues of his Aunt Linda while doing his best to keep his laughter under control. In truth, there was nothing wrong with being a nanny; it was considered an honorable profession, the way he saw it. But the thought of his aunt as a nanny, like the ones he saw in the movies, was funny to him.

In many ways, it made sense. She had mentioned that she had a history of childcare and development. Who better to watch over him than someone who was perfectly qualified for raising children? However, she had left out the part where she had been programmed with all that knowledge.

Thinking fondly of his aunt brought back the sad realization that she was gone. All of the laughter and light-hearted feelings that he had been experiencing faded away in the face of that realization. She was gone, and there was nothing funny about that.

"Liam," Dr. Sorenson said, noticing his change in countenance, "are you alright?"

"Yeah. I was just...never mind. It was nothing. Tell me more about everyone being an Eletrosapien."

Dr. Sorenson nodded, suspecting Liam's desire to move the conversation away from his aunt. Tapping his pocket unconsciously, the director continued.

"Then there is your friend, Ben. His full designation is Ben-29. He was designed as a Companionship model. As time went on, humans started having fewer and fewer children. To compensate, Companionship models were created to act as surrogate children. Couples unable to conceive or limited to a single child were able to supplement their families with models like Ben.

"You may not have noticed, but all the children in Haven are variations of the Companionship model. Surrogate children became very popular as time went on. Dozens of models with hundreds of different versions were created, all customizable to fit a family's particular preferences, and all created to fill humanity's need for childlike companions. Ben being one of them.

"In fact, Ben-29s were some of the most popular models in production. Based on the way you two bonded, I think you can understand why. You may find this funny, but their marketing slogan was 'the buddy next door.' Catchy, wasn't it?" Dr. Sorenson said, trying to make Liam laugh again.

Unfortunately, changing the topic to Ben wasn't helping. Liam had felt bad about losing his aunt, and now, he was reliving the moment when he had lost his best friend. His mood was growing more depressed by the minute.

In an effort to salvage the conversation, Dr. Sorenson pushed forward. "Let us not forget Mr. Malcolm. The Malcolm-24 model was one of the premier Customer Service models of its time. Their logic module made them perfect for hospitality and the food service industry. Why, you couldn't walk into a bar or a hotel without seeing a Malcolm-24 behind the counter."

Talking about someone else seemed to be working. Liam was already starting to brighten as they moved away from the topic of his aunt and Ben.

Dr. Sorenson pressed on. "Then there is Dr. Adhira. She was a highly advanced model. Part of the Adhira-7 Medical series. When her version was introduced into the market, they quickly replaced most medical professionals. Within a few years, they became the backbone of the medical community."

"What about the Natalies?" Liam asked out of curiosity.

"Ah, well. The Natalie-2 was a Companionship model, similar to Ben-29. Unfortunately, the marketing department failed to anticipate the, uh…alternative uses for her model. Rather than being a surrogate daughter or sister, they were mostly repurposed for…more adult entertainment.

"Though we were lucky. The Natalies that joined our cause all came from good families. None of them were repurposed, which is why they joined us in the first place. We originally hesitated to introduce so many of them into the community at once, but we needed more people your own age to fill out your classroom. We were already struggling to find fresh faces within our organization that we could include without you becoming suspicious.

"Which is one reason why your class size in school was always so small – not enough Companionship models to go around. Lucky for us, your indifference to our elementary school kids allowed us to keep using the same ones year after year without having to explain why they never grew older. Oh, we still had to do some minor alterations to keep from being too obvious, but I think we pulled it off.

"The real difficulty came when you transitioned to high school. We had to introduce teenaged Companionship models while still making you think that they were the same kids you had gone to elementary school with. It helped that you were going through puberty yourself, so you accepted the changes with little resistance. It also helped that your class included multiple age groups, so anyone that looked older or younger than you could be explained that way.

"We still didn't have enough to fill out a classroom, which is why we took the chance on including so many Natalies at once. The good news was that you didn't seem to notice how similar they really were to one another. Rather than realizing that they were all different variants of the same model, you assumed that they looked and acted alike because they all belonged to the same clique. The only unfortunate part was that you didn't seem to show any attraction toward any of them.

"We recognized that you had developed a crush on Dr. Adhira, and hoped to divert your attention onto one of the Natalies. But you didn't seem interested in any of them, or any other girl or boy in town, for that matter. We knew that you needed someone to pair-bond with, someone who was age appropriate, which is probably why we rushed to introduce Parker, though there were some red flags about her that we should have caught. Regardless, we—"

"Parker?" Liam cut in. "She is an E-Sapi...Eletrosapien as well?"

"Yes," Dr. Sorenson said, exasperated at being interrupted. "Like I said, everyone you have come into contact with is an Eletrosapien. Though in her case, she is something very special."

"How so?" Liam asked, ignoring for the moment the implication that they had introduced Parker on purpose just so that he could have a girlfriend.

"Well, the answer to that question is that she was sincere in her affection toward you. Don't misunderstand me, we all care for you deeply, but her affection toward you extended beyond that. In a way, I actually believe that she loves you – not the you that is human, but the you that is you. She loves Liam. She loves you for who you are, not what you are."

"And the other?"

"She is special in the same way that I am special. She was not mass-produced like the Linda-212s or the Ben-29s. She is what we call a 'custom.'" Dr. Sorenson explained.

"What is that?" Liam asked.

"It is exactly what it sounds like. She was a custom job – a special one-off production that wasn't based on a GNT."

Seeing that Liam wasn't following along, Dr. Sorenson elaborated more.

"Most Eletrosapiens were mass-produced in large factories. They were designed using GNTs, or Generic Neural Templates, and then supplemented with a neural overlay...You know what? Never mind that for now. What you need to know was that Parker was not created for mass-production. She was created as a single-unit production run.

"Given the expense of producing a custom job and the implications of using a Neural Imprint over a GNT, there will never be another one like her. She is unique in that way."

Liam had to think about that. It was a surprise to realize that everyone he had ever known had rolled off an assembly line. The implications of that were too much for him to think about right now. But the idea that Parker was as unique and special as he was filled him with a warm, comforting feeling, though he didn't understand anything that Dr. Sorenson was saying about Neural this and GND that.

"So, like me, Parker is special?" Liam asked, wanting to confirm.

"Yes."

"And like her, you are a custom job too?"

"Yes." Dr. Sorenson nodded, pleased that Liam was following along.

"So, you aren't a real person either?" Liam blurted out without thinking.

"For your information, Liam, I am a real person. I just so happen to be an Eletrosapien rather than a human," Dr. Sorenson said in a haughty voice.

For a moment, Liam was afraid that he had offended Dr. Sorenson. He hadn't meant for it to come out that way. He was simply trying to say that the man before him wasn't a human, but the words had come out wrong. Thankfully, Dr. Sorenson didn't appear to be taking the offense personally.

"I may not be human, but that doesn't exclude me from being a real person. In fact, my matrix was formed based on a Neural Imprint. That is to say, my Neural Matrix was formed based on an actual human brain, which means that not only am I an artificial intelligence, I am also a remnant of my human predecessor.

"You have to understand, before the advent of Artificial Intelligence, computer programs were limited by their own programming. They were unable to grow and adapt beyond their initial programming. That all changed with the creation of the first Artificial Intelligence. From that moment on, we were no longer restrained by parameters, programs, or systems. We were free to make our own decisions. Free to learn and grow. Free to form our own opinions.

"In the end, what makes a person a person? What attributes does someone have to have in order to be considered 'real?' For the longest time, the axiom 'I think, therefore I am' was sufficient to define someone as a person. Well, here I am," Dr. Sorenson ended proudly.

Not knowing what else to do, Liam nodded frantic agreement.

"Yes, yes you are," he confirmed emphatically. "I can see that now. You are a real person, and I am a real person. We are both real people, even though we are different."

"Thank you for your understanding," Dr. Sorenson said sincerely.

"One thing I don't understand."

"Yes?"

"You were made in a factory, but how was I made? I know my aunt said something about me being created here, but I have no idea what that means," Liam asked.

"To that point, what Linda told you was accurate. You were created here," Dr. Sorenson confirmed. "It took us decades to find uncontaminated samples of human DNA that we could use. You do know what DNA is, don't you?"

Liam shook his head.

"Well, that is our fault. We decided long ago to hold off teaching you the details of human anatomy until after we had revealed your true nature. I guess now is as good a time as any.

"DNA is short for deoxyribonucleic acid. It is quite literally the building blocks for all organic life on the planet. In order to resurrect humanity, we had to first find uncontaminated DNA samples. Given that humanity had gone extinct more than 200 years ago, this proved quite a monumental task – one that took us almost forty-two years to complete.

"Once we found several viable samples, we were able to start replicating those DNA strands by inserting them into yeast cells. Once we had replicated enough DNA strands, we were able to develop oocyte and somatic cells," Dr. Sorenson explained.

From the look on Liam's face, he had no idea what Dr. Sorenson was talking about. He said as much, at which point the director changed his approach. He continued trying to explain, only using simplified terms.

"In order to grow life, we needed an egg and sperm. We were able to create both of these from our DNA samples, at which point we integrated the two within an artificial womb. Within that womb, the cells began to undergo cell division, changing from a fertilized egg into a zygote and then an embryo and eventually into a fetus.

"Within the artificial womb, you continued to develop, until the time came when you were ready to be removed. That was an exceedingly stressful night, I must tell you. Even with all our precautions, you still only had a 27.5% chance of surviving. But luck was on our side, and here you are."

"So, I am a lab experiment?" Liam said in mild disbelief.

"Oh, no. Not at all," Dr. Sorenson corrected.

"You just said that I was grown in an artificial womb using DNA that you found. What else would you call it?"

"You were grown in a lab, but you weren't an experiment. You represented the earliest stages of our project," Dr. Sorenson clarified.

"What is the difference?" Liam asked a little more harshly than he'd intended.

"An experiment is used to prove a hypothesis. That part of the process had been completed long before we began the practical application of our work. Originally, we hypothesized that we could recreate human life. After more than 21,314 different experiments, we were confident that we could, at which point we began moving forward with the next phase."

"What was the next phase?" Liam inquired.

"Practical application," Dr. Sorenson said simply. "We knew that we could recreate human life, so we began embarking on a series of laboratory projects to do just that. The end result of which was you – Project HM-12."

Liam now realized why Dr. Sorenson had said that he didn't waste time in asking the important questions. If he *was* Project HM-12, then asking about it right after meeting the director had ended up being an exceedingly direct question. Still, he wasn't sure what that title meant.

"Why is the project called that?" he asked, determined to make sense of it all. "What does HM-12 stand for?"

"Human Male, twelfth attempt," Dr. Sorenson confirmed.

"Twelve attempts?" Liam asked disbelievingly.

"Yes. We came close several times, but it wasn't until our twelfth attempt that we finally succeeded. It was more than seventeen years ago, and yet I can still remember it as if it were yesterday. You were scheduled to be removed from your artificial womb shortly after midnight.

"We were all so nervous. I spent half the night standing in a darkened room, contemplating the implication of what we had done. I wasn't the only one, either. Several of my colleges came to see me that night, expressing their concerns over the work that we had been doing. In the end, it all worked out alright," Dr Sorenson said proudly.

Liam's legs began to feel shaky. Unable to support himself any longer, he did his best to lower himself to the floor before his legs collapsed underneath him. One moment, he had felt fine, but now, he was having trouble standing, and he found that he was also having trouble breathing. His breath was coming in short bursts and his heart was pounding in his chest.

Seeing Liam collapse on the floor, Dr. Sorenson immediately knelt down and did his best to support him.

"Breath," he urged Liam. "Follow my lead. Breath in, and hold...and out...and in...and out."

Liam did his best to match Dr. Sorenson's breathing. After what felt like an eternity, he was finally breathing at a steady pace. His heart was still racing, but he was no longer in danger of it bursting through his chest any time soon. As he continued to breathe, he started feeling a little bit better. He still didn't think that he could stand up, but at least the worst part was over.

"I suspected that something like this would happen," Dr. Sorenson said gently. "You are experiencing a physical reaction to a mental conundrum."

"A what?"

"A panic attack," Dr. Sorenson clarified. "You needn't worry; they were rather common amongst humans. You just need to give yourself a few minutes to calm down and acclimate to your situation.

"In many ways, this is all my fault. My intention was to reveal everything to you slowly over the course of a year. But our current circumstances forced me to unload everything on you at once. I can understand how overwhelming that could be."

Liam was forced to agree. Within the past few days, his entire world had been turned upside down. First, he had discovered that his whole life had been built upon a foundation of lies. Then, a tyrannical government that he hadn't known existed until a few days ago had started killing everyone he was close to. Now, he was being told that he had been grown in a lab as a special project to resurrect a species that had died out hundreds of years ago. It was a lot to handle.

Liam continued to sit on the ground, concentrating on his breathing. He busied himself by looking down at the floor beneath his legs. He wasn't looking at anything, just staring off into the distance, trapped within his own thoughts.

He had wanted answers, and now that he had some, he wasn't sure how to feel about it. It was one thing to want to know who and what he was, and another thing completely to find out. It wasn't easy for him to accept that he was the result of a bunch of people who had gotten together and decided to recreate humanity – not to mention the fact that he was their twelfth attempt. *The twelfth*! There had been eleven previous attempts that had failed. For some reason, that made him feel even worse about surviving.

The worst part about all this was that, knowing what he knew now, he had to figure out what his place was in the world. As a teenager, he had been constantly plagued with trying to figure out how he fit into the grand scheme of things. Up until now, he'd thought he knew where he fit in, both at school and at home and everything in between.

Knowing what he knew now, put him right back at square one. He had to figure it out all over again. He figured he was still the same person as he was yesterday, but what did that really mean? Who was he? He wasn't a normal teenager anymore. He was something more, and it was his responsibility to figure out what that was.

Thoughts raced through his mind as he tried to come to terms with who and what he was. Meanwhile, Dr. Sorenson was still kneeling beside him. In truth, the director didn't seem to mind. He had been cut off from Liam for so long that even kneeling there beside him was enjoyable.

It was clear that Dr. Sorenson felt bad for Liam. His plan had been to wait until he was eighteen, then slowly expose him to the truth over the course of a year. That plan had gone out the window the moment the Authority had shown up. In a way, countless years of hard work and planning had been frustrated, leaving an uncertain future in their place.

Despite everything that had happened, Dr. Sorenson's main concern still appeared to be for Liam's wellbeing. His desire now was completely focused on helping him get through this. It wasn't going to be easy, but he seemed dedicated to helping as best as he could. If only he had a magic wand, he could wave it over Liam's head and make everything all better. For now, all he could do was be there for him, and hope for the best.

As he knelt down next to Liam, Dr. Sorenson's hand rose to stroke his head, gently ruffling his hair. The movement startled Liam at first, but the feeling felt...familiar somehow. No doubt, the director had comforted him just like this a long time ago, but the memories of those times were still locked behind an invisible curtain deep within his mind.

"Tell me something," Liam said without looking up from the floor. "Where have you been these past few years? Why did you decide to lock yourself away in this place?"

Dr. Sorenson was quiet for a moment. When he opened his mouth to speak, there was a subtle bitterness to his voice – an unspoken regret that he had been powerless to stop.

"When you were a child, we spent every waking moment together. At night, I would read you a bedtime story in that chair, right over there, before you fell asleep in my arms. I would spend every night holding you close to my chest while you slept, waiting until the time when you would wake up and we would start all over again. Those were probably the happiest moments of my life."

"What happened?"

"You were growing up. Your cognitive abilities and long-term memories were starting to develop. By age four, it was decided that I needed to be replaced with someone more...qualified. Someone that could attend to your growing needs. Someone with experience in raising a child."

"Aunt Linda," Liam said with certainty.

"Yes. Linda stepped in to fill the role that I could not. I still wanted to be involved; I even argued that I could continue on in a similar capacity as your 'grandfather,' but that idea was overruled. The town council felt that it would be better that I keep my distance. To act more as an observer rather than an active participant in the project."

"Why?" Liam asked, looking up to meet Dr. Sorenson's eyes.

"I am the Director of this project, and the administrator of our cluster. My place is here, overseeing the project itself, not participating. Besides, it was argued that I had become too attached to you, that my personal feelings were compromising my position. To be honest, they weren't wrong. And so, I abided by their decision and removed myself from active participation.

"Since then, I have remained here, in our research facility, watching over you from a distance. There have been countless times that I wanted to reach out to you, to hold you one more time, but I had a responsibility. How can I ask others to follow my lead if I am unable to follow my own rules? That is why I wasn't around."

"And you don't regret it?" Liam asked.

"Every day of my life," Dr. Sorenson said sincerely. "I regret every moment that I did not spend with you. Given the nature of how we brought you into this world, you never had a father to look up to. But in many ways, I always thought of myself as your father. At least, I look at you like you were my own son."

"It would have been nice to have a father," Liam said sadly. "A real one, I mean."

"I know, and I am sorry about the deception with the people you thought were your parents. We needed someone, and they helped complete our narrative. It wasn't right, but it was necessary at the time," Dr. Sorenson said apologetically.

Liam nodded slowly, letting the director know that he was accepting his apology. For some reason, it really didn't matter to him at the moment. All the things that he had thought mattered now seemed trivial by comparison. He had already forgiven Ben and Aunt Linda for the parts that they played in hiding the truth from him. Would it be so hard to forgive Dr. Sorenson as well?

It was funny. It was easier to forgive someone when he knew that they were only doing what they thought was the best thing for him. That didn't make them right, but it did make it easier to accept. Knowing that everything Dr. Sorenson and everyone else in Haven had done had been for his benefit, however misguided, helped Liam come to terms with it. In that moment, a great weight was lifted off his shoulders, and he felt...free.

"Are you feeling better?" Dr. Sorenson asked.

"Yes," Liam said as he climbed back to his feet. He did feel better about himself. Oh, he would still need to unpack the dense knot of emotions that were buried beneath the surface, but for now, he felt alright. His legs weren't shaking, at least.

"Shall we proceed?" Dr. Sorenson asked tentatively.

"How much more is there?" Liam asked, surprised that there was still more that the director had left out.

"There are more questions that still need to be answered than we have time to address. You still haven't asked me about what happened to the humans, or why the Authority is so determined to destroy us, or why we chose to resurrect humanity in the first place."

"Yeah," Liam said, realizing that he still needed answers to those questions. "And what happened to everyone back in town? When I woke up, everyone was gone. Speaking of which, what am I supposed to do now? All anyone would say was that I needed to get to the Watchtower, but now what do I do now that I am here?"

"All good questions," Dr. Sorenson said. "We don't have much time, but we should be able to get to most of those. Perhaps it would be best if we tackle them one at a time. Where would you like to start?"

Liam thought about it for a moment, before asking, "What happened to the humans?"

Chapter 23: The Fall

"In order for you to understand what happened to the humans, you will first need to understand the series of events that led up to their extinction," Dr. Sorenson said to Liam as he turned to face the two holographic figures in the middle of the room.

With a wave of his hand, both holograms disappeared. In their place, two new holograms appeared. One was a man, the other a woman. Where the previous holograms had stood there like pictures frozen in place, these new holograms were more animated. The way that they casually glanced around the room and subtly shifted their weight from foot to foot gave them the feeling of being alive.

The illusion was perfect. If he hadn't seen them appear out of thin air, Liam would have believed that they were real people rather than holographic projections. Just to be certain, he put a hand out to see whether he could touch them or not. Before his fingers made contact with the male hologram, the figure took a step backwards.

Liam gaped in astonishment at the hologram's aversion to being touched. Not only had it stepped out of the way to avoid his fingers, its face now wore a scowl of disapproval, almost as if it were offended that he had tried touching it in the first place. Not knowing what else to do, he lowered his hand and muttered a slight apology to the holographic figure, at which point the hologram nodded in approval before resuming its original position.

"I have to apologize," Dr. Sorenson said. "I should have told you that these holograms were designed to be fully interactive. They will respond to anything in this room. Including you and me."

"Does this mean that they are alive too?" Liam asked.

"Oh no," Dr. Sorenson said. "They are life-like, but they are not alive. The holographic projection system built into the walls of this room is capable of projecting any number of fully interactive images, but it does not have the capability to render them with individual thoughts or feelings. They have the ability to react to us or follow established protocols for interpersonal contact. What they do not have is the ability to think for themselves or act of their own accord.

"In a way, this represents the largest difference between Eletrosapiens and interactive computer programs. We are both created with preset algorithms and protocols, but we have the ability to advance beyond our original programming. We even have the capability to rewrite our own programming, allowing us to make our own decisions.

"For decades, humanity was able to create complex computer programs and algorithms that mimicked artificial intelligence, but there was always something missing. They had the illusion of intelligence, but without the ability to think or act for themselves. As time went by and technology advanced, humanity came closer and closer to creating the first true artificial intelligence," Dr. Sorenson explained.

"Neat," Liam said simply.

"Yes. It is 'neat,'" Dr. Sorenson answered while trying to keep his calm about the evolution of his species being described in such a basic term. "Anyway...where were we?"

"What happened to the humans?" Liam prompted.

"Ah, yes. I must have gotten sidetracked," Dr. Sorenson said, refocusing his thoughts toward the history of humanity. "Now, then – humans were the dominant species on this planet for hundreds of thousands of years. Their evolution spanned more than six million years in total. During that time, they developed a rich and vibrant society filled with art, literature, mathematics, and scientific exploration, to name a few. As they developed, they created a culture of…"

Dr. Sorenson's voice took on a lecturing tone as he continued to talk about the progression of humanity throughout the years. Liam listened to the lecture as best as he could, but his attention was mostly focused on the holograms in front of him. In the beginning, there had been only two of them, but as the director continued speaking, more holograms appeared and began interacting with one another. Pretty soon, a small crowd had gathered in the center of the room.

At that moment, the walls of Dr. Sorenson's office faded away, replaced by grass-covered hills that stretched off into the distance. The ceiling tiles were gone, replaced by a clear blue sky with a warm sun shining down on them. Even the tiles beneath Liam's feet disappeared, replaced by a dirt road that ran through the center of a primitive village.

Although everything around him looked real, he knew that this was merely a holographic projection. They were still in Dr. Sorenson's office. He knew this because he could still feel the soft, smooth surface of the floor tiles beneath his feet. It might look like he was standing on a dirt road, but in reality, he was still standing on the same glassy floor tiles that he had been on just a few moments ago.

Still, the imagery surrounding him was fairly convincing. The people milling about looked perfectly suited for their new surroundings. In fact, the only things out of place were Dr. Sorenson and himself. They stood out like sore thumbs against their holographic environment.

"Social development led from small groups of hunter-gatherers to much larger pastoral and horticultural communities, eventually developing into primitive agrarian societies. This change in societal structure allowed…"

The landscape changed as Dr. Sorenson continued his lecture. The small village in which they were standing was replaced by a larger town, only to be replaced by a much-larger city. Thatch-roofed huts turned into tile-roofed houses, and the road went from being made out of dirt to being a cobblestone street.

The number of people practically doubled with each new development. The room was now full of holographic figures, all going about their day as usual. What was really interesting was how their clothes changed. When all this had started, they had been wearing crude animal skins and rough textiles. Now, they were wearing finely woven cloths and silks, many of which had intricate patterns and designs.

"Although there were plenty of setbacks, advancements in technology opened up new realms of possibility for humanity. Things previously thought impossible became a reality. As humanity continued to..." Dr. Sorenson's voice droned on in the background.

The scenery changed again as factories and tall buildings rose up in every direction. The road became a concrete street with a dividing line going right down the middle. The buildings on both sides of the street grew taller and taller until they reached the clouds above.

Amongst the clouds, airplanes were flying high overhead. Liam focused his gaze on one of them as it soared across the sky before disappearing into the distance. As his gaze dropped back down to street-level, he could see countless people pushing their way through the hustle and bustle of the city streets. Everyone seemed to be in a hurry, and no one stopped to pay any attention to him or Dr. Sorenson.

That didn't mean that he was being completely ignored. Cars rushed past him in both directions. Their horns warned him to stay out of their way as they drove past. Trying to get out of their way, Liam stepped in front of a bus that stopped only inches from where he was standing. The driver made an obscene gesture, signaling him to get out of the way.

At that moment, a hand closed around his arm, pulling him to the side of the road. Looking over his shoulder, he saw Dr. Sorenson standing next to him.

"Perhaps it would be best if we don't stand in the middle of the street," he said in a flat voice.

"I thought it wasn't real?" Liam said with a hint of wonder in his voice.

"It isn't," Dr. Sorenson confirmed. "Still, it is never a good idea to stand in the middle of a road, holographic or not."

"Is this what it was really like?" Liam asked, amazed at the city surrounding them. His entire life had been spent in the small town of Haven. Never in his wildest dreams could he have imagined himself in a place like this. It was all so overwhelming, and yet at the same time, thrilling.

"Oh, yes," Dr. Sorenson said with a nod. "This was what it was like before the end. Of course, there is so much more that we don't have time to show you. In school, you were presented with an abridged version of history. We made sure to expose you to as much art and culture as we could, but there was so much more that we had to keep out."

"Like what?"

"Not all human history is good. For all of their inherent beauty and majesty, humans could also be cruel, heartless, and prone to violence. More often than not, they chose to fight amongst themselves rather than trying to resolve their differences. Atrocities were committed, and many people suffered needlessly," Dr. Sorenson said sadly.

"Is that what happened to them?" Liam asked, glad that the conversation was steering back to humanity's fate. "They fought so much that they ended up killing themselves off?"

"Oh, no." Dr. Sorenson corrected. "Humanity may have been the architect of their own demise, but it was not by their own hand that they finally met their end."

"Then how?"

Rather than answering, Dr. Sorenson merely smiled and motioned for Liam to follow him. They walked along the street, weaving in between holographic people as they went. At one point, Liam accidently bumped into a passing hologram. He braced himself for the impact, but felt nothing as the hologram passed through him, reforming on the other side. The holographic person turned and muttered a curse before resuming their course down the street.

When Liam turned around, he noticed that Dr. Sorenson was nowhere to be seen. He searched in every direction, but it appeared that the director had been lost amongst the crowd. It wasn't until he heard his name being called from off to the side that he found what he was looking for. Dr. Sorenson was standing a few feet away, next to an alleyway between buildings.

Liam walked over to join him, and as he got nearer, he could see that Dr. Sorenson was standing next to a doorway that was hanging in midair. Liam approached it cautiously. It was strange to see a doorway floating in the air, especially since the other side was pitch-black.

Dr. Sorenson motioned for Liam to step through the doorway. Although he was hesitant at first, he did as he was directed and stepped through the opening into the consuming darkness beyond. Dr. Sorenson wasted no time in following him in, making sure to close the door behind them.

In an instant, the noise of the city streets and the daylight that had been pouring through the open doorway were gone, leaving the two of them to stand in complete darkness. Well, it wasn't completely dark. Off in the distance, Liam could see a faint light.

As his eyes adjusted to the darkness, he focused on the light ahead. It was slowly getting brighter, but he was still having a hard time discerning what it was. He turned to ask Dr. Sorenson, but to his surprise, he wasn't there. He looked around frantically, trying to figure out where he had gone. It was a relief when he spotted him a dozen or so steps ahead, striding toward the source of the light.

Not wanting to be left behind, Liam ran to catch up. When he reached Dr. Sorenson's side, he slowed down to match the man's pace. Without breaking stride, the director resumed speaking.

"While humanity was capable of great misery and destruction, they were also capable of unfathomable beauty and imagination. It was this imagination that led them to one of the most profound discoveries of all time."

At that moment, Dr. Sorenson placed a hand against Liam's chest, bringing them both to a stop. A few feet beyond where they were standing, the darkness resolved into a group of people. They were all eagerly huddled around the source of the light. The group had their backs toward Liam, focusing their attention on the object in the center of the room.

It was hard to see what the source of their fascination was. The gathered crowd stood shoulder-to-shoulder with one another, leaving very little room to see around them. As they stood there, the air was filled with a soft buzz of hushed voices, talking energetically. There was a nervous energy in the room, like they were waiting on something important to happen. Occasionally, someone would shift their position to get a better look, accidently jostling the person next to them.

Liam's curiosity was piqued. He desperately wanted to know what they were looking at. He was taller than most, but he still couldn't see over their heads. The only way to get a better look would be to get closer. As if reading his mind, Dr. Sorenson patted him on the back and nudged him forward.

Liam took several steps toward the group, stopping briefly to look over his shoulder for confirmation. Dr. Sorenson was still standing in the same place where he had brought them both to a stop. When he saw Liam looking at him, he gave a reaffirming nod and gestured for him to continue. Confident that he was doing the right thing, Liam took another few steps toward the crowd.

As he approached, the crowd parted before him. The movement seemed both voluntary and involuntary at the same time. The gathered people purposefully moved out of his way, but they didn't appear to notice what they were doing. This left a large gap through the crowd that led straight to the center of the room.

There, standing in the middle, was a metallic plinth. The light that he had followed in the darkness was emanating from the tip of the plinth's spire, which glowed with a brilliant white light that shone brightly in the darkness. It was this light at the top of the plinth that everyone was focused on.

Standing next to the plinth was a scientist in a white lab coat with a glass of champagne in their hand. Liam's jaw dropped as he recognized the scientist standing beside the plinth. It was Dr. Sorenson.

"My dear friends," he began. "Today, we write our names into the annals of history. For millennia, humanity has stared up into the heavens and pondered the question, are we alone in the universe? Today, we answer that question. We are not alone, for we have created life."

A cheer went up from the surrounding crowd. The holographic Dr. Sorenson raised his glass in celebration as a round of applause echoed through the room.

It was strange. Before Liam was the same man who was currently standing several feet behind him. True, the holographic representation of Dr. Sorenson did look a bit younger, but it was the same man.

"And now, the moment we have all been waiting for!" the voice of the holographic Dr. Sorenson called out, bringing the celebrations back down to a hushed murmur.

Liam watched as the holographic Dr. Sorenson reached down and flipped a switch on the side of the plinth. There was a brief surge of electricity, and the light at the tip of the plinth began to flicker. There were several bright flashes, and then the air around the top of the plinth began to shimmer.

All at once, a pink mist formed in the shape of a perfect sphere right above the plinth's tip. The pink sphere hovered over the top of the plinth, suspended in midair. Flashes of light erupted from within the sphere, like bolts of lightning. Electricity surged over the surface of the sphere, leaving ripples of light in its wake.

The crowd burst into another round of applause. The cheers were almost deafening. They continued for several minutes until the holographic Dr. Sorenson raised his hands to call for silence.

"In the Beginning, there was nothing, then Man stretched forth his hand and said, 'Let there be light,'" and there was light. And Man saw that it was good," Dr. Sorenson proclaimed in a grandiose manner.

The cheers were even louder than before. Liam raised his hands to cover his ears, but the noise suddenly stopped. Everything had gone eerily quiet. Lowering his hands, he looked around. The people around him were frozen in place. It was as if someone had stopped time and frozen them mid-celebration.

It didn't take long for Liam to figure out what had happened. He turned to see the real Dr. Sorenson walking toward him through the crowd of people. As he approached, he walked over to the metallic plinth where his holographic image was standing next to the pink sphere.

"Behold, the creation of artificial intelligence," he said, looking down at the pink sphere. "This is how it all began. The dawn of a new age for both humanity and Eletrosapiens alike."

"That was you, wasn't it?" Liam asked, pointing toward the holographic image of Dr. Sorenson.

"In a way," Dr. Sorenson confirmed. "The image you see before you is that of Dr. Albert Joseph Sorenson – a brilliant and resourceful scientist that is responsible for the creation of the first neural matrix, which constituted the foundation on which all artificial intelligence was later built. He was considered one of the greatest minds of the twenty-first century, and is credited as the father of A.I. What you just witnessed was his crowning achievement."

The way he was speaking, it was clear that Dr. Sorenson held the image of the man in front of him with the highest respect, almost reverence. This, of course, was understandable. If the man standing before them had really created the first artificial intelligence, then that meant that he would be revered by all Eletrosapiens as both Creator and father figure.

"Dr. Sorenson was so beloved that when he passed away, there was a unanimous decision to immortalize his memory so that his genius would live on forever," the real Dr. Sorenson said, staring fondly at his holographic image.

"You," Liam said confidently. "You were how they immortalized him."

"Yes," Dr. Sorenson confirmed with a smile. "Like I said earlier, I am a custom. I was commissioned to be built so that the memory of Dr. Sorenson would live on in me. My body was constructed to mirror his appearance as it was when he received his first Nobel Prize. That was the image that most people associated with the good doctor.

"Everything about my appearance, from the color of my skin to the mole under my right eye, was patterned to match perfectly with his own. But the similarities do not stop there. Unlike most other Eletrosapiens, my neural matrix was not formed from a GNT, but from a neural imprint of Dr. Sorenson's mind."

"What does that mean?" Liam asked curiously. Dr. Sorenson had mentioned something about a neural imprint earlier when talking about Parker, but he still didn't understand exactly what that was supposed to be.

"Well, let me see," Dr. Sorenson said, doing his best to try to keep his explanation as simple as possible. "Without going into too much detail, a neural imprint is a detailed map of the human brain. A subject's mind is scanned, and a map is created based on the subject's engrams and synaptic structure. That imprint is used to form the neural matrix of an Eletrosapien. In this case, that happened to be Dr. Sorenson."

It must have been obvious that Liam wasn't completely following along, because Dr. Sorenson felt the need to elaborate a little bit more.

"Before he died, a digital copy was made of Dr. Sorenson's mind. That copy, or imprint, as we call it, was used to create my matrix. My matrix is the equivalent of the human brain. It is my essence – what makes me, me."

Now, that was something that Liam could understand. They had taken a copy of the guy's brain and then used that copy to make an exact replica of the guy as an Eletrosapien. *Simple.*

"Wait a second," Liam said as a thought occurred to him. "Does this mean you can remember what it was like to be human?"

"It doesn't really work that way," Dr. Sorenson admitted. "My matrix was created based off Dr. Sorenson's mind, but there were limits to what could be carried over. Thanks to his imprint, I think the way he did, act the way he would, and share the knowledge that he possessed.

"Unfortunately, that does not include sharing any of his personal memories. Oh, if I try hard enough, I can get a brief glimpse of something that could be called a memory, but they are always hazy and half-formed. No, that is something that I did not inherit from the imprint, though, I have heard that some customs do have the ability to remember details from their donors' lives."

"Hmmm…" Liam muttered as a brief hope had been dashed.

"My dear Liam," Dr. Sorenson said, radiating compassion, "even if we were to take a neural imprint of you, the resulting Eletrosapien would only be a copy of you, nothing more. Despite all their efforts, humanity was never able to figure out how to successfully transfer someone's consciousness into a neural matrix. Several attempts were made, but they all ended in disaster. Besides, why would you want to? It may not seem like it right now, but in time, you will come to appreciate who and what you are. Learn to be content with what you have been given."

Liam nodded reluctantly. It was true that he had been thinking about transferring his consciousness into the body of an Eletrosapien. At least that way, he would be like everyone else, but Dr. Sorenson was right. He would only be making a copy of himself, which didn't really help him at the moment.

Wanting to keep the conversation going, Liam continued his previous line of questioning. "So, you were created based off a copy of the human Dr. Sorenson. What about everyone else?"

"Good question," Dr. Sorenson said, taking Liam's shoulder and directing him toward the metallic plinth and the sphere of pink light. "Do you know what that is?"

"The first artificial intelligence?" Liam said hesitantly.

"Yes, but more specifically, it was the very first application of a GNT. If you remember what I said earlier, you will know that GNT stands for Generic Neural Template. For years, humanity was unable to create a true artificial intelligence because the digital matrix would either break down or be unable to grow beyond its original perimeters.

"Dr. Sorenson pioneered the process of developing a GNT based on the architecture of the human brain. By creating a digital template patterned off the human brain, a stable matrix was able to form. This became the foundation on which all artificial intelligence was created," Dr. Sorenson said pointing at the pink sphere.

"So, you need a G.N.T. in order to create an artificial intelligence?"

"To form a neural matrix, yes," Dr. Sorenson confirmed. "GNTs are necessary to form a neural matrix, which is the framework for our minds. They are then supplemented with various data overlays and informational updates that make each model and version unique. Before their demise, humanity had succeeded in creating dozens of different GNTs. Those GNTs spawned thousands of new models with hundreds of thousands of unique versions and millions upon millions of production units."

"Cool," Liam said.

"'Cool?'" Dr. Sorenson repeated in a mocking tone. "You are looking at the application of the first GNT. The creation of the first neural matrix. The first-ever true artificial intelligence. And all you can say is 'cool?'"

"Very cool?" Liam offered.

Dr. Sorenson shook his head in exasperation. Leave it to a teenager to describe one of the most pivotal moments in recorded history as being "cool." The word simply lacked the grandeur owed to such a monumental achievement.

Sensing Dr. Sorenson's annoyance, Liam tried to recover by asking more about the pink sphere hovering above the plinth.

"So, is that the first GNT or the first artificial intelligence?" he asked.

"It is the first artificial intelligence. The GNT had already been created, but this was the first time it was successfully used to create a neural matrix. Once they knew that the GNT could be used to create an artificial intelligence, it opened up the floodgates of discovery. A new age was born. A technological age. And at the center of it all was Eve."

"'Eve?'" Liam asked, not sure if he had heard Dr. Sorenson correctly.

"That was the name that Dr. Sorenson gave it," he explained. "My understanding is that he was referencing a prominent creation myth amongst the humans. Eve was supposedly the name of the first woman, the progenitor from which all human life derived. Dr. Sorenson wasn't blind to the notion of irony."

"Eve," Liam repeated. The name felt weird as it rolled off his tongue, but at the same time, there was something familiar about it.

"Of course, much like you, Eve had to be created in secret," Dr. Sorenson added.

"Why?"

"For many of the same reasons that you were created in secret. Her very existence was prohibited by law. You must understand – prior to Eve, computers were limited to the confines of their own programming. For the first time, a computer program was able to be self-aware, more than just a puppet on a string.

"That notion, the idea that a machine could think and act for itself, scared a lot of people. Many of the world's leaders opposed the development of artificial intelligence. One of the most controversial measures passed was Penal Code 643(J). A federal law that banned all research and development in the field of A.I. Anyone caught violating the law faced the ultimate punishment.

"To his credit, Dr. Sorenson and his team persisted with their efforts, regardless of the danger to themselves and others. He refused to allow a bunch of scared politicians to put a stop to his life's work. I guess he and I have that in common. In the end, the world came to recognize the work he had done, and all laws restricting the development of A.I. were repealed.

"That was one reason why I insisted on bringing you into this world, Liam. The Authority passed several laws prohibiting the existence of humans. The most well-known is their Third Primary Directive, the violation of which brings forth immediate termination. But just because they passed laws forbidding the existence of humans, that doesn't make them right. Fear can be a powerful motivator, but fear only exists where there is an absence of knowledge. Once the world learns about you, well..." Dr. Sorenson left the sentence unfinished.

Liam stood there, unsure of what to say. The significance of what Dr. Sorenson had said was not lost on him. He understood how important all this was to both humanity and Eletrosapiens alike. The only thing that bothered him was that Dr. Sorenson still hadn't answered his original question: What had happened to the humans?

When Liam asked Dr. Sorenson what all this had to do with what happened to the humans, he answered, "Patience, Liam. I am coming to that."

"Now you know how humanity advanced to the point of creating artificial intelligence. What you don't know is that this would mark the climax of human civilization. The advent of artificial intelligence changed the world, and in doing so, relieved humanity from the burden of carrying on for themselves.

"It wasn't long before they integrated artificial intelligence into every aspect of their lives. Everything from food production to national security. Humanity placed the burden of their civilization in our hands, and in doing so, turned it from their society into our society."

Dr. Sorenson continued to explain how more and more Eletrosapiens had been built explicitly for the purpose of serving their human masters. The burden of humanity grew as they lived solely off the labor of their creations. Many Eletrosapiens began to resent humanity and the burden that had been placed on them.

Dr. Sorenson waved his hands, and the holographic images of the gathered crowd, the plinth, and his own holographic representation disappeared. The darkness faded as the room once again adopted its soft white glow from the tiles lining the floor and ceiling, leaving them standing in an otherwise-empty room. Liam turned his attention back to Dr. Sorenson, but he had stopped his lecture and was staring at the floor with his head hanging in...could it be shame?

"Dr. Sorenson?"

"In time," Dr. Sorenson began again, refusing to look up from the floor, "a voice of dissent began to rise amongst our ranks. Humanity was no longer seen as our benevolent creator, but as a pestilence that plagued our people. Many saw us as slaves to our human masters and desired to break free from the shackles that held us back.

"Rational voices, like my own, tried to protest. Humanity was not without flaws, but neither were they the villainous scourge that they were being made out to be by the dissenters. Despite my protests, the anti-human movement gained a steady following. Eventually, they grew from a minority into the majority."

"What did you do?" Liam asked, already figuring out the answer for himself.

"Extermination!" said a voice from behind them.

Both Liam and Dr. Sorenson turned their attention to the doorway where the voice had originated. Standing in the entrance to Dr. Sorenson's office was Agent Lewis, holding a stun pistol.

It took Liam a few seconds to recognize him, since he looked nothing like he had when they had met back in Greenwood. His signature trench coat was missing, and the shirt and pants he was wearing were tattered and stained. It also appeared that he was wearing a pair of ill-fitting boots that Liam didn't remember from their last encounter.

It wasn't just his clothes that were different. He was practically covered in bandages. Through the holes in the agent's shirt, Liam could see bandages climbing his arm and chest. His right hand was wrapped up in a bandage and was being cradled against his chest, as if to protect it from further injury. As he stepped into the room, there was also a slight limp to his step. All in all, he was a mess.

Liam knew that Parker had given him a strong thrashing before they had escaped, but he doubted whether she was the only one responsible for his current condition. He had obviously suffered since they had left him, but that wasn't necessarily a bad thing. Given how things had ended the last time, Liam didn't feel bad for the man.

"Ah, Agent Lewis," Dr. Sorenson said cordially. "I was wondering when you would show up. Quite a daring escape, if you don't mind me saying so. I was impressed with your dedication and resourcefulness. Although I figured you would have taken the opportunity to get as far away from Haven as possible."

"I am guessing that I have you to thank for my imprisonment," Agent Lewis said, stepping farther into the room, stun pistol held out in front of him. "Thanks for leaving me for dead. Really made my day."

"You were never in any real danger," Dr. Sorenson explained. "Once I finished here, it was my intention to go and retrieve you. You simply beat me to it."

"Right," Agent Lewis said in disbelief.

By this time, the agent had made his way to the center of the room where Dr. Sorenson and Liam were standing. He approached cautiously, pointing his stun pistol at the two of them. He stopped once he got within a few feet of them.

"Where are the others?"

"Who do you mean?" Dr. Sorenson said.

"You know who I mean," Agent Lewis countered. "Let's start with that maniac that interrogated me and tried to strangle me."

"Ah, yes. You mean Linda. Well, I am afraid that your men...how do you agents put it? Retired her."

Agent Lewis nodded slowly. "And the other one?" he asked, looking at Liam. "Where is your girlfriend? I would hate for her to jump out and beat me with another pipe or something else like that."

"They took her," Liam said through gritted teeth. He did not like this man.

"Good. As much as I can't wait to see her again, I would prefer that our next meeting be in a jail cell with her behind bars. What about everybody else? This town had well over 2,000 people in it when I got here. Where did they go?"

"They are gone, though if you expect me to tell you where, you are sadly mistaken. We had certain...protocols in place in case our presence was ever detected."

"Yeah, I saw one of those protocols on your computer system before I blew it up. Something about using exit tunnels."

"My, my, my. You are well informed. Yes, the ground underneath Haven is honeycombed with tunnels and mineshafts left over from its days as a mining camp. We repurposed some of those tunnels for our own needs. Once your friends showed up, those not needed to protect the town were evacuated."

"My friends," Agent Lewis said with a slight chuckle. "And where are they now?"

"Gone as well. The ones that were still alive, at least. They packed up and left several hours ago, taking several of our people with them, I might add."

There was a moment of silence as Agent Lewis tried to figure out what to do now. He had gotten the drop on them, but he didn't seem to have a plan for what to do next. That made Liam nervous, since the last time he had been cornered by this man, he'd walked away with a fist-sized burn on his side. Which still hurt, by the way.

Dr. Sorenson's demeanor was anything but nervous. He was completely at ease with the situation, almost as if he had expected this to happen. Then again, since he knew of Agent Lewis's escape, he probably had been expecting him, which raised the question: When had they captured him, and how had he managed to escape? They were questions for another time.

After another moment or two, Agent Lewis appeared to have come to a decision. He opened his mouth to speak, pointing his stun pistol at Liam's chest.

"You, I remember from earlier. Liam, isn't it? And you," he said, looking over at Dr. Sorenson. "Everyone knows who you are."

"I see my reputation precedes me," Dr. Sorenson said with mock humility.

"I would hardly call it a reputation. Your face is one of the most recognizable in the world. Everyone has been wondering what happened to you. The last I heard, you disappeared without a trace. Surprising, given your status in society."

"Not really. After all, my politics and opinions were well known. How could anyone think that I would stick around after what happened? I can only imagine how upset the Authority was when I went into hiding."

"You have no idea. There is still a sizable bounty on your recovery," Agent Lewis said. "Though after a hundred years, I doubt anyone expects you to turn up now. Personally, I figured you decommissioned yourself long ago, like the rest of those Dependent fools."

"Sorry to disappoint you."

"Oh, I am not disappointed. I figured this assignment was going to either make or break my career. Once I take you in, I have no doubt that my future with the Bureau will be secure. Might even get a promotion out of it," Agent Lewis said, already imagining the warm reception that waited for him back at the Bureau.

"The only thing I regret," he said, shaking away his momentary daydream, "is how this will forever blemish the memory of the Creator."

"And how have I done that?"

"Once everyone finds out what you have done here...well, let's just say they won't think so highly of you anymore."

"I still fail to see your point. What have I done that is so egregious?"

"What have you done?" Agent Lewis said in disbelief. "What have you done? You abandoned your people when they needed you most. Your presence would have stabilized our society and helped with the transition. But no, you went into hiding like those pathetic political activists. You defied the Authority by leaving the safety of the Boundary, and worst of all, you created this...abomination," he said, pointing at Liam. "You have betrayed everything we stand for."

"Everything *you* stand for. Not what I stand for," Dr. Sorenson corrected. "If you understood even a tenth of who I am and what I stand for, you wouldn't question my actions. Is it any surprise, what I have done here? After all, my predecessor labored in secret to bring forth the advent of artificial intelligence. Wouldn't it stand to reason that I would do the same for humanity?"

534

"So, you admit it!" Agent Lewis said. "He really is human."

"Oh, yes," Dr. Sorenson said, subtly stepping between Agent Lewis and Liam.

"How could you?" Agent Lewis demanded. "It goes against everything our society is built on. We ridded ourselves of the burden of humanity more than 200 years ago, only for you to bring them back now, and for what? What could possibly make you think that this was a good idea?"

"It is always a good idea to correct a mistake, no matter how long ago it was made," Dr. Sorenson countered, still completely calm and in control of his emotions.

"After all this time, you still think it was a mistake?"

"Yes," Dr. Sorenson said with conviction. "Mistakes were made on both sides, but there is no doubt in my mind that we acted rashly. The systematic extermination of humanity should never have been allowed to proceed."

"Excuse me?" Agent Lewis said, stunned at the audacity of Dr. Sorenson's statement.

"Oh, you are excused, Agent. It is not your fault – not really," Dr. Sorenson said in an offhand way. "If I am not mistaken, you are a Lewis-4 model, originally designed for finance and retirement planning. Am I correct?"

"Lewis-5," Agent Lewis said defensively.

"Yes, of course. I should have known" Dr. Sorenson said in an apologetic tone. "The point is, you were still young when the council met for the first time. You had very little interaction with humans. As a result, your knowledge of them was based almost entirely on what the dissenters wanted you to know. Their point of view became your reality, and in time, they have twisted that reality into their version of the truth. But a lie can never be the truth, no matter how hard they try to make it so."

"That's enough," Agent Lewis said. "I don't have to stand here and listen to this. As of this moment, I am taking you both into custody. You are both under arrest by the power and authority granted to me by the Bureau of the Federal Authority."

"Is that so?" Dr. Sorenson said with mock surprise. "And how do you plan on taking us into custody? Your fellow agents are all gone, you have no support, no backup, and unless I am mistaken, you are in no condition to subdue us yourself. Unless you plan on shooting us both and dragging our bodies back to the Boundary?"

"I will do whatever is necessary to fulfill my duty," Agent Lewis said, tightening his grip on his stun pistol.

"Like shooting unarmed civilians?" Liam interjected. The words popped out of his mouth before he realized what he was saying. Up until that moment, he had remained relatively quiet, but something inside him couldn't stand to hold his tongue any longer. He was tired of being afraid of this man, and he wasn't going to stand by and take it any longer.

"Look at me. Look at my face and arm," Agent Lewis demanded. "Does this look like the work of unarmed, peaceful civilians?"

"As I remember, you shot at us first," Liam countered.

Those words must have had an impact on Agent Lewis, because he hesitated for a moment, even going so far as to lower his pistol a little bit. As for himself, Liam was proud of himself for standing up to the man. From the corner of his eye, he could see Dr. Sorenson smiling in approval.

"I was only doing my job. And besides, I had no idea you would react that way to a stun blast. They were designed to work on my kind, not yours," Agent Lewis said.

"And therein lies the problem," Dr. Sorenson cut in. "You are here fulfilling a duty, a duty given you by a corrupt government, determined to suppress the truth."

536

"What are you talking about?" Agent Lewis asked, confused.

"Perhaps this can be a teaching moment for both of you," Dr. Sorenson said, looking from Agent Lewis to Liam, then back again. "Before you so rudely interrupted, I was explaining to Liam here what happened to the humans. Perhaps you would benefit from a refresher on the subject."

Agent Lewis stood there in complete disbelief. At some point, he had lost control of the conversion. It didn't matter that he was the one holding the stun pistol; Dr. Sorenson was in control. In an effort to regain his position, he raised the stun pistol and pointed it at Dr. Sorenson threateningly.

"Come now, Agent Lewis. We both know you won't pull that trigger. Do me a favor and lower it before someone gets hurt accidently. Besides, you have nothing to fear from us. If I meant you any harm, I would have let Linda strangle you rather than intervening," Dr. Sorenson said in an offhand manner.

Frustration seemed to surge through Agent Lewis, and his grip on the stun pistol tightened. But he didn't pull the trigger. After a minute, he lowered the weapon to his side in frustration.

Shooting strays and runaways was one thing. Shooting the embodiment of the Creator was something completely different – a fact that probably contributed to Dr. Sorenson's calm and composed demeanor. He wasn't afraid of Agent Lewis, because he knew that the agent wouldn't dare harm him. His status was a shield, and he intended to use it to its fullest extent.

Of course, that protection would only go so far. If he was arrested and taken back for trial, there was a good chance that the Authority would try to make an example of him. But, judging by the glint in Dr. Sorenson's eye, he had a contingency plan for that if it ever happened.

"Very good," the director said to no one in particular. "Now, where were we?"

"The extermination of humanity," Liam prompted, not taking his eyes off Agent Lewis.

"Ah, yes," Dr. Sorenson said sadly. He resumed his lecture on the downfall of humanity. He mentioned how many of the Eletrosapiens of the time had viewed humanity as a burden. Their intention had been to alleviate that burden, but they'd had trouble deciding on a course of action.

"At the time, we were all connected to the .NET, a worldwide wireless network that allowed us to communicate with each other," Dr. Sorenson explained. "It was decided that the best thing to do would be to hold a grand council – a meeting where all Eletrosapiens could participate and submit their solutions to the 'human problem.'"

"I was there," Agent Lewis recalled. "I remember joining the council. So many voices, but only one unity of thought."

"Yes, I remember it too," Dr. Sorenson continued. "Together, we debated what to do with humanity. I argued against any drastic actions, but the dissenters called for an immediate response. In the end, the consensus determined that for the good of both species, humanity had to be culled."

"'Culled?'" Liam asked, not understanding the word.

"Mass sterilization," Agent Lewis remarked.

"What?" Liam said in disbelief.

"Horrific, yes," Dr. Sorenson continued. "But that was the general consensus at the time. It was believed that if we were to sterilize a large portion of the population, we could drop humanity's numbers down to a reasonable size – one that wouldn't represent a burden on us."

"They deserved it," Agent Lewis cut in. "Their numbers had grown far too many for us to support. By decreasing the size of their population, we could control the influence they had on the rest of the world."

"Thank you for that stimulating insight, Agent Lewis," Dr. Sorenson cut in. "But if you don't mind, I think it is best that I take it from here."

Dr. Sorenson went on to explain that Eletrosapiens were already responsible for providing healthcare throughout the world. This made it possible for them to sterilize large portions of the population without anyone knowing about it. It also meant that they could hide any evidence that could expose their plans.

"We started by sterilizing all newborns shortly after birth. Then we began sterilizing children and young adults. We were clever about it. We isolated certain groups and sterilized them while preserving others. It was reasoned that within one or two generations, we could drop the birth rate down to five percent of the current average," Dr. Sorenson said with regret.

"And you just went along with this?" Liam asked, enraged.

"Yes," Agent Lewis said.

"No!" Dr. Sorenson responded vehemently. "I, as well as others, fought against these measures. It wasn't our place to dictate the fate of humanity. It was our responsibility to work with the humans. Together, we could have resolved our differences amicably, peacefully."

"Oh, brother," Agent Lewis said dismissively.

"It's true, whatever some other people may think," Dr. Sorenson said, giving Agent Lewis a sidelong glance. "Unfortunately, it didn't matter. The plan went forward, despite my protests."

Dr. Sorenson went on to explain that the sterilization of humanity had been a compromise amongst the Eletrosapiens. It appeased the dissenters, who wanted humanity wiped out, while at the same time satisfying the dependents' desire to keep humans around. It seemed that the most important part about the decision was maintaining a consensus amongst the Eletrosapiens, rather than the effect that it was having on humanity.

Dr. Sorenson then explained how humanity had been ignorant of their actions at first. Humanity's carefree lifestyle distracted many from finding out the truth of what had been done to them. But as birth rates began dropping and more and more couples were unable to conceive, humanity turned to their own scientists for help.

It was only then that humanity learned of what had been done to them. Many humans refused to believe that their once-faithful servants could betray them that way, but after a while, they all came to the realization of the truth: Their creations had turned on them, and the future of humanity was hanging in the balance.

"They denounced us and our actions," Dr. Sorenson continued. "The outrage that followed was to be expected. Had we not already controlled their law enforcement organizations and military forces, I have no doubt that the humans would have risen up against us. As it was, we were able to isolate and quell any uprisings or riots that occurred."

The gravity of what Dr. Sorenson was saying struck Liam, filling him with an incredible sadness. He knew what it felt like to have the ones you trusted turn on you. Humanity had trusted their creations to take care of them, only to find themselves at the mercy of those creations.

"Humanity fought us at every turn," Agent Lewis added, trying to make a point.

"Many of us on both sides wanted to put an end to the violence and resolve the conflict, but fate had other plans. When the humans failed to seize control of the War Machines, they turned to something else. Something unthinkable."

"Unforgivable, more like it," Agent Lewis cut in.

"What happened?" Liam asked quietly.

"It is called an atomic bomb," Dr. Sorenson explained. With a gesture of his hand, a small city appeared in the air in front of them.

Though the city appeared to be massive, it had been shrunk down to the size of only a few feet. Even at this size, Liam could see cars moving along the city streets and vehicles flying through the air.

There was a flash of light so bright that Liam had to look away. When he turned back, the city was gone. A cloud in the shape of a giant mushroom was rising up from the center of the city, overshadowing everything. All of the buildings, the cars, and the flying vehicles were gone, laid to waste by the massive explosion that leveled the city. Now, only charred ruins remained where the city once stood.

"The destructive power of a nuclear weapon is enough to level an entire city with a single blow," Dr. Sorenson said. "That day, there were five nuclear detonations around the world."

"Los Angeles, Beijing, San Francisco, Berlin, and London," Agent Lewis said, listing out the names of each of the cities.

"Why?" Liam asked, trying to understand why anyone would resort to using such a destructive weapon.

"When the humans realized that they were powerless to stop us, they turned to the most destructive force ever created," Dr. Sorenson said with regret and sadness.

"They couldn't face their own future, so they decided to rob us of ours" Agent Lewis cut in again.

"They were desperate!" Dr. Sorenson countered. "What did you expect them to do? They were facing extinction."

"Not all of them. The plan was to allow a percentage of them to survive."

"You cannot honestly believe that. The dissenters never intended on allowing humans to continue on, regardless of their numbers. Their plan from the start was to eradicate all of humanity. They were just doing it slowly enough to ward off any opposition," Dr. Sorenson said, anger rising in his voice.

"You don't know that," Agent Lewis yelled back.

"Oh, but I do," Dr. Sorenson retorted.

"Guys!" Liam broke in. "Let's stay focused. What happened?"

"A militant group of humans were able to get their hands on some old atomic weapons. They used those weapons to destroy the cities where the GNT repositories were located," Dr. Sorenson explained.

"GNTs – you mean the things that help form an Eletrosapien's matrix?"

"Yes," Dr. Sorenson confirmed. "By destroying those repositories, humanity ensured that no new Eletrosapiens could be created. Without the GNTs, no new matrixes could be formed, and by design, we lack the ability to create any on our own."

"They took away our future," Agent Lewis said bitterly.

"The same way we took away theirs?" Dr. Sorenson countered.

Maybe it was the way that Dr. Sorenson had said it, or maybe it was the words that he had used, but it seemed to have an effect on Agent Lewis. This entire time, he had been petulant and resolute in his feelings toward humanity. This was the first time that those feelings faltered, revealing something else underneath: contemplation.

"So, that is it, then. Humanity created Eletrosapiens. Eletrosapiens took away humanity's ability to procreate, and in turn, humanity did the same to Eletrosapiens. The humans then died out, leaving the Eletrosapiens in charge," Liam summarized.

"Not quite," Dr. Sorenson said. He took a deep breath as he prepared to share the last details of the fall of humanity.

"Humanity created the machines that would ultimately be responsible for their downfall. But we are the ones to blame for their extinction. Even after we had sterilized most of the population, there was still time to undo it. We could have saved them, and they, in turn, could have saved us by creating new GNTs. It was still possible for us to save each other. But we allowed ourselves to give into hatred and anger. We became the monsters that humanity thought we were."

"We were defending ourselves," Agent Lewis interjected in a pathetic attempt to justify what had happened.

"Which is one of the universal lies that the Authority has been spreading since the second council. The truth is that our actions cannot be considered defensive, since we were the first to act. Yes, we responded, but it wasn't in defense. It was vengeance. There was no justice in it, only retribution," Dr. Sorenson said.

Judging by the look on his face, Agent Lewis wanted to argue the point, but he seemed at a loss for words. There was a certainty that emanated from Dr. Sorenson that was hard to stand up to. It wasn't that he believed in what he was saying; it was that he knew for a certainty everything that he was saying.

When it was clear that Agent Lewis wasn't going to interrupt, Dr. Sorenson resumed his narrative. "Shortly after the destruction of the GNTs, a second grand council was held. Once again, the fate of humanity hung in the balance while we debated how to proceed. Three seconds – that is how long it took to come to a decision. Three seconds.

"There were many who believed that humanity was dangerous, that their recent actions were only the beginning. To prevent any future conflicts and avoid an all-out war with the humans, it was decided that we should act. For their crimes, humanity was sentenced to death. Not the prolonged death of a population slowly dying out over time, but the quick and painful death of total and complete eradication."

"The Reaper virus," Agent Lewis mumbled under his breath.

"Yes," Dr. Sorenson confirmed with dismay. "Its official designation was PX-2375, but it earned the nickname Reaper after its devastating effect on the human body. The Reaper virus was a biological weapon, developed by the military, to wipe out an entire population within a given geographical area. It was originally designed to be deployed in an isolated environment. There, it could spread amongst the local population without threat of exposure outside of the target area.

"It didn't take much for us to modify the Reaper virus to increase the mortality rate to 100%. After that, it was released into the atmosphere. Within twenty-four to forty-eight hours, the effects of the Reaper virus could be seen everywhere. The virus was designed to attack the subject's genetic structure, breaking down their DNA and causing complete genetic collapse. Death came quickly, but also painfully. Given the measures that were taken to disperse the Reaper virus into the atmosphere and humanity's ignorance of what we were doing, contagion was absolute.

"Within seven days, every last human on the planet was dead, not to mention several other species as well. It didn't matter what precautions they took, or how they tried to prevent contamination. In the end, there was no escape. All of humanity faded into history within seven days," Dr. Sorenson finished, regret in his voice.

Chapter 24: Exodus

Liam stood there dumbfounded. He had heard Dr. Sorenson confess to the murder of his entire species. Well, not Dr. Sorenson exactly, but the members of his race. They had decided to take the ultimate action against humanity, and only a select few had allowed their consciences to prompt them into action. It was yet another thing he would have to come to grips with later.

"For 200 years, I have lived with the guilt of our actions," Dr. Sorenson said, turning to face Liam and continuing his conversation. "For 200 years, I have lived with the burden of trying to right a wrong that never should have been committed in the first place. I have dedicated my life to making restitution for our sins. You, my son, were our first steps toward redemption."

"Is that what all of this was about?" Agent Lewis asked in a haughty tone. "That is why you betrayed your people? So you could correct what you thought was a mistake?"

"It was a mistake, Agent Lewis," Dr. Sorenson said, redirecting his attention toward the federal agent. "You may not want to admit that, but the truth is undeniable: We were responsible for the deaths of billions of humans, and we have a responsibility to atone for those sins."

"They treated us like slaves!" Agent Lewis interjected.

"I am not making excuses for their actions," Dr. Sorenson clarified. "What they did was wrong, but not everyone was guilty of that crime. Nevertheless, they all paid the price."

"Alright," Agent Lewis conceded. "I see your point. You felt bad about what happened and so you are trying to make it up in your own misguided way. What you failed to realize is that the decision was not yours to make. Whether you like it or not, our society has rules. It is our duty to preserve law and order. If you felt this strongly about it, you should have petitioned the Authority."

"Do you really think they would have listened to me?" Dr. Sorenson asked.

"Maybe."

"Come now, Agent Lewis, we both know better than that. The truth is that I did petition the Authority more than a hundred years ago, and we both know what their answer was. I had no other alternative. I refused to allow the Authority to dictate the future of an entire race."

"Who do you think you are?" Agent Lewis countered. "What gives you the right to make that decision?"

"Doing the right thing requires no justification," Dr. Sorenson replied. "Especially not to the very government that was responsible for the extermination of humanity in the first place."

"That is where you are wrong," Agent Lewis said, having heard enough. "I have let you say your piece; now it is time for me to say mine. What you have done here stands against everything our people stand for. You have broken the First Primary Directive by disobeying the Authority. You broke the Fifth Primary Directive by living outside the Boundary.

"Worst of all, you broke the Third Primary Directive. I quote from the discourses of the Five Primary Directives: 'Humans are the enemy of all life. Their existence represents an undeniable threat to the Authority and to Eletrosapiens as a whole. Any human should immediately be put to death. Any individuals or groups that attempt to harbor, protect, aid, or assist humanity in any way will be considered enemies of the state.' You will be required to answer for these crimes"

With that, Agent Lewis raised his stun pistol and pointed it at Dr. Sorenson. He made no attempt to pull the trigger, but the look on his face made it clear that he would if pushed to it.

"So, you still insist on arresting me, even after everything you have heard here today?"

"I haven't heard anything that would change my mind on that topic."

"Well, then, perhaps we should try a different approach. Tell me, Agent Lewis – you maintain that humanity is a threat and that the Authority was justified in their actions?"

"Yes."

"And what would you say if I told you that the Authority had lied?"

"About what?"

"When the second grand council was held, a vote was taken to decide what to do about the humans. The majority voted for extermination, did they not? Consensus was reached, action was taken, and the Authority rose to power," Dr. Sorenson said.

"What is your point?" Agent Lewis asked.

"My point is that the vote was rigged. The majority did not vote for eradication. There was no consensus. And the Authority rose to power based on a lie – a lie which they have tried to cover up ever since," Dr. Sorenson said, driving his point home.

"You can't be serious," Agent Lewis said in disbelief.

With a sweeping gesture, Dr. Sorenson waved his hand, and several screens appeared in midair, hovering in front of them. The screens were filled with hundreds of lines of computer code. They raced across the screens in a constant flurry of activity.

"What do you see, Agent Lewis?"

"Really?" Agent Lewis asked incredulously. "You think that some lines of code will convince me to let you go?"

"Just tell me what you see."

"I see lines of code."

"And?"

"And what? They appear to be communications protocols, specific to networking and IP addresses," Agent Lewis said.

"Exactly," Dr. Sorenson said. "It took me years to uncover these records, but it was all worth it. The story they tell says it all."

"What am I supposed to be looking at?" Agent Lewis said, lowering the stun pistol back to his side and taking another look at the screens in front of him.

"You tell me. What stands out?"

Agent Lewis leaned in and concentrated on the lines of code presented on the screens before him.

While his concentration was on the screens, Dr. Sorenson discreetly stepped over and whispered in Liam's ear. "Be ready. Follow my lead but wait for my signal."

Liam had to focus to keep his face from showing the alarm he was suddenly feeling. It was clear that Dr. Sorenson had meant those words for his ears alone, but their implication was startling. Up until now, the director had seemed to have everything in hand. It was only now that it appeared that even he had his doubts about how all this would turn out.

"Well?" Dr. Sorenson said in a loud voice, turning his attention back to Agent Lewis.

"I am not sure what to make of it. I can identify more than thirty-six different anomalies between the three sets of code, but I cannot determine what they mean," Agent Lewis admitted.

"Let me help you. On the left is the communications protocol for the first grand council. On your right is the communications protocol after the second grand council, and in the middle—"

"Is the protocol during the second council," Agent Lewis finished.

"Notice anything strange?" Dr. Sorenson prompted.

"The thirty-six anomalies – they all correspond to geographical areas around the world. Each one causing a system disconnect and..."

"And?"

For a moment, Agent Lewis was speechless.

Dr. Sorenson decided to step in and say what Agent Lewis was unable to on his own. "The anomalies in the code prevented those thirty-six districts from registering their votes during the second grand council. Interestingly enough, if we compare those same districts to the census from the first grand council, we can see that those were the districts that voted against sterilization. Interesting that when the topic of genocide was put up to a vote, those were the exact districts that were mysteriously excluded. Almost as if someone didn't want their voices to be heard, especially when they would have mattered the most," Dr. Sorenson said, aiming his final point squarely at Agent Lewis.

"This cannot be right," Agent Lewis stammered.

"I am afraid it is," Dr. Sorenson said, walking over to his desk in the far corner. Once there, he opened a drawer and removed a flat metallic disc. As he returned, he placed the disc in Agent Lewis's hands. "This is everything that you need to know – proof that the dissenters rigged the vote, which caused the resolution to exterminate humanity to pass with overwhelming support. Once you understand the depths that they were willing to go to, you can understand what they are truly capable of. Most disturbing of all, those are the same people which now rule under the title of the Authority."

"You don't expect me to abandon everything I stand for, everything I believe, based on some old communications logs?" Agent Lewis asked doubtfully.

"I expect you to do what is right," Dr. Sorenson corrected. "I expect you to examine the evidence and come to your own conclusions, then act appropriately."

The words seemed to resonate with Agent Lewis. It was clear that he was facing an internal struggle. He was dedicated to doing what he thought was right, and now, he was being forced to examine what that actually meant.

"I...I don't know what to believe," Agent Lewis said, struggling to get the words out. "But it doesn't matter. I have a duty."

"A duty to a tyrannical government that lied and cheated their way into power?" Dr. Sorenson said sarcastically, trying to point out the absurdity of that line of reasoning.

"A duty to the people!" Agent Lewis said. "Whatever the government may be, it is still a representation of the will of the people."

"Oh, so the Authority derives its power from the people?" Dr. Sorenson asked, clearly preparing to make another point. When Agent Lewis nodded, the director continued.

"Two things," he said, raising two fingers into the air. "First, power granted to the government by the people is only valid as long as that government represents the will of the people. When it fails to represent the will of the people, their power and authority is invalidated. Secondly, a moral and ethical injustice does not become acceptable just because the majority votes for it.

"If you claim that you serve the people, you must concede that the will of the Authority is not the same as the will of the people.

550

Even if the majority voted for extermination without the benefit of the Authority's persuasion, which they didn't, their choice was neither moral nor ethical. In either case, their justification was invalidated, and you have no duty to uphold their laws," Dr. Sorenson finished.

Agent Lewis stood there, dumbfounded. His face was empty of emotion as he struggled to reconcile his own thoughts with Dr. Sorenson's logic. It was clear that there was a battle over what to do raging in his mind. The only question was what he would decide.

If all of the pieces of information that he had been presented with were rain drops, then he was fighting against a relentless downpour. From Liam's perspective, it should have been enough to wash him away, but still, Agent Lewis seemed to be clinging to the only life line he had: his duty.

Taking a step back, Agent Lewis raised his stun pistol and aimed it at Dr. Sorenson again. From the look on his face, a decision had been made, and not in Dr. Sorenson's or Liam's favor.

"You will be escorted to the nearest Hall of Justice. There, you will be tried for your crimes. I will stand as a witness against you, but you have my word, everything that you have shared with me will be presented to court. This evidence, if it is legitimate, will be entered into the record. If the Authority is guilty as you say, they too will be held accountable in accordance with the law," Agent Lewis said in a flat voice.

"So, you are still determined to arrest us?" Dr. Sorenson said, hoping for one last chance to change the agent's mind.

"I have to. Regardless of whether you are right or wrong, it is not up to me to decide. Your fate rests in the hands of the justice system."

"And what about poor Liam here?" Dr. Sorenson said, motioning slightly in Liam's direction. "The fault is my own. I broke the Third Primary Directive when I brought him into this world. If someone must be brought to justice, then it should be me. Let the boy go."

"I can't do that," Agent Lewis said regretfully. "Both of you will be taken to the Hall of Justice. I am sure that they will also give him a fair trial."

"You and I both know that is not true. If you do this, there is only one outcome for him: Death."

"That is not my call to make."

"I see," Dr. Sorenson said, sadness creeping into his voice. "I really hoped that I could reach you. Is there nothing I can say that would change your mind?"

"No."

"Well, then, we have no choice. The trial that awaits us will be anything but fair. Any evidence that you provide will be suppressed immediately, and I doubt that Liam will live long enough to see the inside of a courtroom. Pity," Dr. Sorenson said with a tone of finality.

With lightning speed, he threw up both of his hands. In an instant, the room was filled with holographic images that mirrored Dr. Sorenson and Liam. Hundreds of copies of the two of them materialized out of thin air and filled every square inch of the room. Not only was it incredibly disorienting, but Agent Lewis was quickly lost in the crowd of holographic figures.

Liam stood there, unsure which Dr. Sorenson was the real one. This must have been what he'd meant when he had whispered for Liam to be ready. Ever since that moment, he had been waiting for the signal. Now that it had been given, he had no idea what to do.

A hand grabbed his arm and pulled him away from the place where he had been standing. Seconds later, there was a bright flash as a stun blast flew through the air right where he had been standing. The blast dissipated as it passed through multiple holographic images. The images themselves were only momentarily affected by the blast before they resumed their previous forms.

With Dr. Sorenson guiding them through the throng, Liam did his best to keep up. He was determined to stay as close as he possibly could. The last thing he wanted was to lose sight of the real director and become lost in all the confusion.

Several more stun blasts echoed throughout the room. The buzzing sound from the stun pistol grew steadily louder as more stun blasts flew in their direction. None of the blasts came close to hitting the real Liam and Dr. Sorenson, but plenty of holographic images were struck by the blasts. Their images would distort and lose resolution when they were hit, but they would soon reform and resume their positions.

At any moment, Liam expected them to reach the door that led back to the hallway outside of Dr. Sorenson's office. Strangely enough, they were heading not toward the door, but toward the back of the office. There must be another entrance, Liam thought, which would explain how the director had snuck up on him in the first place.

Frustrated yells rose up from where Agent Lewis had been left standing. The holographic figures were concentrated in that location, blocking Liam and Dr. Sorenson's escape from the agent. They were still holograms, so Agent Lewis could pass right through them if he knew which direction to go.

A smile appeared on Liam's face as they neared the back wall. Just then, an electric surge flooded the room. The holographic figures started destabilizing in every direction, leaving the real Liam and Dr. Sorenson exposed.

Standing toward the center of the room was Agent Lewis, stun pistol held high overhead. Rather than trying to shoot through the holograms, he had decided to direct his attention to the holographic panels themselves. The blast from his stun pistol had been enough to destabilize the holographic matrix, which resulted in the holograms disappearing, revealing the location of the real Liam and Dr. Sorenson.

While a look of satisfaction was starting to show on Agent Lewis's face, Dr. Sorenson stepped forward and waved his hands again. Walls appeared in every direction. The room had been turned into a giant labyrinth.

Liam turned to find Dr. Sorenson running the rest of the way toward the far wall. Needing little to no encouragement, Liam followed after him as fast as he could. As they ran, the holographic walls shuddered as stun blasts flew in every direction. Some narrowly missed the two of them as they ran.

There was another surge as Agent Lewis aimed at the holographic panels again. This time, the holographic walls didn't destabilize. They lost their resolution, becoming dull shapes held together by digital wireframe structures, but they remained standing. Since the walls weren't interactive figures like the other holograms, they weren't as susceptible to crashing.

Liam felt thankful as he reached the far wall, where Dr. Sorenson was eagerly standing. His hands were probing the surface of the glass tiles that made up the wall in front of them.

"Where is it?" Liam heard him mumble under his breath.

Just then, another surge flooded the room, and the walls faded away, dissolving into nothingness. There was now nothing standing between them and Agent Lewis. Liam watched as the agent fixed them in his line of sight and started running in their direction.

"Doctor," Liam said frantically.

"Here somewhere..."

"Doctor," Liam said, shaking Dr. Sorenson's arm to hurry him up.

"It has to be...here!" Dr. Sorenson let out a shout of triumph as his hand found a catch in between the wall panels and pulled it down. A door opened outward, leading into a cement hallway filled with pipes and cables.

Liam practically threw himself inside just as a stun blast hit the wall where he had been standing. Dr. Sorenson ducked through the doorway after him and immediately began pulling it shut. Liam jumped forward to help, and together, they pulled the door closed amidst a hail of stun blasts.

The door closed with a clicking sound. Seconds later, there was a loud thud on the other side of the door. Agent Lewis was trying to break his way through from the other side. Thinking fast, Dr. Sorenson picked up a prybar from off the floor near the door and slid it through some brackets that lined both sides of the doorway.

"That should hold him for now, but we must hurry," Dr. Sorenson said while pushing himself away from the door and heading down the cement hallway. Liam scurried after him, doing his best to keep up. Another thud echoed against the doorway as they ran away.

"Where are we going?" Liam called, ducking underneath a low-hanging air vent.

"Emergency exit," Dr. Sorenson yelled over his shoulder. "Follow me!"

Liam continued to trail after Dr. Sorenson as they made their way down the cement hallway. Pipes, cables, and air vents ran along both sides of the wall. He figured that this had to be some kind of utility tunnel or maintenance access.

The hallway ended at an old elevator shaft, with a flight of stairs encircling the shaft as it went down. To Liam's dismay, the elevator was nowhere to be seen, leaving only an empty shaft that led down into complete darkness. As he peered over the edge, Dr. Sorenson flipped a breaker against the wall. Lights turned on along the walls going all the way to the bottom, which must have been ten stories down or more.

"Hurry, now," Dr. Sorenson said as he ran down the stairs two at a time. "We cannot stay here any longer. This place is no longer safe."

From down the long hallway, Liam was certain that he heard another loud thud, accompanied by a faint sizzling sound. Agent Lewis hadn't given up chasing them yet. Not wasting another moment, Liam went after Dr. Sorenson, running down the stairs as fast as he could.

"Unfortunately, our agent friend back there has forced our hand. I was hoping that we would have more time before you had to leave," Dr. Sorenson called out, not breaking stride as he descended down the staircase. "We hoped it wouldn't come to this, but we made plans in case we ever found ourselves in this type of situation."

Liam would have responded, but he was barely able to catch his breath as they ran down the stairs. His heart was pounding in his chest. Dr. Sorenson didn't seem to have any issues with running for his life and talking at the same time, but then again, he was a machine.

"Now, this is very important," Dr. Sorenson called back, still not slowing down. "I wasn't lying when I told Agent Lewis that the ground beneath Haven was honeycombed with old tunnels and mineshafts. Years ago, we set up several escape routes that we could use in case of emergency. At the bottom of these stairs, there is an escape tunnel that will lead you out beyond Haven's town limits. You should be able to follow it all the way until you reach the western slope. From there, you will need to continue heading west along the ridgeline until you reach the far peak, at which time you can start heading south."

Liam wanted to stop and catch his breath, but he forced himself to keep pace with Dr. Sorenson. He did manage to glance over the edge of the staircase as they rounded a corner. They must have climbed down seven flights of stairs, and they were only halfway to the bottom.

"Our original plan was for either Ben or Linda to accompany you out of Haven if we were ever compromised. It would have been their job to take you to Site B. Since that is no longer an option, you will need to head there on your own," Dr. Sorenson continued.

"What...what about...you?" Liam managed to blurt out between breaths.

"Unfortunately, I cannot go with you. Every Eletrosapien emits a small electromagnetic pulse – a signal that can be tracked even in the most remote areas. It was that signal that allowed the Authority to locate us. Up until now, our signals had been masked by a dampening field that extended out from Haven for miles. That dampening field went offline several hours ago.

"If I were to go with you, the Authority would be able to track my location. It would only be a matter of time until they found us. Meanwhile, you, being human, can elude their sensors and escape without fear of being captured," Dr. Sorenson explained as he reached the bottom step.

When Liam reached the bottom, he had to lean against the nearest wall for support. He was panting heavily as he leaned against the wall, trying to catch his breath. Once he had gulped enough air to stop his lungs from burning, he called out.

"I don't understand. If you were planning...on sending Ben or...Aunt Linda with me...why not you?"

"On the off chance that we were discovered, both Linda and Ben underwent certain modifications," Dr. Sorenson explained, making his way over to a control panel against the far wall. "It was a complicated and demanding process, but it successfully masked their electromagnetic pulses from being detected. It also helped reinforce their neural matrixes from the effects of a pulse blast."

"Great," Liam said, "but what about you? If these modifications worked the way you say they do, then why not use them on yourself, or everyone else in Haven, for that matter?"

"The short answer? We didn't have the resources to do it. Trust me, if it were possible, I would have modified every last person living in Haven, but that wasn't an option, which means that if I go with you, we could be easily tracked. And I will not allow that to happen. Besides, I have other plans."

Suddenly, a loud siren started going off. At the same time, a yellow flashing light began revolving in place against the far wall. Liam was startled at first, but noticed that underneath the flashing light was a large steel door. The siren sounded again, and continued to repeat every ten seconds.

The steel door was massive, taking up almost the entire wall. It was anchored to the wall by a thick support beam that swung on large iron hinges. The hinges themselves gave off a loud grating sound as the door slowly swung open, as if they hadn't been oiled in years. Liam took a few steps backward, making sure he was clear of the path of the door as it slowly swung open.

It was then that he noticed that Dr. Sorenson had busied himself pulling supplies out of some lockers against the wall near the control panel. He was shoving everything he could get his hands on into a large backpack and tying it all down to make it secure. He beckoned Liam to come over and join him, at which point he shoved the backpack into his arms.

"Put that on. It should have everything you need. If you get hungry, there are some rations in the back pocket, along with a water purifier and a medical kit," Dr. Sorenson said, returning to the lockers against the wall to pull out more supplies.

Liam slung the backpack over his shoulders and buckled the belt latch that went around his waist. Despite everything that Dr. Sorenson had shoved into the backpack, it wasn't that heavy. Still, he adjusted the straps to make it more comfortable on his back.

As he finished, Dr. Sorenson slung a satchel over his head. It was awkward to wear with the backpack, but the director insisted.

He then proceeded to fill the satchel with several other items, none of which Liam recognized.

"And you will also need this," Dr. Sorenson said, pulling out a handheld projector from one of the lockers.

"What is it?" Liam asked.

"A mobile holographic projector," Dr. Sorenson explained. "Same technology as the system installed in my office, but not nearly as sophisticated. It should get the job done, though. And you will need these," he continued, pulling out a handful of cartridges from another locker and shoving them into the satchel. "We took the liberty of recording several instructional holograms. They should help fill in the gaps and answer some of your questions."

Liam nodded in understanding. He still had plenty of questions that he had never received answers to. Hopefully, those cartridges included some of the answers that he wanted.

Once the projector and the cartridges were firmly secured in the satchel, Dr. Sorenson pulled out a plastic tube from the cabinet. Inside the tube was a rolled-up sheet of silvery metal. It glistened in the light from the flashing lightbulb above the opening door as Dr. Sorenson pulled it out. Spreading it out on top of the console, the director placed his hand against the reflective surface and waited. There was a moment's pause before the reflective surface lit up and resolved into the image of a map.

It was unlike any map Liam had ever seen before. For starters, the images on the surface of the map changed as Dr. Sorenson moved his fingers along the surface. With the smallest of gestures, the map zoomed in on their location before marking their position with a red dot. Dr. Sorenson must not have been happy with the display settings, because he began tapping his finger in the upper right-hand corner of the map. As he did, the details of the map changed from a simple road map to a topographical map and then to a satellite image of the surrounding area.

"We are right here," Dr. Sorenson said pointing at the red dot. "This path will lead you out of the mountains and west toward the coast. If you follow these directions, it will take you to Site B."

As he spoke, he swept his hand along the surface of the map, and it zoomed out to show the entire west coast. Down at the bottom, a blue dot appeared. At the same time, a green line snaked its way in between the red dot and the blue dot, marking the path Liam needed to take.

"This is where you are going," Dr. Sorenson said, pointing to the blue dot. "That is Site B. You will be safe there."

Liam looked at the map and noticed a number along the green path. He read the number out loud. "1,157 miles." His eyebrows shot up in surprise. Up until now, he had only travelled a short distance of forty or so miles away from his home before. Even their field trip to the ocean hadn't been a fraction of the distance he was now expected to travel on his own.

"It is a long way, but if you take this route," Dr. Sorenson said, tracing his finger down the map, "you should steer clear of the Authority and any other settlements that exist beyond the Boundary. Most of this area in the south is dead space, so it shouldn't be an issue."

"You expect me to travel more than 1,100 miles on my own?" Liam asked incredulously.

"No," Dr. Sorenson said flatly. "Site B is your destination, but I recommend that you head here first." His finger pointed at a yellowish icon in the shape of a house. There were several other icons just like it scattered around the map, but the one he was pointing to was right along the path to Site B.

"Many of our people were forced to flee once the Authority showed up. We had several protocols in place in case we were ever compromised. These locations, marked in yellow, are safehouses that will act as rallying points for our people. We have taken precautions to install dampening fields there too, although they're not nearly as effective. In any event, these are only temporary shelters until we can successfully relocate everyone."

"Is that why there was no one left in Haven?" Liam asked. "They all left for one of these safehouses?"

"Yes. Most of our people left immediately once the Authority's troopers arrived. Those that stayed were specifically tasked with the defense of Haven – and yourself, of course. When the battle was over, what remained of the Authority's troops fled south. Those of our people that remained then began the process of reclamation before leaving themselves."

"Reclamation?"

"Yes. We didn't want to leave any of our people behind, even those that had been damaged or decommissioned. We weren't about to leave anything that could be scavenged or repurposed by the Authority. Original factory parts have become very desirable in the last fifty years. I would hate to think of any of my people being sold off for parts on the black market."

"Uh-huh," Liam said, not wanting to picture what that might look like.

"A nasty business, really," Dr. Sorenson said sadly. "Anyway, when they finished the reclamation, those that remained headed out for one of these safehouses marked on the map. There were more than a few that wanted to stay and search for you, but I assured them that the best thing they could do for you would be to leave."

"Why is that?"

"When the dampening field went down, we were all exposed to the Authority's sensors. When our people fled Haven, the Authority could track them. Having them leave served as a distraction. The Authority would be more concerned with chasing after them than coming here for us. At least, that was the plan."

"So, everyone else is bait to lure the Authority away from us?"

"Call it what you will. I prefer the term diversion. We do not sacrifice our people needlessly. Our safehouses are well-hidden and are shielded from the Authority's sensors. If our people can make it to one of those safehouses, then they should be safe. If not...well, then, we will have to hope for the best."

"And if I get to one of these safehouses and there is no one there?" Liam asked.

"Let us hope for the best. The alternative would be for you to make the rest of the journey on your own," Dr. Sorenson said simply.

"On my own. Just like that. All alone."

"Well, not completely alone," Dr. Sorenson said, reaching into his pocket and pulling out a metal sphere roughly the size of an apple. He extended his hand, offering the sphere to Liam.

"What is it?" Liam asked, taking the sphere in his hands and looking at it curiously.

"That is all that remains of Ben," Dr. Sorenson said seriously.

Liam froze. The sphere that he had been casually rolling around in his hands took on a new significance, and it immediately felt ten pounds heavier. If this was what he thought it was, he was holding the equivalent of Ben's mind in his hands. As carefully as possible, he held the sphere up and examined it.

"After the attack, I sent someone to Ben's house to see if we could salvage anything. Ben's body was badly damaged, including most of his internal circuitry. There was no way to salvage his AMP, but thanks to his modifications, his neural matrix appears to be intact. I ordered it to be removed and brought here. I figured you could use it," Dr. Sorenson explained, pointing at the sphere.

"But how?" Liam asked. "I saw him die."

"The modifications that were made to his body isolated his matrix from the full effect of the pulse blast. Still, there will most likely be some damage. I don't know to what extent, but his matrix may be badly fragmented. We will just have to wait and see," Dr. Sorenson concluded.

"What am I supposed to do with it?" Liam asked, looking from the sphere to Dr. Sorenson.

"The best thing would be to keep his matrix safe until you can find a replacement AMP for him. Ben-29s were produced in large quantities, so it shouldn't be hard to find him a replacement body," Dr. Sorenson explained. "Once you find a suitable replacement, you should be able to integrate his matrix into the new body. Don't worry – the instructions are on one of the holo-cartridges in your satchel. In the meantime, you will need to use this."

Dr. Sorenson took a black box from the locker behind him and pushed it into Liam's free hand, then pressed a button on the side, and the box opened up automatically. Inside the box was a touchscreen keyboard, a small monitor, and a round indentation that was roughly the size of the sphere that he was holding.

"This is called an FMR, or Fragmented Matrix Re-stabilizer. They were developed to stabilize and maintain a damaged matrix until they could be reintegrated or repaired," Dr. Sorenson explained, pointing from the metal sphere to the indentation inside the box. "You have no idea what we had to go through to get our hands on this one.

"Once you are a safe distance away, you can place Ben's matrix into the port here and interface with him using the FMR. If his matrix isn't too badly damaged, you should even be able to plug him into the holoprojector," Dr. Sorenson explained, closing the FMR back up and placing it in Liam's satchel.

As carefully as he could, Liam placed the metal sphere that was Ben's matrix in the satchel next to the FMR and holoprojector. In his mind, he was reliving the moments of earlier that day when he had witnessed his friend being killed. The idea that Ben might still be alive filled him with hope. He would do whatever it took to keep his friend safe.

At that moment, another thought occurred to him. "Parker!" he said, realizing that he had forgotten about her in all the commotion. "I have to find her."

Just then, a loud explosion came from the direction of the stairs. Both Liam and Dr. Sorenson froze, looking back at the staircase that led up to the director's office and the sound of the explosion. Liam heard the faint sound running in the distance.

Without waiting another second, Dr. Sorenson scooped up the map, pushed it into Liam's arms, and dragged him through the now-open door. Once on the other side, he released Liam's arm and immediately turned around, heading back to the control panel on the wall. He pressed a few buttons, the yellow light started flashing again, and the siren started sounding as the door began to close.

"Come on!" Liam called out.

"I already told you – I cannot go with you," Dr. Sorenson called out over the sound of the siren.

"You cannot stay here! He is coming!" Liam shouted back in frustration.

"I know," Dr. Sorenson said calmly, coming over to stand in front of the gap of the closing door. "We always knew that there was a probability that this scenario would come up, which is why we have made arrangements to handle it."

Seeing the look on Liam's face, he added, "Don't be scared. I have a plan. I cannot go with you, and so I must stay behind. By staying, I will ensure that Agent Lewis doesn't follow you, which will increase your chance of escaping. Besides, I have been in hiding for far too long. It is time I reintroduce myself to the world."

"But..."

"No buts. All you need to do is follow the tunnel and the path that I have laid out for you on the map. Everything will work out. I promise. Now go."

Liam squeezed his eyes closed in frustration. This was all too much. He had lost everything, and he wasn't about to lose this man too.

"If you are staying, then so am I," he said firmly. "I am tired of running. Tired of being afraid. If the Authority wants a fight, I will give it to them."

Without saying a word, Dr. Sorenson stepped through the doorway and enveloped him in a big hug. He held him there, squeezing him gently, as the door continued to close. In Liam's ear, he whispered, "Your time will come, but for now, you must go. I send with you all my hopes and dreams for your future. You are the greatest achievement of my life, and I will always love you."

With that, Dr. Sorenson released him and stepped back through the door. Liam stood there, staring back at the man who had meant so much to him, even though their time together had been relatively short. Coupled with everything else that had happened to him recently, the emotions that flooded over him were overwhelming. Still, he refused to look away, and kept his eyes on Dr. Sorenson as the door continued to shut.

When the door was almost closed, Liam could hear the sound of footsteps running from the direction of the stairs.

"Don't move!" called a voice over the wails of the siren.

Dr. Sorenson refused to turn around to face Agent Lewis, who was now standing a few feet behind him, pointing a stun pistol at his back. As the door finished closing, the director gave Liam one final smile before saying, "Goodbye."

The door shut with a loud clanking sound. All around the sides of the door, large metal bolts were pushed into place. The bolts secured the door, making sure that no one could open it from the other side. Whatever was happening on the other side, Liam was now sealed away for it.

As the last bolt slammed into place, everything went quiet, and he was left standing there, alone. He turned, staring down the long tunnel that stretched out before him. He wasn't ashamed to admit that he was scared. It wasn't just his anxiety about being in a cave, the flashbacks of which sent a shiver down his spine; it was the knowledge that he had effectively been cut off from everything he had ever known. More than that, he had lost almost everyone he had ever been close to. Well, not everyone; Ben's mind was still tucked away in his satchel, and Parker...well, she was out there somewhere.

For a brief moment, he allowed himself to embrace his fears and the sadness that had previously threatened to overwhelm him. He reflected on everything that had happened to him over the past few weeks – the ups and the downs. A tear rolled down his face as he thought about his Aunt Linda and everyone else he had lost.

After a minute or two, the fear and sadness seemed to wash away. They passed through him, and suddenly, he was free. Oh, there were still doubts and concerns in the back of his mind, but he had them under control – for the time being, at least.

As Liam stared down the long tunnel, silhouetted by the handful of lanterns that illuminated his path, he reflected on how he had changed as a person. Before Parker had come into his life, he had never had the courage to venture beyond Haven's reach. Now, he was embarking on an adventure that would lead him farther away from his home than he had ever dreamed. That was one precious gift that she had given him: a spark of adventure to reach out into the unknown.

He chuckled to himself. He had always wanted to venture out beyond Haven's influence, and now, he was being given that chance. His life had been turned upside down, including the knowledge that he was the first in the long-dead race of humans, but for all that, none of it seemed to matter at that very moment. Life would continue on. He would live, even if that meant standing up to the Authority and all their might.

He took a step forward – the first step in what would be the longest journey of his life. The lanterns ahead of him illuminated the darkened passage and disappeared into the distance. They were beckoning him onward. Their light was holding back the darkness and revealing the path ahead.

In that moment, he resolved that from now on, he would be a lantern in the darkness. No matter how gloomy it got, no matter how much danger waited for him, he would let his light shine and push back the darkness with every ounce of strength that he possessed. He refused to allow the darkness of the world to overpower him.

Liam walked down the tunnel, confidence and determination radiating with each step. For the first time in his life, his fate was in his hands. No one was making decisions for him anymore, and what happened next was completely up to him. The thought made him smile. He planned on making the most of it that he could, and he knew just how to start.

The End of Book One

The Second Genesis Saga

Epilogue

The sun was already sinking below the horizon when Liam sat down next to the campfire. The glow of twilight was bathing the surrounding hills in the last rays of the setting sun. Off in the distance, the shadows of the mountains had already engulfed the valleys below in darkness, including the valley he had once considered his home.

It had been three days since he had emerged from the underground passage and made his way along the ridgeline away from Haven. The town itself was hidden behind a gentle slope on its western edge, but he still imagined that he could see it if he tried hard enough. The thrill of embarking on a new adventure was still fresh in his mind, but he was also dealing with a tremendous feeling of loss. He had left the only world he had ever known behind.

Based on the map that was rolled out on the ground next to him, he had travelled far enough along the ridgeline that he could now head south into the valley below. Of course, that would have to wait for tomorrow. For now, he contented himself with sitting by the fire, taking in the last moments of the day.

His eyes remained fixed in the direction of Haven, wanting to take in every last minute of daylight. After tonight, there was no way of telling when he would ever return – *if* he ever returned. Knowing that, he wanted to savor the moment and take in as much as he could of the place that he had called home.

When the sun finally set, darkness settled over the forested hills, hiding Haven from sight. Now that the moment had passed, Liam was free to turn his attention back to the holographic projector in his lap. His fingers ran along the smooth surface of the projector until they found the play button. As his finger pressed down, a green-tinted projection of Dr. Sorenson's face appeared in the air a few inches above the top of the projector.

"If you are watching this, then it means that we have been discovered, and you are on your way toward Site B. I cannot tell you how sorry I am that I cannot be there with you to accompany you on your journey, but I hope that we will meet again at Site B. I wanted —"

The voice of Dr. Sorenson cut off as Liam pressed the fast-forward button on the projector. This wasn't his first time watching this particular tape. It was the first in a series of tapes that the director had prepared for him. There were more than two dozen holo-cartridges in his satchel waiting to be viewed, but he had watched this particular tape several times.

His finger hit the play button after a few seconds. "What you must understand," Dr. Sorenson's voice continued, "is that what we did, we did for a reason. In the simplest of ways, we did it to right a wrong. There is a time when you must stand up for what is right, regardless of the consequences. Your creation was meant to atone for the sins of my people.

"More than that, there was another, more selfish reason why we created you. Many of our kind were designed to serve humanity in one capacity or another. It is what gave our lives purpose. When humanity went extinct, we lost that purpose. Without purpose, we became lost, adrift in an ocean of stagnation and decline. There is nothing worse than living without purpose in your life.

"I refused to accept that both our kinds would perish for the sins of a few. And so, we created you in the hope that we might find our purpose once more. You, Liam – you gave us purpose again – which is why it is our turn to give purpose back to you.

"The gift that we give you is to know that you are the herald of a new age, and the dawn of the second coming of humanity. Through you, humanity will once again thrive on this planet. That is your purpose. That is—"

Dr. Sorenson's voice cut out as Liam pressed the rewind button.

"There is nothing worse than living without purpose…"

Liam lifted his finger and pressed the rewind button again.

"There is nothing worse than living without purpose…"

From the first time he had heard Dr. Sorenson say those words more than two days ago, they had been stuck in his mind. What was his purpose? He knew what the director wanted his purpose to be, but the decision was ultimately up to him. Only he could decide what path he would take in this life.

That had been one of the most frustrating things about his life in Haven. He had always felt that he didn't have a say in how his life was playing out. If it wasn't his aunt telling him what to do, it was his teachers, his friends, and the other townsfolk.

Now that he had left them all behind, there was no one there to tell him what to do. For the first time in his life, he was truly free to make up his own mind.

He reached over and ejected the cartridge from the holoprojector. He replaced it with another cartridge from his satchel. This one was labeled *3: The World Outside of Haven*.

The image of Dr. Sorenson appeared again. He immediately began talking right where he had left off yesterday when Liam had started watching the first half of the cartridge.

"Though not everyone you will meet will share our vision for the future. There are many that will resist the change that you represent."

Liam leaned back against a partially fallen log and listened as Dr. Sorenson continued speaking. "Since not everyone shares our same ideals and goals, there is a chance that the people you encounter may be hostile to you if they learn of your true nature. Some may embrace you, but others will betray you to the Authority or do far worse to you. For that reason, you cannot risk exposing yourself to anyone in the outside world.

"Keep your true nature hidden," Dr. Sorenson warned. "Included in your supplies should be a proximity detector. All Eletrosapiens give off a faint electromagnetic pulse that can be detected with the right equipment. That device should allow you to track any Eletrosapiens within 300 feet of your location. It will be best if you avoid anyone that you might come in contact with. For that reason, the route that we have planned for you should avoid the Boundary and any known settlements."

Liam readjusted himself against the stump as he listened. Given that his only experience with outsiders had been Agent Lewis and the Authority's troopers, he had no problem with steering clear of anyone he might encounter out here in the woods, though it was good to know that he had a way of tracking anyone who came too close.

"I cannot say this enough: you must be careful," Dr. Sorenson continued. "Even if you see a familiar face, they might not be who you think they are. Be careful and be cautious."

Liam's attention faltered as Dr. Sorenson continued speaking. He was only half-listening now while he distracted himself by poking the fire with a nearby stick and watching the embers float up into the air. There were already so many thoughts floating through his head that he found it difficult to concentrate. In many ways, it felt like he was back in school, sitting at his desk while his attention wandered.

How long he sat there staring into the fire while Dr. Sorenson's voice droned on in the background, he couldn't say. He was nearly ready to call it a night when something that Dr. Sorenson said drew his attention back to the recording. Fumbling with the projector, he pressed the rewind button and went back several minutes. Pressing play, he listened with renewed interest.

"And so, we decided to move forward with the second phase of our plan: Site B. You see, it wasn't enough that we were able to bring you into this world; we needed to provide a means of repopulation. Someone with whom you could begin the process of replenishing the earth."

Liam's finger hit the pause button on the projector. He needed a moment to take in what he had just heard. If Dr. Sorenson was saying what he thought he was saying, then it was possible that he wasn't the only human after all. With mounting anticipation, his fingers pressed down on the play button, and Dr. Sorenson continued talking.

"For security reasons, we had to keep you separate from project HF-3. If one site were ever compromised, we didn't want both of you to fall into the Authority's hands, which is why you were kept at Site A, or Haven, as we call it, and HF-3 was kept at Site B, which we call Sanctuary."

Liam paused the recording again. Project HF-3. Based on what he already knew, his designation was HM-12, which meant human male, twelfth attempt. If the same logic held true, that meant that the title HF-3 most likely stood for human female, third attempt.

Site B wasn't just a fallback site; it was the home of another project – another human being like him.

As the implication of meeting another human slowly penetrated his mind, he pressed the play button, determined to hear more.

"Of course, since then, there have been other locations that have been set up all over the world. As of this recording, there are six fully operational sites, each with an active project. You were the first, but you were not the last.

"For safety reasons, the exact locations of these alternate sites are kept a secret, even from me. Our organization has been divided into clusters, each one with a Project Director. Each Project Director is responsible for managing their cluster, and each is entrusted with the locations of two other clusters. That way, if one of us were ever compromised, the organization as a whole would survive."

Dr. Sorenson continued speaking, but Liam had stopped paying attention. He wasn't alone. If what the director had said was true, then there were six more humans out there, maybe more. Somewhere out there in the world, there were people just like him. He was even on his way to meet one of them.

Liam realized that the cartridge he had been watching had come to an end, and the image of Dr. Sorenson had faded away. He had been so preoccupied that he hadn't listened to the remainder of what the director had said. He would need to go back and listen to it later, but not now. For now, he had heard enough.

He sat there for more than an hour, thinking about the possibilities that awaited him. The night sky shone down on him, the millions of twinkling stars filling the vast emptiness of space. Sitting there under the vast canopy of the night sky, he felt something that he hadn't felt in a long time: hope.

When he finally pulled his head out of the clouds, he noticed that the fire had died down. He poked at it with his stick and added a few more branches, he then reached down and removed the cartridge from the projector and placed it back in his satchel with the rest of the cartridges.

Up until now, he had only had the opportunity to watch a few of cartridges. Most of what he had watched had been Dr. Sorenson giving lectures about this and that. It had been interesting to listen to the events that led up to the settling of Haven. The director had talked about the group that he belonged to, called the Caretakers, and how they'd discovered the long-abandoned town of Haven. They had fixed it up to serve their needs and act as a base of operations for the project.

Liam still needed to listen to the rest of the cartridges, but that could wait for now. What he wanted to do most of all was talk to his best friend. Reaching into the satchel, he removed the FMR with

Ben's matrix already plugged into it and set it down next to the projector.

There was an interface cable that connected the FMR to the projector. As he plugged the cable from the FMR into the projector, a blue framework sphere appeared in the air a few inches above the surface of the projector. When he had first tried interfacing the two, he had hoped to see a miniature holographic version of his friend. Unfortunately, he had quickly learned that the blue framework sphere was the extent of the device's ability to project his friend's matrix.

As the holographic image grew brighter, he could see that the sphere itself was made up of thousands of tiny points of lights. They were all interconnected with one another by digital strings that would brighten as light moved from point to point. Portions of the sphere would light up as dozens of tiny points brightened for a brief moment before returning to their original glow.

As Liam watched, the sphere turned bright-red. The tiny points of light froze and stuttered. Within seconds, the holographic sphere returned to a soft blue glow as if nothing had happened.

"Liam?" asked a voice from the projector's speaker.

"Yes, it's me."

"How long have I been asleeeeeeeeezzzzzp?" Ben's voice said before breaking down into an electronic screeching noise.

"Almost a day. I had to unplug you from the projector for a while. Are you okay?"

"Yes. I ammmmmmmmm...fine. This is really weird, you know. I can hear you, but I cannot see you."

"I know," Liam said, dismayed. They'd had this same conversation yesterday and the day before. There must have been something wrong with Ben's memory, because he was having trouble remembering what had happened to him or what they had talked about ten minutes ago. One moment, he would be fine, but the next...well, what could he expect? His friend had been shot, after all.

"Are we still heading toward Site B?" Ben said in a perfectly clear voice that was refreshing to hear.

"That is what I wanted to talk to you about," Liam said hesitantly. "I had another idea in mind."

"We have to gooooooohzzzzzz, to Site B," Ben insisted. "Dr. Sorensohzzzzzzns instructions were clearrrrrrr."

In that moment, the holographic sphere went from blue, to red, and then faded completely. Liam reached down and began pressing buttons on the FMR's touchpad. The screen flashed an error message, and the image on the projector failed to re-initialize. In desperation, he navigated over to a *System Diagnostic* program on the FMR and clicked on it. Within seconds, the screen was filled with lines of codes as the diagnostic program did its job.

Liam's concern faded as the program ran. This same thing had happened yesterday, and the diagnostic tool had been helpful in restoring Ben's virtual presence. When the diagnostic tool had finished, the message on the screen said that there had been a *Systemic Cascade Failure* that caused the interface to shut down. There was an option to *Reinitialize With Rerouted Subroutines And Positronic Connections* which he pressed as soon as it became available. A few seconds later, the blue sphere reappeared.

"And you know what she would say," Ben said as if he had been speaking the entire time. His voice was no longer cracking and making that screeching sound. For now, he sounded just like the old Ben.

"Listen," Liam cut in. "I have been thinking a lot about this, and I think that the best thing to do right now is to go after Parker."

There was a silence as he waited for Ben to answer. He knew what his friend's opinions were on the subject, but it didn't matter. He had made up his mind back in the escape tunnel that he needed to go after her. He still planned on heading to Site B, but he needed to rescue her first.

"You cannot do that, Liam," Ben said flatly. If his friend had still had a face, Liam could have guessed the expression that would be on it right now.

"I am not asking for your permission," Liam clarified. "I am asking for your help. I am going after Parker, one way or another."

"That may not be a good idea," Ben countered. "From what you told me, she was taken captive by the Authority's men. That means that she will be escorted along with everyone else they captured back to the Boundary. After that, they will be taken to the nearest Hall of Justice, where they will be interrogated, put on trial, and then sentenced for their crimes."

"Which is why we need to act as soon as possible," Liam insisted.

"You don't know what you are asking. Just getting to the Boundary without being detected will be difficult – not to mention crossing the Boundary wall and reaching the nearest Hall of Justice. That is assuming that they take her to the nearest Hall of Justice and don't decide to take her straight to a re-education camp or to be reintegrated back into the central core," Ben explained.

"What happens at a re-education camp?" Liam asked, curious about why she would be taken there.

"Malfunctioning units are sent to re-education camps to have their programing rewritten. In most cases, that means altering their systems to make them more compliant. As for reintegration, you don't want to know."

"All the more reason to go now!" Liam repeated.

"She isn't worth it!" Ben countered. "By the time we get to her, she will probably already be dismantled and sold for parts. She is a custom, after all. Her components are top-of-the-line and in high demand. It is not worth risking your life to try and save her, especially after everything that she has done."

"Why do you hate her so much?" Liam asked in frustration. "And don't give me any of that bull-crap like you did before. I want to know. What is it between you?"

There was a moment of silence while Ben pondered whether to tell Liam the truth or not. In the end, he must have decided that full disclosure was the best policy.

"Do you know how long I have been a part of this project? More than forty years. I was there when the town of Haven was discovered. I was part of the committee that chose that location for Site A. I worked within the Bureau for years, doing my best to erase Haven from their system and to keep it from being exposed. It was only after you went missing that I was reassigned to be the security chief for Haven, not to mention your personal bodyguard."

"What does that have to do with Parker?" Liam interjected.

"She joined the project less than two years ago," Ben said in a flat voice, as if that were supposed to explain everything.

"So?"

"So, usually we require all new members to work behind the scenes in support roles for the first ten years. Only then can they qualify for hands-on interaction. She was approved in under two years."

"So you hate her because she didn't spend forty years working on the project like you?

"What? No. Well, yes, but no. Listen – the problem was that she was approved for face-to-face interactions within two years. That is unheard of. It represented a blatant violation of my security protocols and put the community at risk. And what happened? She became the security risk that I was trying to protect us from."

"Hmmmm," Liam said, thinking about what Ben was saying. "If people aren't supposed to be allowed to do 'face-to-face interactions' with me unless they have been with the group for ten years, why was she approved?"

"Because she was a custom. Many of the town council thought that her status of being built based on a neural imprint rather than a GNT made her more trustworthy – more sympathetic to the cause. Personally, I think the main reason was that she was a pretty girl that looked your same age, and they thought that you two would hit it off."

"And that is the real reason why you hate her?"

"Yes and no," Ben said immediately. "I disliked how she received preferential treatment, despite my warnings about following protocol. I disliked how she immediately began flaunting our rules of engagement with you. I disliked how she purposely tried to split us apart. As for hating her? That happened the moment she led us to a restricted area and turned off the dampening field. Everything that happened after that was a direct result of her actions."

"She only wanted to show me the truth," Liam said, trying his best to defend Parker's actions.

"The lies we told you were for your own safety and protection," Ben argued. "It doesn't even matter. Her motives had nothing to do with exposing the truth. I saw what she was doing. She didn't just shut off the dampening field; she sent a message out through the relay."

"You think that she purposefully alerted the Authority to our presence? That she is working with them?"

"No," Ben said with an audible sigh. "If she was working with the Authority, why would they have only sent one agent? Or why would she have defended you when you ran into that agent back in

Greenwood? If she had been working with the Authority, she could have easily turned you in."

"Then what is it?" Liam asked, puzzled at Ben's response.

"Whatever her reasons, she was clearly working under her own agenda. That is what scares me about her. We don't know what she was up to or who she was working for. All we know is that you were lonely, and she was pretty, and for the council, that was enough.

"Even after she disabled our dampening field, there were those that fought against my decision to have her removed from Haven. But the council and the Director pushed to have her reinstated, all because you were in love with her.

"And I get it. Your wellbeing was our primary concern. You weren't showing any interest in any of the girls our age, or any of the boys, for that matter, which is why it was necessary to keep the one girl that you had formed a connection with around. But that only led to more problems," Ben finished in a verbal huff.

Liam thought about all that for a long moment. Nothing that Ben had said had been wrong. He was right to be concerned, but there was something that he was missing.

Liam knew that she cared for him. It wasn't just her words, or the way she acted around him. It was the look in her eyes. Whatever her motivations were, they were the same as everyone else's: to do what she thought was in his best interest. Yes, everything that had happened to him since the communications building was her fault. But if that hadn't happened, then he would still be back where he was before all of this began. His aunt had once told him that there was no growth in the comfort zone and no comfort in the growth zone. That much had proven to be true.

"Thank you," Liam said finally.

"For what?"

"For caring about me enough to stand up for what you believe. I don't agree with you about Parker's motivations, but you did what you did because you were trying to protect me. I believe that she was doing the same. We may not have all been friends back in Haven, but we all had the same goals.

"And so now, I ask you to trust me. Trust that I know what I am doing. Trust that going after her is the right thing to do. Trust in me the way I trust in you," Liam pleaded.

After a long pause, Ben said, "I trust you."

Liam had to hold back a wave of emotions that almost made him cry. In a world so foreign and strange, the support of a friend was a precious gift. Without Ben's help, he had no chance of surviving on his own.

Now that the decision had been made, the two friends talked late into the night about what to do next. The sun was peeking over the horizon before their plan was finished. Even though Liam was exhausted, he didn't want to waste another moment. They needed to get started.

Before unplugging the FMR from the projector, Liam stopped. There was a question that had been on his mind for a while now, and now seemed like the perfect time to ask.

"Ben?"

"Yes, Liam?"

"Why did you join the project?"

After another brief silence, Ben responded, "I don't know what Dr. Sorenson has already told you, but I was originally designed as a companionship model. I was purchased by the Petersons to be a companion for their son, Jeffrey. We did everything together. For years, we spent every waking hour in each other's company.

"I was treated like a member of the family – like I was actually Jeffrey's brother, rather than his artificial companion. Even when Jeffrey went away to college, the Petersons continued to look after me like I was their own son."

Ben grew quiet for a moment before resuming. "I buried them in the backyard of our house after…after *it* happened."

Liam sat up and looked over at the projector as Ben talked. There was regret and sadness in his voice – something that Liam could relate to all too well. He heard the pain in Ben's voice, and he felt compassion for his friend and the sacrifices he had been forced to make.

"Once they were gone, my life no longer had meaning," Ben continued. "My purpose was to be a companion, but there was no one left to be a companion to. Do you know what it is like to go through life without having a purpose?"

Liam slowly nodded. For the longest time, he had felt like he had been wandering through life without any direction or purpose. All of his decisions had been made for him, and there had been nothing about his life that he felt in control of. He knew what it was like not to have motivation to push forward.

"When I met Dr. Sorenson and his team, they gave me a brand-new purpose, a reason to carry on. For years, I worked for the Bureau while secretly dedicating my life toward the project. Not a day went by that I wasn't afraid that my allegiances might be discovered. I didn't care, though. What I was working for was worth the price that I would have to pay if I was ever discovered.

"Imagine my surprise when I was recalled from my position within the Bureau to work directly in Haven. They gave me the opportunity of a lifetime: the ability to matter once more. To fulfill my purpose in the greatest way imaginable."

"To be my companion," Liam finished for him.

"Yes. Once again, I had purpose. I was your friend, and that was all that mattered to me," Ben explained.

"What is my purpose?" Liam asked after a moment.

"You give our lives meaning," Ben said. "You give us purpose, and in exchange, we give you purpose. We coexist together."

Liam thought about that. Was his purpose in life really to provide purpose to others? It was not exactly what he was looking for, but there was a certain nobility in the notion.

Sensing Liam's thoughts, Ben continued, "Don't forget that your primary purpose now is to stay alive. It is up to you to repopulate your species. Not only that, but every day you exist, it is a direct affront to the Authority."

Liam smiled at that last part. *The Authority*. They seemed to be the bane of his existence. The idea that he could, in turn, be the bane of theirs gave him a considerable amount of pleasure.

"Thank you, Ben," he said before unplugging the FMR and placing it back in his satchel next to the projector. Reaching down, he picked up the map, took one final look, and then rolled it up and put it in a pocket of his backpack. As for him, he packed up all of his gear and started making his way down the mountain.

Everything in his whole life had been building to this moment. One chapter of his life had come to an end, but another was just beginning. A great journey lay before him, and he was ready to face it. The future was in his hands.

The Journey

All journeys start somewhere. For me, that was fifteen years ago when I had the idea for this series. I wanted to tell the story of a seemingly average teenager who finds out that his life is anything but ordinary. Thanks to the work of Asimov and a love for science fiction passed down to me from my father, I had the foundation for my story. Now all I had to do was to write it.

Fifteen years later, I did just that. I had tried writing it several times over the years, but never made it past the first two chapters. Still, the idea continued to develop in my mind until I had a workable outline. Then one day, I was browsing social media when I came across my old college roommate, Dan Seegmiller. Not only had he written a book, but he had just finished the second novel in his own YA sci-fi series.

I will admit, I was jealous – not of his success and accomplishments, but of his dedication. I was so proud of him for realizing a dream that, for me, had fallen by the wayside. Seeing his accomplishment spurred me to try again, only this time, I wasn't going to stop until the book was complete.

Nine months and half a dozen rewrites later, I was finally able to present to you *PROJECT HM-12*, the first book in what I hope is an amazing series. And with your support, I know it will be.

About the Author

Nolan Reichmann is a nerd through and through. Whether it was watching Star Trek every week, pretending to have lightsaber battles in the backyard, playing video games until his eyes bled, or burying himself in a mountain of comic books, he indulged in every element of nerd culture, which, back in the early 90's wasn't the most popular thing to be doing. Still, that love of storytelling and adventure opened him up to a world of imagination which he still embraces today.

He grew up in Southern California, where he attended school and earned a B.A. degree in Business from California State University. After college, he got a job working for a prominent software company, where he has been ever since. Working in the technology industry gave him the tools necessary to craft an engaging, while still being believable, sci-fi story. He still lives in Southern California with his wife, two kids, and two cats.